festival of Shadows

A Japanese Ghost Story

Atelier Sentō

TUTTLE Publishing

Tokyo | Rutland, Vermont | Singapore

Prologue

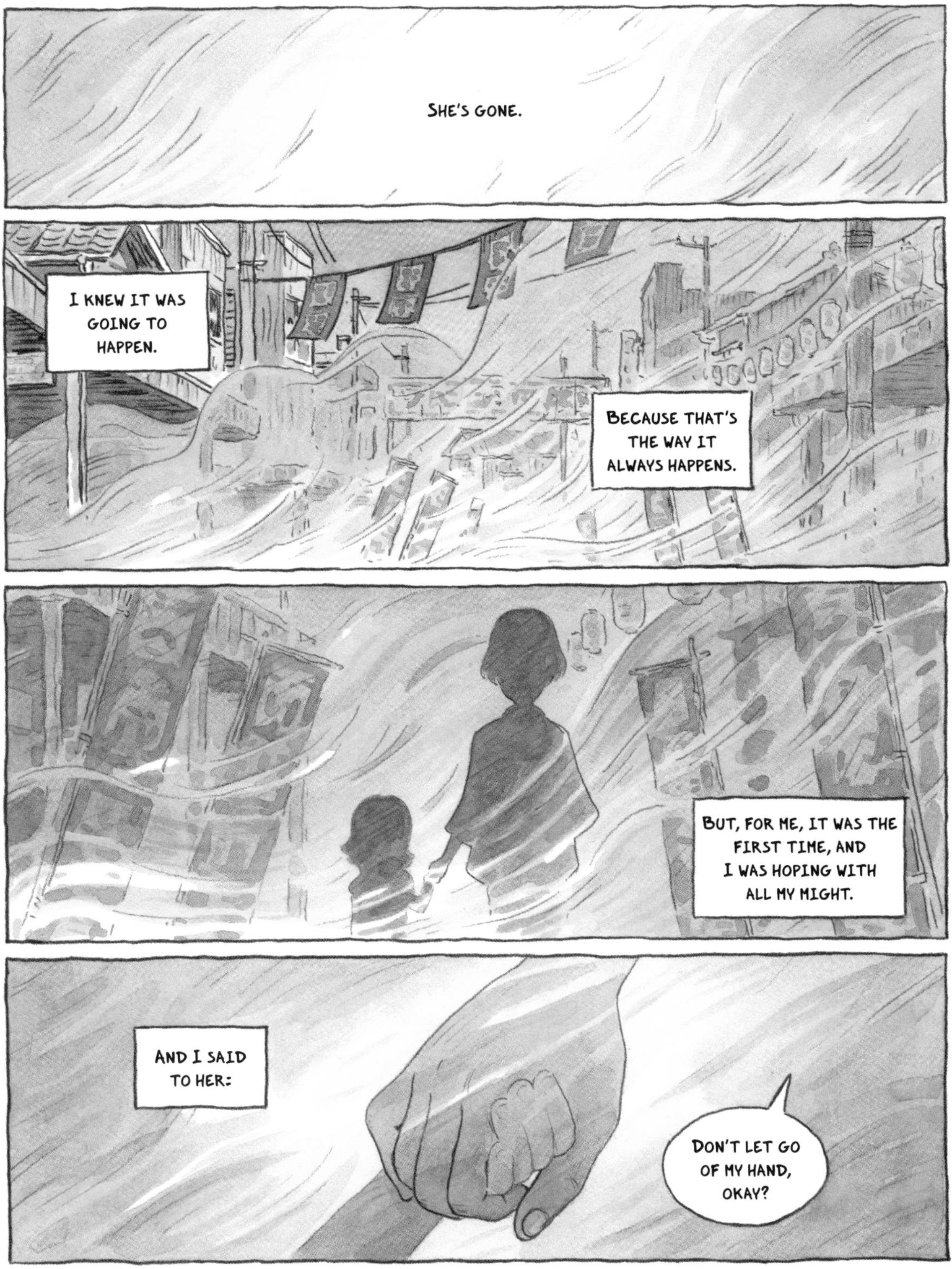
SHE'S GONE.
I KNEW IT WAS GOING TO HAPPEN.
BECAUSE THAT'S THE WAY IT ALWAYS HAPPENS.
BUT, FOR ME, IT WAS THE FIRST TIME, AND I WAS HOPING WITH ALL MY MIGHT.
AND I SAID TO HER:
DON'T LET GO OF MY HAND, OKAY?

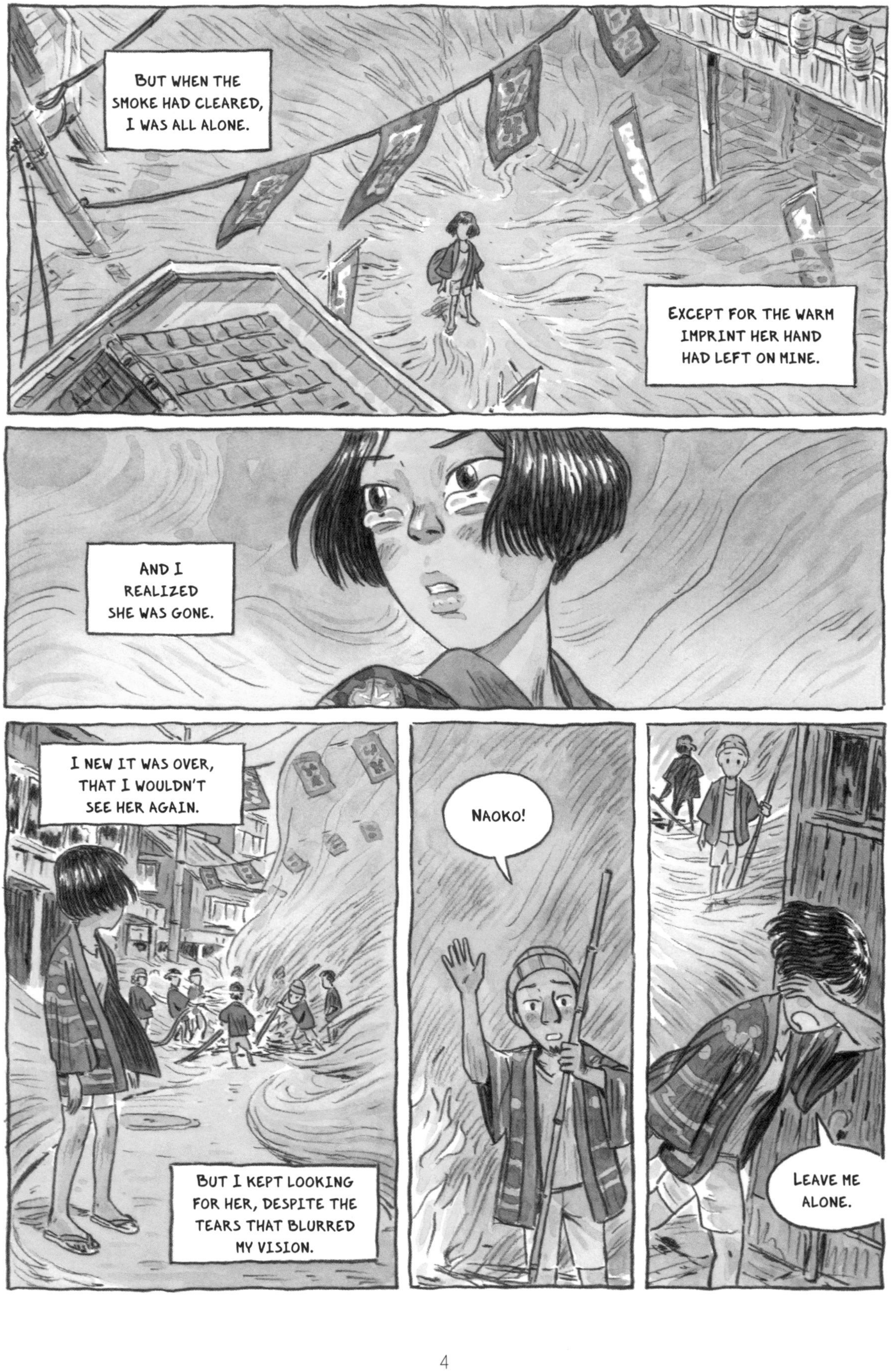
BUT WHEN THE SMOKE HAD CLEARED, I WAS ALL ALONE.
EXCEPT FOR THE WARM IMPRINT HER HAND HAD LEFT ON MINE.
AND I REALIZED SHE WAS GONE.
I NEW IT WAS OVER, THAT I WOULDN'T SEE HER AGAIN.
BUT I KEPT LOOKING FOR HER, DESPITE THE TEARS THAT BLURRED MY VISION.
NAOKO!
LEAVE ME ALONE.

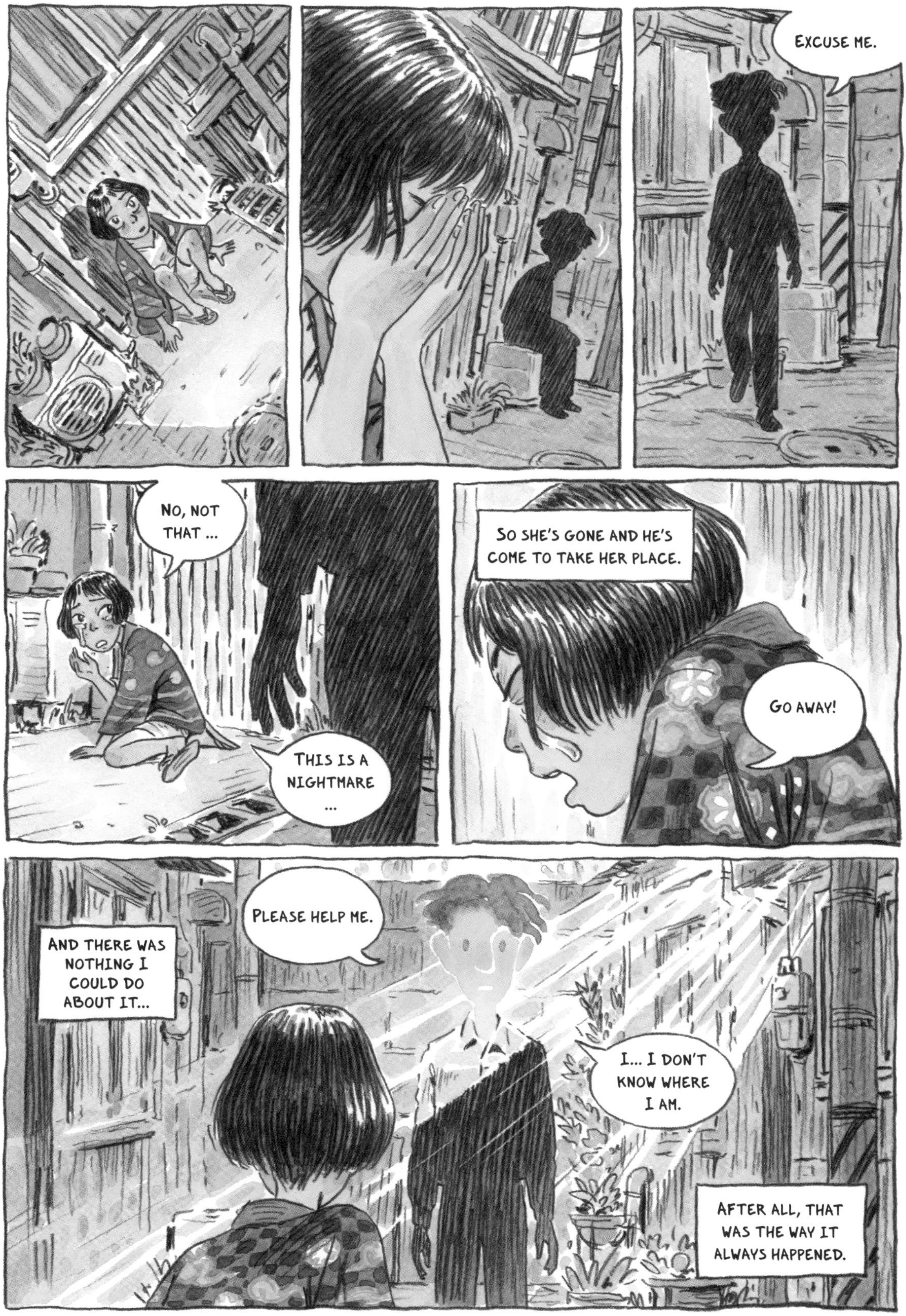
EXCUSE ME.
NO, NOT THAT ...
THIS IS A NIGHTMARE ...
SO SHE'S GONE AND HE'S COME TO TAKE HER PLACE.
GO AWAY!
AND THERE WAS NOTHING I COULD DO ABOUT IT...
PLEASE HELP ME.
I... I DON'T KNOW WHERE I AM.
AFTER ALL, THAT WAS THE WAY IT ALWAYS HAPPENED.

Part one

秋

Fall

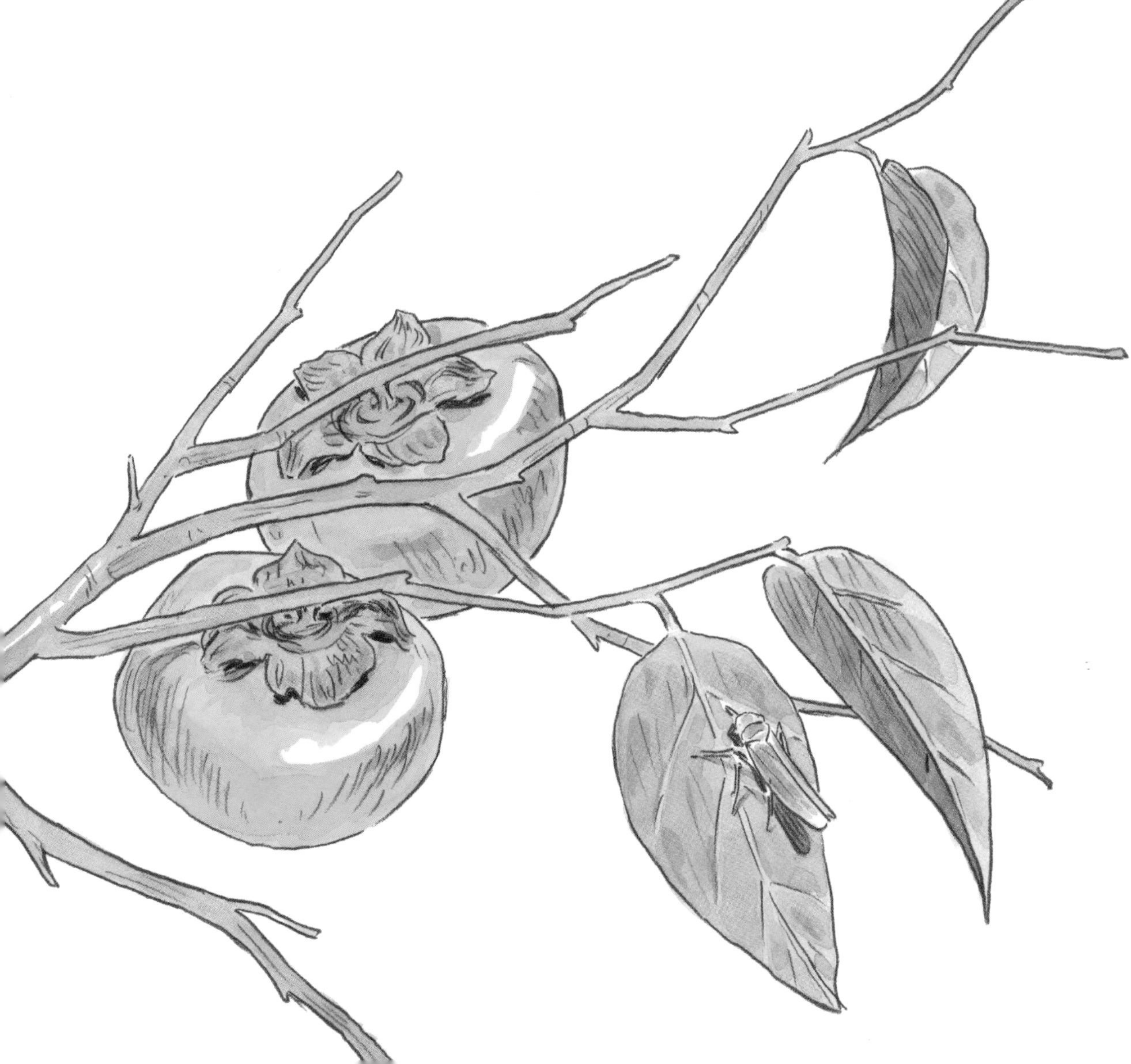

The old women

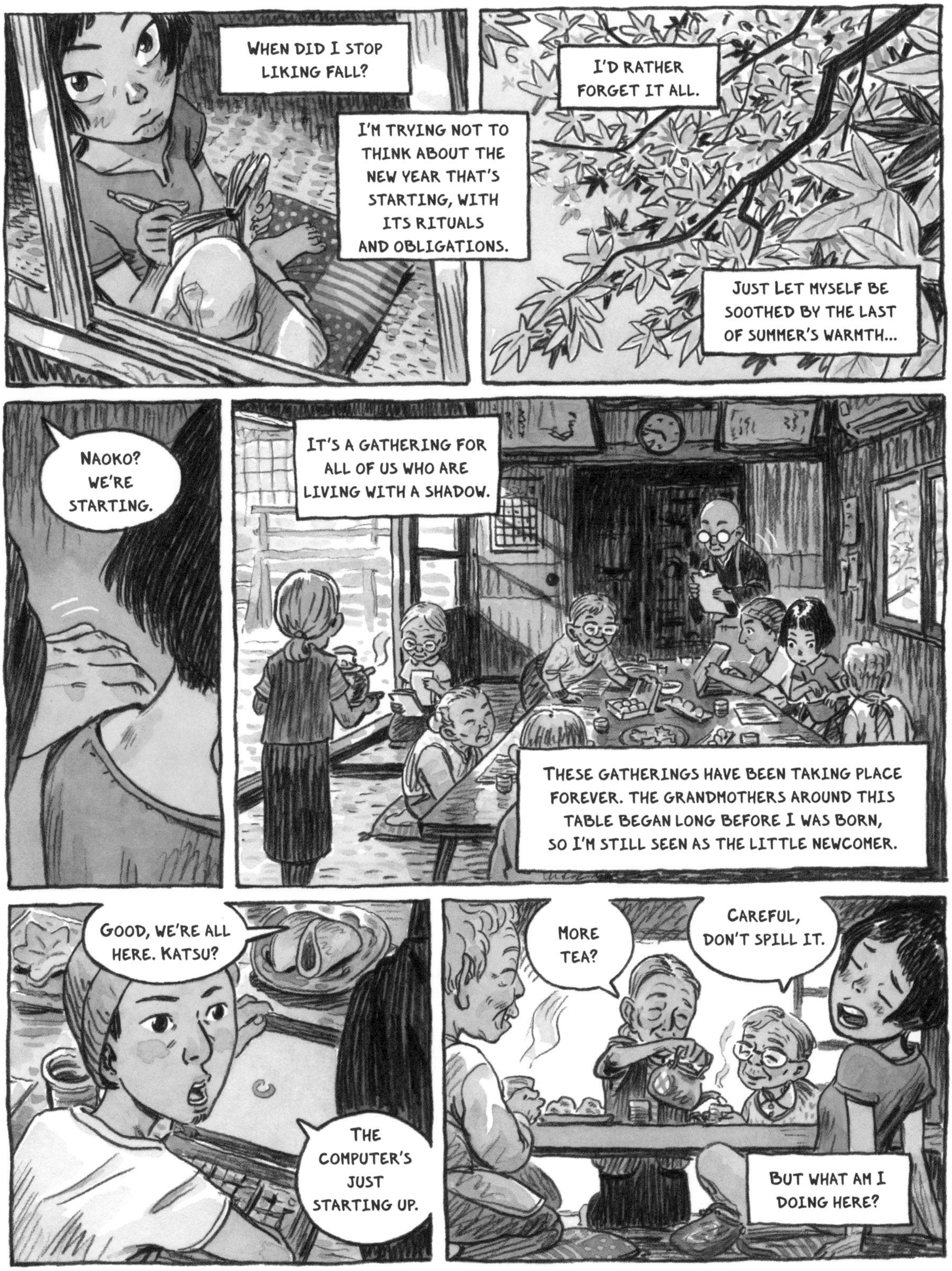
WHEN DID I STOP LIKING FALL?
I'M TRYING NOT TO THINK ABOUT THE NEW YEAR THAT'S STARTING, WITH ITS RITUALS AND OBLIGATIONS.
I'D RATHER FORGET IT ALL.
JUST LET MYSELF BE SOOTHED BY THE LAST OF SUMMER'S WARMTH...
NAOKO? WE'RE STARTING.
IT'S A GATHERING FOR ALL OF US WHO ARE LIVING WITH A SHADOW.
THESE GATHERINGS HAVE BEEN TAKING PLACE FOREVER. THE GRANDMOTHERS AROUND THIS TABLE BEGAN LONG BEFORE I WAS BORN, SO I'M STILL SEEN AS THE LITTLE NEWCOMER.
GOOD, WE'RE ALL HERE. KATSU?
THE COMPUTER'S JUST STARTING UP.
MORE TEA?
CAREFUL, DON'T SPILL IT.
BUT WHAT AM I DOING HERE?

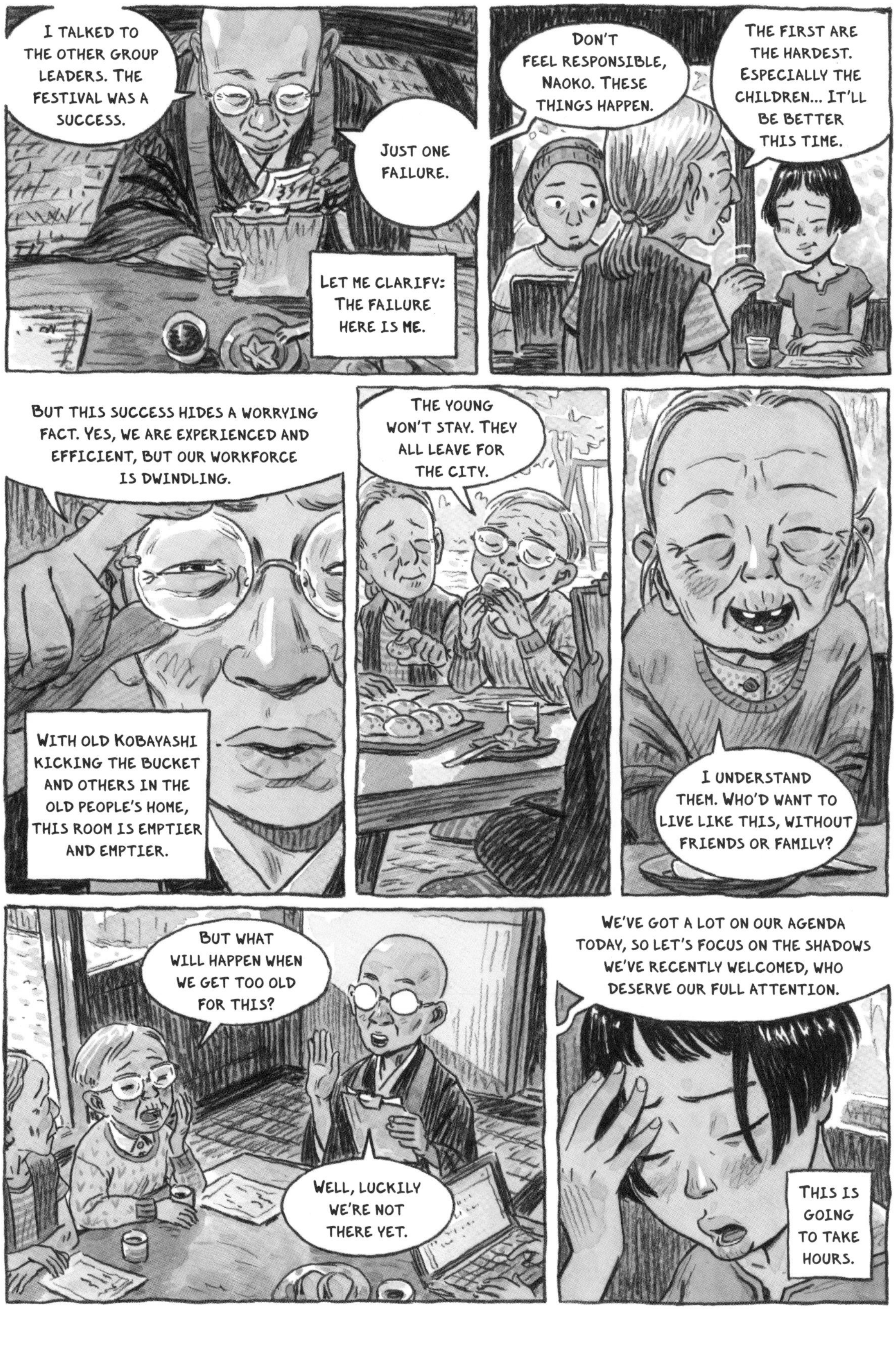
I TALKED TO THE OTHER GROUP LEADERS. THE FESTIVAL WAS A SUCCESS.
JUST ONE FAILURE.
LET ME CLARIFY: THE FAILURE HERE IS ME.
DON'T FEEL RESPONSIBLE, NAOKO. THESE THINGS HAPPEN.
THE FIRST ARE THE HARDEST. ESPECIALLY THE CHILDREN... IT'LL BE BETTER THIS TIME.
BUT THIS SUCCESS HIDES A WORRYING FACT. YES, WE ARE EXPERIENCED AND EFFICIENT, BUT OUR WORKFORCE IS DWINDLING.
WITH OLD KOBAYASHI KICKING THE BUCKET AND OTHERS IN THE OLD PEOPLE'S HOME, THIS ROOM IS EMPTIER AND EMPTIER.
THE YOUNG WON'T STAY. THEY ALL LEAVE FOR THE CITY.
I UNDERSTAND THEM. WHO'D WANT TO LIVE LIKE THIS, WITHOUT FRIENDS OR FAMILY?
BUT WHAT WILL HAPPEN WHEN WE GET TOO OLD FOR THIS?
WELL, LUCKILY WE'RE NOT THERE YET.
WE'VE GOT A LOT ON OUR AGENDA TODAY, SO LET'S FOCUS ON THE SHADOWS WE'VE RECENTLY WELCOMED, WHO DESERVE OUR FULL ATTENTION.
THIS IS GOING TO TAKE HOURS.

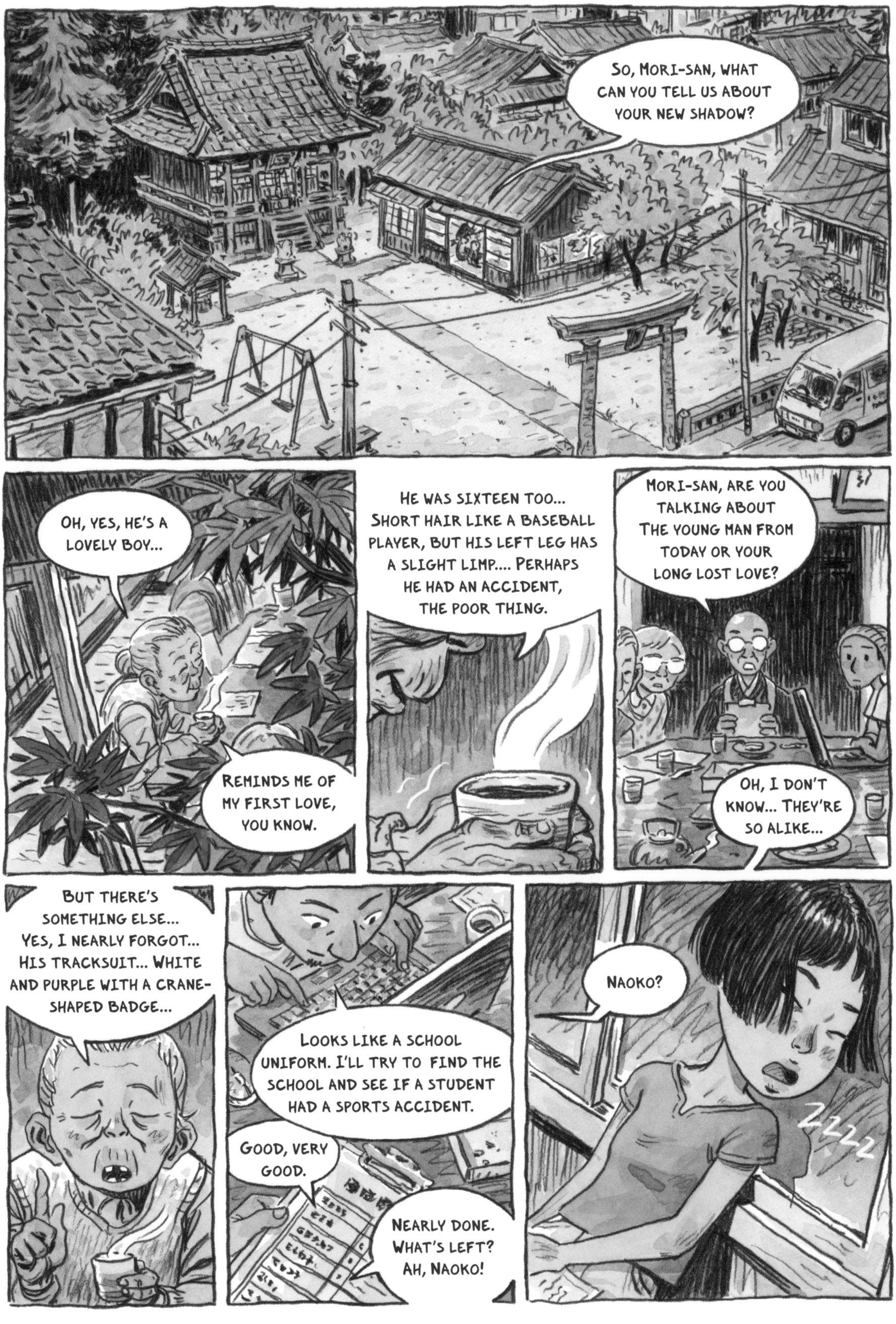

So, Mori-san, what can you tell us about your new shadow?
Oh, yes, he's a lovely boy...
Reminds me of my first love, you know.
He was sixteen too... Short hair like a baseball player, but his left leg has a slight limp.... Perhaps he had an accident, the poor thing.
Mori-san, are you talking about the young man from today or your long lost love?
Oh, I don't know... They're so alike...
But there's something else... Yes, I nearly forgot... His tracksuit... White and purple with a crane-shaped badge...
Looks like a school uniform. I'll try to find the school and see if a student had a sports accident.
Good, very good.
Nearly done. What's left? Ah, Naoko!
Naoko?
ZZZZ

The road home from school

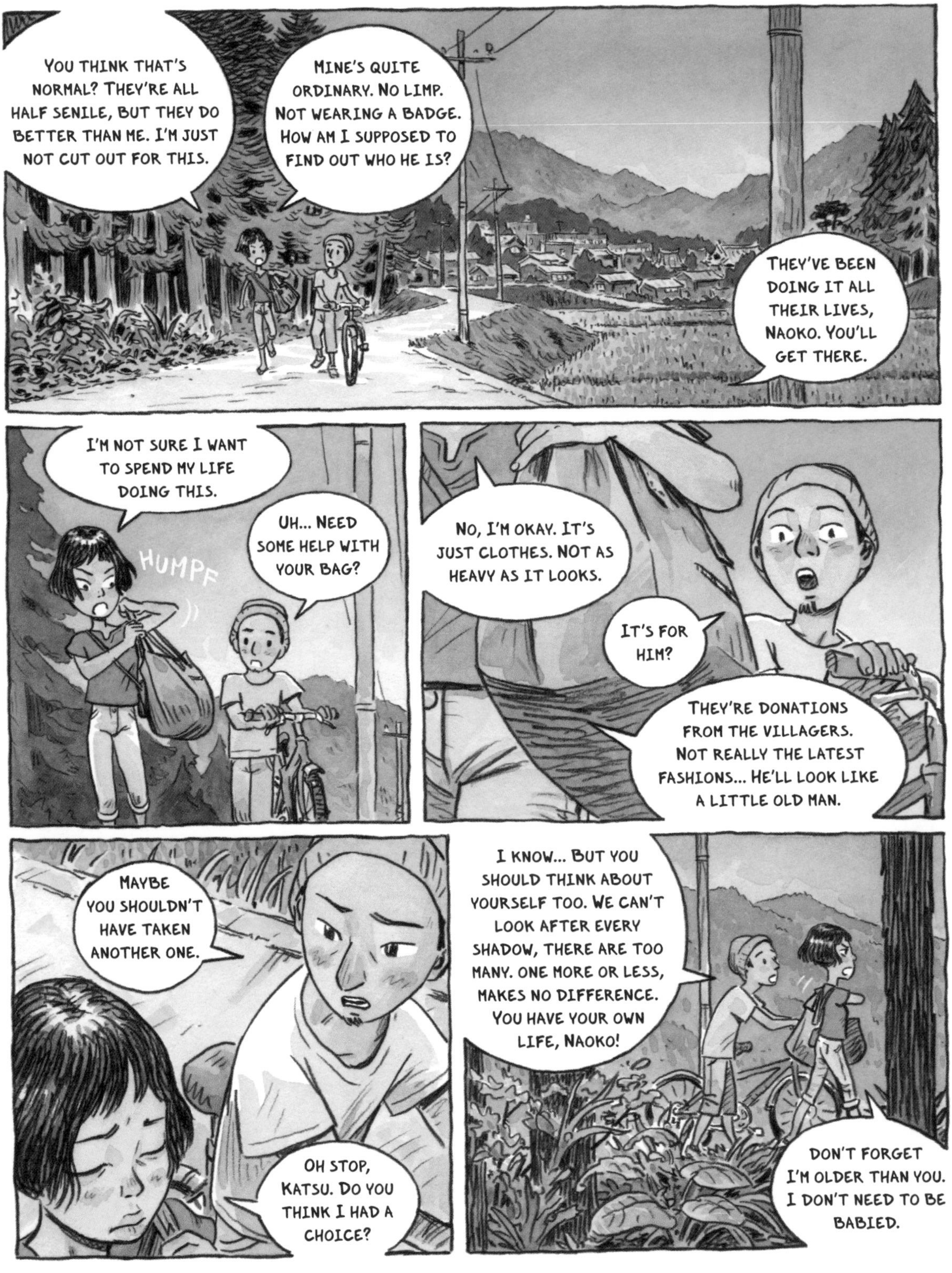

YOU THINK THAT'S NORMAL? THEY'RE ALL HALF SENILE, BUT THEY DO BETTER THAN ME. I'M JUST NOT CUT OUT FOR THIS.
MINE'S QUITE ORDINARY. NO LIMP. NOT WEARING A BADGE. HOW AM I SUPPOSED TO FIND OUT WHO HE IS?
THEY'VE BEEN DOING IT ALL THEIR LIVES, NAOKO. YOU'LL GET THERE.
I'M NOT SURE I WANT TO SPEND MY LIFE DOING THIS.
HUMPF
UH... NEED SOME HELP WITH YOUR BAG?
NO, I'M OKAY. IT'S JUST CLOTHES. NOT AS HEAVY AS IT LOOKS.
IT'S FOR HIM?
THEY'RE DONATIONS FROM THE VILLAGERS. NOT REALLY THE LATEST FASHIONS... HE'LL LOOK LIKE A LITTLE OLD MAN.
MAYBE YOU SHOULDN'T HAVE TAKEN ANOTHER ONE.
OH STOP, KATSU. DO YOU THINK I HAD A CHOICE?
I KNOW... BUT YOU SHOULD THINK ABOUT YOURSELF TOO. WE CAN'T LOOK AFTER EVERY SHADOW, THERE ARE TOO MANY. ONE MORE OR LESS, MAKES NO DIFFERENCE. YOU HAVE YOUR OWN LIFE, NAOKO!
DON'T FORGET I'M OLDER THAN YOU. I DON'T NEED TO BE BABIED.

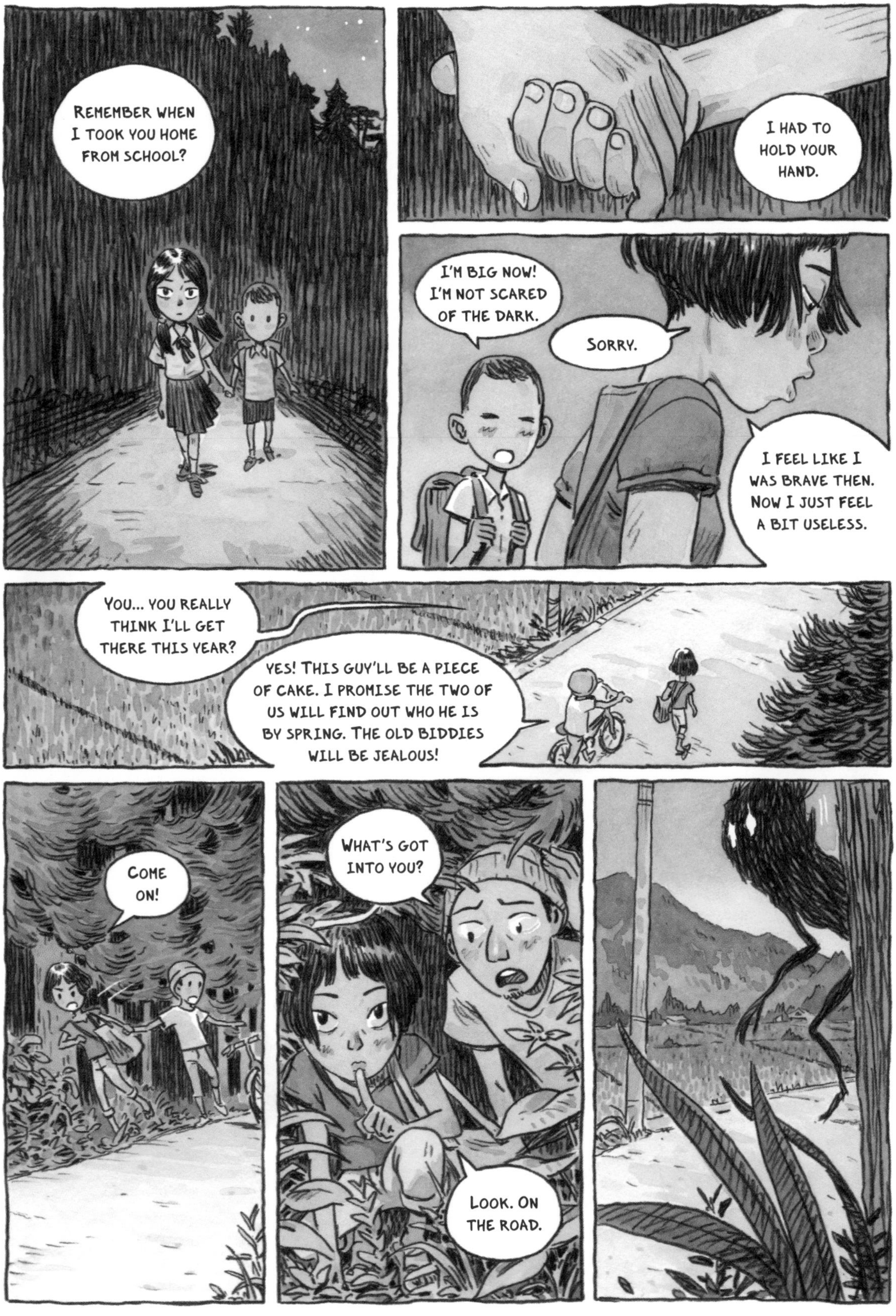
REMEMBER WHEN I TOOK YOU HOME FROM SCHOOL?
I HAD TO HOLD YOUR HAND.
I'M BIG NOW! I'M NOT SCARED OF THE DARK.
SORRY.
I FEEL LIKE I WAS BRAVE THEN. NOW I JUST FEEL A BIT USELESS.
YOU... YOU REALLY THINK I'LL GET THERE THIS YEAR?
YES! THIS GUY'LL BE A PIECE OF CAKE. I PROMISE THE TWO OF US WILL FIND OUT WHO HE IS BY SPRING. THE OLD BIDDIES WILL BE JEALOUS!
COME ON!
WHAT'S GOT INTO YOU?
LOOK. ON THE ROAD.

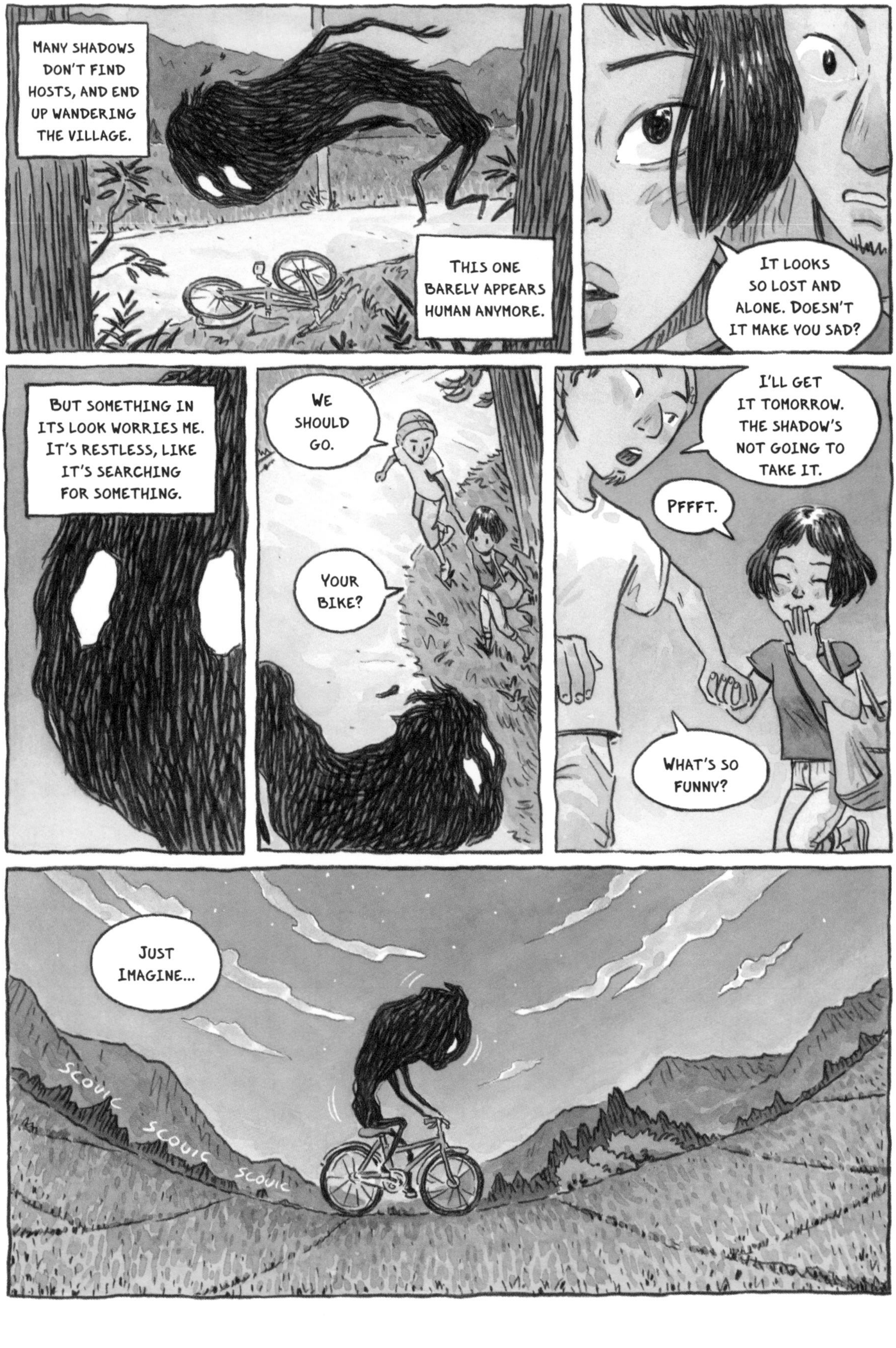

MANY SHADOWS DON'T FIND HOSTS, AND END UP WANDERING THE VILLAGE.
THIS ONE BARELY APPEARS HUMAN ANYMORE.
IT LOOKS SO LOST AND ALONE. DOESN'T IT MAKE YOU SAD?
BUT SOMETHING IN ITS LOOK WORRIES ME. IT'S RESTLESS, LIKE IT'S SEARCHING FOR SOMETHING.
WE SHOULD GO.
YOUR BIKE?
I'LL GET IT TOMORROW. THE SHADOW'S NOT GOING TO TAKE IT.
PFFFT.
WHAT'S SO FUNNY?
JUST IMAGINE...
SCOUIC
SCOUIC
SCOUIC

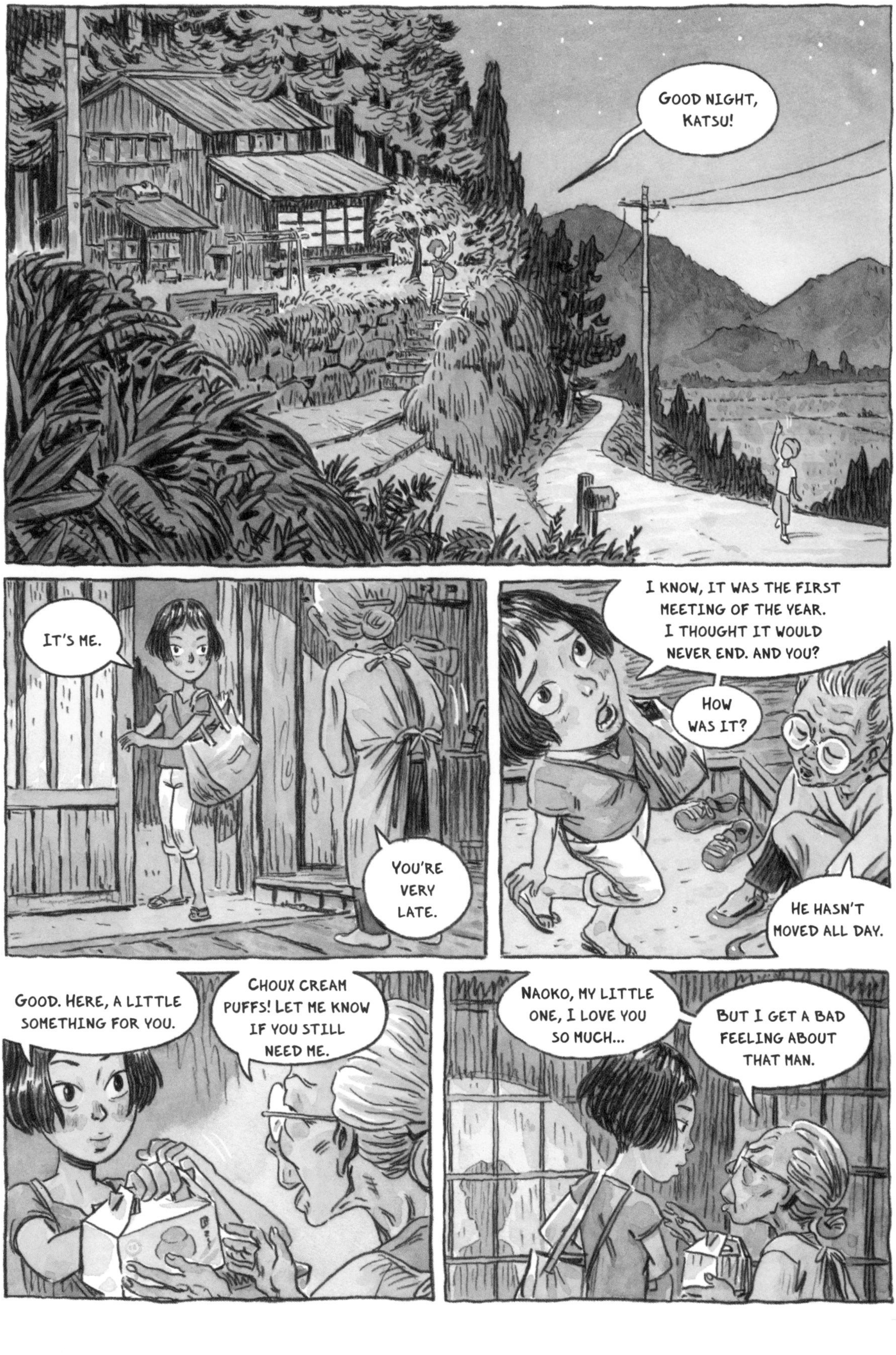
GOOD NIGHT, KATSU!
IT'S ME.
YOU'RE VERY LATE.
I KNOW, IT WAS THE FIRST MEETING OF THE YEAR. I THOUGHT IT WOULD NEVER END. AND YOU?
HOW WAS IT?
HE HASN'T MOVED ALL DAY.
GOOD. HERE, A LITTLE SOMETHING FOR YOU.
CHOUX CREAM PUFFS! LET ME KNOW IF YOU STILL NEED ME.
NAOKO, MY LITTLE ONE, I LOVE YOU SO MUCH...
BUT I GET A BAD FEELING ABOUT THAT MAN.

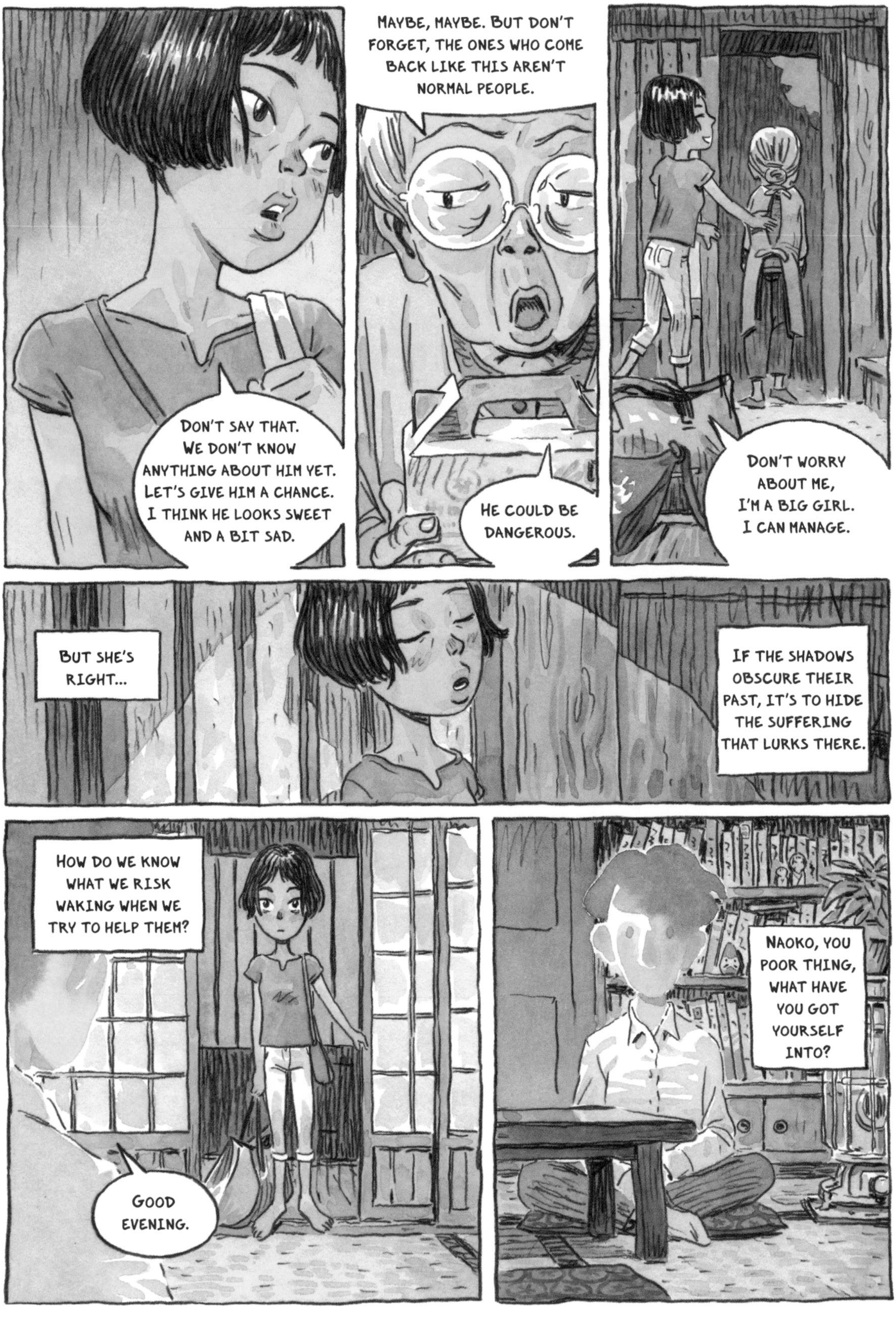
Maybe, maybe. But don't forget, the ones who come back like this aren't normal people.
Don't say that. We don't know anything about him yet. Let's give him a chance. I think he looks sweet and a bit sad.
He could be dangerous.
Don't worry about me, I'm a big girl. I can manage.
But she's right...
If the shadows obscure their past, it's to hide the suffering that lurks there.
How do we know what we risk waking when we try to help them?
Good evening.
Naoko, you poor thing, what have you got yourself into?

Like a star

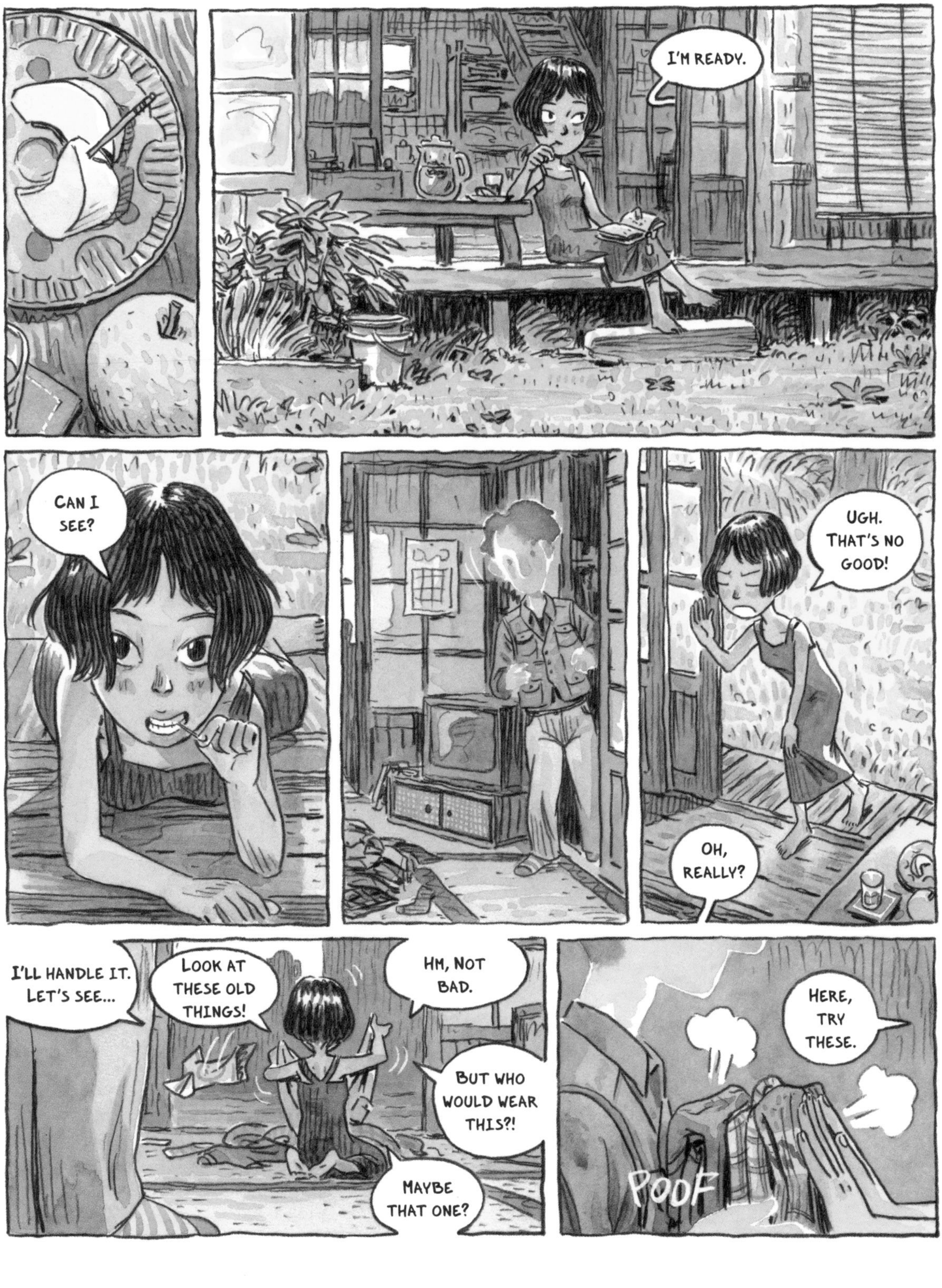
I'M READY.
CAN I SEE?
UGH. THAT'S NO GOOD!
OH, REALLY?
I'LL HANDLE IT. LET'S SEE...
LOOK AT THESE OLD THINGS!
HM, NOT BAD.
BUT WHO WOULD WEAR THIS?!
MAYBE THAT ONE?
HERE, TRY THESE.
POOF

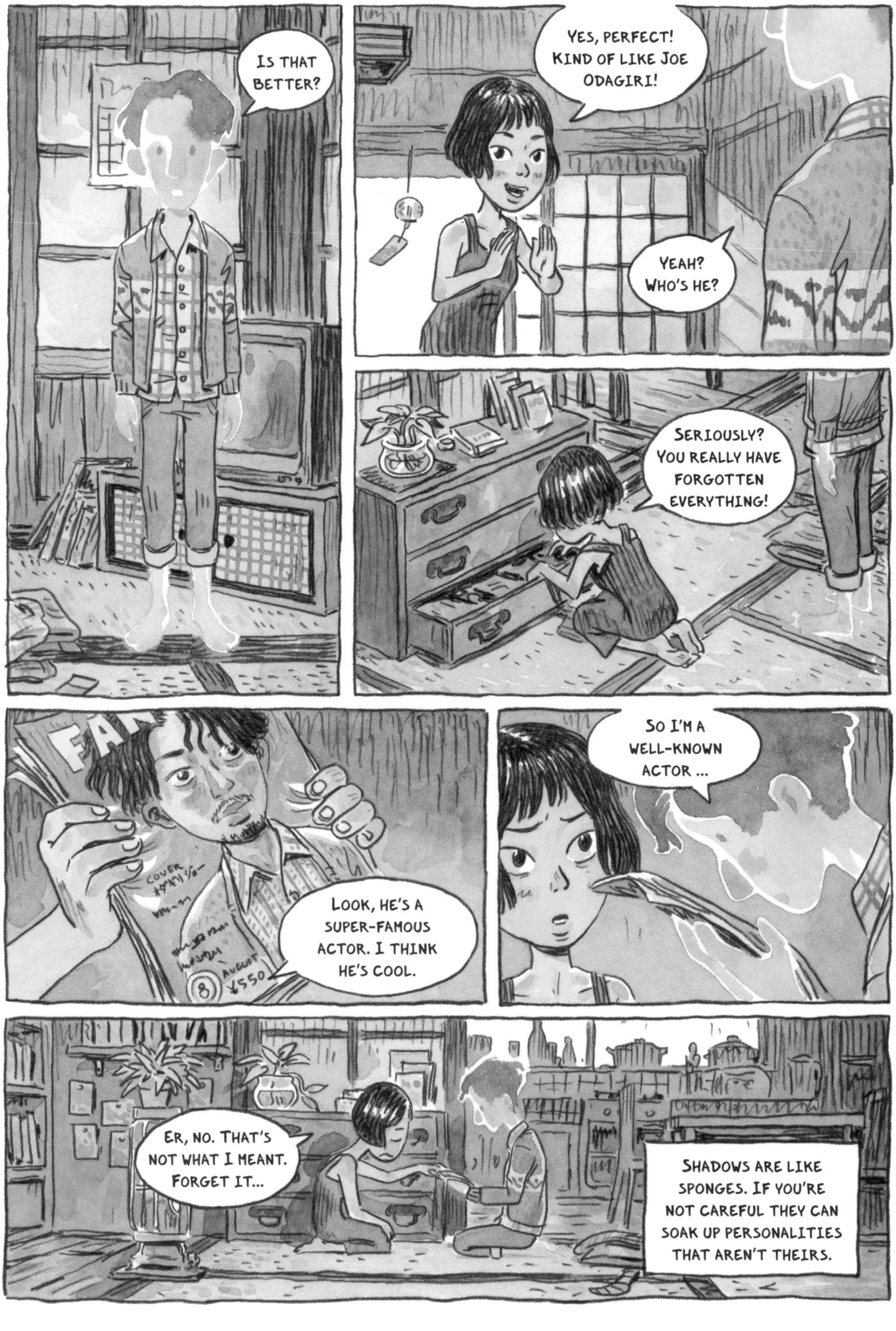
IS THAT BETTER?
YES, PERFECT! KIND OF LIKE JOE ODAGIRI!
YEAH? WHO'S HE?
SERIOUSLY? YOU REALLY HAVE FORGOTTEN EVERYTHING!
LOOK, HE'S A SUPER-FAMOUS ACTOR. I THINK HE'S COOL.
COVER
AUGUST
¥550
SO I'M A WELL-KNOWN ACTOR ...
ER, NO. THAT'S NOT WHAT I MEANT. FORGET IT...
SHADOWS ARE LIKE SPONGES. IF YOU'RE NOT CAREFUL THEY CAN SOAK UP PERSONALITIES THAT AREN'T THEIRS.

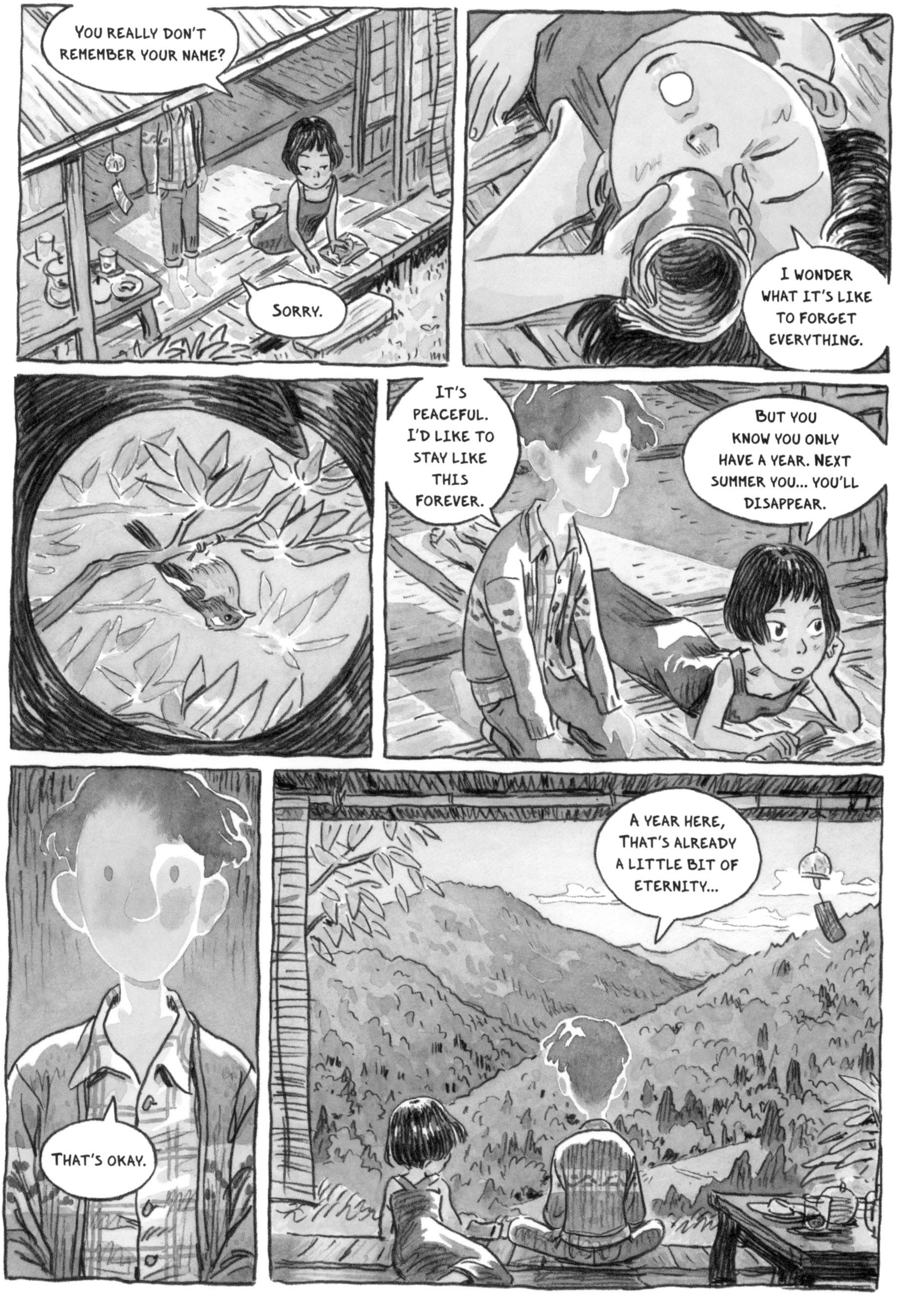
YOU REALLY DON'T REMEMBER YOUR NAME?
SORRY.
I WONDER WHAT IT'S LIKE TO FORGET EVERYTHING.
IT'S PEACEFUL. I'D LIKE TO STAY LIKE THIS FOREVER.
BUT YOU KNOW YOU ONLY HAVE A YEAR. NEXT SUMMER YOU... YOU'LL DISAPPEAR.
THAT'S OKAY.
A YEAR HERE, THAT'S ALREADY A LITTLE BIT OF ETERNITY...

Eternity

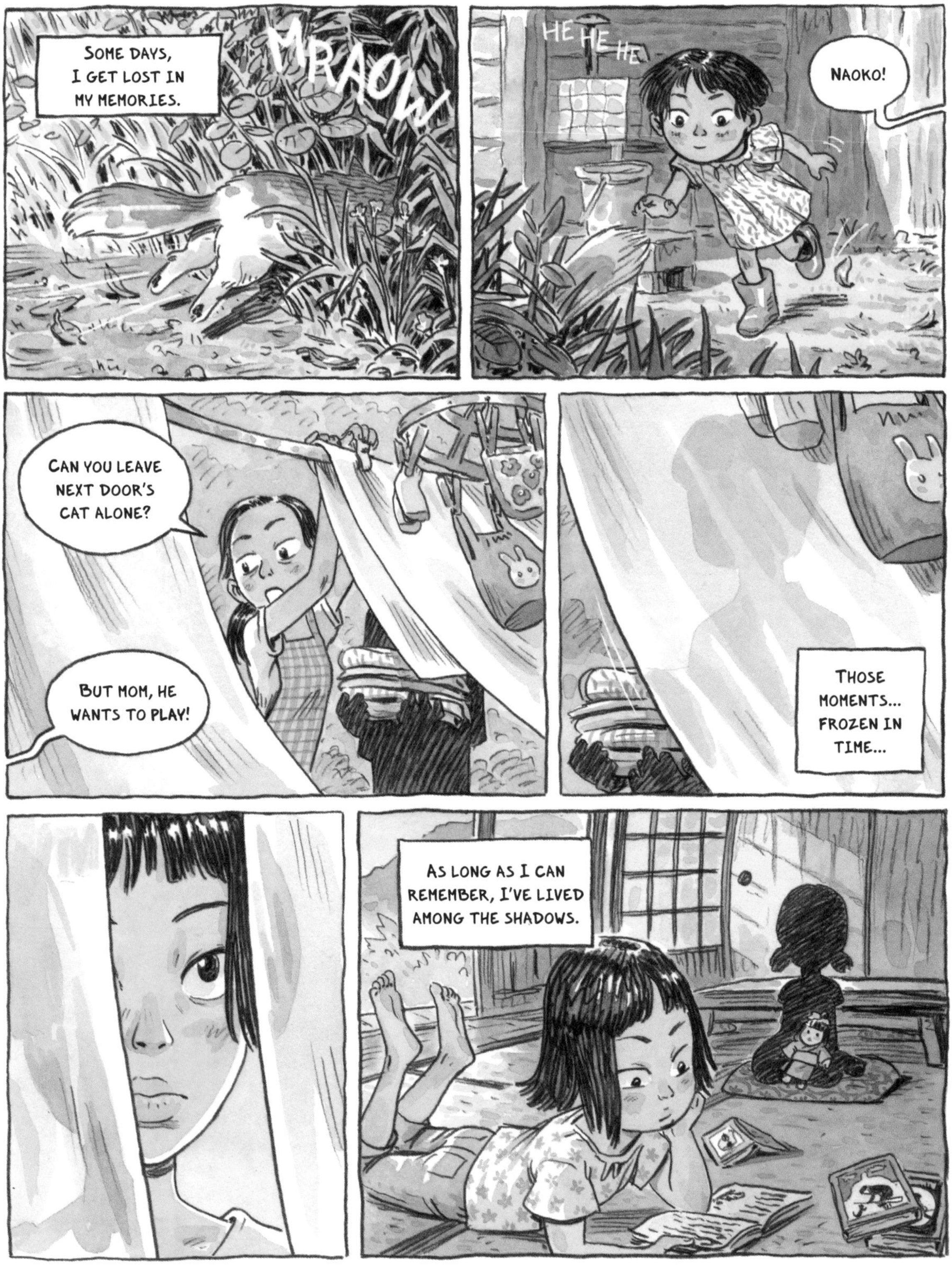
SOME DAYS, I GET LOST IN MY MEMORIES.
MRAOW
HE HE HE HE
NAOKO!
CAN YOU LEAVE NEXT DOOR'S CAT ALONE?
BUT MOM, HE WANTS TO PLAY!
THOSE MOMENTS... FROZEN IN TIME...
AS LONG AS I CAN REMEMBER, I'VE LIVED AMONG THE SHADOWS.

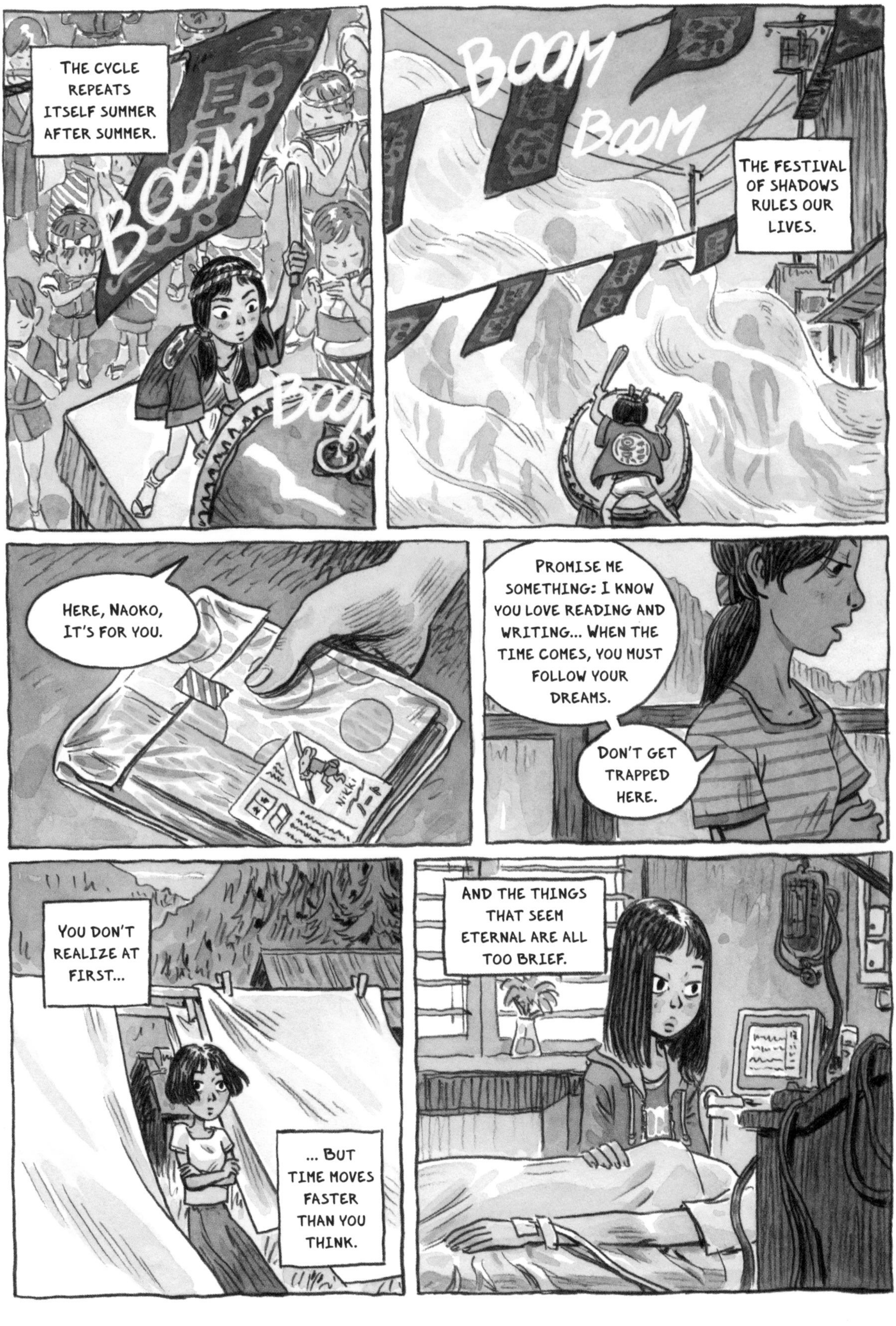

THE CYCLE REPEATS ITSELF SUMMER AFTER SUMMER.
BOOM
BOOM
BOOM
BOOM
BOOM
THE FESTIVAL OF SHADOWS RULES OUR LIVES.
HERE, NAOKO, IT'S FOR YOU.
PROMISE ME SOMETHING: I KNOW YOU LOVE READING AND WRITING... WHEN THE TIME COMES, YOU MUST FOLLOW YOUR DREAMS.
DON'T GET TRAPPED HERE.
YOU DON'T REALIZE AT FIRST...
... BUT TIME MOVES FASTER THAN YOU THINK.
AND THE THINGS THAT SEEM ETERNAL ARE ALL TOO BRIEF.

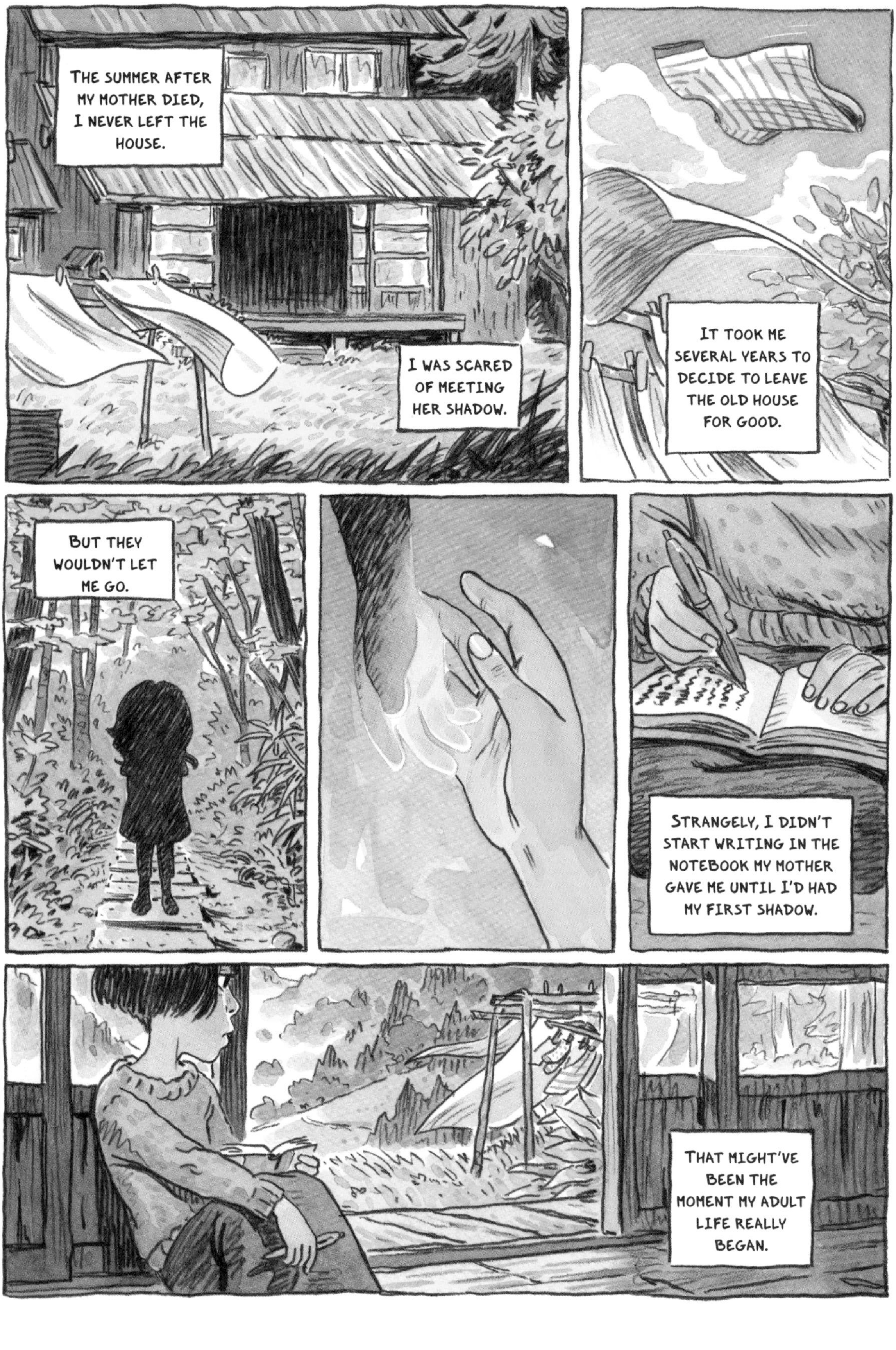
THE SUMMER AFTER MY MOTHER DIED, I NEVER LEFT THE HOUSE.
I WAS SCARED OF MEETING HER SHADOW.
IT TOOK ME SEVERAL YEARS TO DECIDE TO LEAVE THE OLD HOUSE FOR GOOD.
BUT THEY WOULDN'T LET ME GO.
STRANGELY, I DIDN'T START WRITING IN THE NOTEBOOK MY MOTHER GAVE ME UNTIL I'D HAD MY FIRST SHADOW.
THAT MIGHT'VE BEEN THE MOMENT MY ADULT LIFE REALLY BEGAN.

Persimmon season

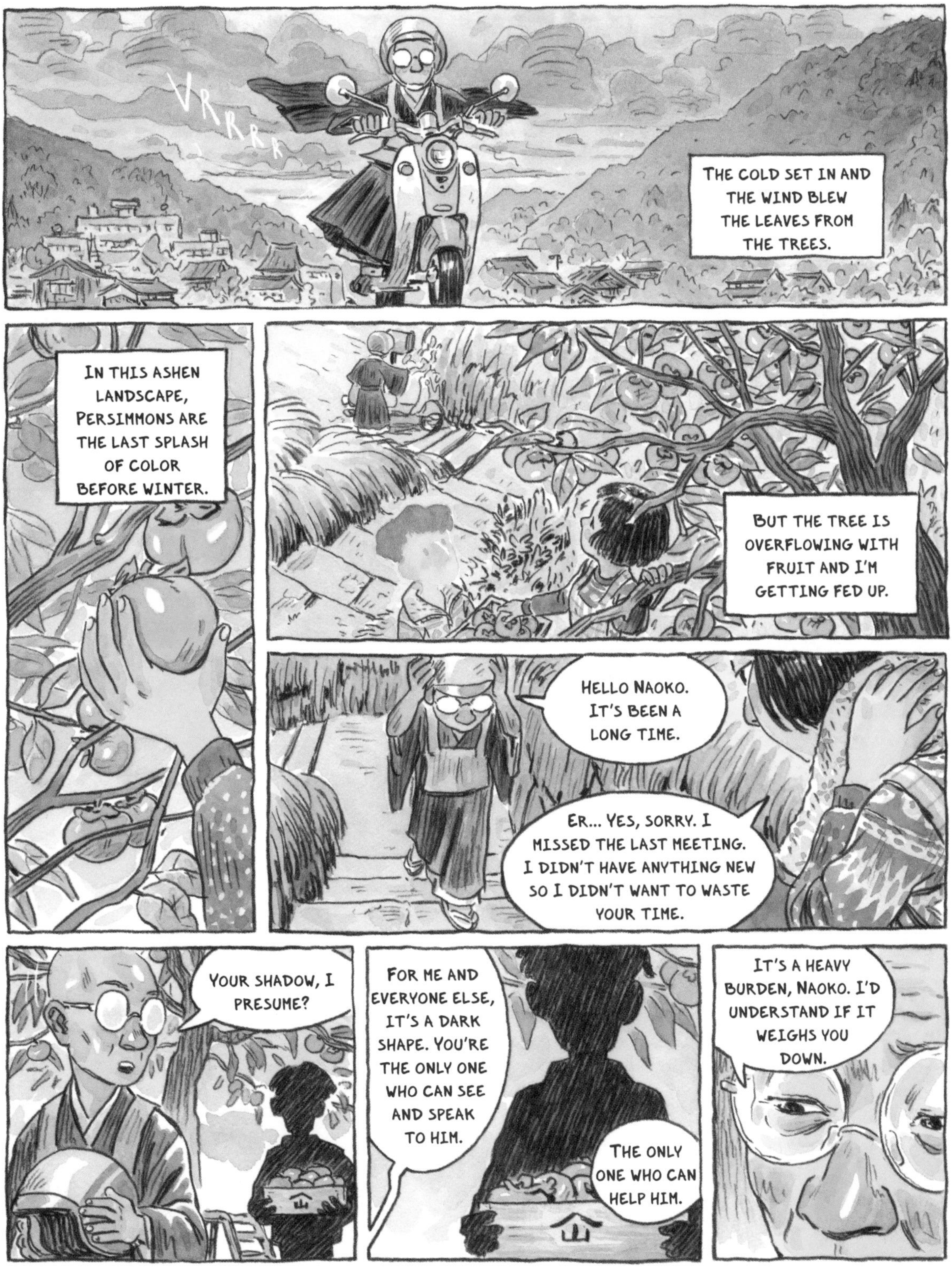
VRRRRR
THE COLD SET IN AND THE WIND BLEW THE LEAVES FROM THE TREES.
IN THIS ASHEN LANDSCAPE, PERSIMMONS ARE THE LAST SPLASH OF COLOR BEFORE WINTER.
BUT THE TREE IS OVERFLOWING WITH FRUIT AND I'M GETTING FED UP.
HELLO NAOKO. IT'S BEEN A LONG TIME.
ER... YES, SORRY. I MISSED THE LAST MEETING. I DIDN'T HAVE ANYTHING NEW SO I DIDN'T WANT TO WASTE YOUR TIME.
YOUR SHADOW, I PRESUME?
FOR ME AND EVERYONE ELSE, IT'S A DARK SHAPE. YOU'RE THE ONLY ONE WHO CAN SEE AND SPEAK TO HIM.
THE ONLY ONE WHO CAN HELP HIM.
IT'S A HEAVY BURDEN, NAOKO. I'D UNDERSTAND IF IT WEIGHS YOU DOWN.

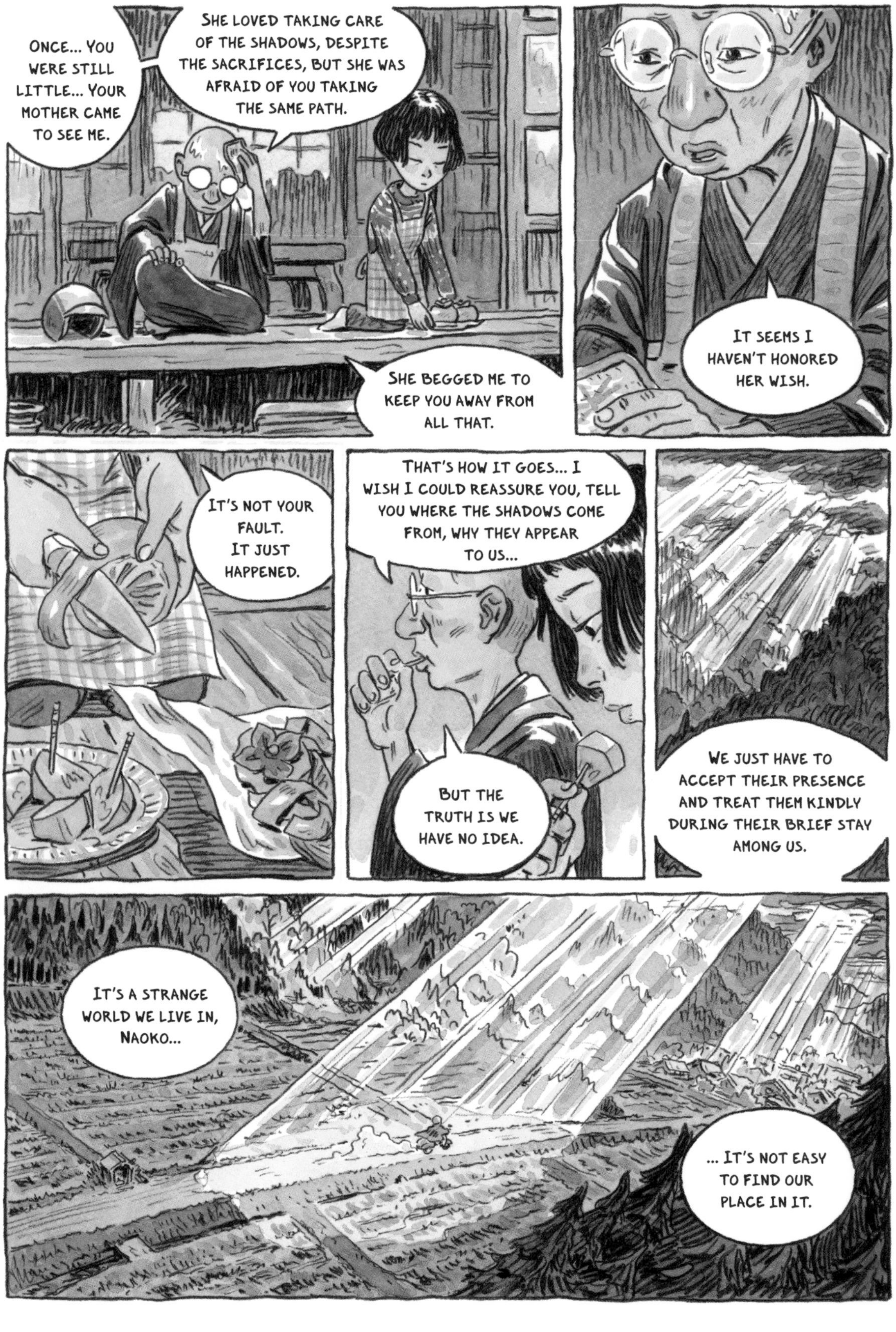
ONCE... YOU WERE STILL LITTLE... YOUR MOTHER CAME TO SEE ME.
SHE LOVED TAKING CARE OF THE SHADOWS, DESPITE THE SACRIFICES, BUT SHE WAS AFRAID OF YOU TAKING THE SAME PATH.
SHE BEGGED ME TO KEEP YOU AWAY FROM ALL THAT.
IT SEEMS I HAVEN'T HONORED HER WISH.
IT'S NOT YOUR FAULT. IT JUST HAPPENED.
THAT'S HOW IT GOES... I WISH I COULD REASSURE YOU, TELL YOU WHERE THE SHADOWS COME FROM, WHY THEY APPEAR TO US...
BUT THE TRUTH IS WE HAVE NO IDEA.
WE JUST HAVE TO ACCEPT THEIR PRESENCE AND TREAT THEM KINDLY DURING THEIR BRIEF STAY AMONG US.
IT'S A STRANGE WORLD WE LIVE IN, NAOKO...
... IT'S NOT EASY TO FIND OUR PLACE IN IT.

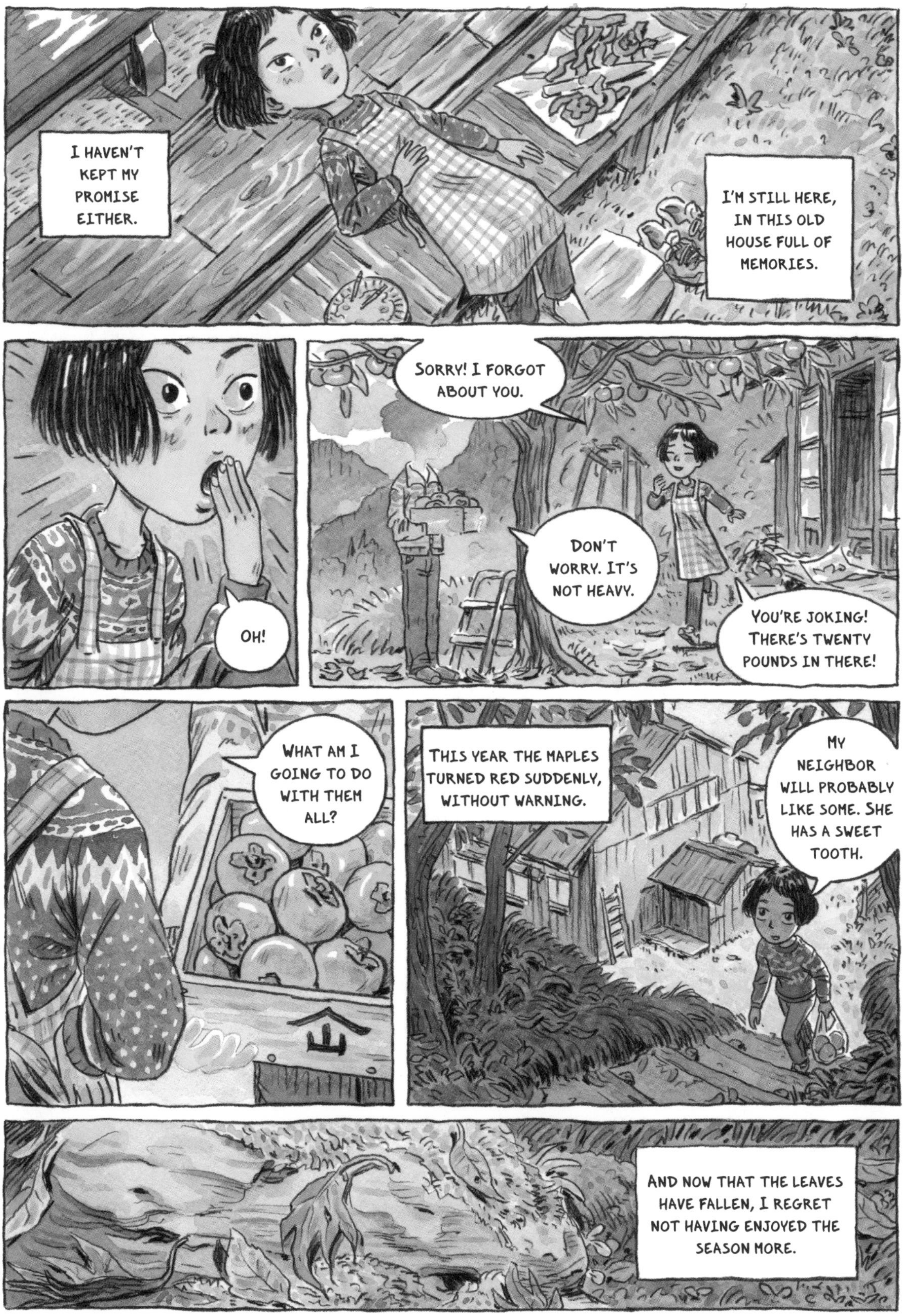
I HAVEN'T KEPT MY PROMISE EITHER.
I'M STILL HERE, IN THIS OLD HOUSE FULL OF MEMORIES.
OH!
SORRY! I FORGOT ABOUT YOU.
DON'T WORRY. IT'S NOT HEAVY.
YOU'RE JOKING! THERE'S TWENTY POUNDS IN THERE!
WHAT AM I GOING TO DO WITH THEM ALL?
THIS YEAR THE MAPLES TURNED RED SUDDENLY, WITHOUT WARNING.
MY NEIGHBOR WILL PROBABLY LIKE SOME. SHE HAS A SWEET TOOTH.
AND NOW THAT THE LEAVES HAVE FALLEN, I REGRET NOT HAVING ENJOYED THE SEASON MORE.

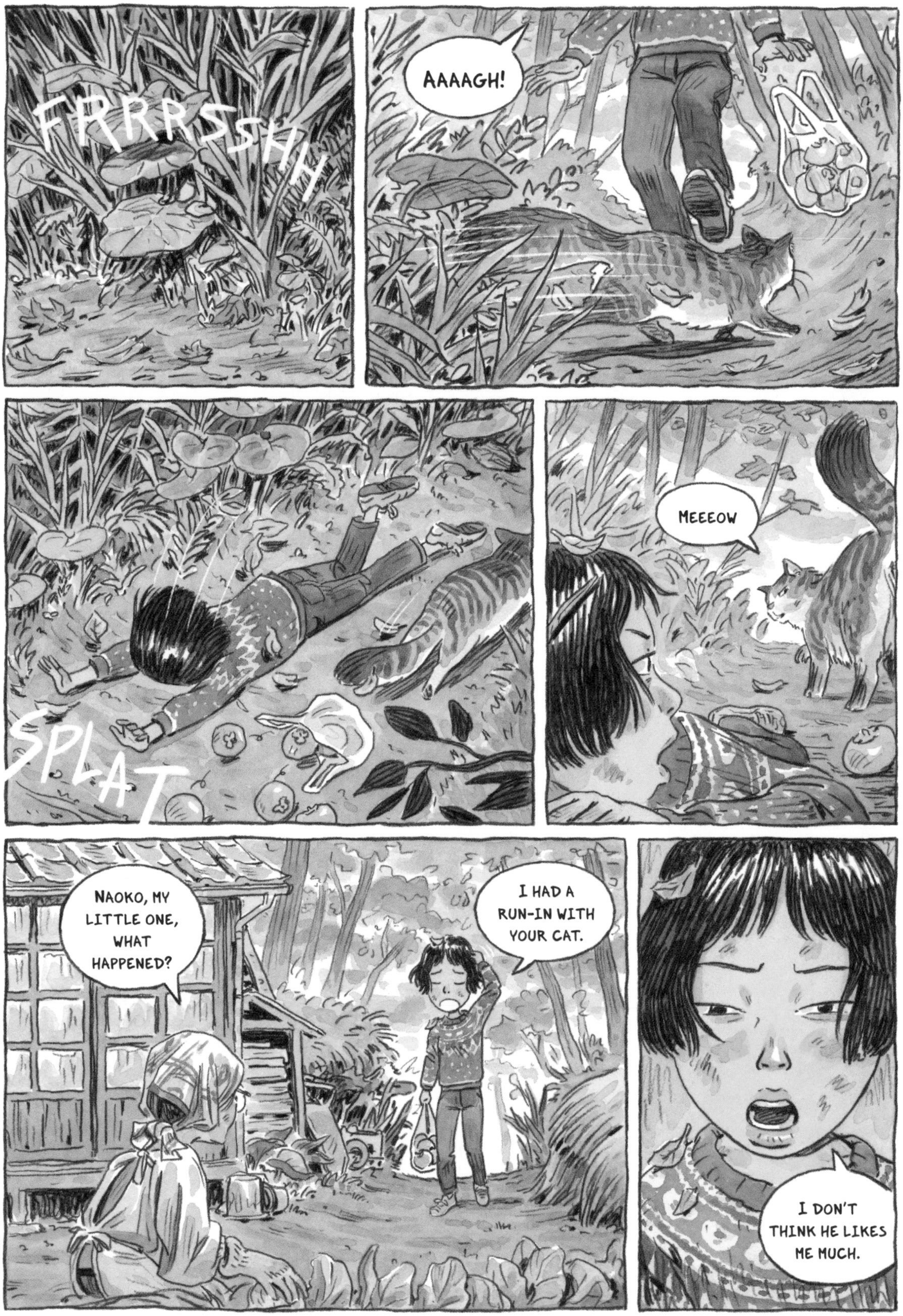
FRRRSSHH
AAAAGH!
SPLAT
MEEEOW
NAOKO, MY LITTLE ONE, WHAT HAPPENED?
I HAD A RUN-IN WITH YOUR CAT.
I DON'T THINK HE LIKES ME MUCH.

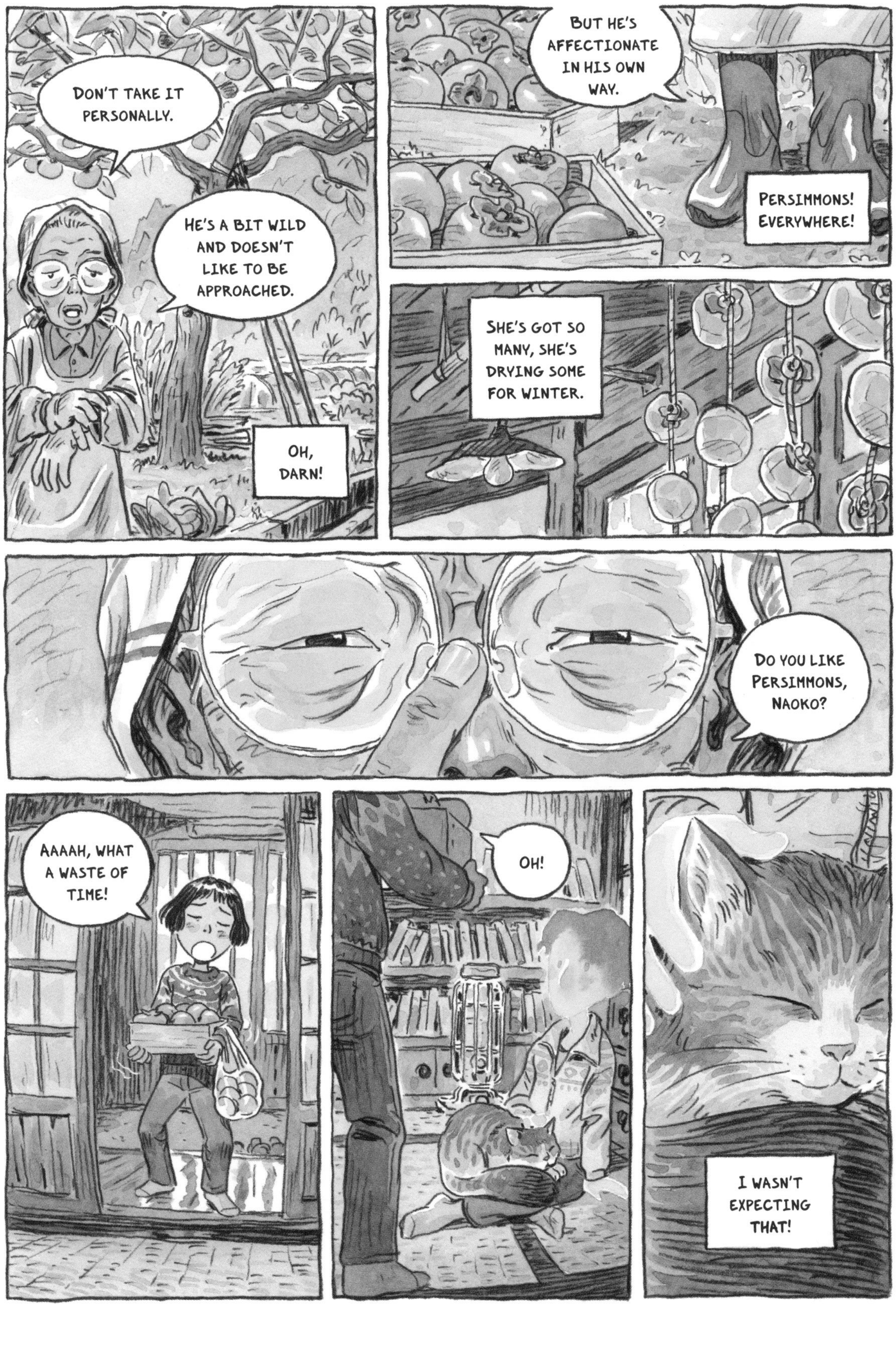

DON'T TAKE IT PERSONALLY.
HE'S A BIT WILD AND DOESN'T LIKE TO BE APPROACHED.
OH, DARN!
BUT HE'S AFFECTIONATE IN HIS OWN WAY.
PERSIMMONS! EVERYWHERE!
SHE'S GOT SO MANY, SHE'S DRYING SOME FOR WINTER.
DO YOU LIKE PERSIMMONS, NAOKO?
AAAAH, WHAT A WASTE OF TIME!
OH!
I WASN'T EXPECTING THAT!

The great escape

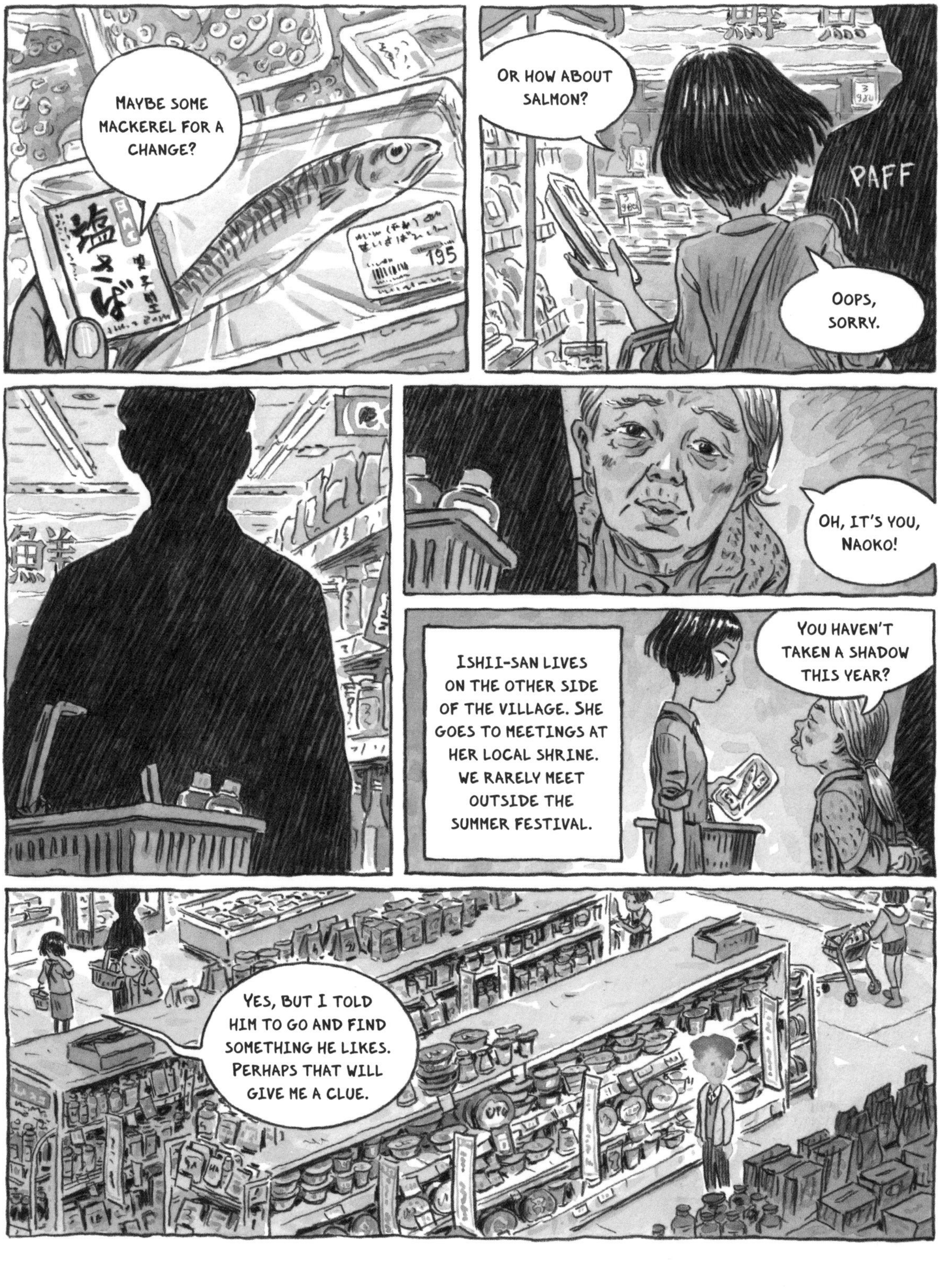
MAYBE SOME MACKEREL FOR A CHANGE?
OR HOW ABOUT SALMON?
PAFF
OOPS, SORRY.
OH, IT'S YOU, NAOKO!
ISHII-SAN LIVES ON THE OTHER SIDE OF THE VILLAGE. SHE GOES TO MEETINGS AT HER LOCAL SHRINE. WE RARELY MEET OUTSIDE THE SUMMER FESTIVAL.
YOU HAVEN'T TAKEN A SHADOW THIS YEAR?
YES, BUT I TOLD HIM TO GO AND FIND SOMETHING HE LIKES. PERHAPS THAT WILL GIVE ME A CLUE.

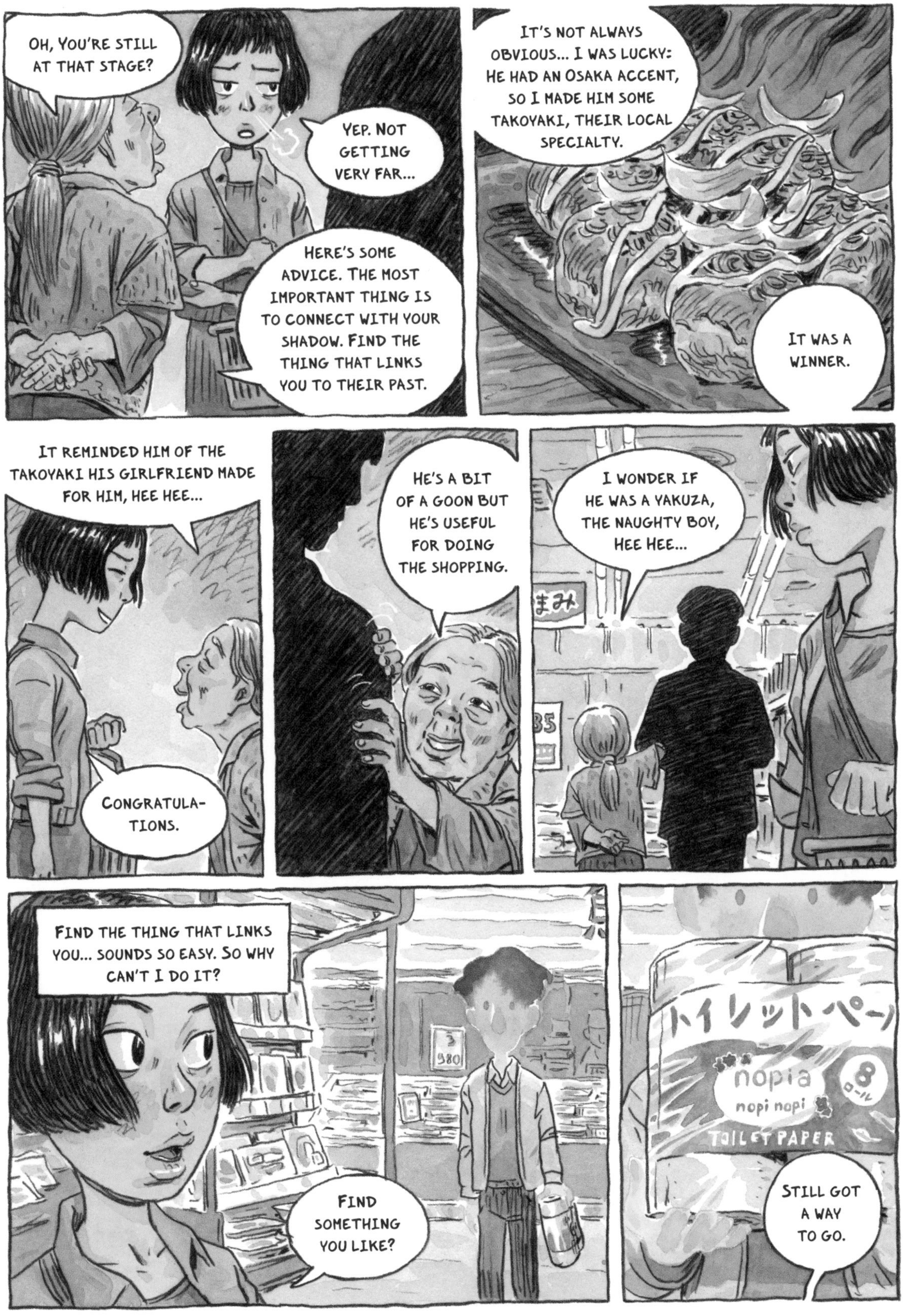
OH, YOU'RE STILL AT THAT STAGE?
YEP. NOT GETTING VERY FAR...
HERE'S SOME ADVICE. THE MOST IMPORTANT THING IS TO CONNECT WITH YOUR SHADOW. FIND THE THING THAT LINKS YOU TO THEIR PAST.
IT'S NOT ALWAYS OBVIOUS... I WAS LUCKY: HE HAD AN OSAKA ACCENT, SO I MADE HIM SOME TAKOYAKI, THEIR LOCAL SPECIALTY.
IT WAS A WINNER.
IT REMINDED HIM OF THE TAKOYAKI HIS GIRLFRIEND MADE FOR HIM, HEE HEE...
CONGRATULA-TIONS.
HE'S A BIT OF A GOON BUT HE'S USEFUL FOR DOING THE SHOPPING.
I WONDER IF HE WAS A YAKUZA, THE NAUGHTY BOY, HEE HEE...
FIND THE THING THAT LINKS YOU... SOUNDS SO EASY. SO WHY CAN'T I DO IT?
FIND SOMETHING YOU LIKE?
トイレットペー
nopia
nopi nopi
8 ロール
TOILET PAPER
STILL GOT A WAY TO GO.

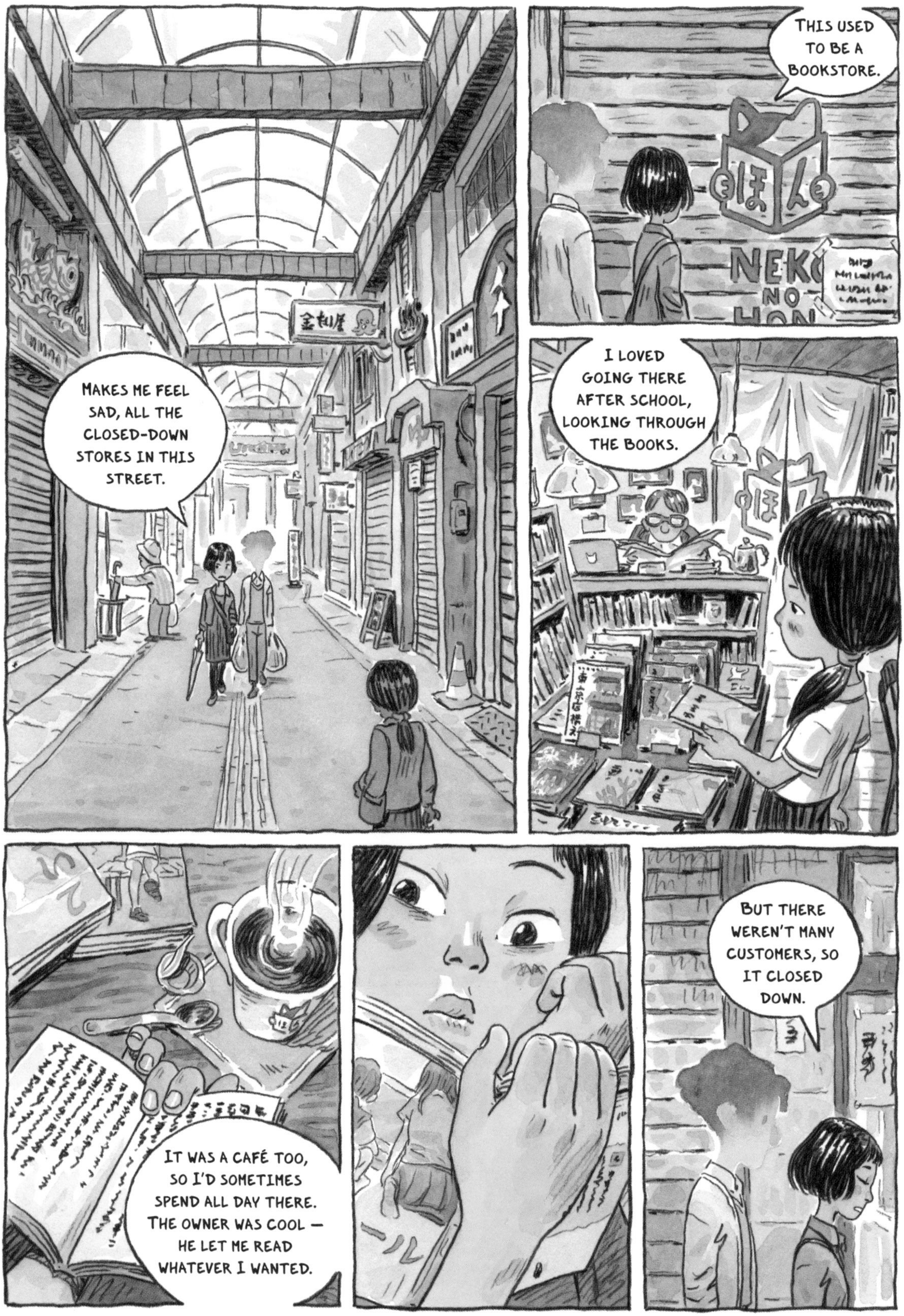
MAKES ME FEEL SAD, ALL THE CLOSED-DOWN STORES IN THIS STREET.
THIS USED TO BE A BOOKSTORE.
I LOVED GOING THERE AFTER SCHOOL, LOOKING THROUGH THE BOOKS.
IT WAS A CAFÉ TOO, SO I'D SOMETIMES SPEND ALL DAY THERE. THE OWNER WAS COOL — HE LET ME READ WHATEVER I WANTED.
BUT THERE WEREN'T MANY CUSTOMERS, SO IT CLOSED DOWN.

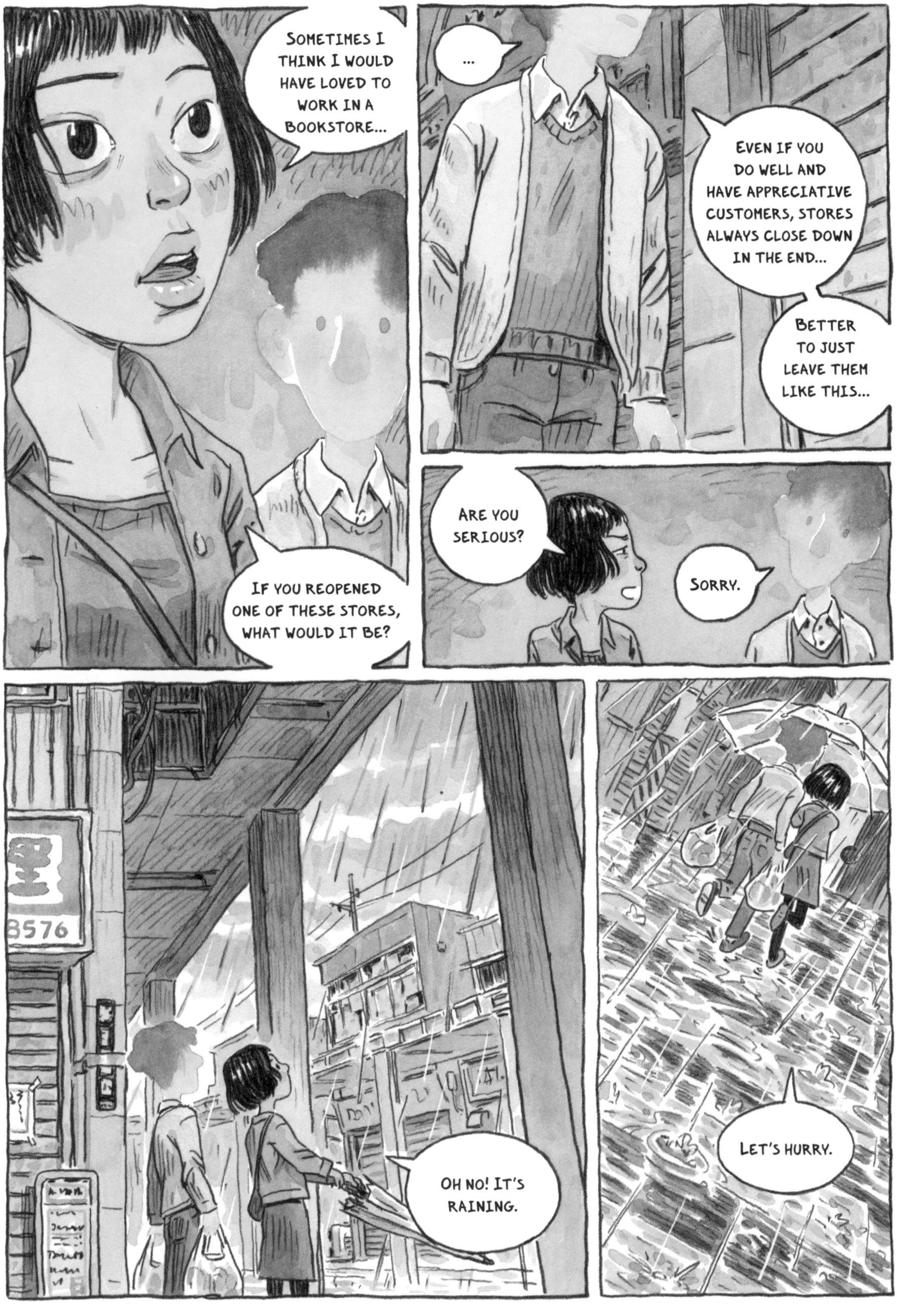
Sometimes I think I would have loved to work in a bookstore...
If you reopened one of these stores, what would it be?
...
Even if you do well and have appreciative customers, stores always close down in the end...
Better to just leave them like this...
Are you serious?
Sorry.
3576
Oh no! It's raining.
Let's hurry.

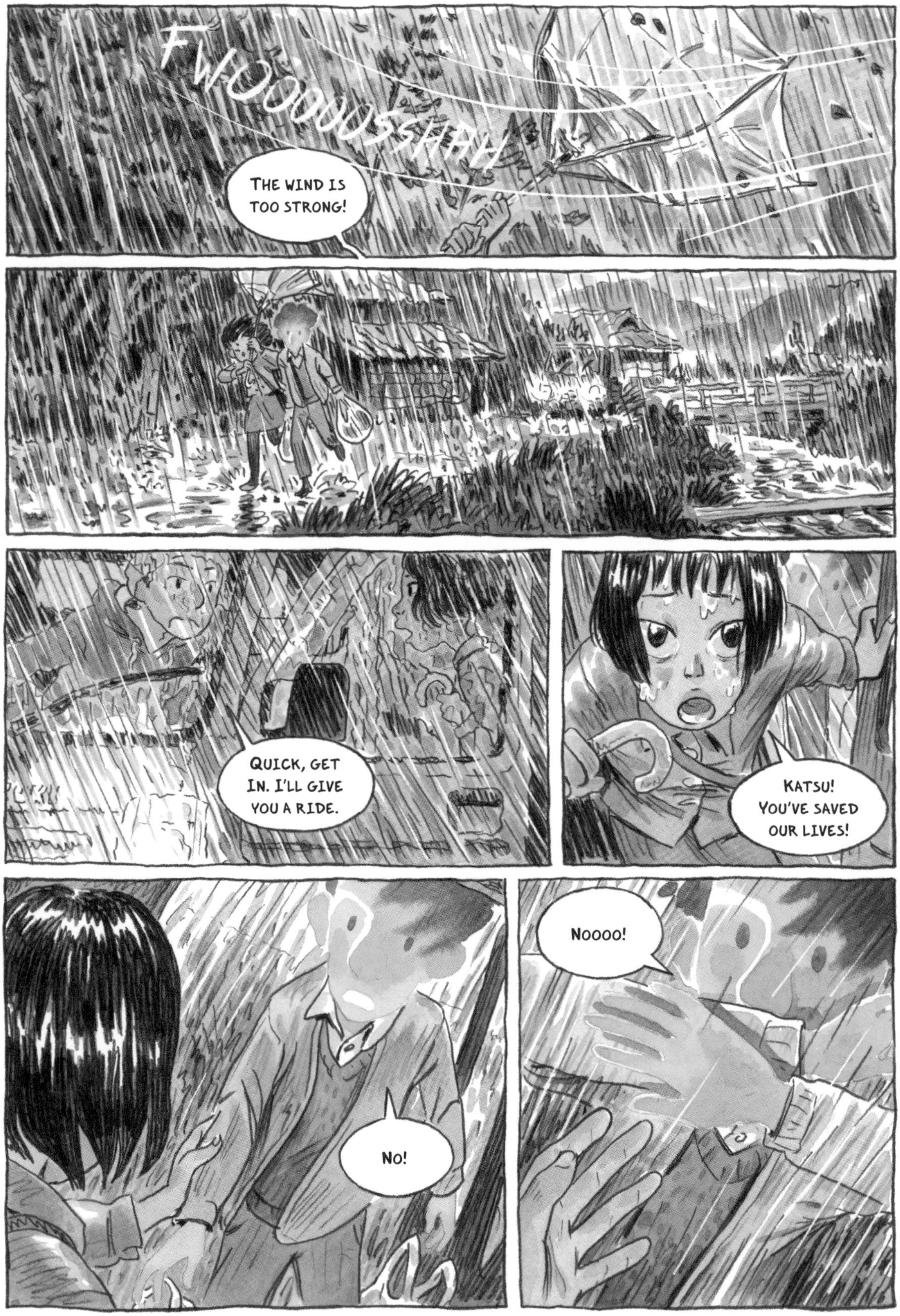
FWOOOOUSSHHH
THE WIND IS TOO STRONG!
QUICK, GET IN. I'LL GIVE YOU A RIDE.
KATSU! YOU'VE SAVED OUR LIVES!
NO!
NOOOO!

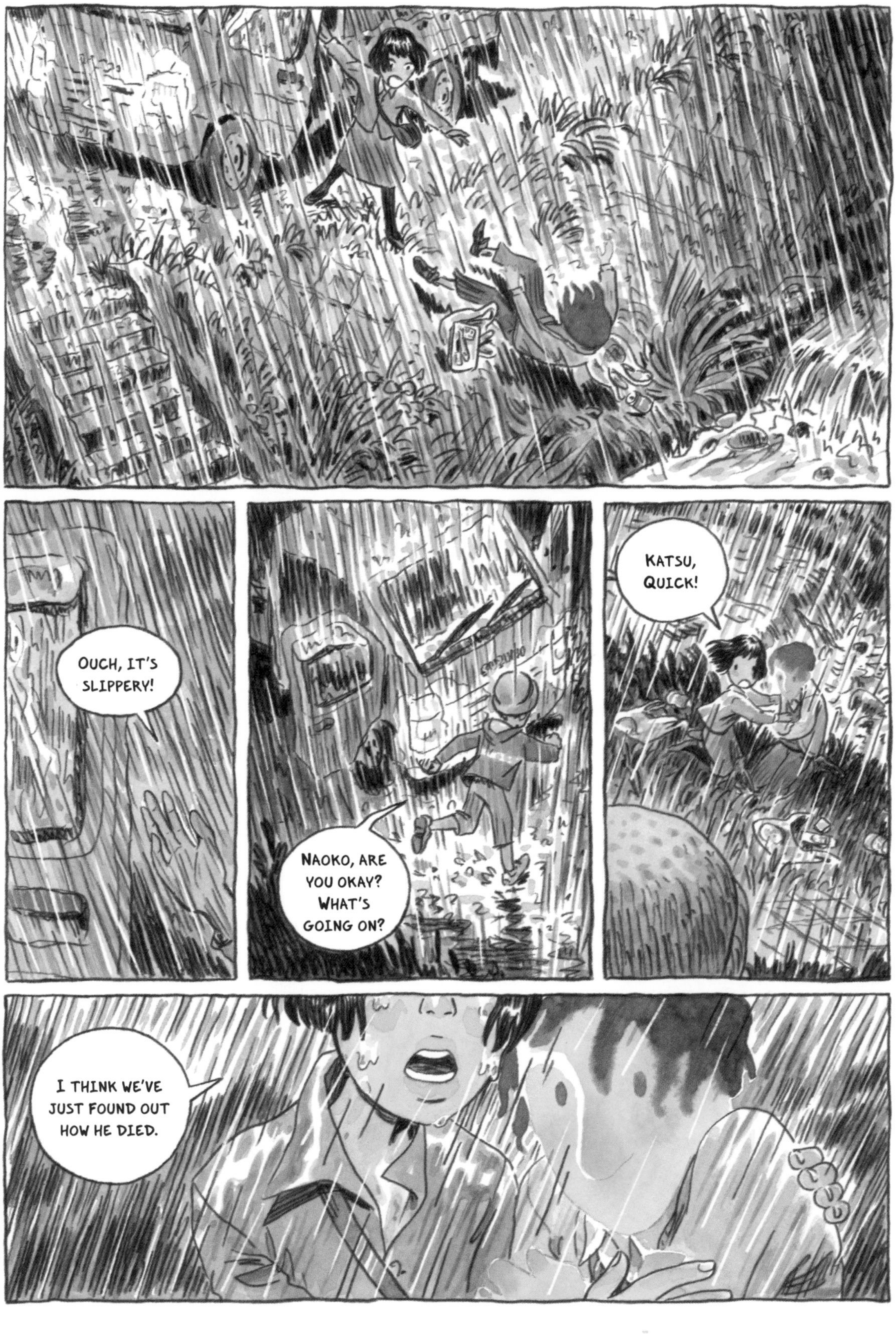
OUCH, IT'S SLIPPERY!
NAOKO, ARE YOU OKAY? WHAT'S GOING ON?
KATSU, QUICK!
I THINK WE'VE JUST FOUND OUT HOW HE DIED.

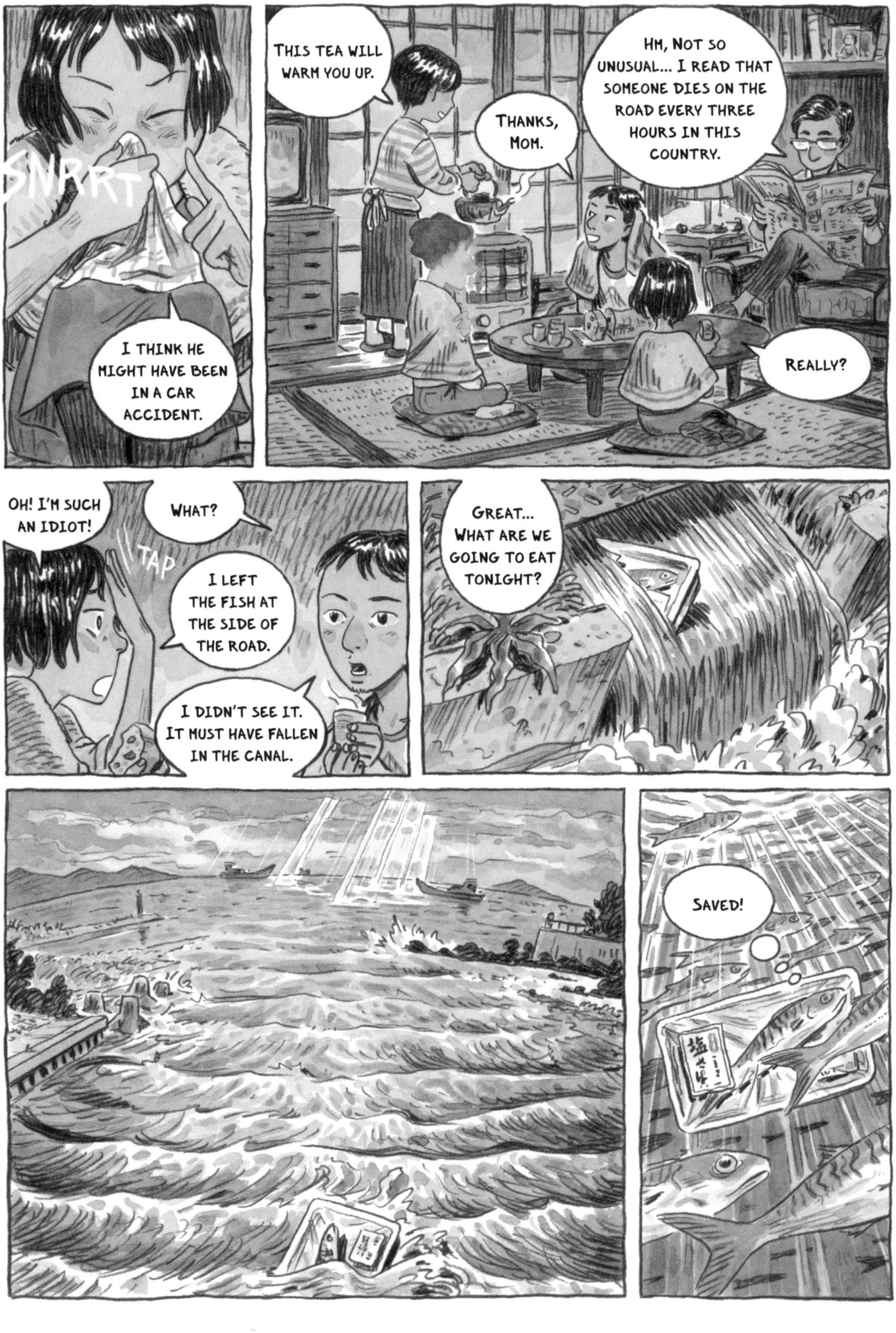
SNRRT
I THINK HE MIGHT HAVE BEEN IN A CAR ACCIDENT.
THIS TEA WILL WARM YOU UP.
THANKS, MOM.
HM, NOT SO UNUSUAL... I READ THAT SOMEONE DIES ON THE ROAD EVERY THREE HOURS IN THIS COUNTRY.
REALLY?
OH! I'M SUCH AN IDIOT!
WHAT?
TAP
I LEFT THE FISH AT THE SIDE OF THE ROAD.
I DIDN'T SEE IT. IT MUST HAVE FALLEN IN THE CANAL.
GREAT... WHAT ARE WE GOING TO EAT TONIGHT?
SAVED!

A sleepless night

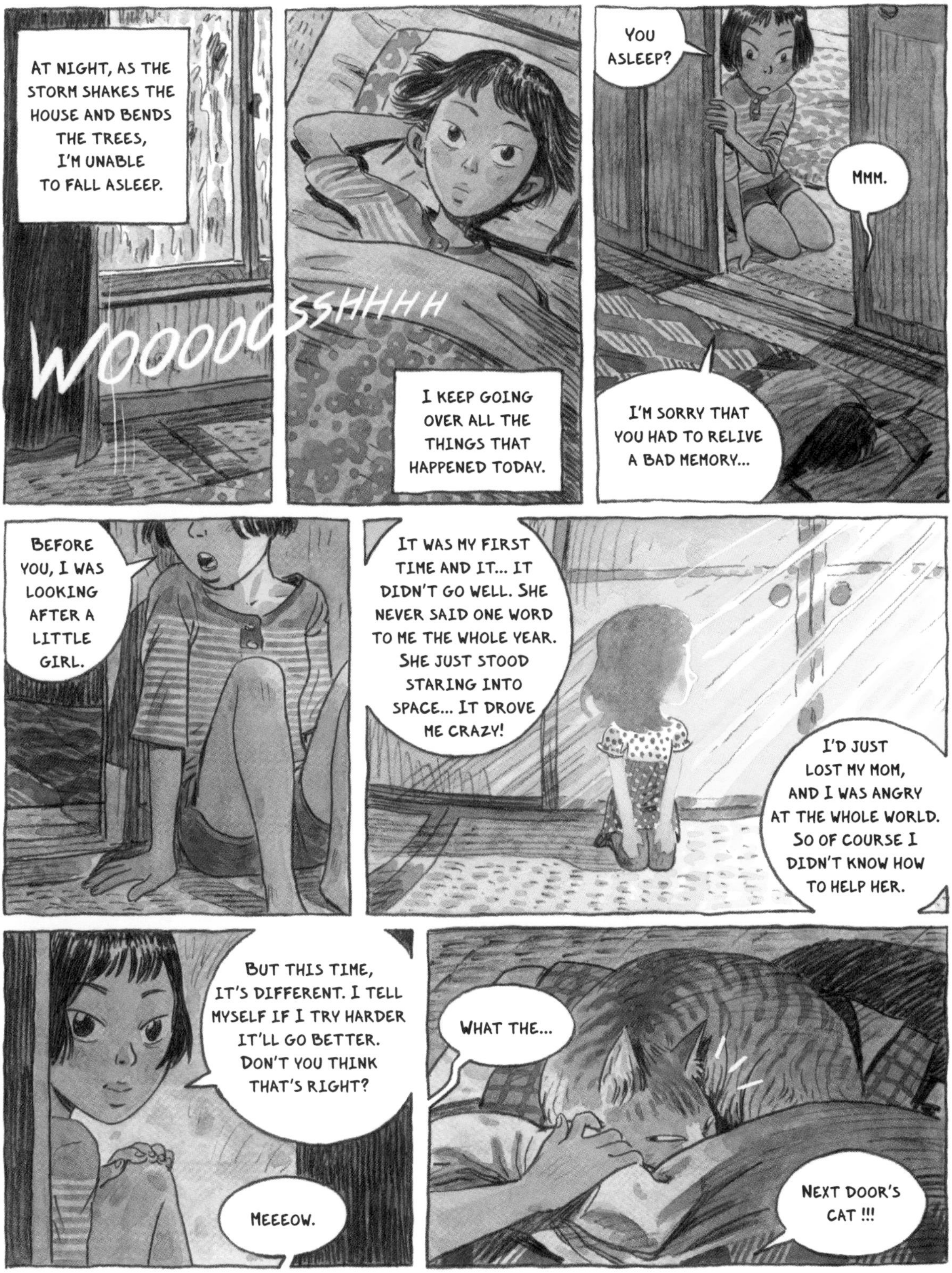

AT NIGHT, AS THE STORM SHAKES THE HOUSE AND BENDS THE TREES, I'M UNABLE TO FALL ASLEEP.
WOOOOOSSHHHH
I KEEP GOING OVER ALL THE THINGS THAT HAPPENED TODAY.
YOU ASLEEP?
MMM.
I'M SORRY THAT YOU HAD TO RELIVE A BAD MEMORY...
BEFORE YOU, I WAS LOOKING AFTER A LITTLE GIRL.
IT WAS MY FIRST TIME AND IT... IT DIDN'T GO WELL. SHE NEVER SAID ONE WORD TO ME THE WHOLE YEAR. SHE JUST STOOD STARING INTO SPACE... IT DROVE ME CRAZY!
I'D JUST LOST MY MOM, AND I WAS ANGRY AT THE WHOLE WORLD. SO OF COURSE I DIDN'T KNOW HOW TO HELP HER.
BUT THIS TIME, IT'S DIFFERENT. I TELL MYSELF IF I TRY HARDER IT'LL GO BETTER. DON'T YOU THINK THAT'S RIGHT?
MEEEOW.
WHAT THE...
NEXT DOOR'S CAT !!!

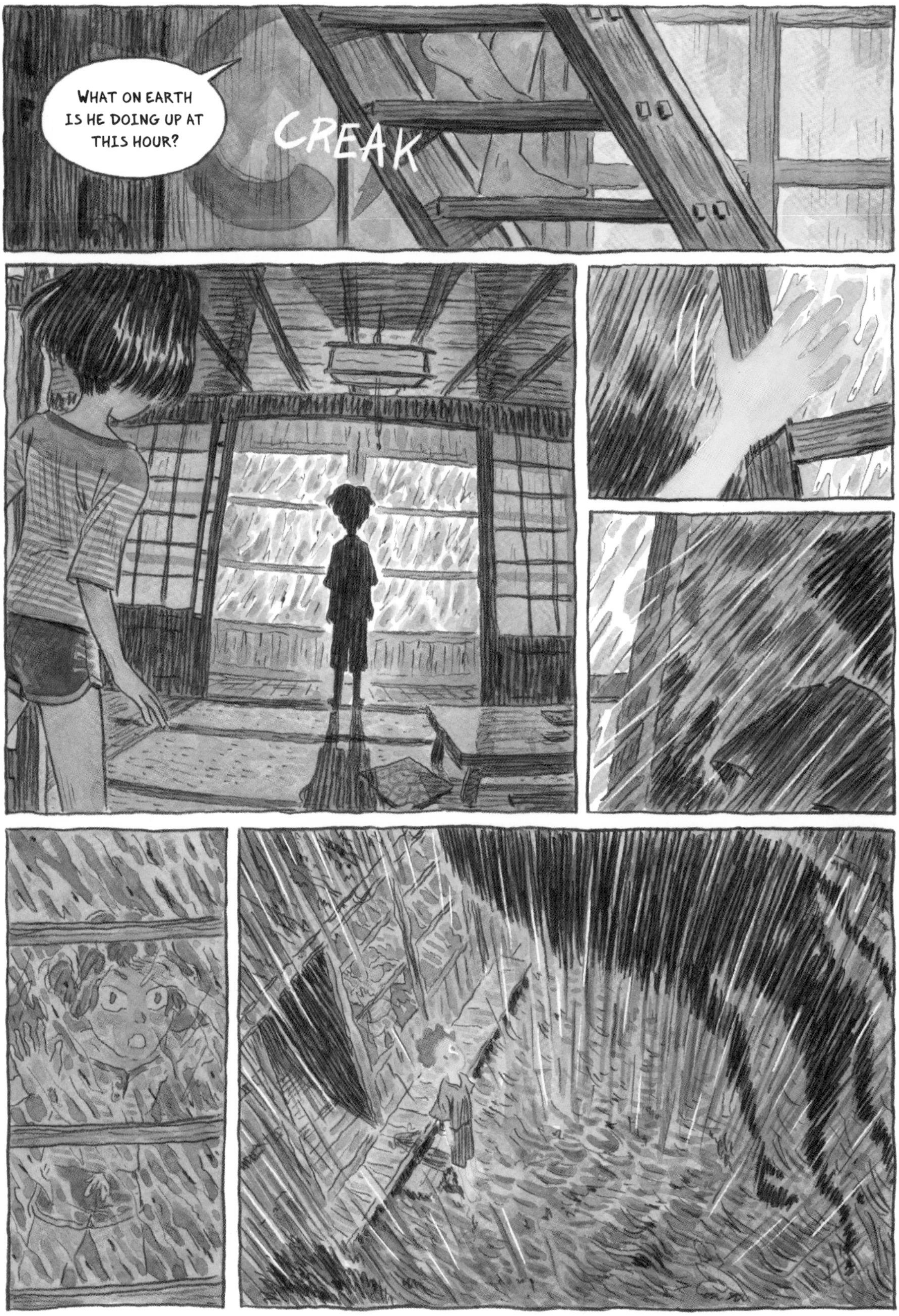
WHAT ON EARTH IS HE DOING UP AT THIS HOUR?
CREAK

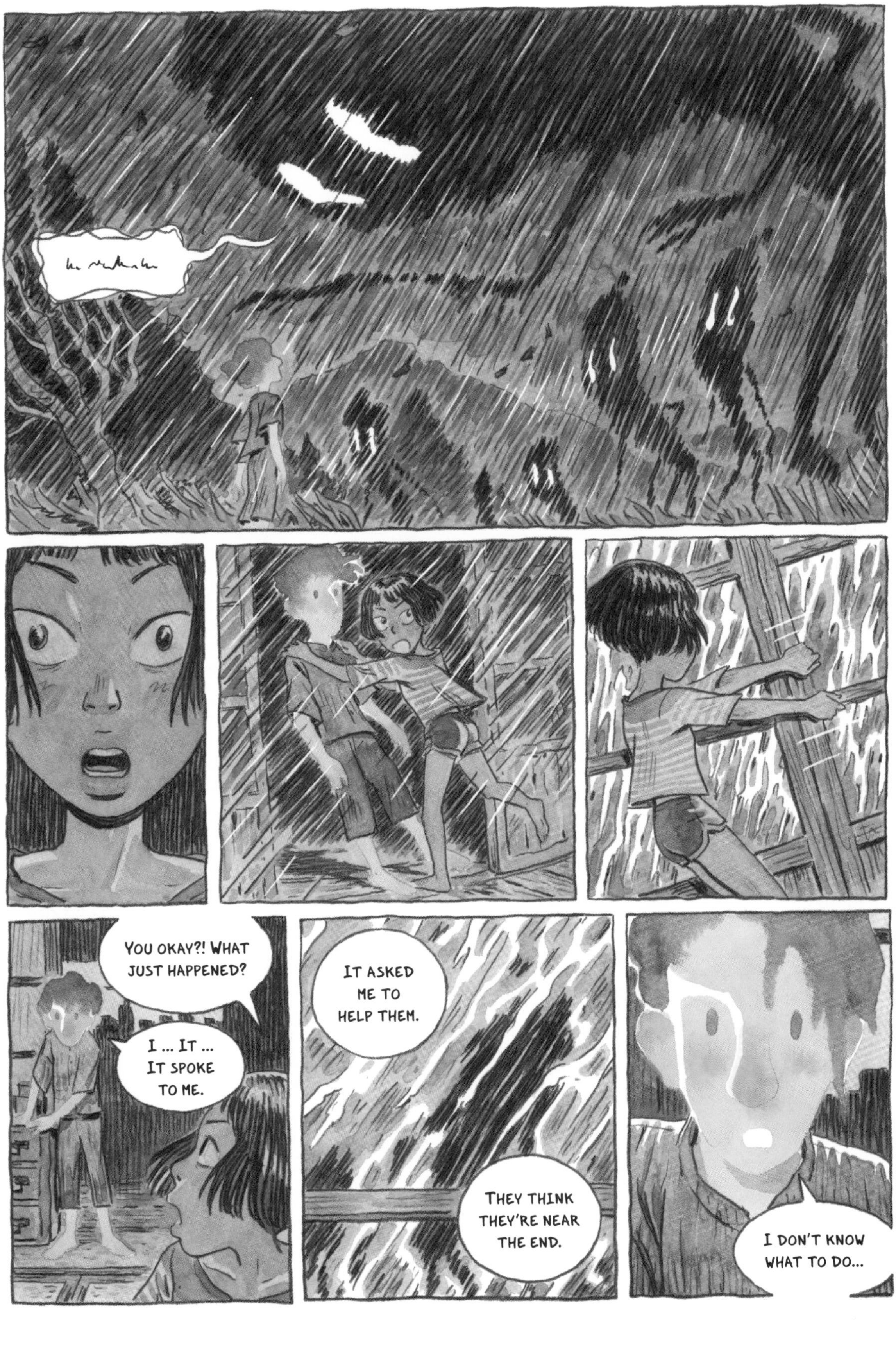
YOU OKAY?! WHAT JUST HAPPENED?
I ... IT ... IT SPOKE TO ME.
IT ASKED ME TO HELP THEM.
THEY THINK THEY'RE NEAR THE END.
I DON'T KNOW WHAT TO DO...

The mist clears

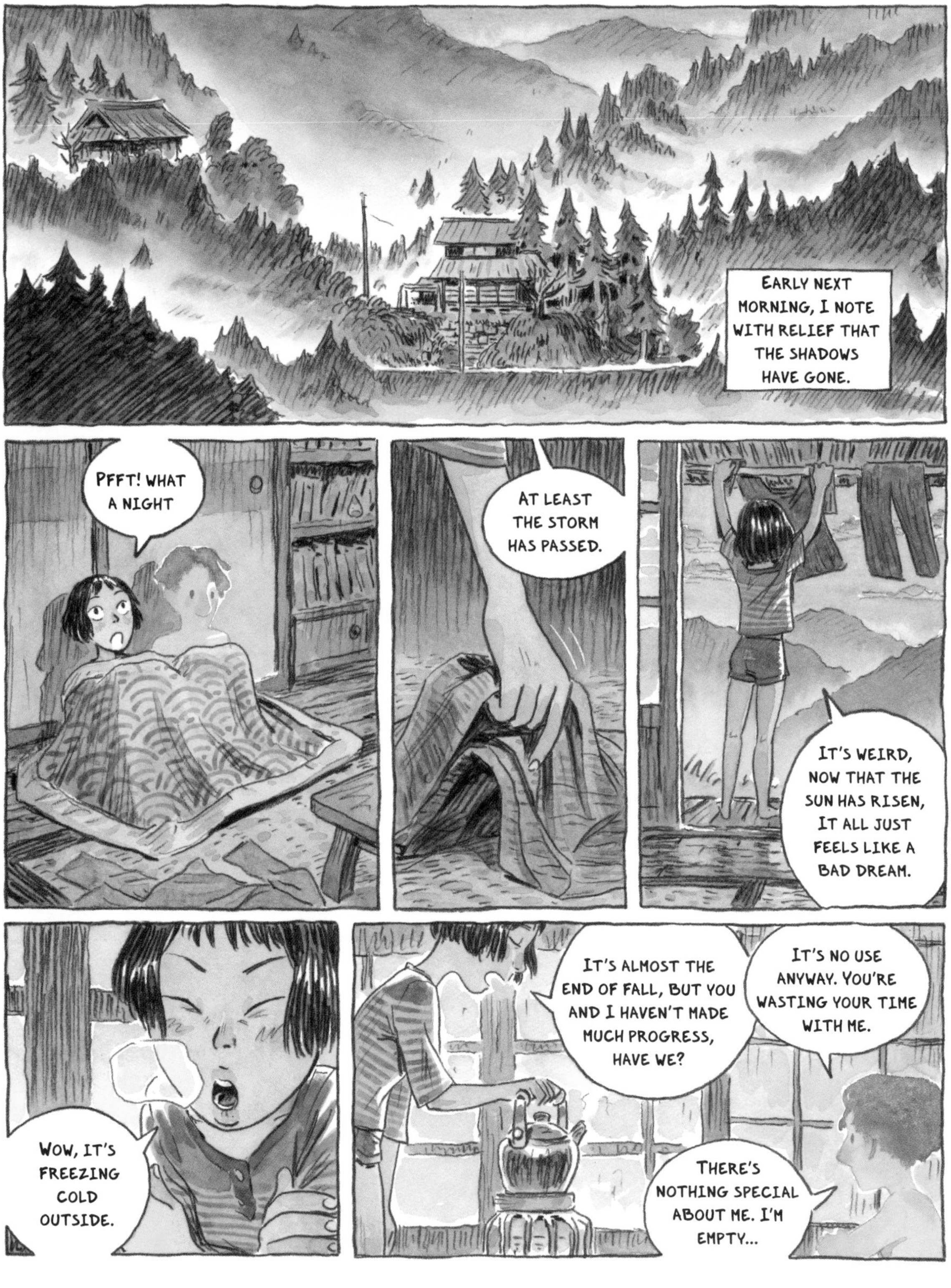
EARLY NEXT MORNING, I NOTE WITH RELIEF THAT THE SHADOWS HAVE GONE.
PFFT! WHAT A NIGHT
AT LEAST THE STORM HAS PASSED.
IT'S WEIRD, NOW THAT THE SUN HAS RISEN, IT ALL JUST FEELS LIKE A BAD DREAM.
WOW, IT'S FREEZING COLD OUTSIDE.
IT'S ALMOST THE END OF FALL, BUT YOU AND I HAVEN'T MADE MUCH PROGRESS, HAVE WE?
IT'S NO USE ANYWAY. YOU'RE WASTING YOUR TIME WITH ME.
THERE'S NOTHING SPECIAL ABOUT ME. I'M EMPTY...

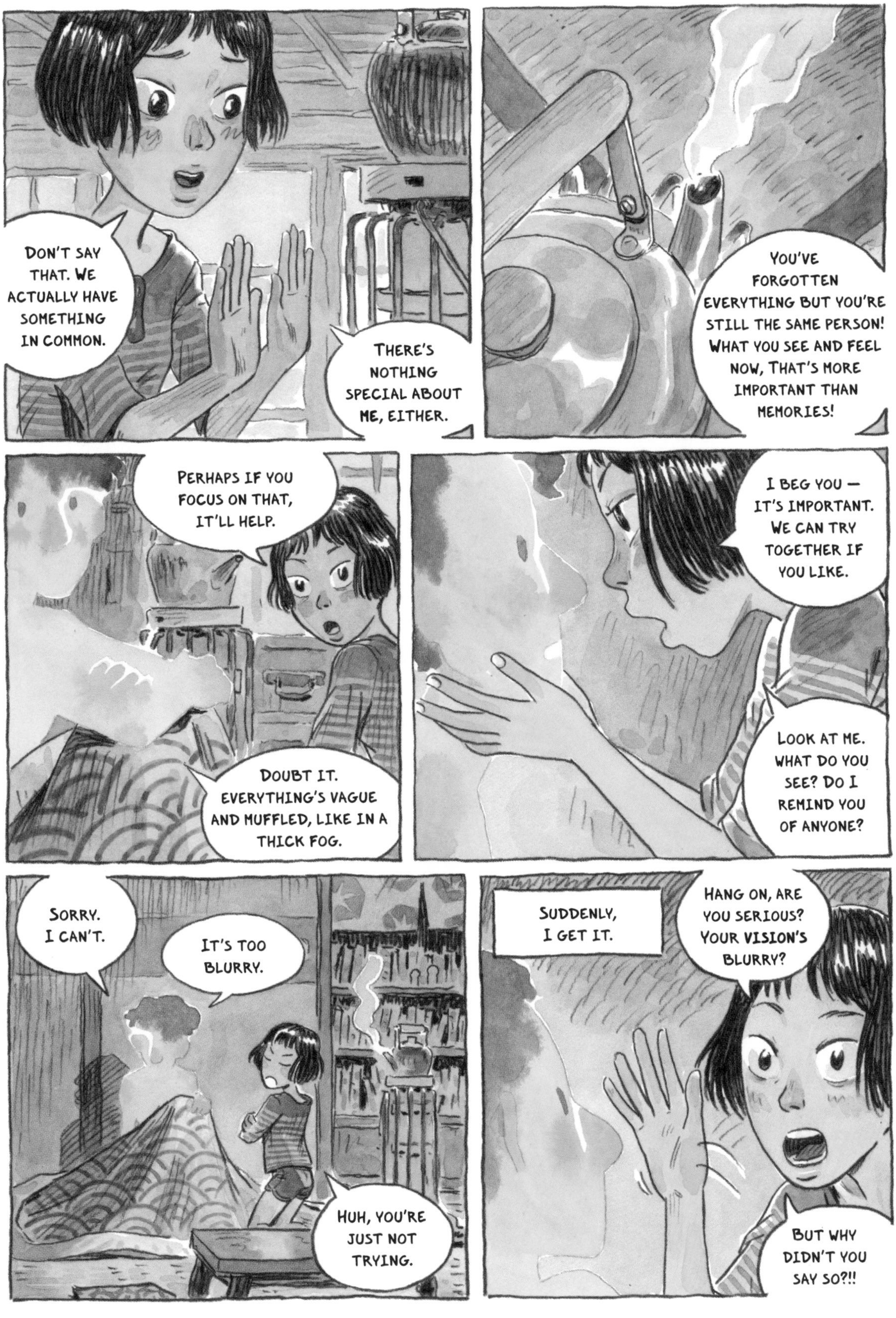
DON'T SAY THAT. WE ACTUALLY HAVE SOMETHING IN COMMON.
THERE'S NOTHING SPECIAL ABOUT ME, EITHER.
YOU'VE FORGOTTEN EVERYTHING BUT YOU'RE STILL THE SAME PERSON! WHAT YOU SEE AND FEEL NOW, THAT'S MORE IMPORTANT THAN MEMORIES!
PERHAPS IF YOU FOCUS ON THAT, IT'LL HELP.
DOUBT IT. EVERYTHING'S VAGUE AND MUFFLED, LIKE IN A THICK FOG.
I BEG YOU — IT'S IMPORTANT. WE CAN TRY TOGETHER IF YOU LIKE.
LOOK AT ME. WHAT DO YOU SEE? DO I REMIND YOU OF ANYONE?
SORRY. I CAN'T.
IT'S TOO BLURRY.
HUH, YOU'RE JUST NOT TRYING.
SUDDENLY, I GET IT.
HANG ON, ARE YOU SERIOUS? YOUR VISION'S BLURRY?
BUT WHY DIDN'T YOU SAY SO?!!

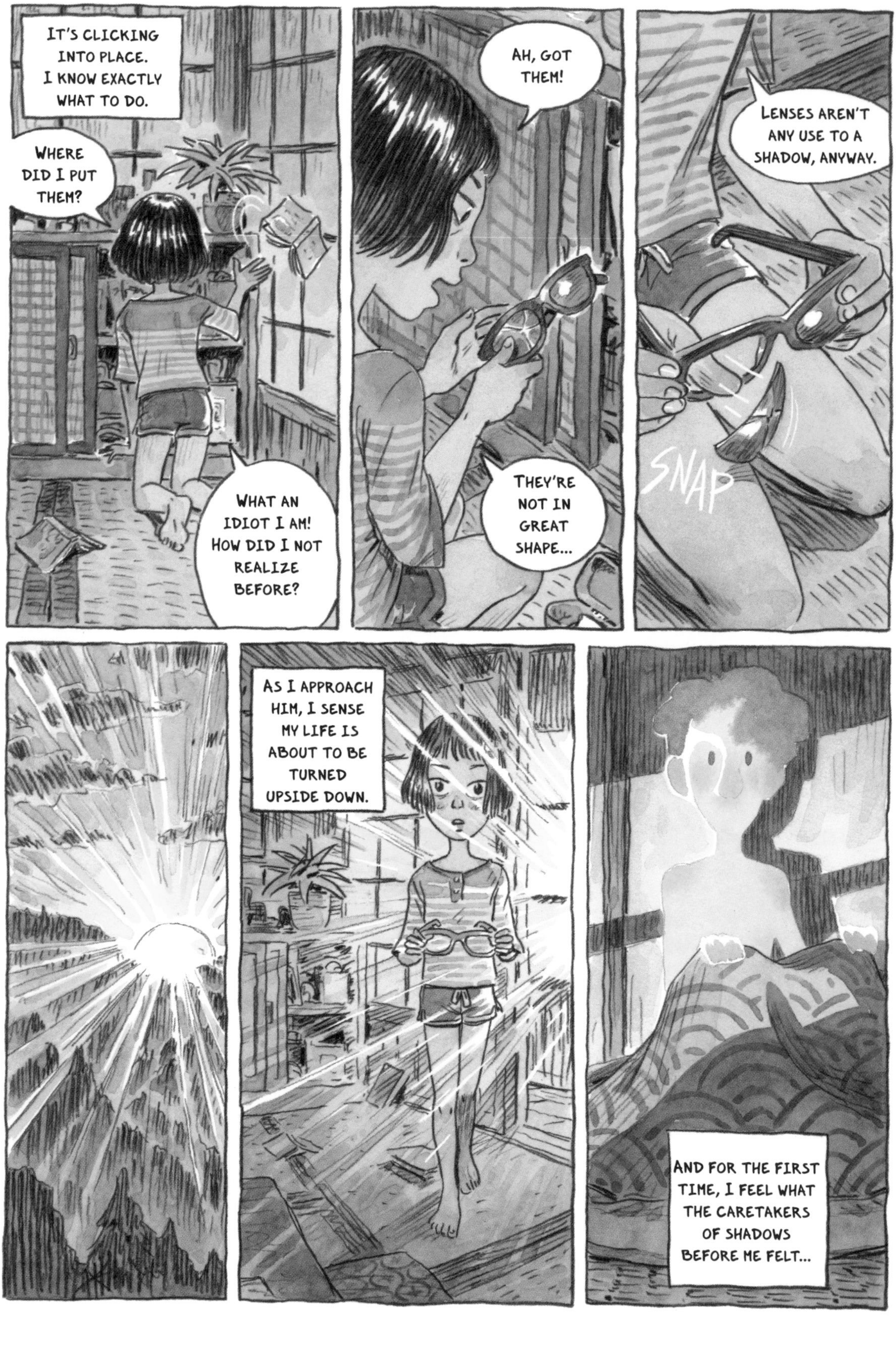
IT'S CLICKING INTO PLACE. I KNOW EXACTLY WHAT TO DO.
WHERE DID I PUT THEM?
WHAT AN IDIOT I AM! HOW DID I NOT REALIZE BEFORE?
AH, GOT THEM!
THEY'RE NOT IN GREAT SHAPE...
LENSES AREN'T ANY USE TO A SHADOW, ANYWAY.
SNAP
AS I APPROACH HIM, I SENSE MY LIFE IS ABOUT TO BE TURNED UPSIDE DOWN.
AND FOR THE FIRST TIME, I FEEL WHAT THE CARETAKERS OF SHADOWS BEFORE ME FELT...

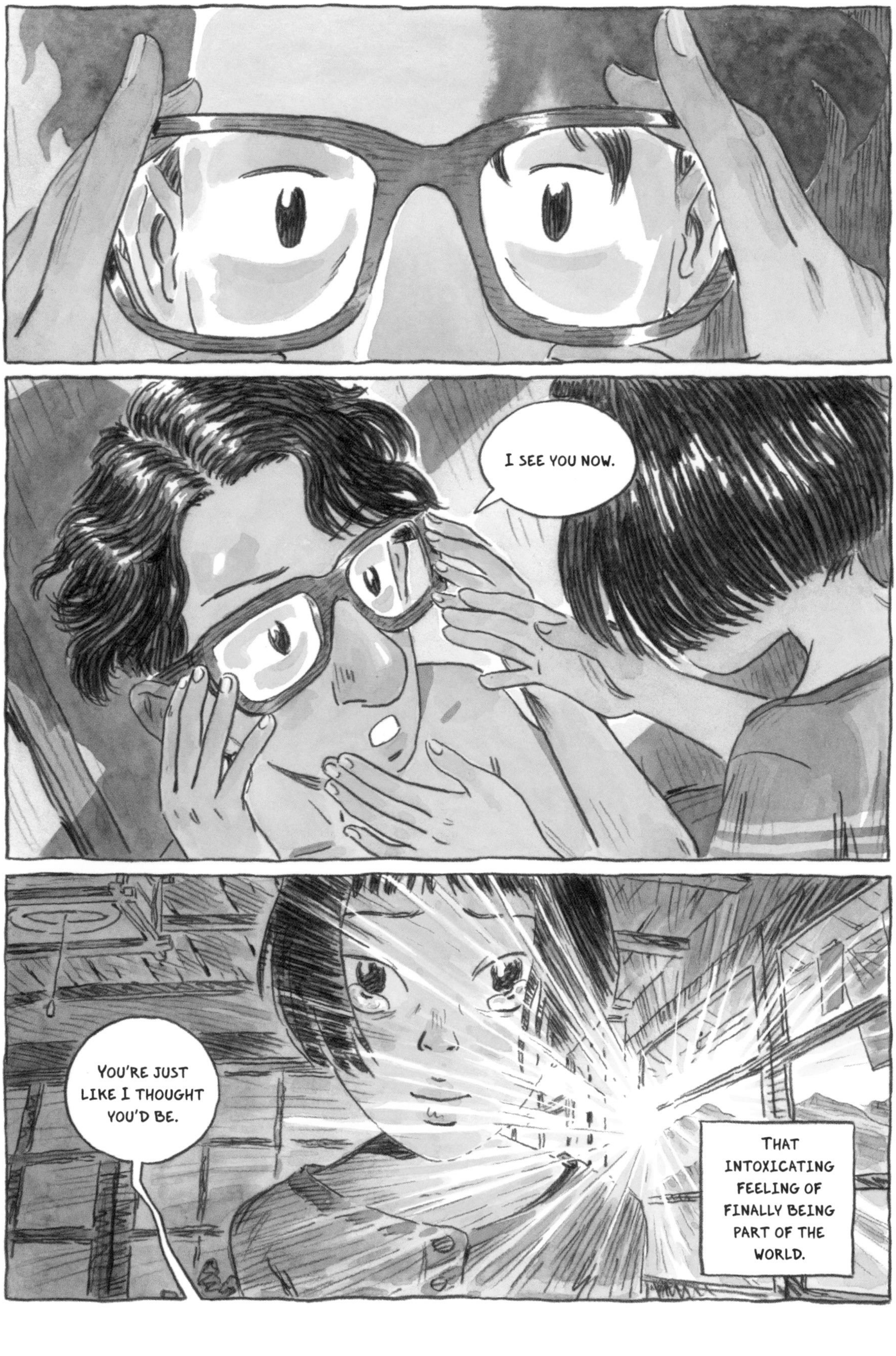
I SEE YOU NOW.
YOU'RE JUST LIKE I THOUGHT YOU'D BE.
THAT INTOXICATING FEELING OF FINALLY BEING PART OF THE WORLD.

冬

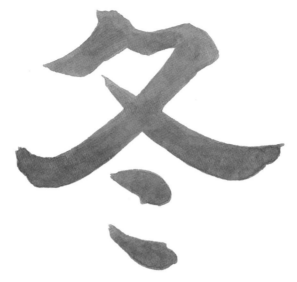

Winter

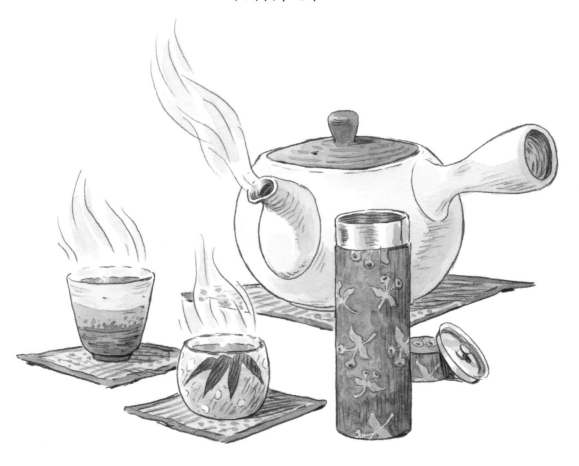

The absentees

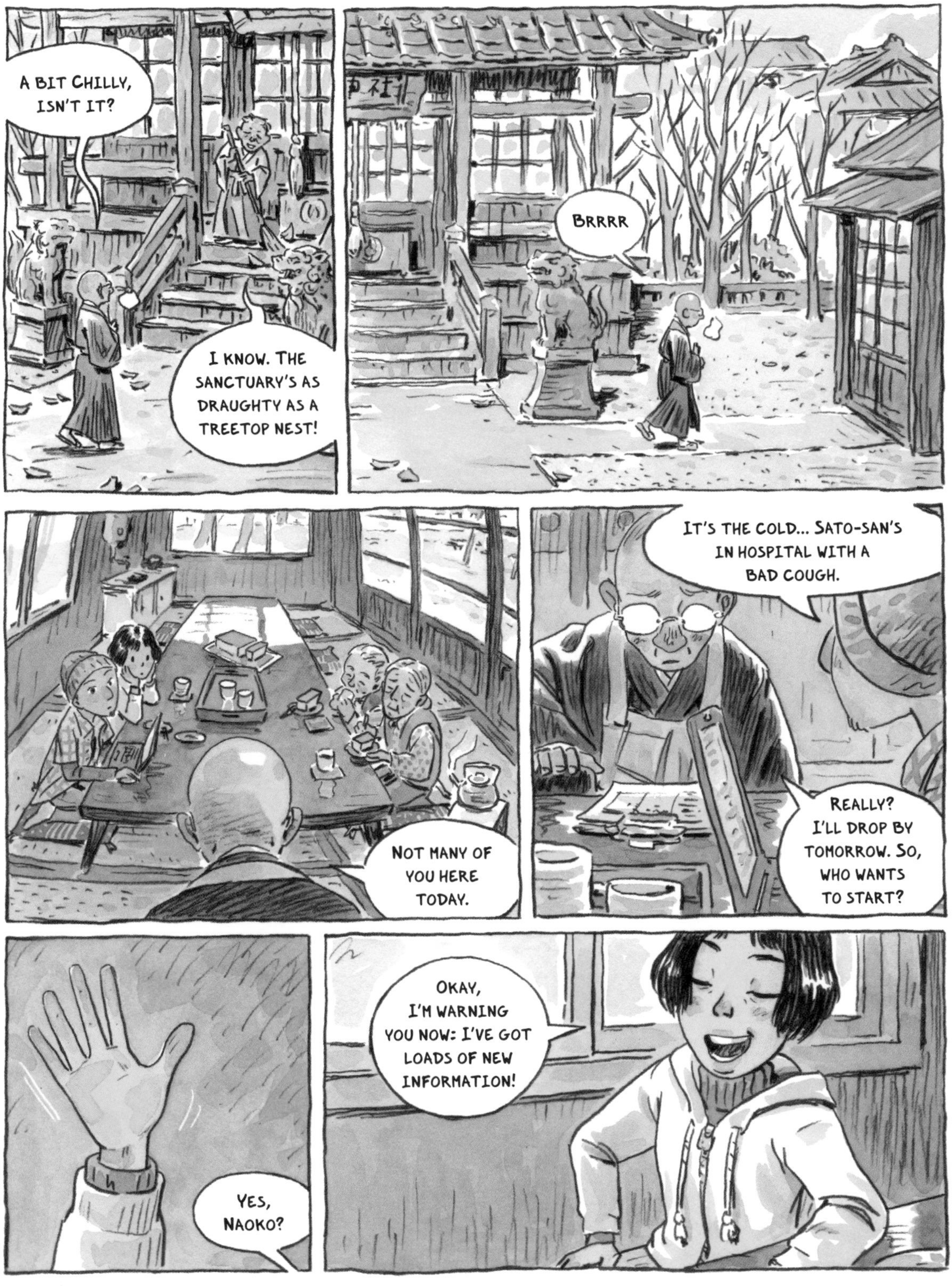
A BIT CHILLY, ISN'T IT?
I KNOW. THE SANCTUARY'S AS DRAUGHTY AS A TREETOP NEST!
BRRRR
NOT MANY OF YOU HERE TODAY.
IT'S THE COLD... SATO-SAN'S IN HOSPITAL WITH A BAD COUGH.
REALLY? I'LL DROP BY TOMORROW. SO, WHO WANTS TO START?
YES, NAOKO?
OKAY, I'M WARNING YOU NOW: I'VE GOT LOADS OF NEW INFORMATION!

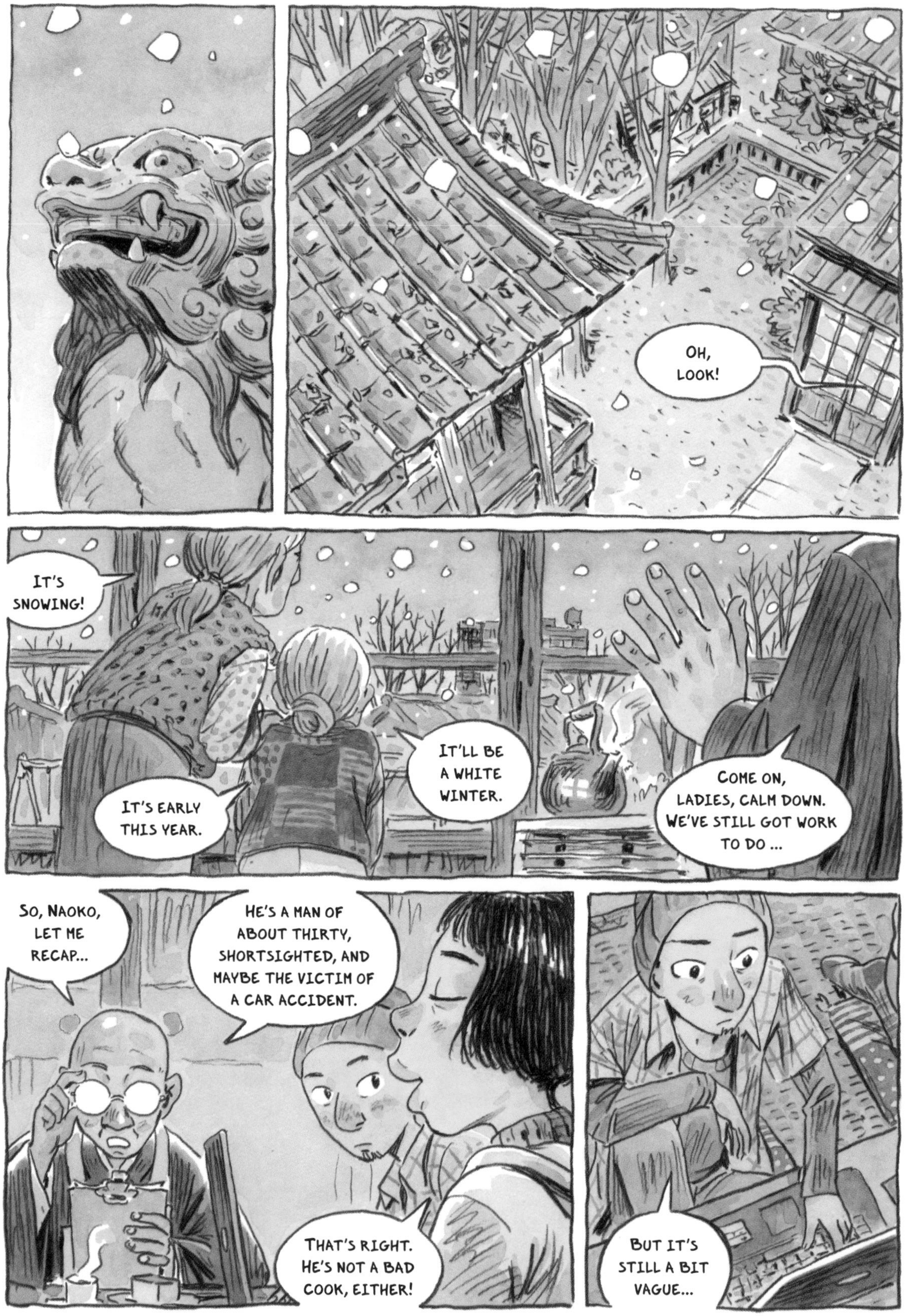
OH, LOOK!
IT'S SNOWING!
IT'S EARLY THIS YEAR.
IT'LL BE A WHITE WINTER.
COME ON, LADIES, CALM DOWN. WE'VE STILL GOT WORK TO DO ...
SO, NAOKO, LET ME RECAP...
HE'S A MAN OF ABOUT THIRTY, SHORTSIGHTED, AND MAYBE THE VICTIM OF A CAR ACCIDENT.
THAT'S RIGHT. HE'S NOT A BAD COOK, EITHER!
BUT IT'S STILL A BIT VAGUE...

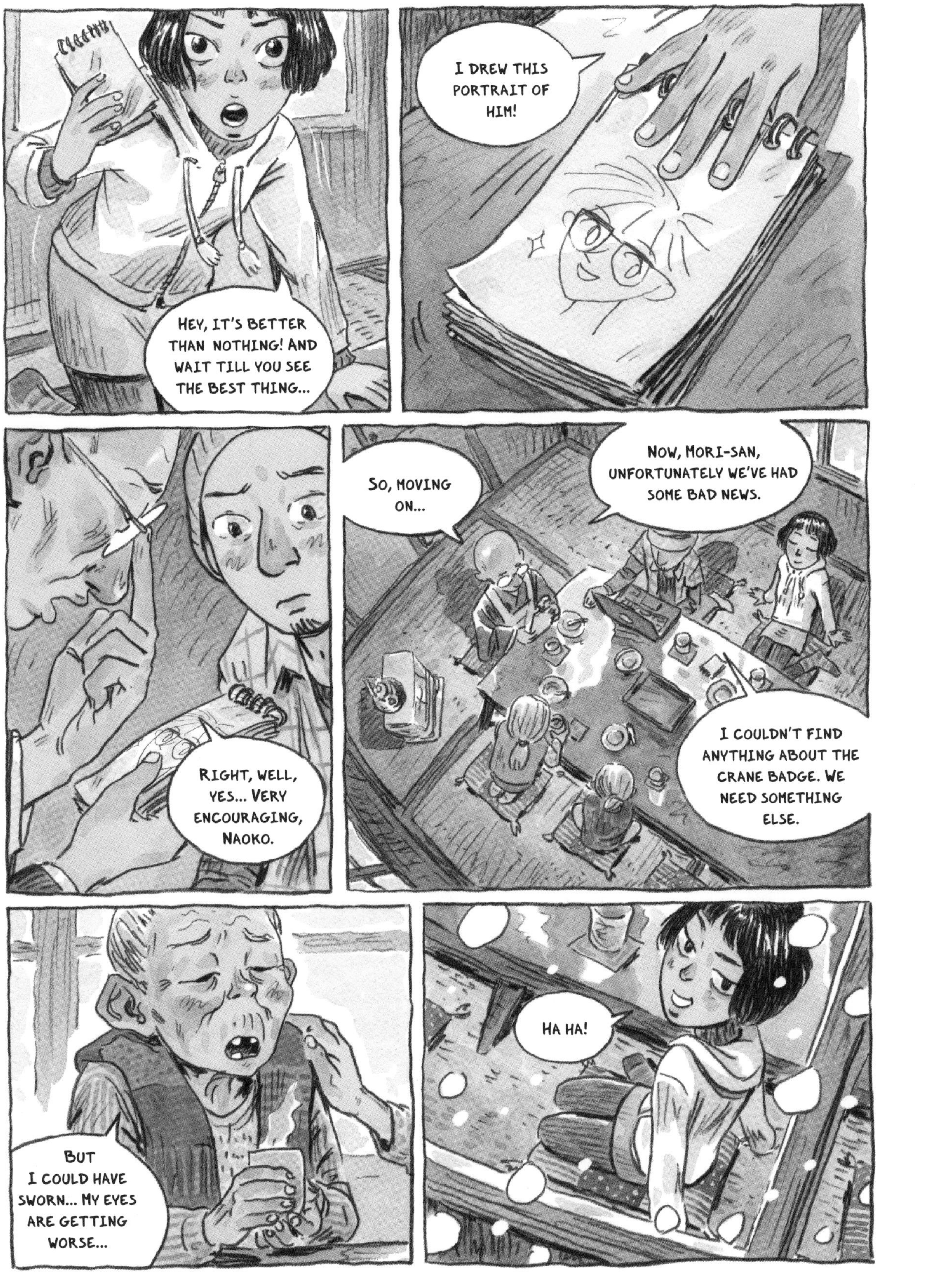
HEY, IT'S BETTER THAN NOTHING! AND WAIT TILL YOU SEE THE BEST THING...
I DREW THIS PORTRAIT OF HIM!
RIGHT, WELL, YES... VERY ENCOURAGING, NAOKO.
SO, MOVING ON...
NOW, MORI-SAN, UNFORTUNATELY WE'VE HAD SOME BAD NEWS.
I COULDN'T FIND ANYTHING ABOUT THE CRANE BADGE. WE NEED SOMETHING ELSE.
BUT I COULD HAVE SWORN... MY EYES ARE GETTING WORSE...
HA HA!

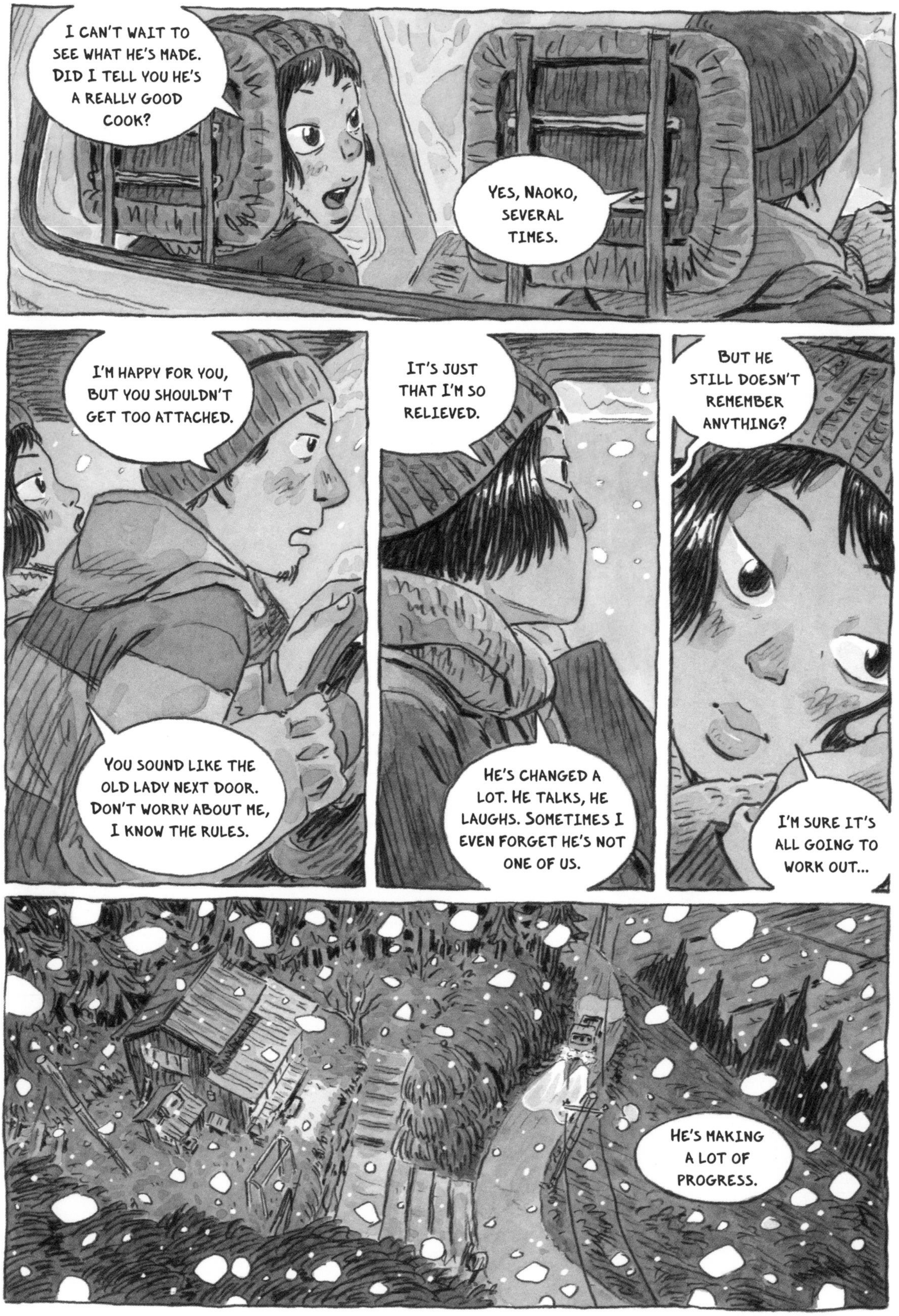
I CAN'T WAIT TO SEE WHAT HE'S MADE. DID I TELL YOU HE'S A REALLY GOOD COOK?
YES, NAOKO, SEVERAL TIMES.
I'M HAPPY FOR YOU, BUT YOU SHOULDN'T GET TOO ATTACHED.
YOU SOUND LIKE THE OLD LADY NEXT DOOR. DON'T WORRY ABOUT ME, I KNOW THE RULES.
IT'S JUST THAT I'M SO RELIEVED.
HE'S CHANGED A LOT. HE TALKS, HE LAUGHS. SOMETIMES I EVEN FORGET HE'S NOT ONE OF US.
BUT HE STILL DOESN'T REMEMBER ANYTHING?
I'M SURE IT'S ALL GOING TO WORK OUT...
HE'S MAKING A LOT OF PROGRESS.

Sukiyaki

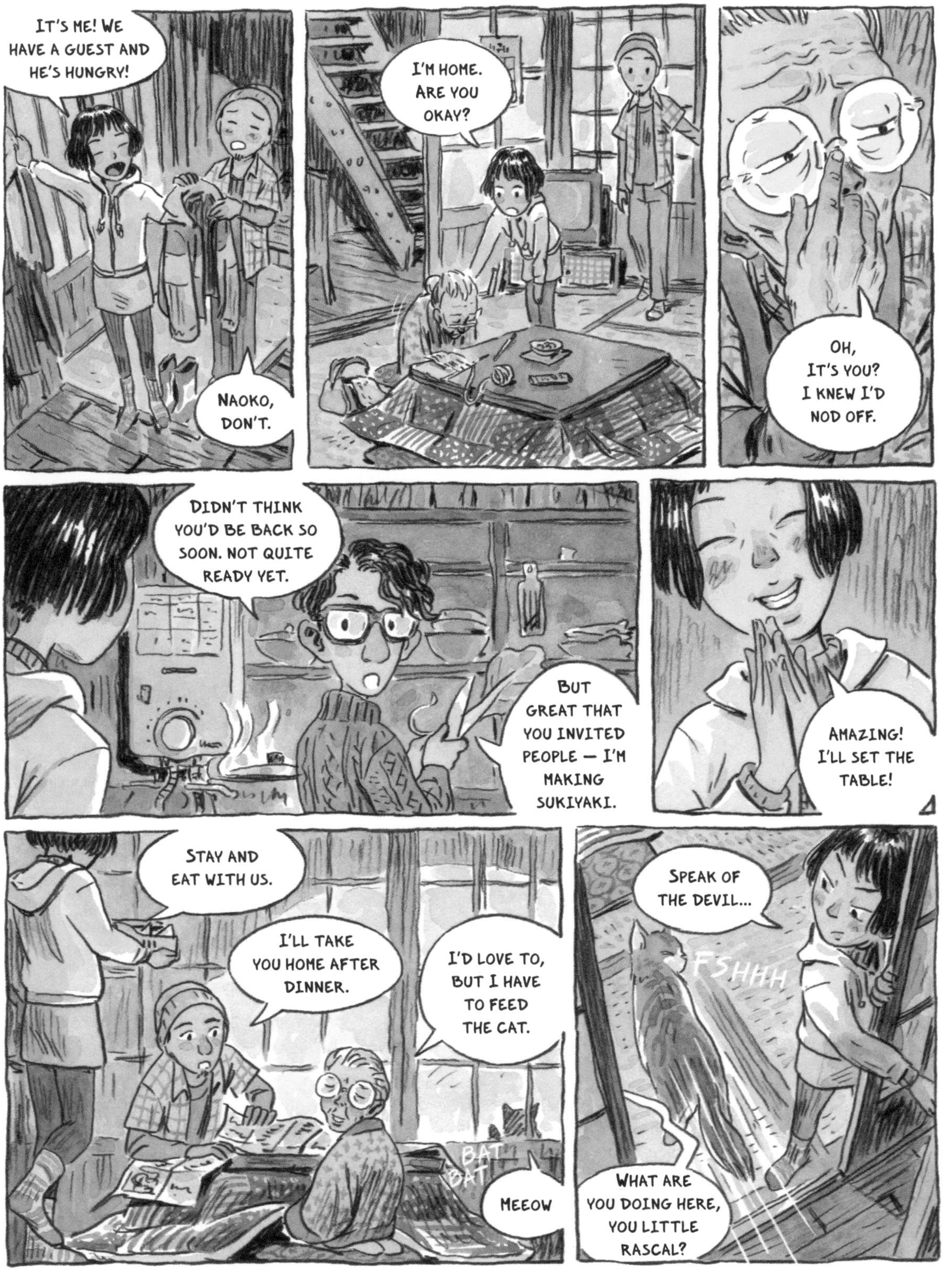
IT'S ME! WE HAVE A GUEST AND HE'S HUNGRY!
NAOKO, DON'T.
I'M HOME. ARE YOU OKAY?
OH, IT'S YOU? I KNEW I'D NOD OFF.
DIDN'T THINK YOU'D BE BACK SO SOON. NOT QUITE READY YET.
BUT GREAT THAT YOU INVITED PEOPLE — I'M MAKING SUKIYAKI.
AMAZING! I'LL SET THE TABLE!
STAY AND EAT WITH US.
I'LL TAKE YOU HOME AFTER DINNER.
I'D LOVE TO, BUT I HAVE TO FEED THE CAT.
BAT BAT
MEEOW
SPEAK OF THE DEVIL...
FSHHH
WHAT ARE YOU DOING HERE, YOU LITTLE RASCAL?

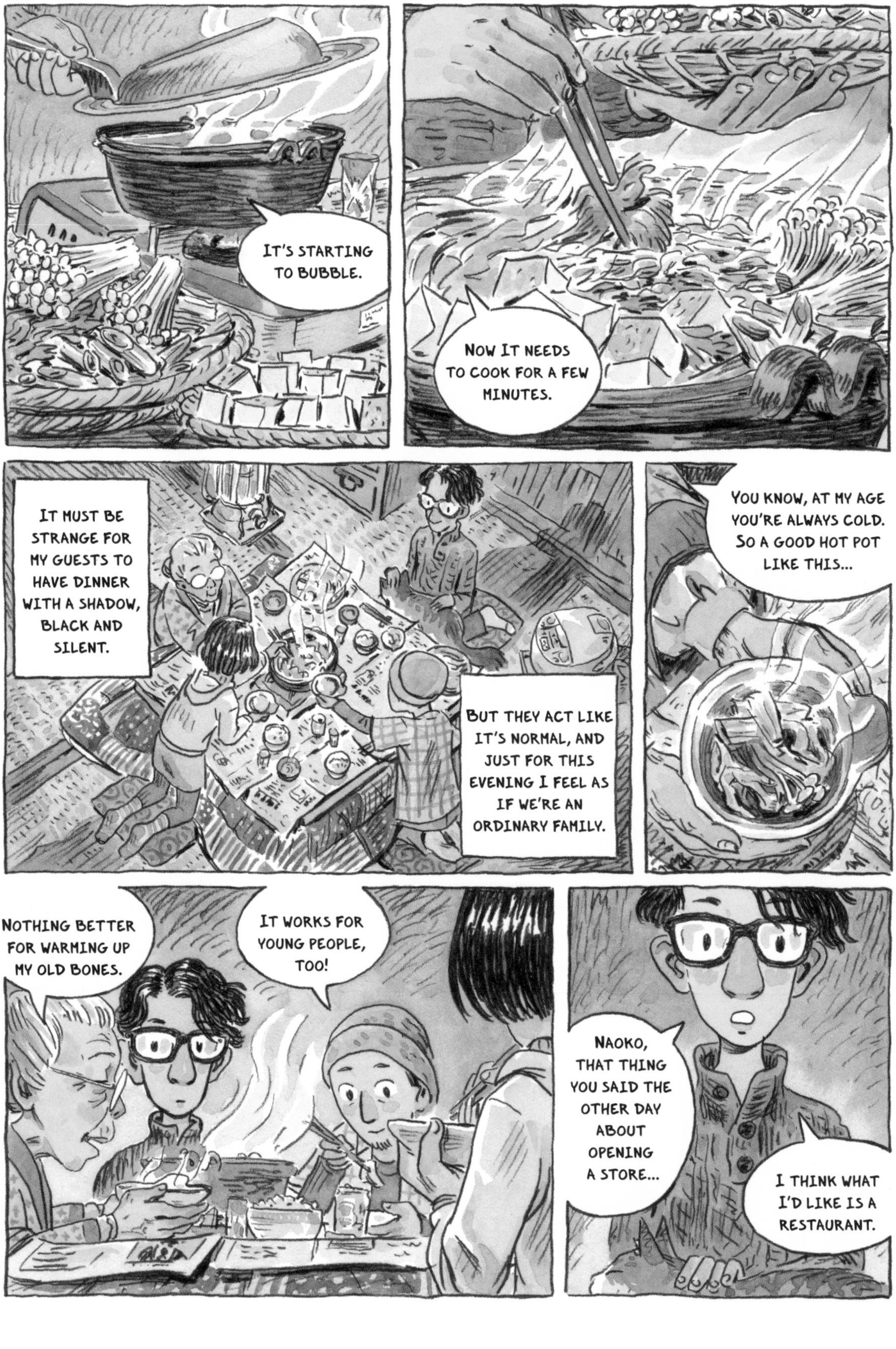
It's starting to bubble.
Now it needs to cook for a few minutes.
It must be strange for my guests to have dinner with a shadow, black and silent.
But they act like it's normal, and just for this evening I feel as if we're an ordinary family.
You know, at my age you're always cold. So a good hot pot like this...
Nothing better for warming up my old bones.
It works for young people, too!
Naoko, that thing you said the other day about opening a store...
I think what I'd like is a restaurant.

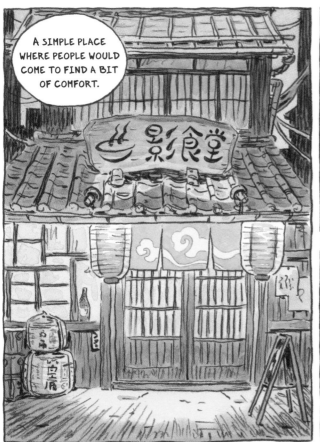

A SIMPLE PLACE WHERE PEOPLE WOULD COME TO FIND A BIT OF COMFORT.

I'D TAKE CARE OF THE FOOD AND YOU COULD SERVE.

WE WOULDN'T HAVE MANY CUSTOMERS AT FIRST...

BUT SLOWLY, THROUGH WORD OF MOUTH...

I KNOW IT WOULD BECOME REALLY POPULAR.

HMM, IS THAT REALLY A GOOD IDEA?

The white expanses

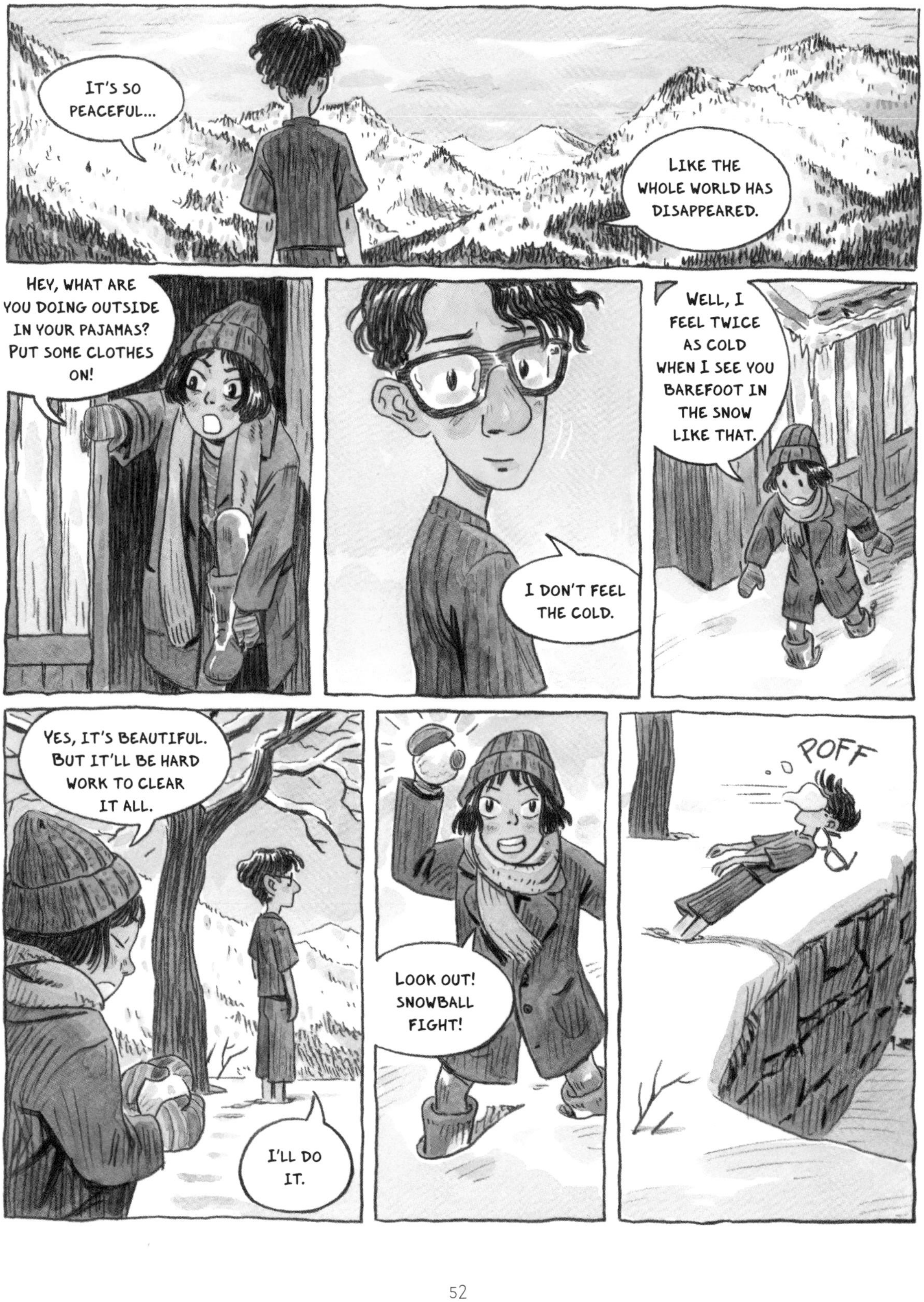
IT'S SO PEACEFUL...
LIKE THE WHOLE WORLD HAS DISAPPEARED.
HEY, WHAT ARE YOU DOING OUTSIDE IN YOUR PAJAMAS? PUT SOME CLOTHES ON!
I DON'T FEEL THE COLD.
WELL, I FEEL TWICE AS COLD WHEN I SEE YOU BAREFOOT IN THE SNOW LIKE THAT.
YES, IT'S BEAUTIFUL. BUT IT'LL BE HARD WORK TO CLEAR IT ALL.
I'LL DO IT.
LOOK OUT! SNOWBALL FIGHT!
POFF

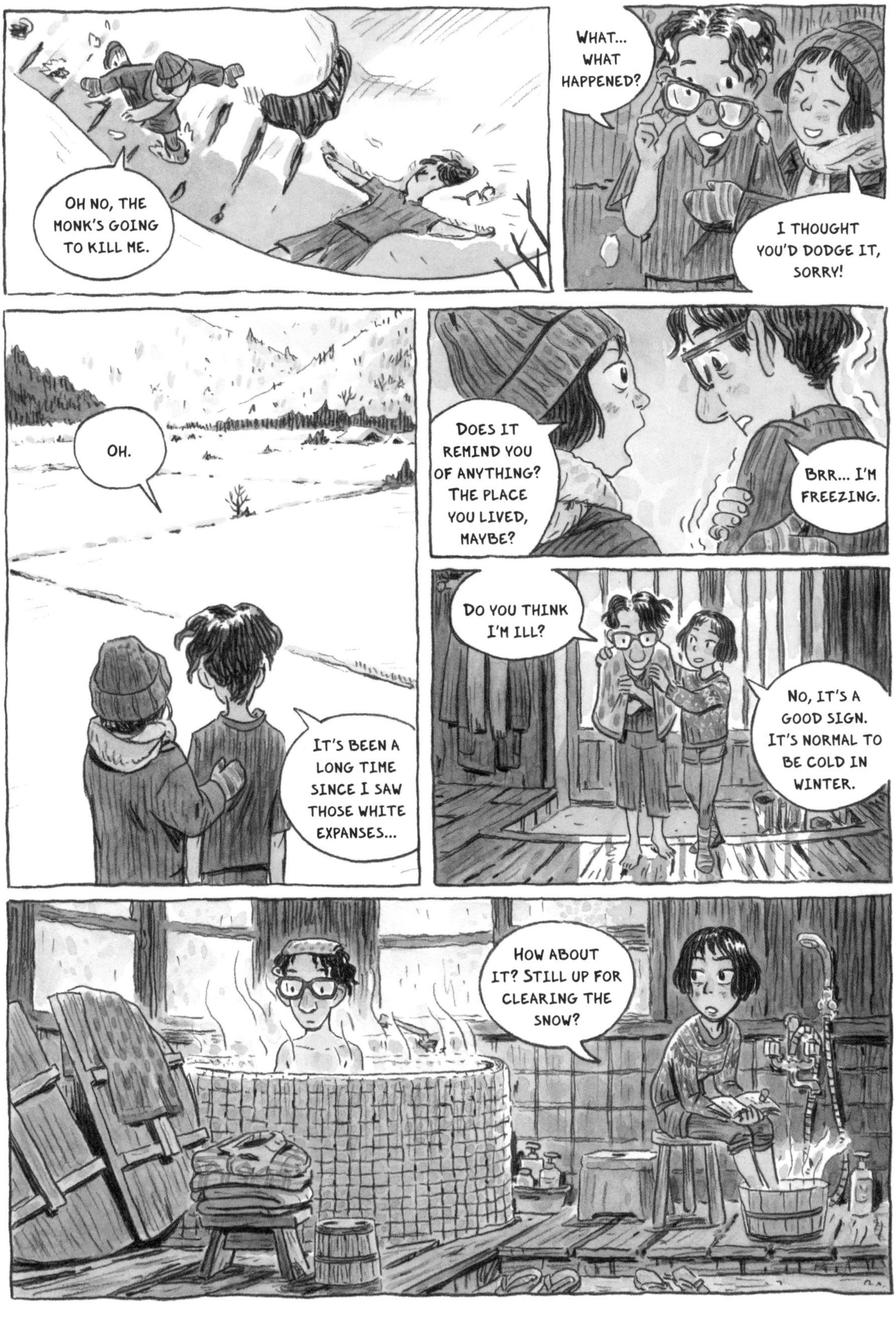
OH NO, THE MONK'S GOING TO KILL ME.
WHAT... WHAT HAPPENED?
I THOUGHT YOU'D DODGE IT, SORRY!
OH.
IT'S BEEN A LONG TIME SINCE I SAW THOSE WHITE EXPANSES...
DOES IT REMIND YOU OF ANYTHING? THE PLACE YOU LIVED, MAYBE?
BRR... I'M FREEZING.
DO YOU THINK I'M ILL?
NO, IT'S A GOOD SIGN. IT'S NORMAL TO BE COLD IN WINTER.
HOW ABOUT IT? STILL UP FOR CLEARING THE SNOW?

Constellations

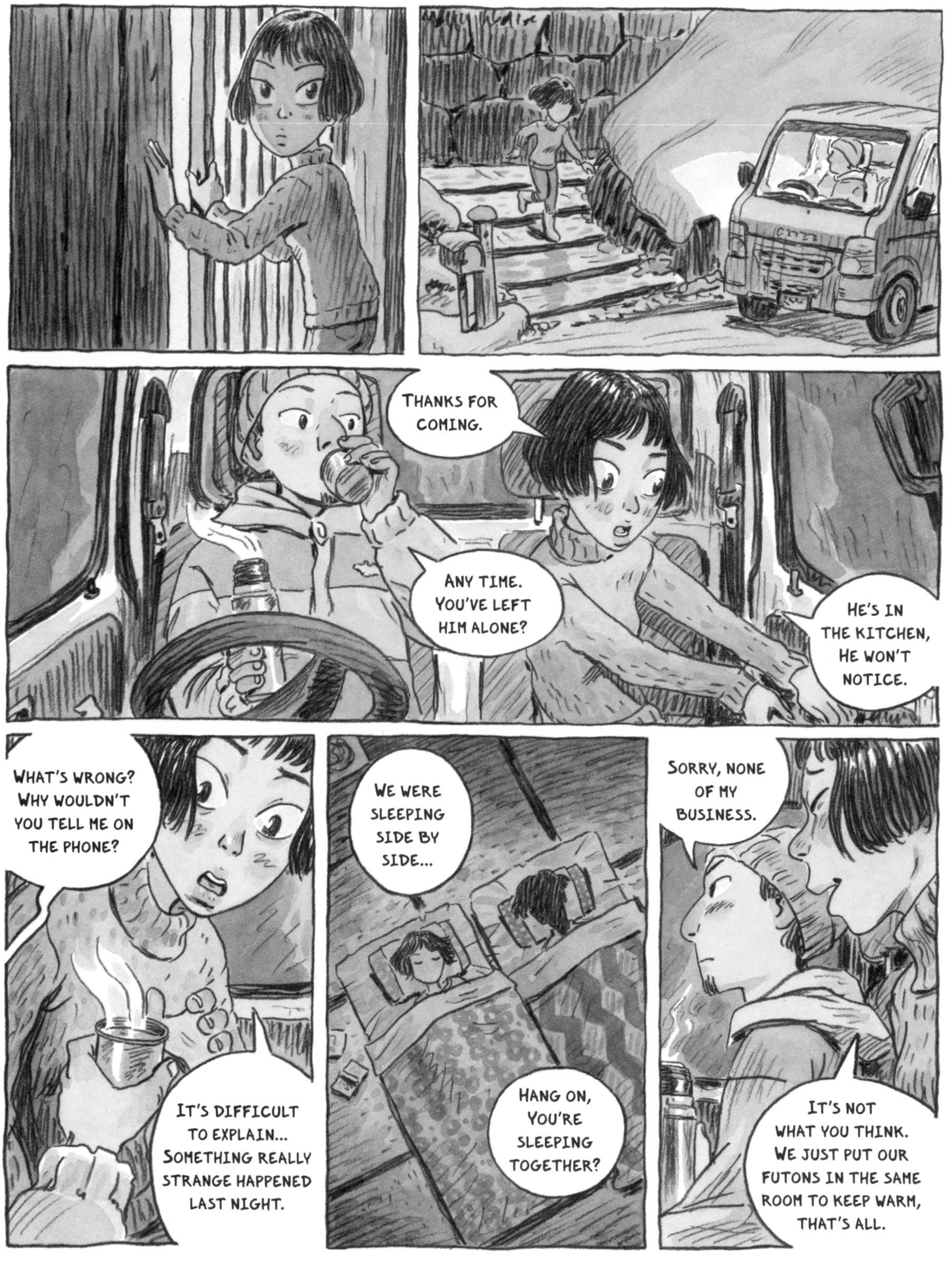
THANKS FOR COMING.
ANY TIME. YOU'VE LEFT HIM ALONE?
HE'S IN THE KITCHEN, HE WON'T NOTICE.
WHAT'S WRONG? WHY WOULDN'T YOU TELL ME ON THE PHONE?
IT'S DIFFICULT TO EXPLAIN... SOMETHING REALLY STRANGE HAPPENED LAST NIGHT.
WE WERE SLEEPING SIDE BY SIDE...
HANG ON, YOU'RE SLEEPING TOGETHER?
SORRY, NONE OF MY BUSINESS.
IT'S NOT WHAT YOU THINK. WE JUST PUT OUR FUTONS IN THE SAME ROOM TO KEEP WARM, THAT'S ALL.

SO, LAST NIGHT, SOMETHING WOKE ME UP.

HE LOSES HIS HUMAN FORM WHEN HE SLEEPS. IT'S LIKE HE TURNS INTO A BLACK WELL.

AND THE MURMURING SEEMED TO BE COMING UP FROM ITS DEPTHS.

A MURMURING IN THE DARKNESS...

I MOVED CLOSER...

AND THEN I SAW THEM, INSIDE HIM...

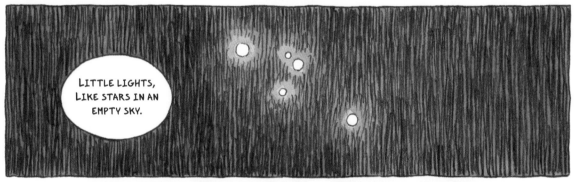

LITTLE LIGHTS, LIKE STARS IN AN EMPTY SKY.

I WAS SO FREAKED OUT, I COULDN'T GET BACK TO SLEEP. NOW I KEEP THINKING ABOUT IT.

LOOKS LIKE IT MEANS SOMETHING IMPORTANT, RIGHT?

IT SEEMS TO BE A CONSTELLATION. I'LL RESEARCH IT.

I DIDN'T UNDERSTAND ONE WORD OF THE MURMURING. BUT ONE THING'S FOR SURE...

IT WASN'T HIS VOICE.

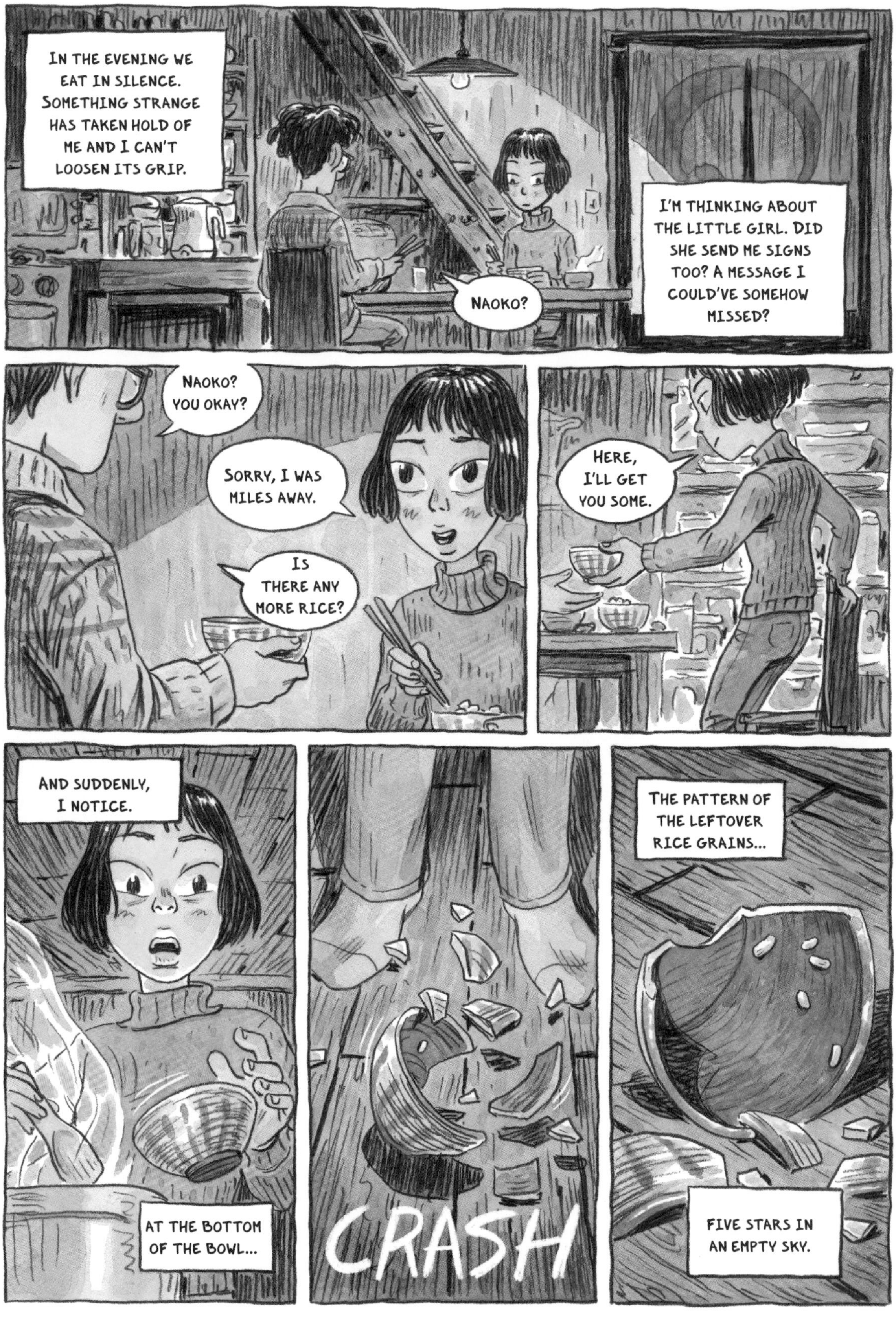

IN THE EVENING WE EAT IN SILENCE. SOMETHING STRANGE HAS TAKEN HOLD OF ME AND I CAN'T LOOSEN ITS GRIP.
NAOKO?
I'M THINKING ABOUT THE LITTLE GIRL. DID SHE SEND ME SIGNS TOO? A MESSAGE I COULD'VE SOMEHOW MISSED?
NAOKO? YOU OKAY?
SORRY, I WAS MILES AWAY.
IS THERE ANY MORE RICE?
HERE, I'LL GET YOU SOME.
AND SUDDENLY, I NOTICE.
AT THE BOTTOM OF THE BOWL...
CRASH
THE PATTERN OF THE LEFTOVER RICE GRAINS...
FIVE STARS IN AN EMPTY SKY.

The call of the blue

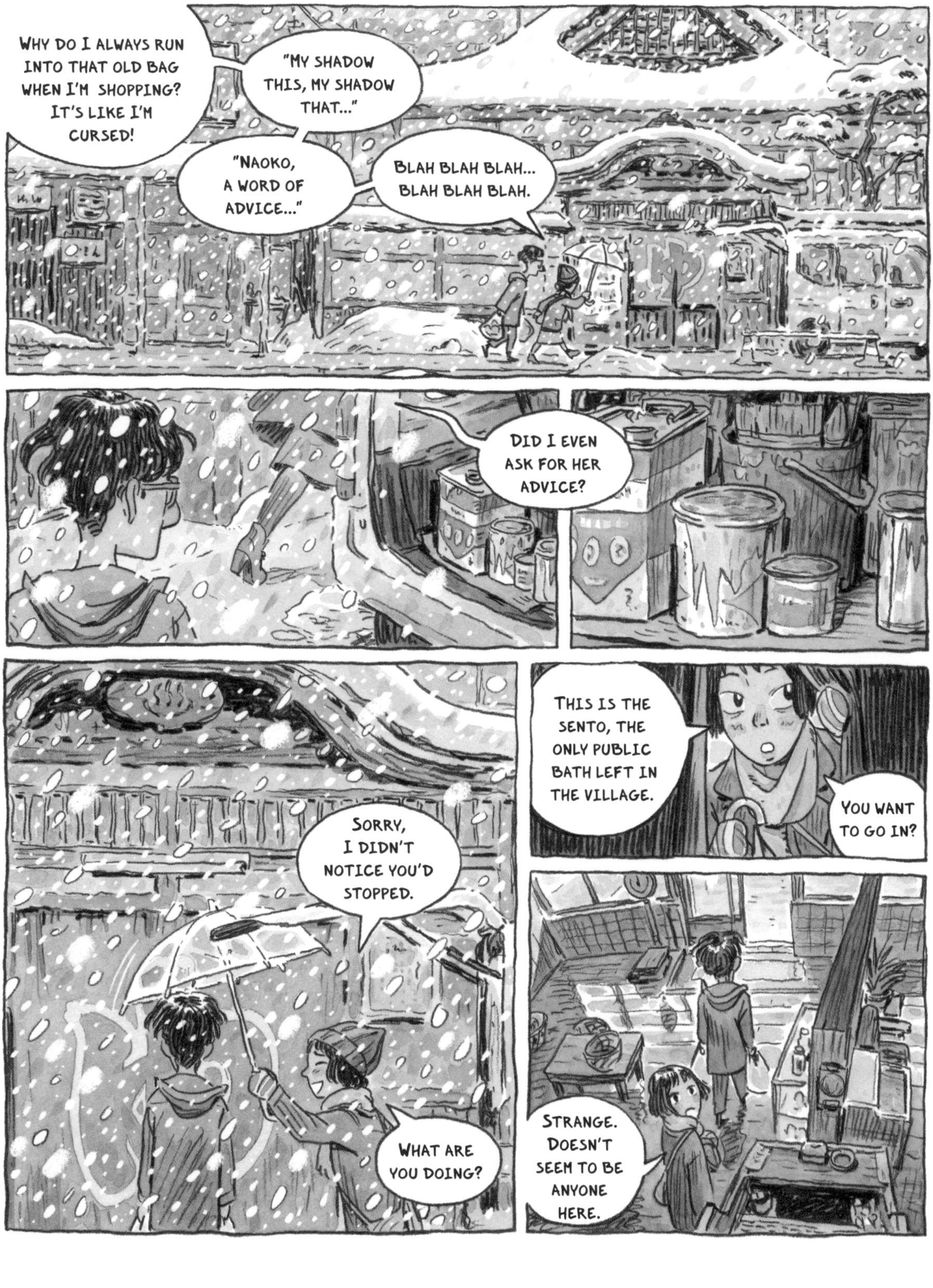

WHY DO I ALWAYS RUN INTO THAT OLD BAG WHEN I'M SHOPPING? IT'S LIKE I'M CURSED!
"MY SHADOW THIS, MY SHADOW THAT..."
"NAOKO, A WORD OF ADVICE..."
BLAH BLAH BLAH... BLAH BLAH BLAH.
DID I EVEN ASK FOR HER ADVICE?
SORRY, I DIDN'T NOTICE YOU'D STOPPED.
WHAT ARE YOU DOING?
THIS IS THE SENTO, THE ONLY PUBLIC BATH LEFT IN THE VILLAGE.
YOU WANT TO GO IN?
STRANGE. DOESN'T SEEM TO BE ANYONE HERE.

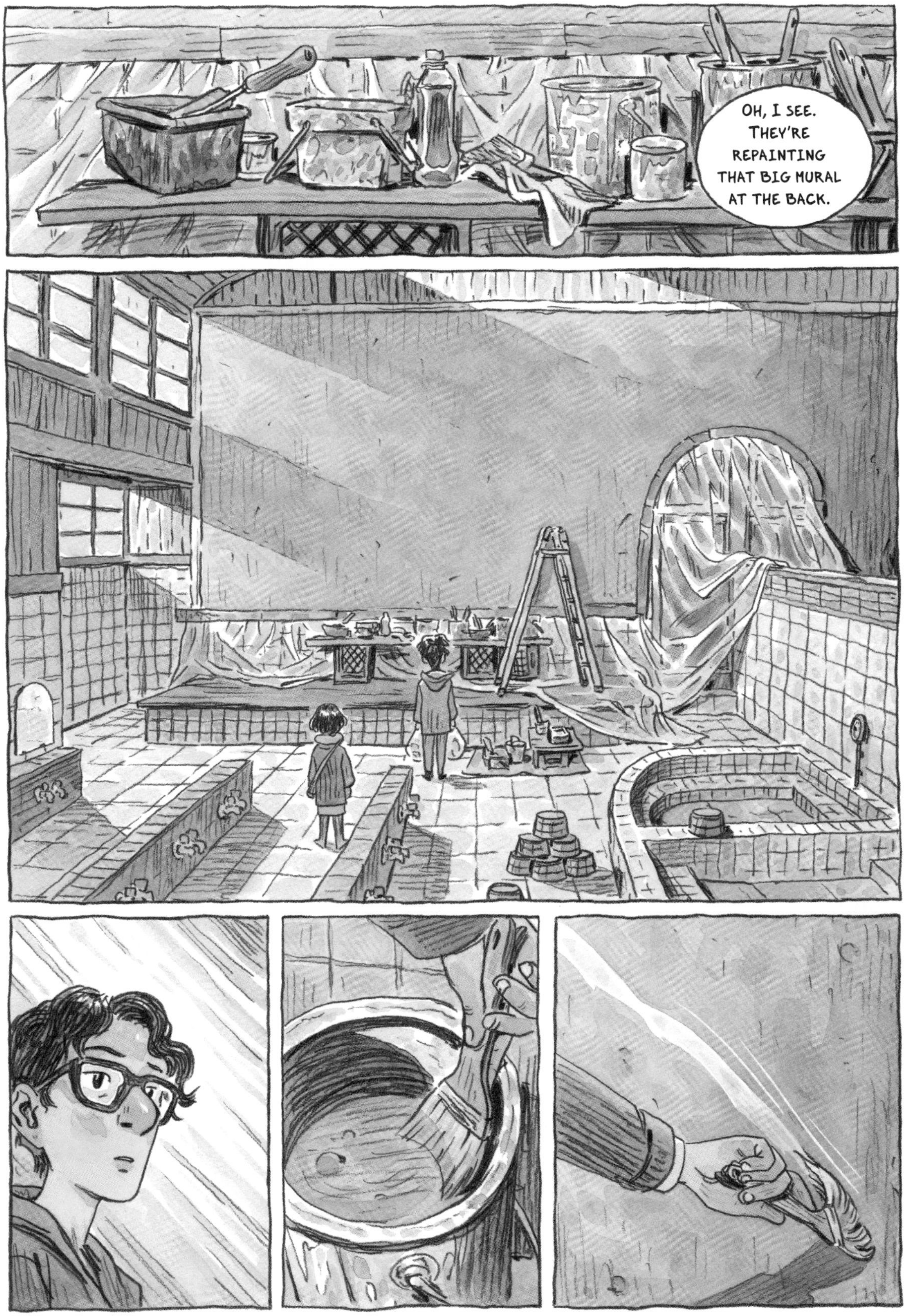
OH, I SEE. THEY'RE REPAINTING THAT BIG MURAL AT THE BACK.

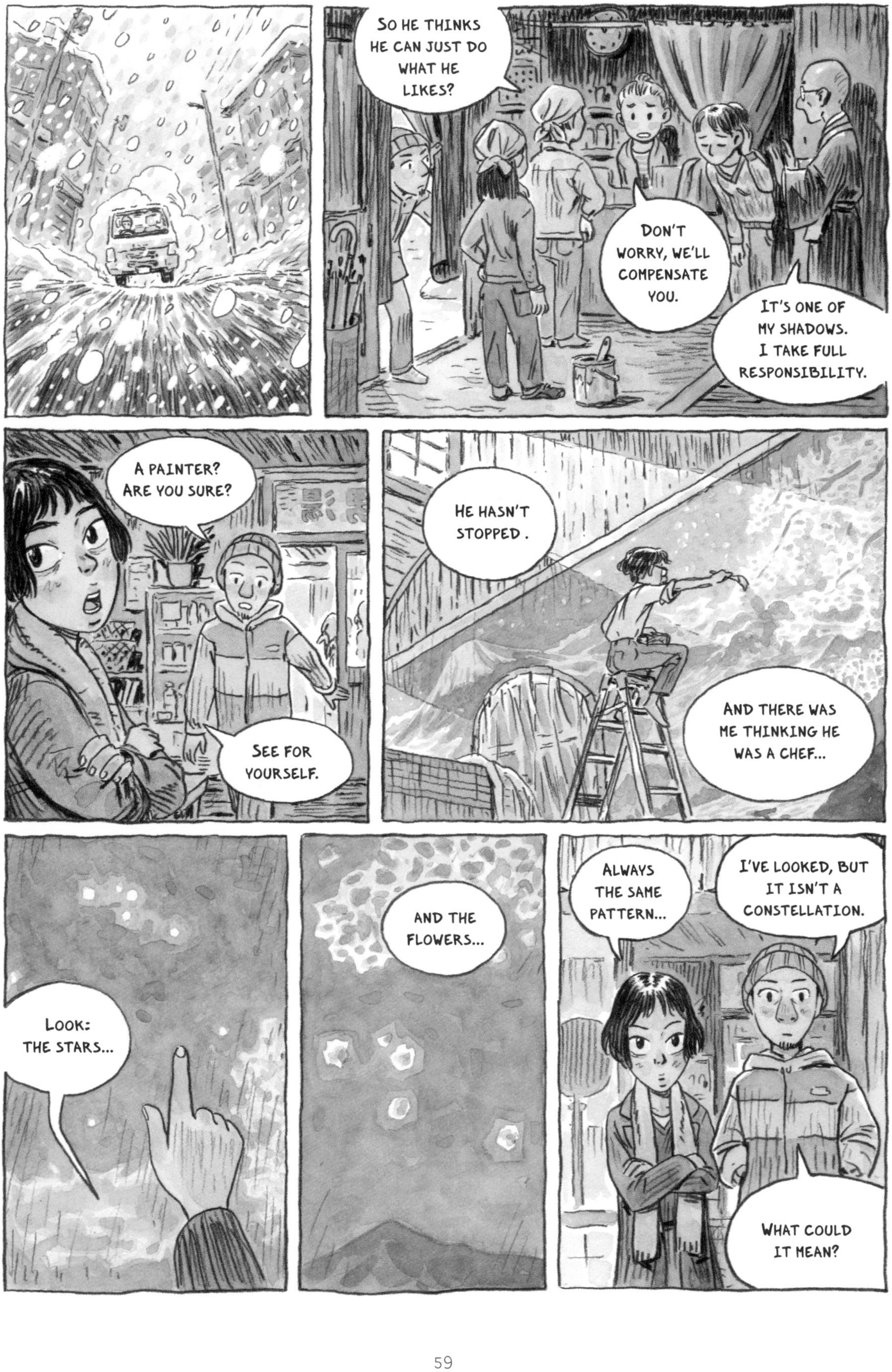
SO HE THINKS HE CAN JUST DO WHAT HE LIKES?
DON'T WORRY, WE'LL COMPENSATE YOU.
IT'S ONE OF MY SHADOWS. I TAKE FULL RESPONSIBILITY.
A PAINTER? ARE YOU SURE?
SEE FOR YOURSELF.
HE HASN'T STOPPED .
AND THERE WAS ME THINKING HE WAS A CHEF...
LOOK: THE STARS...
AND THE FLOWERS...
ALWAYS THE SAME PATTERN...
I'VE LOOKED, BUT IT ISN'T A CONSTELLATION.
WHAT COULD IT MEAN?

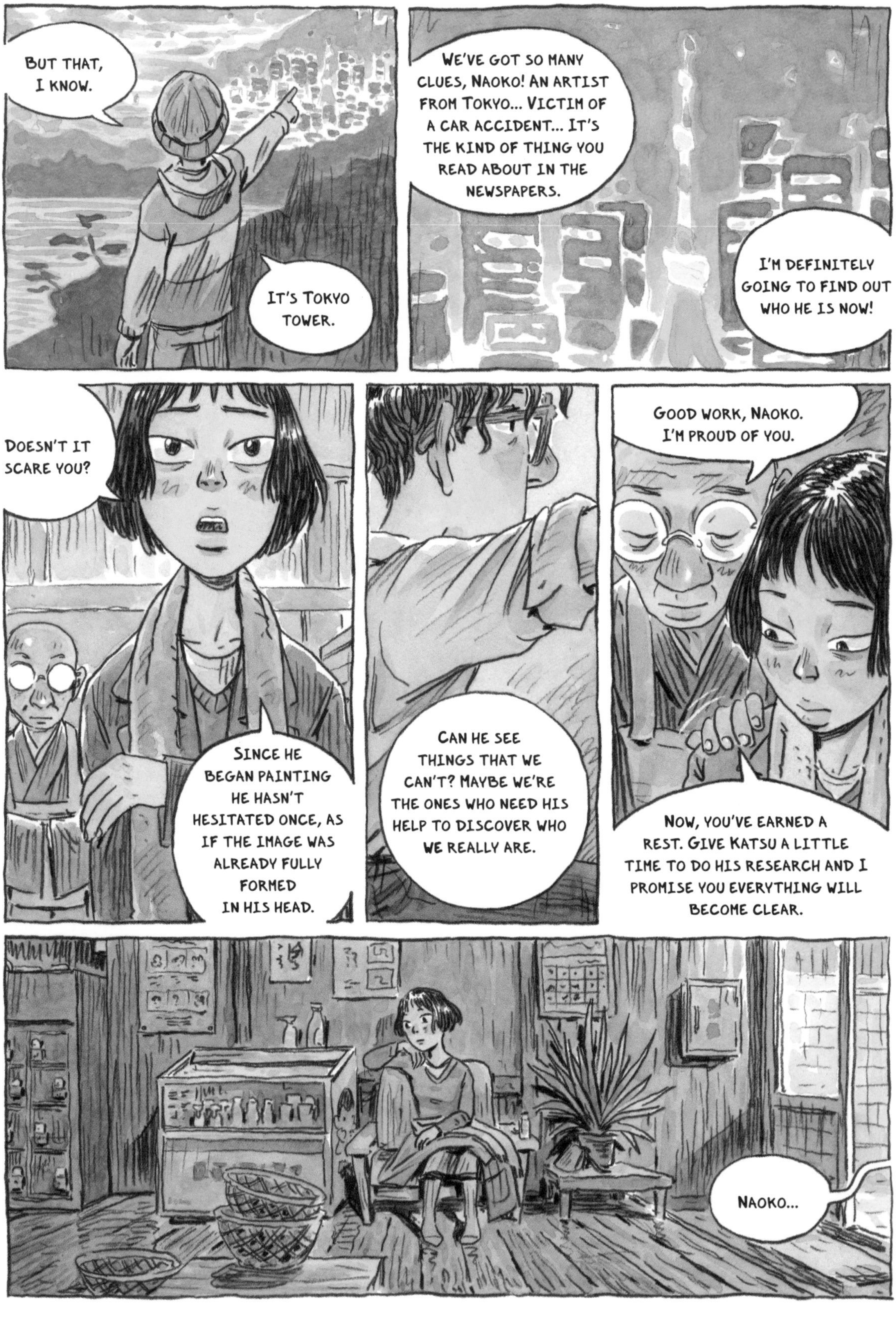
BUT THAT, I KNOW.
IT'S TOKYO TOWER.
WE'VE GOT SO MANY CLUES, NAOKO! AN ARTIST FROM TOKYO... VICTIM OF A CAR ACCIDENT... IT'S THE KIND OF THING YOU READ ABOUT IN THE NEWSPAPERS.
I'M DEFINITELY GOING TO FIND OUT WHO HE IS NOW!
DOESN'T IT SCARE YOU?
SINCE HE BEGAN PAINTING HE HASN'T HESITATED ONCE, AS IF THE IMAGE WAS ALREADY FULLY FORMED IN HIS HEAD.
CAN HE SEE THINGS THAT WE CAN'T? MAYBE WE'RE THE ONES WHO NEED HIS HELP TO DISCOVER WHO WE REALLY ARE.
GOOD WORK, NAOKO. I'M PROUD OF YOU.
NOW, YOU'VE EARNED A REST. GIVE KATSU A LITTLE TIME TO DO HIS RESEARCH AND I PROMISE YOU EVERYTHING WILL BECOME CLEAR.
NAOKO...

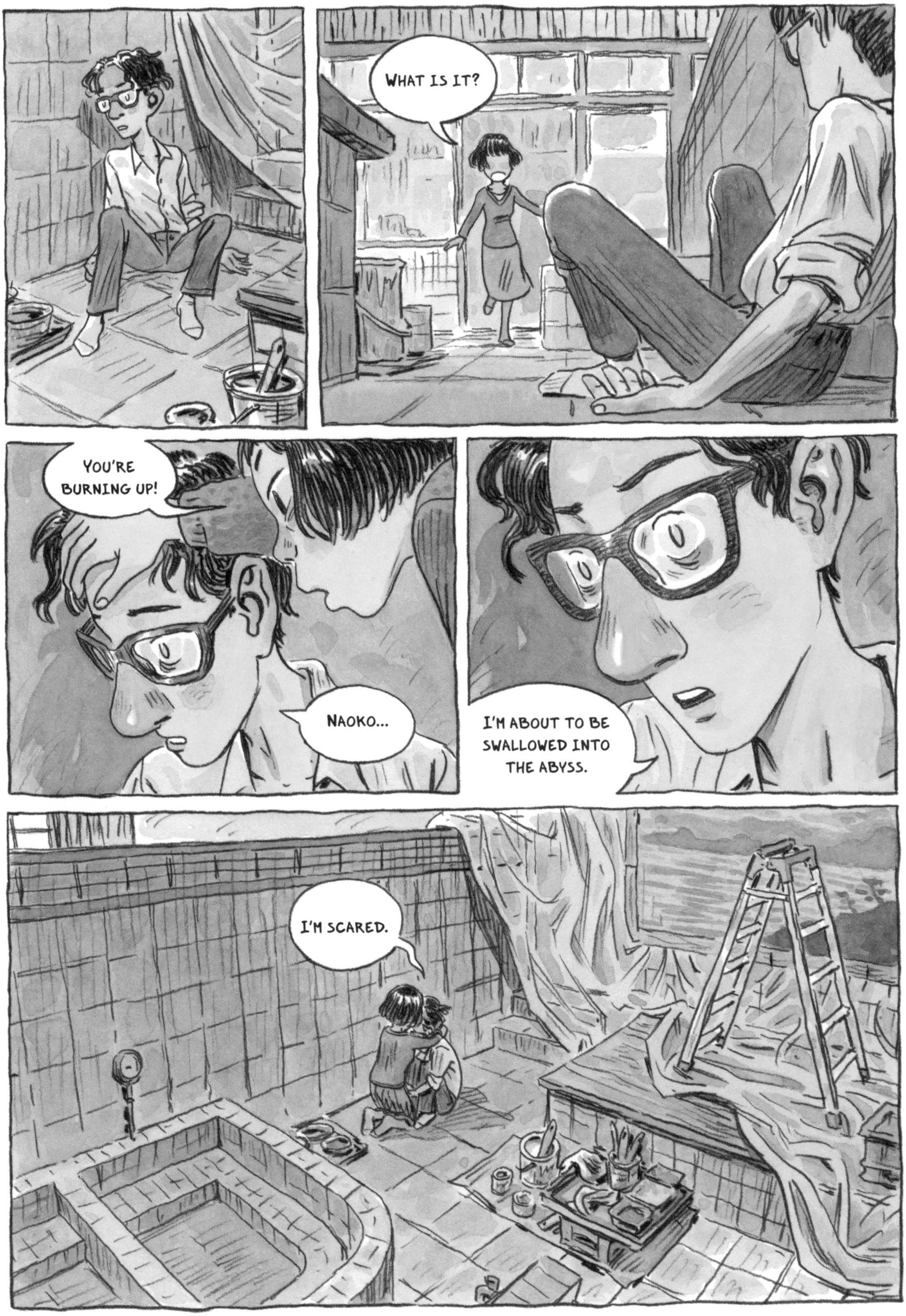
WHAT IS IT?
YOU'RE BURNING UP!
NAOKO...
I'M ABOUT TO BE SWALLOWED INTO THE ABYSS.
I'M SCARED.

The fire ceremony

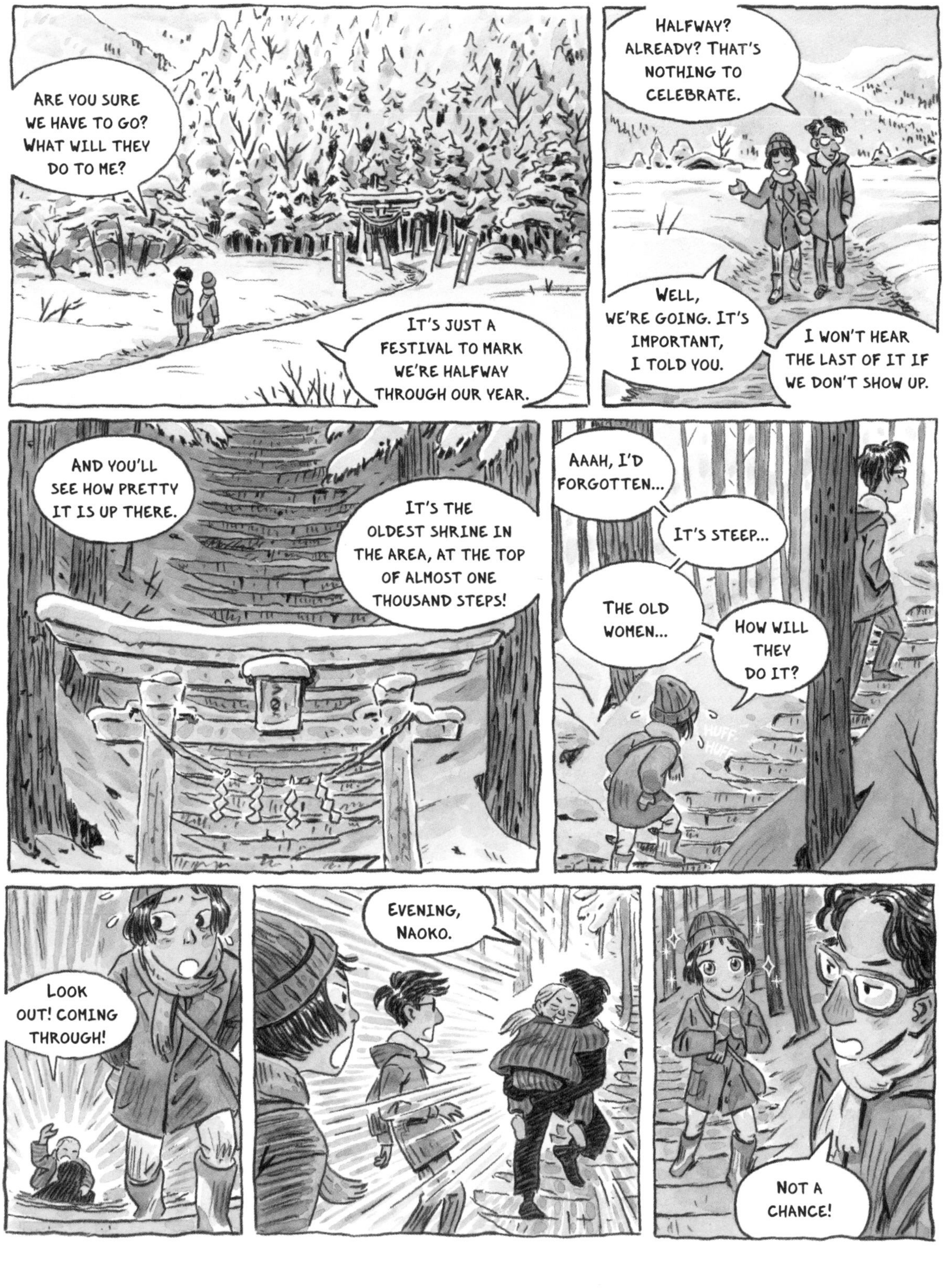
ARE YOU SURE WE HAVE TO GO? WHAT WILL THEY DO TO ME?
IT'S JUST A FESTIVAL TO MARK WE'RE HALFWAY THROUGH OUR YEAR.
HALFWAY? ALREADY? THAT'S NOTHING TO CELEBRATE.
WELL, WE'RE GOING. IT'S IMPORTANT, I TOLD YOU.
I WON'T HEAR THE LAST OF IT IF WE DON'T SHOW UP.
AND YOU'LL SEE HOW PRETTY IT IS UP THERE.
IT'S THE OLDEST SHRINE IN THE AREA, AT THE TOP OF ALMOST ONE THOUSAND STEPS!
AAAH, I'D FORGOTTEN...
IT'S STEEP...
THE OLD WOMEN...
HOW WILL THEY DO IT?
HUFF HUFF
LOOK OUT! COMING THROUGH!
EVENING, NAOKO.
NOT A CHANCE!

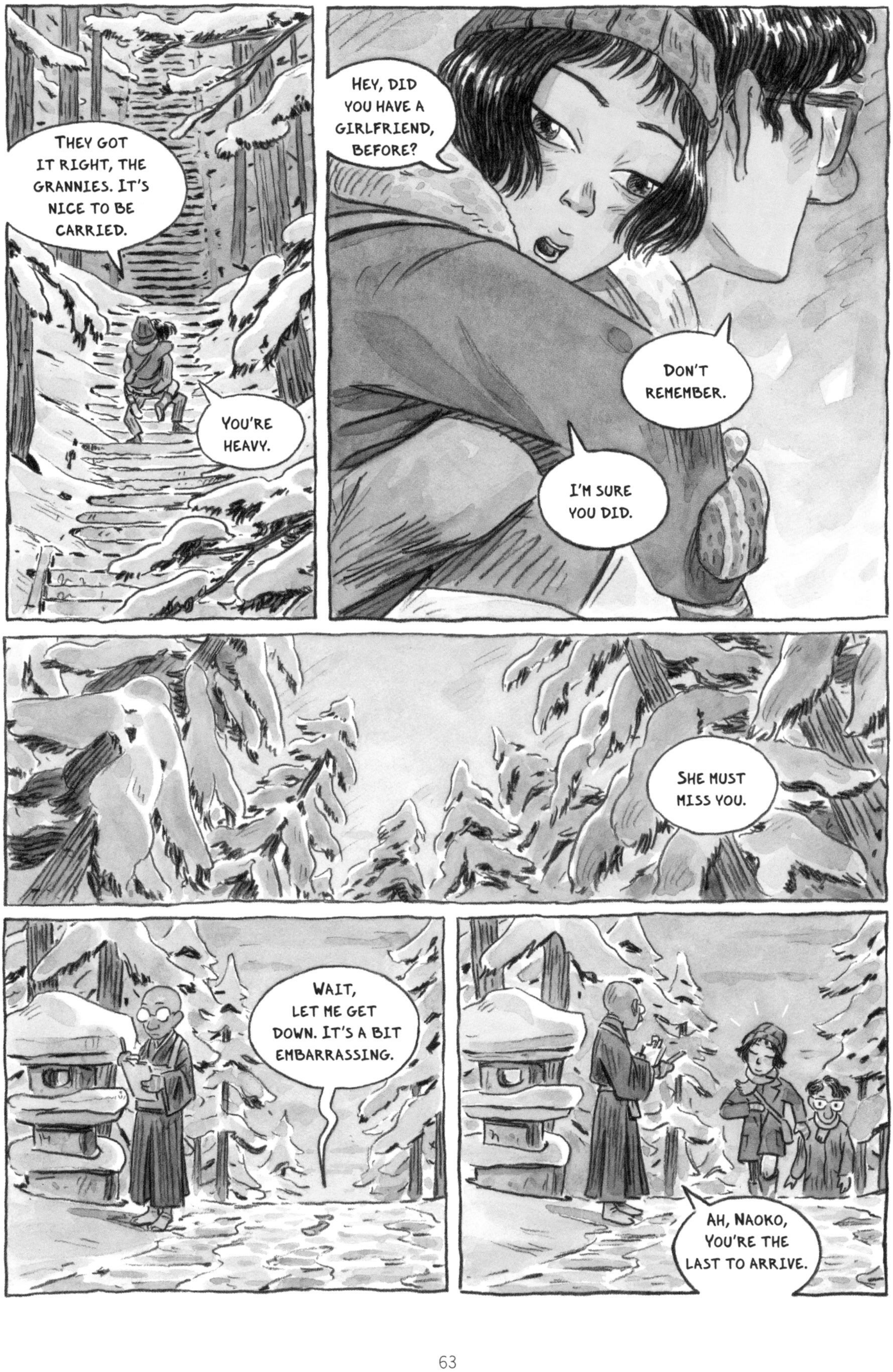
They got it right, the grannies. It's nice to be carried.
You're heavy.
Hey, did you have a girlfriend, before?
Don't remember.
I'm sure you did.
She must miss you.
Wait, let me get down. It's a bit embarrassing.
Ah, Naoko, you're the last to arrive.

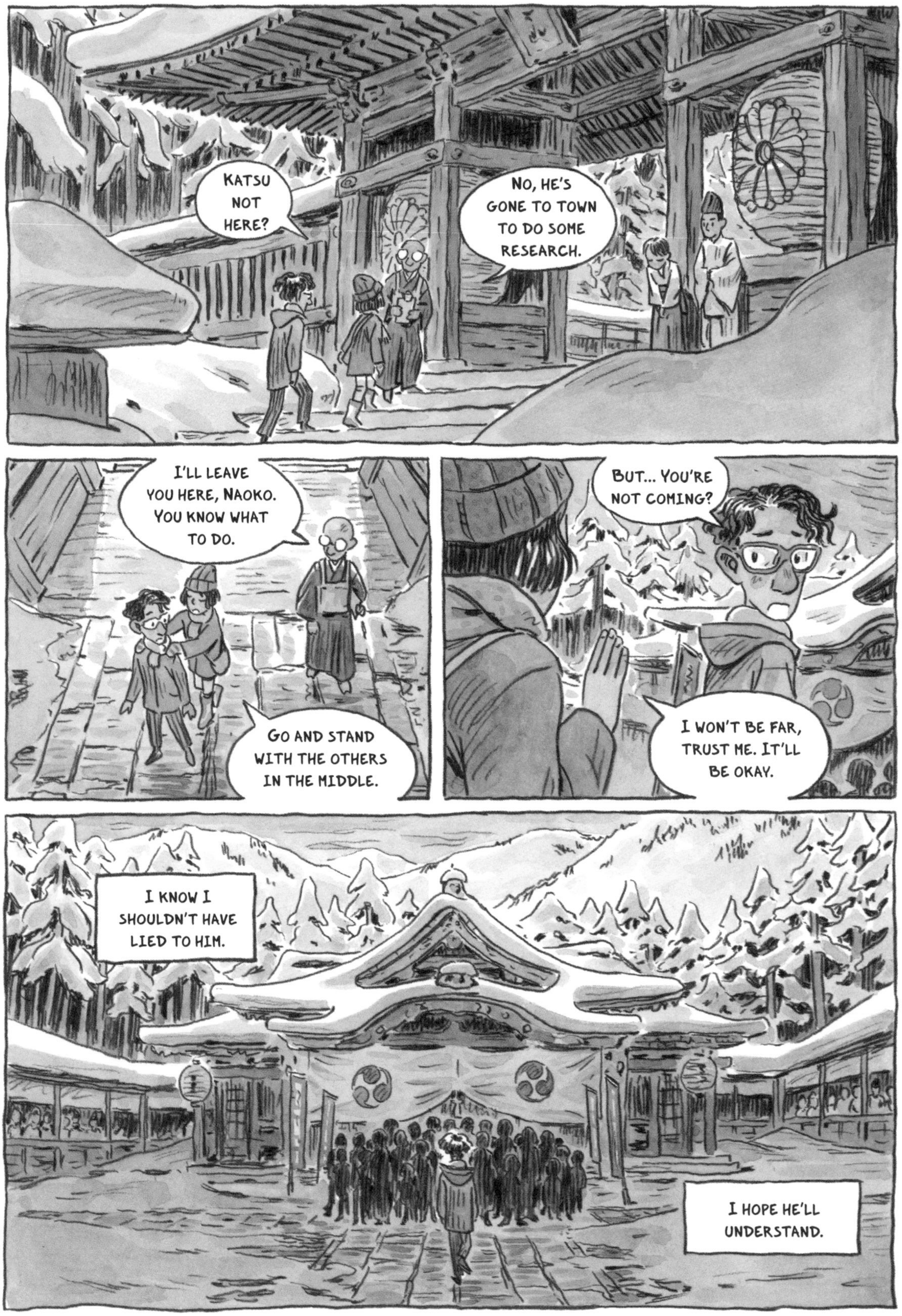
KATSU NOT HERE?
NO, HE'S GONE TO TOWN TO DO SOME RESEARCH.
I'LL LEAVE YOU HERE, NAOKO. YOU KNOW WHAT TO DO.
GO AND STAND WITH THE OTHERS IN THE MIDDLE.
BUT... YOU'RE NOT COMING?
I WON'T BE FAR, TRUST ME. IT'LL BE OKAY.
I KNOW I SHOULDN'T HAVE LIED TO HIM.
I HOPE HE'LL UNDERSTAND.

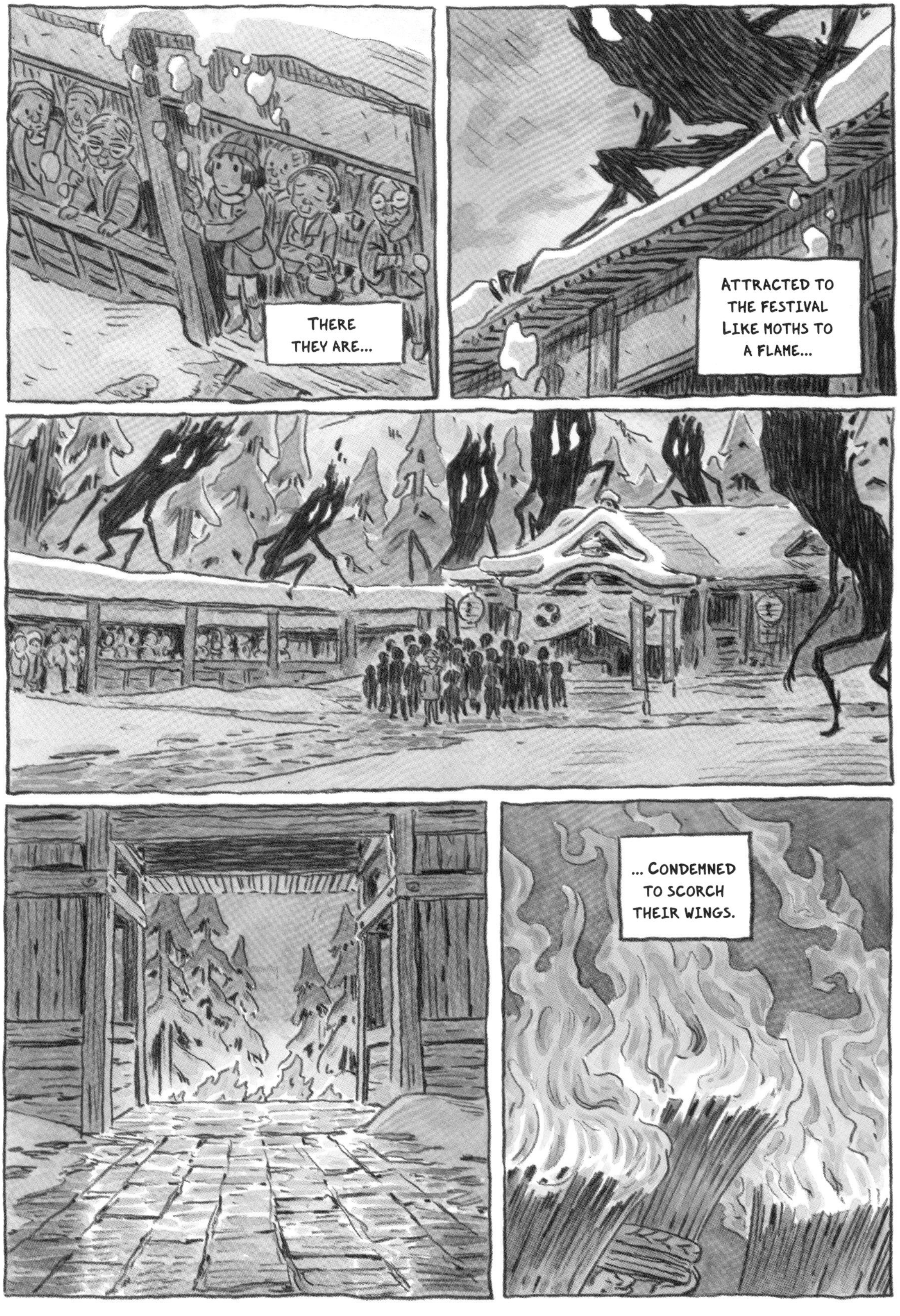
There they are...
Attracted to the festival like moths to a flame...
... Condemned to scorch their wings.

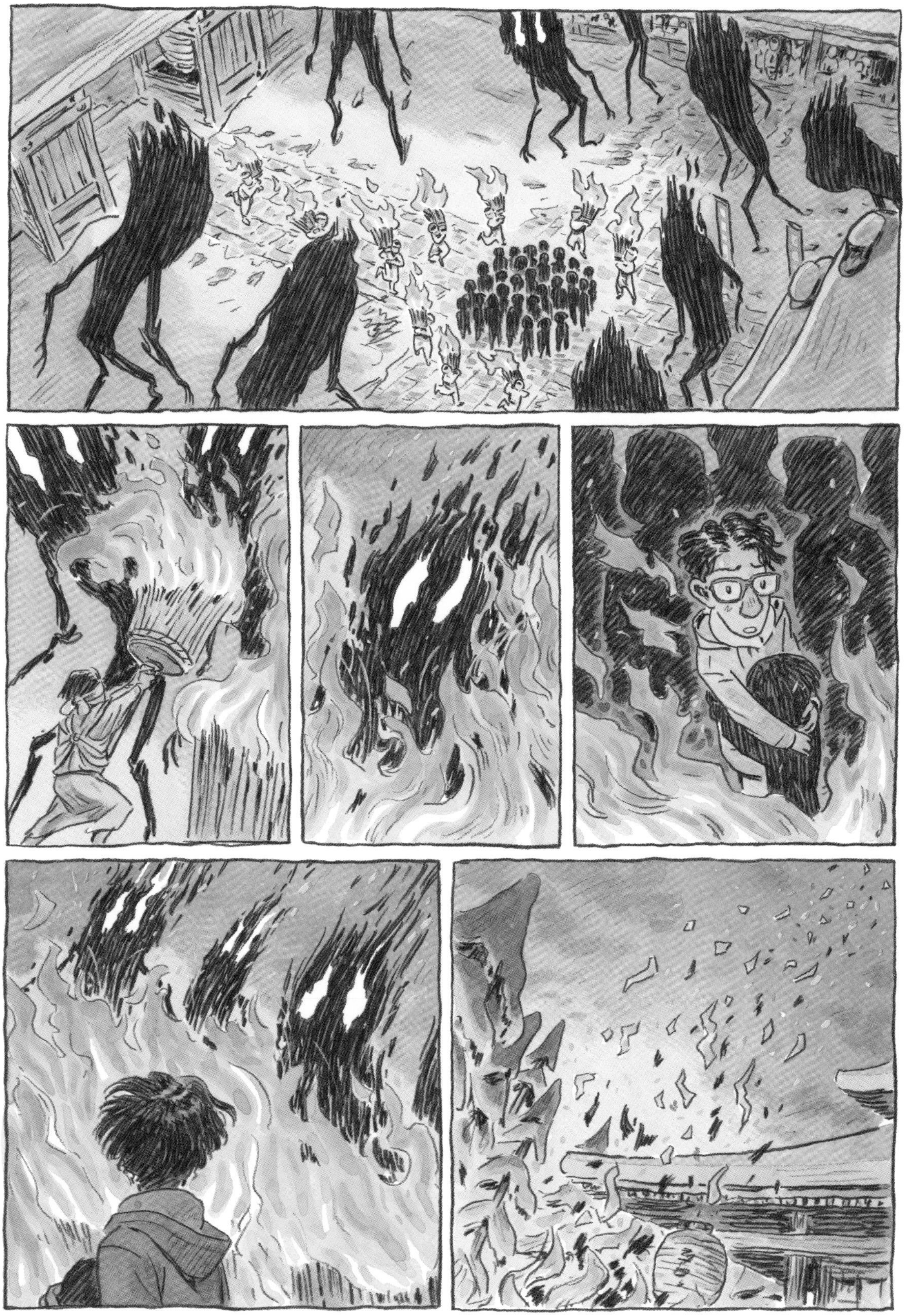

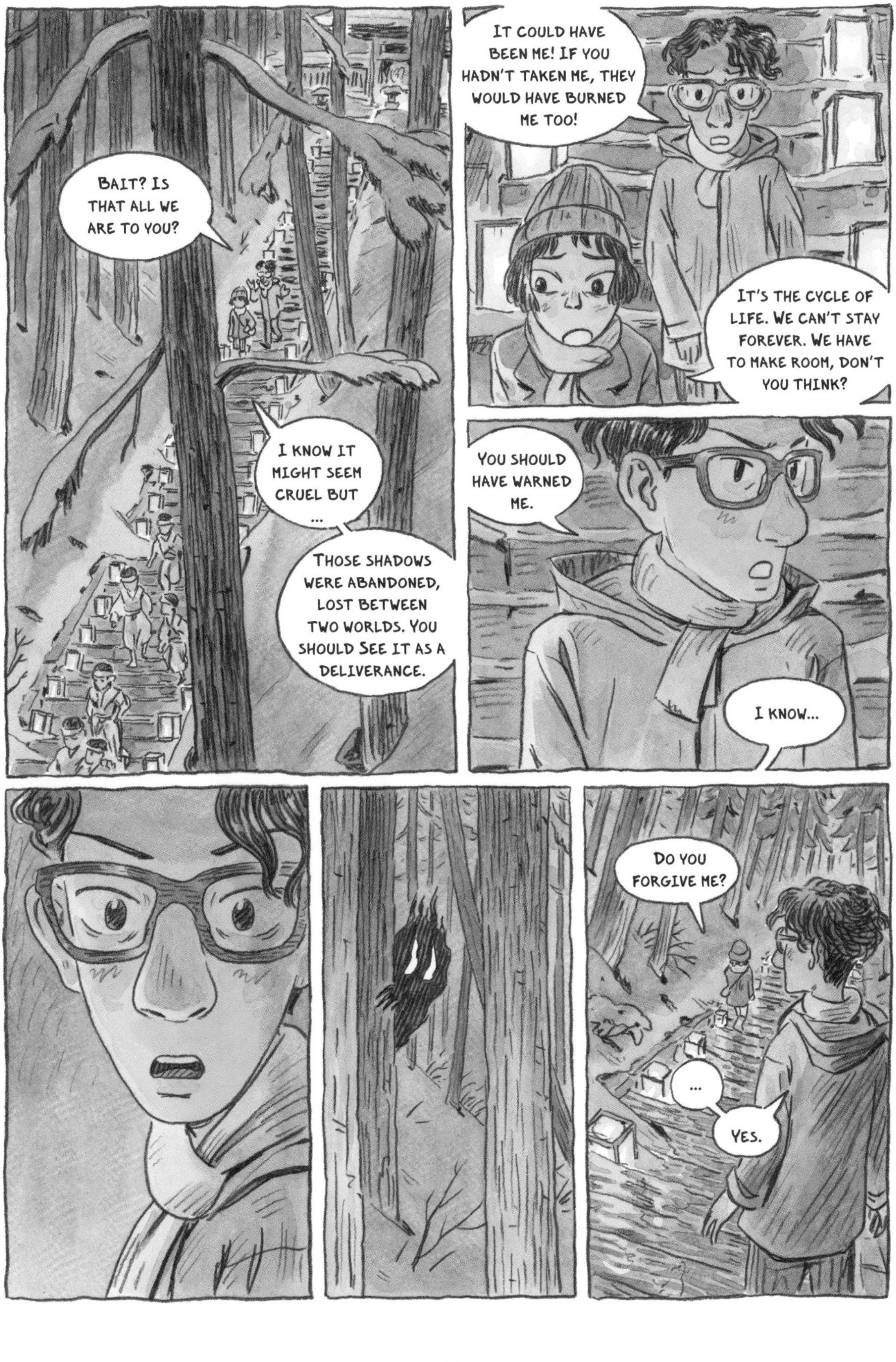
BAIT? IS THAT ALL WE ARE TO YOU?
I KNOW IT MIGHT SEEM CRUEL BUT ...
THOSE SHADOWS WERE ABANDONED, LOST BETWEEN TWO WORLDS. YOU SHOULD SEE IT AS A DELIVERANCE.
IT COULD HAVE BEEN ME! IF YOU HADN'T TAKEN ME, THEY WOULD HAVE BURNED ME TOO!
IT'S THE CYCLE OF LIFE. WE CAN'T STAY FOREVER. WE HAVE TO MAKE ROOM, DON'T YOU THINK?
YOU SHOULD HAVE WARNED ME.
I KNOW...
DO YOU FORGIVE ME?
...
YES.

Shards of light

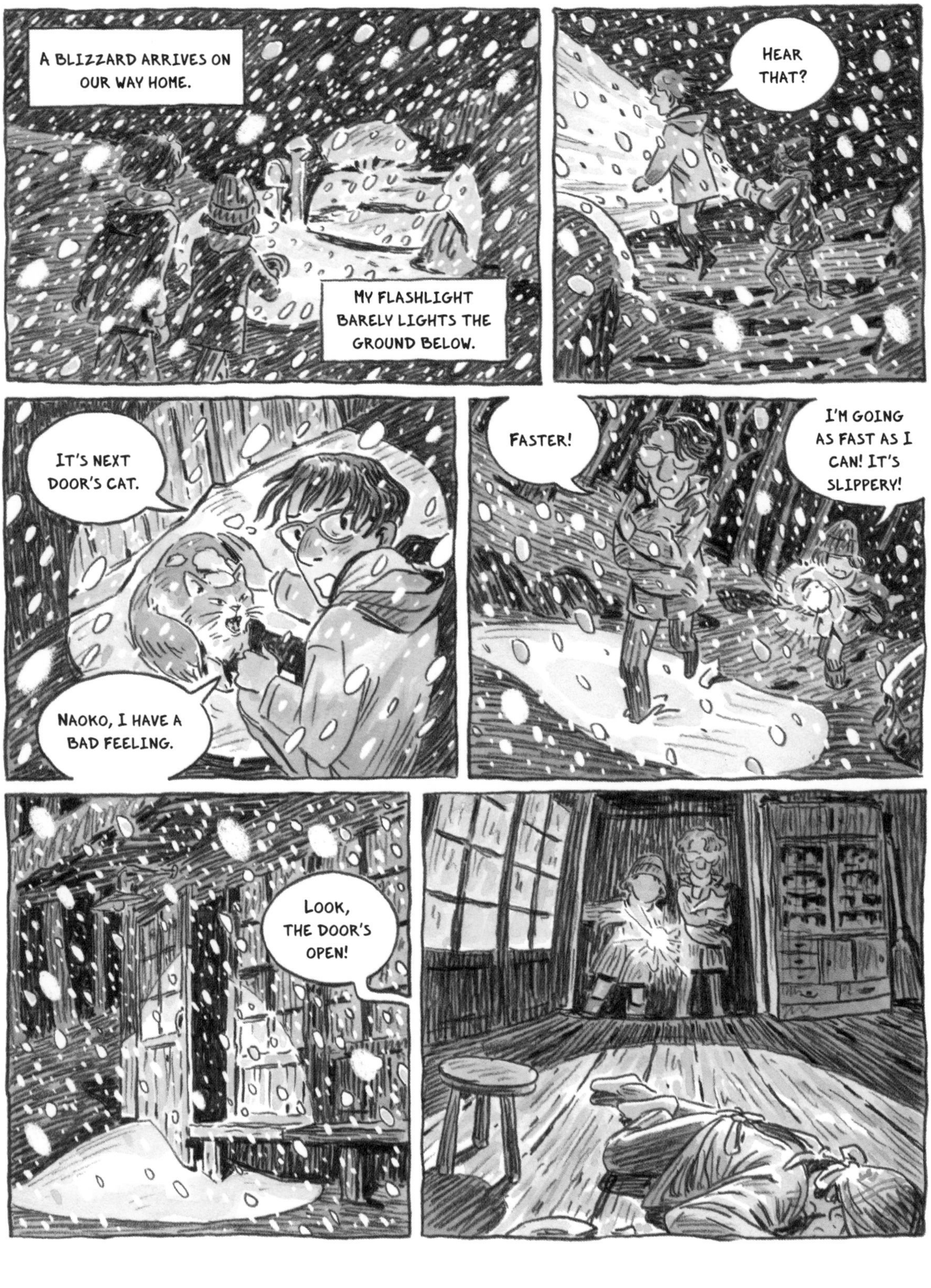
A BLIZZARD ARRIVES ON OUR WAY HOME.
MY FLASHLIGHT BARELY LIGHTS THE GROUND BELOW.
HEAR THAT?
IT'S NEXT DOOR'S CAT.
NAOKO, I HAVE A BAD FEELING.
FASTER!
I'M GOING AS FAST AS I CAN! IT'S SLIPPERY!
LOOK, THE DOOR'S OPEN!

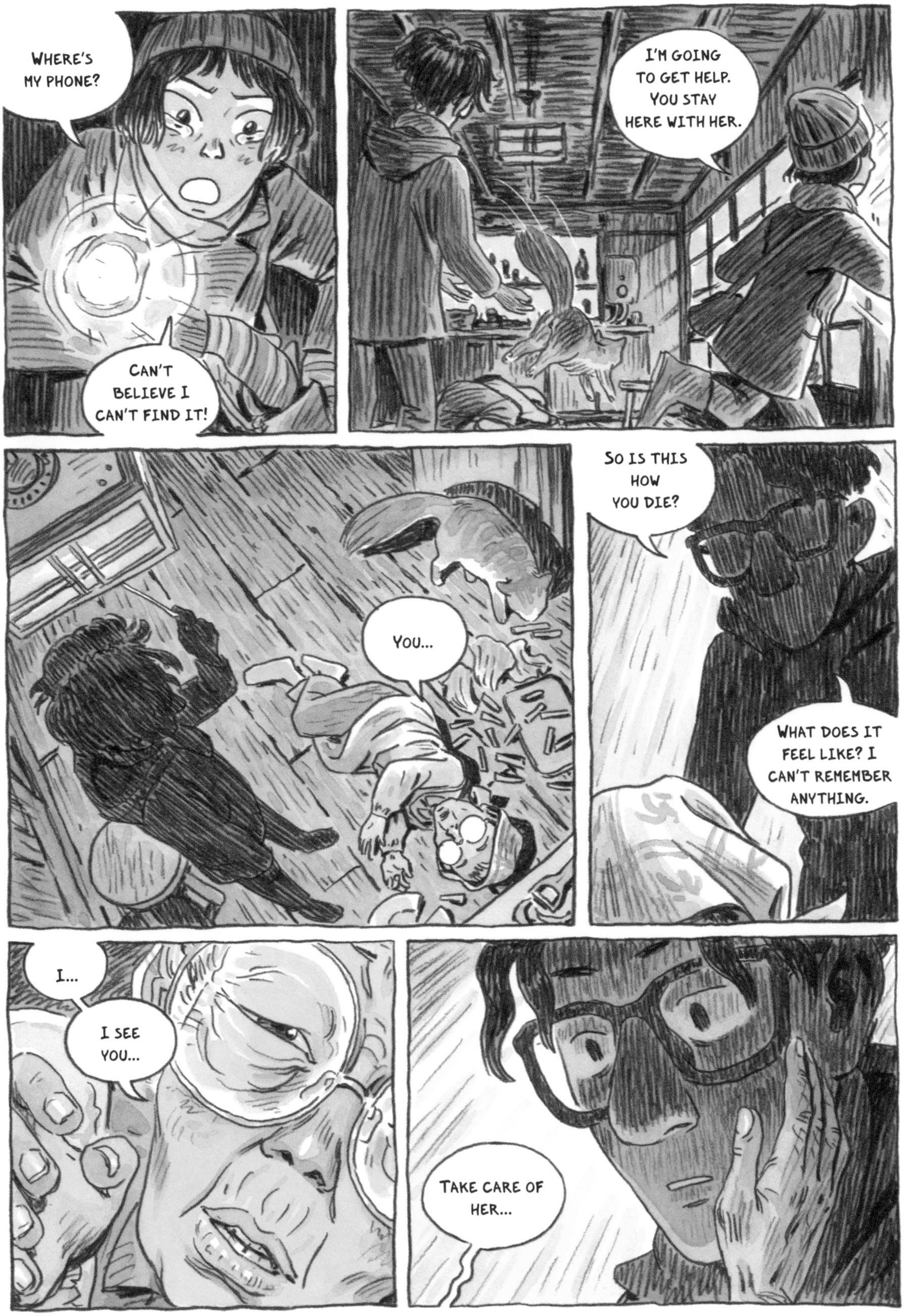
WHERE'S MY PHONE?
CAN'T BELIEVE I CAN'T FIND IT!
I'M GOING TO GET HELP. YOU STAY HERE WITH HER.
YOU...
SO IS THIS HOW YOU DIE?
WHAT DOES IT FEEL LIKE? I CAN'T REMEMBER ANYTHING.
I...
I SEE YOU...
TAKE CARE OF HER...

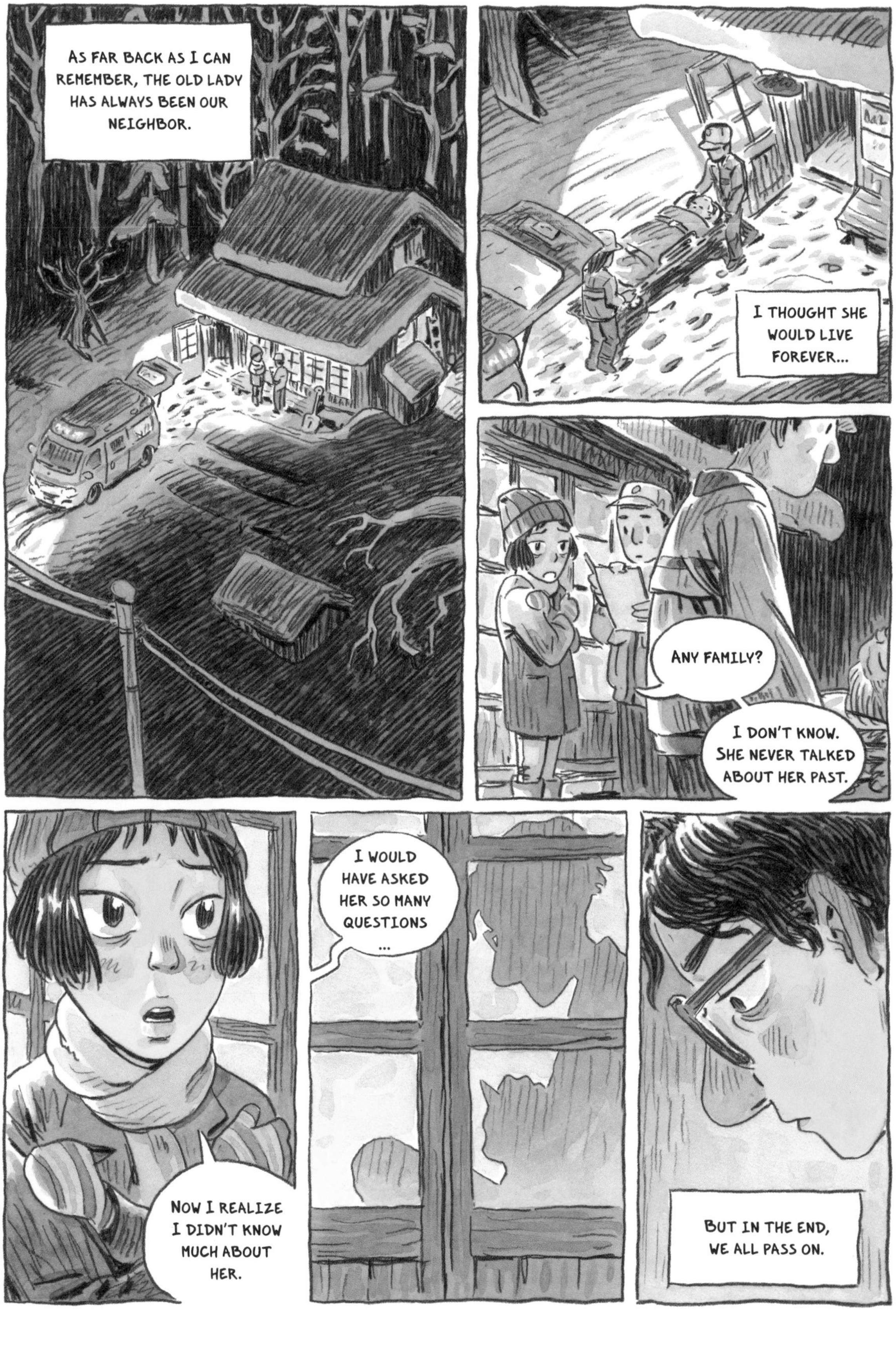
AS FAR BACK AS I CAN REMEMBER, THE OLD LADY HAS ALWAYS BEEN OUR NEIGHBOR.
I THOUGHT SHE WOULD LIVE FOREVER...
ANY FAMILY?
I DON'T KNOW. SHE NEVER TALKED ABOUT HER PAST.
NOW I REALIZE I DIDN'T KNOW MUCH ABOUT HER.
I WOULD HAVE ASKED HER SO MANY QUESTIONS ...
BUT IN THE END, WE ALL PASS ON.

Wounded hearts

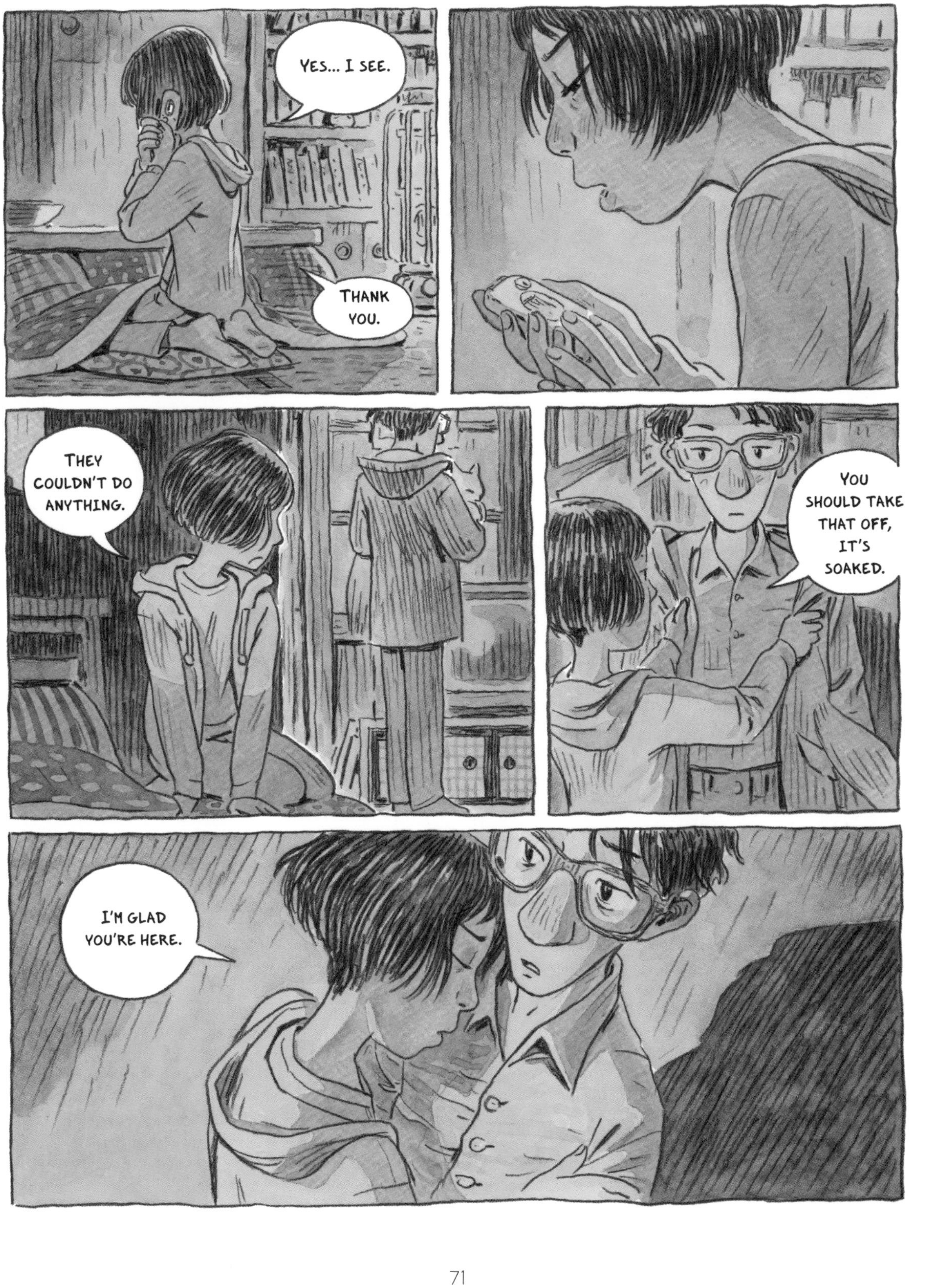
YES... I SEE.
THANK YOU.
THEY COULDN'T DO ANYTHING.
YOU SHOULD TAKE THAT OFF, IT'S SOAKED.
I'M GLAD YOU'RE HERE.

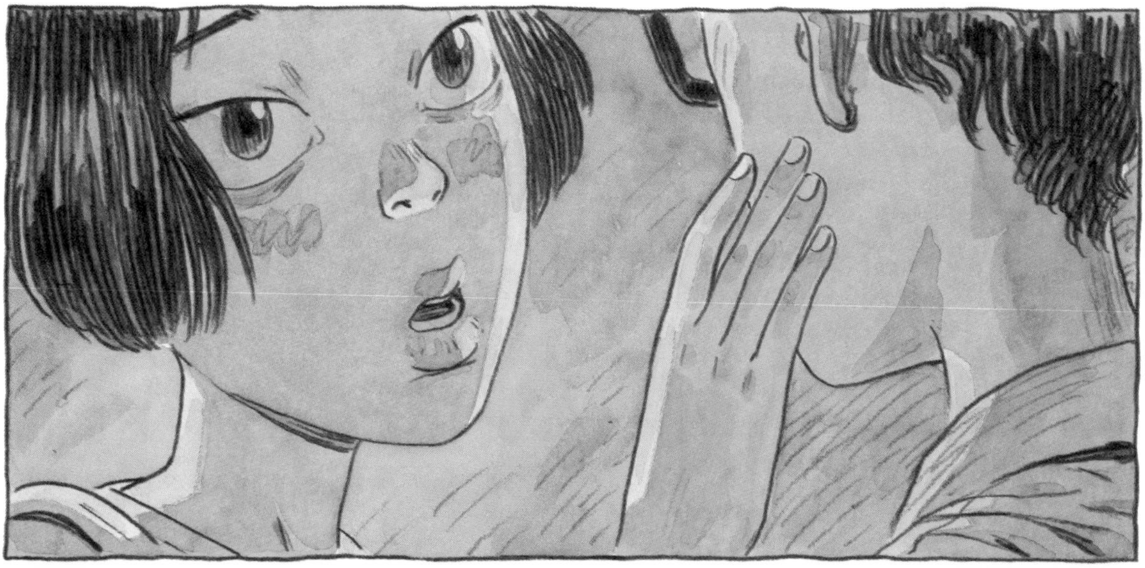

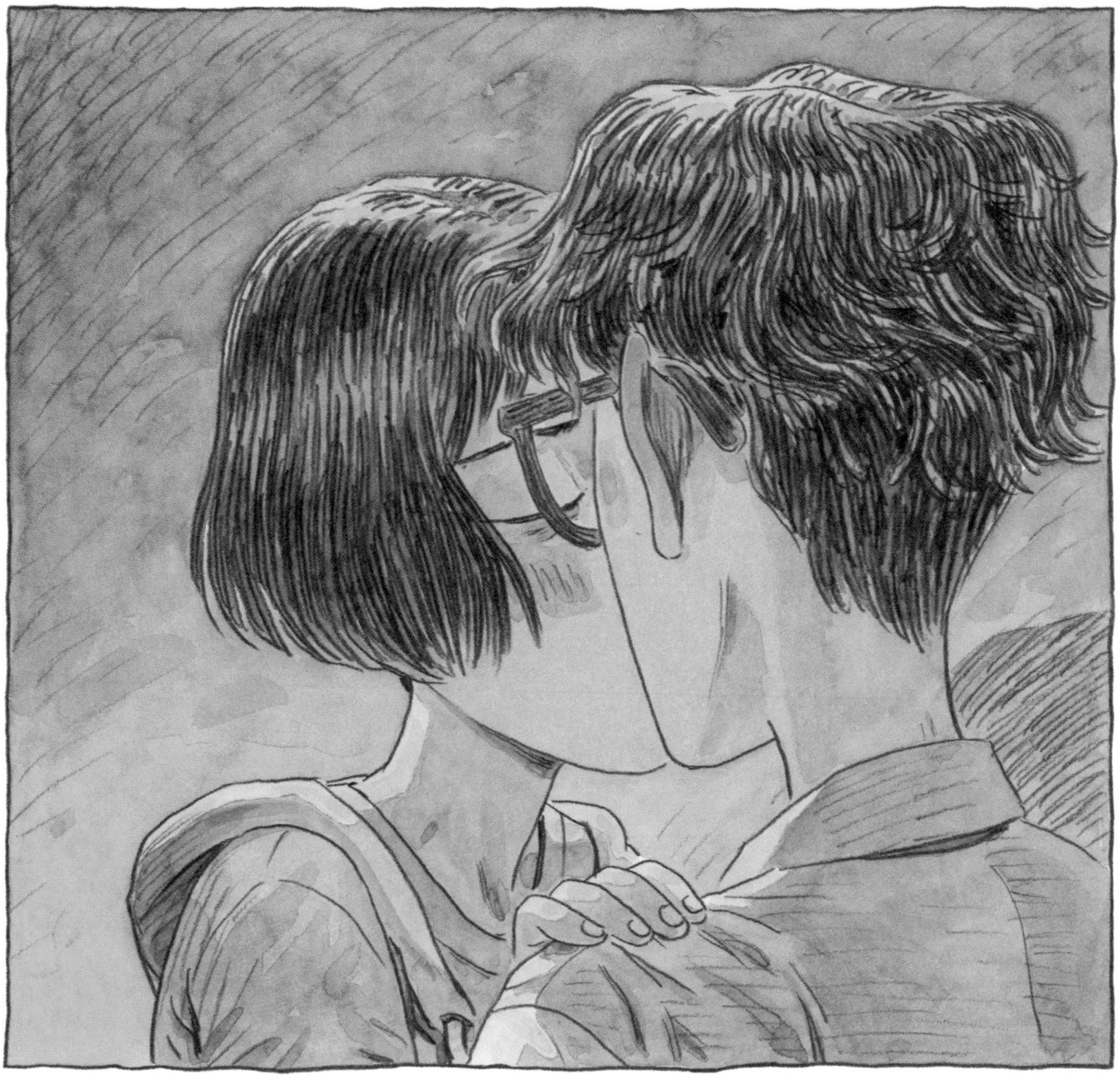

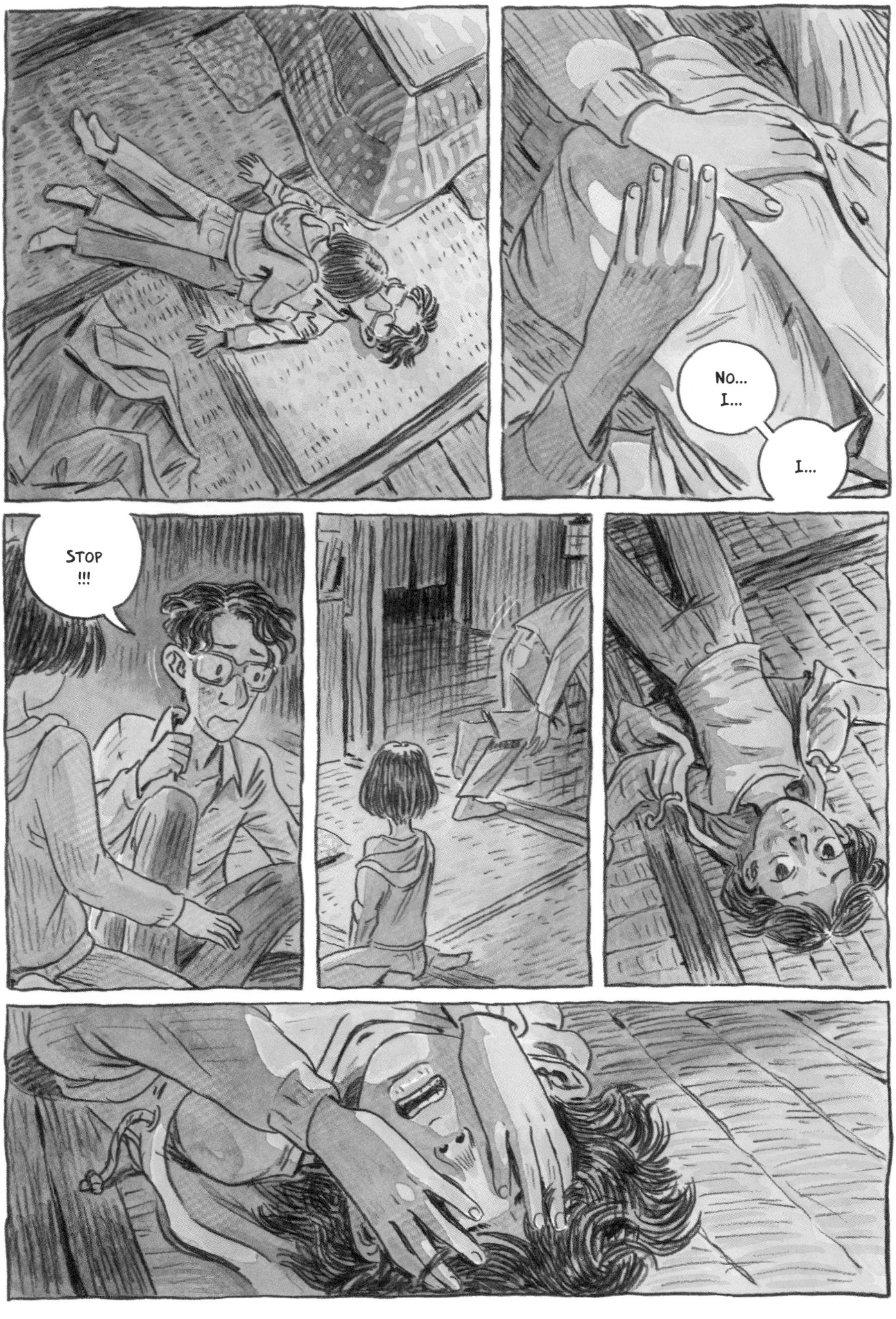

NO...
I...
I...
STOP
!!!

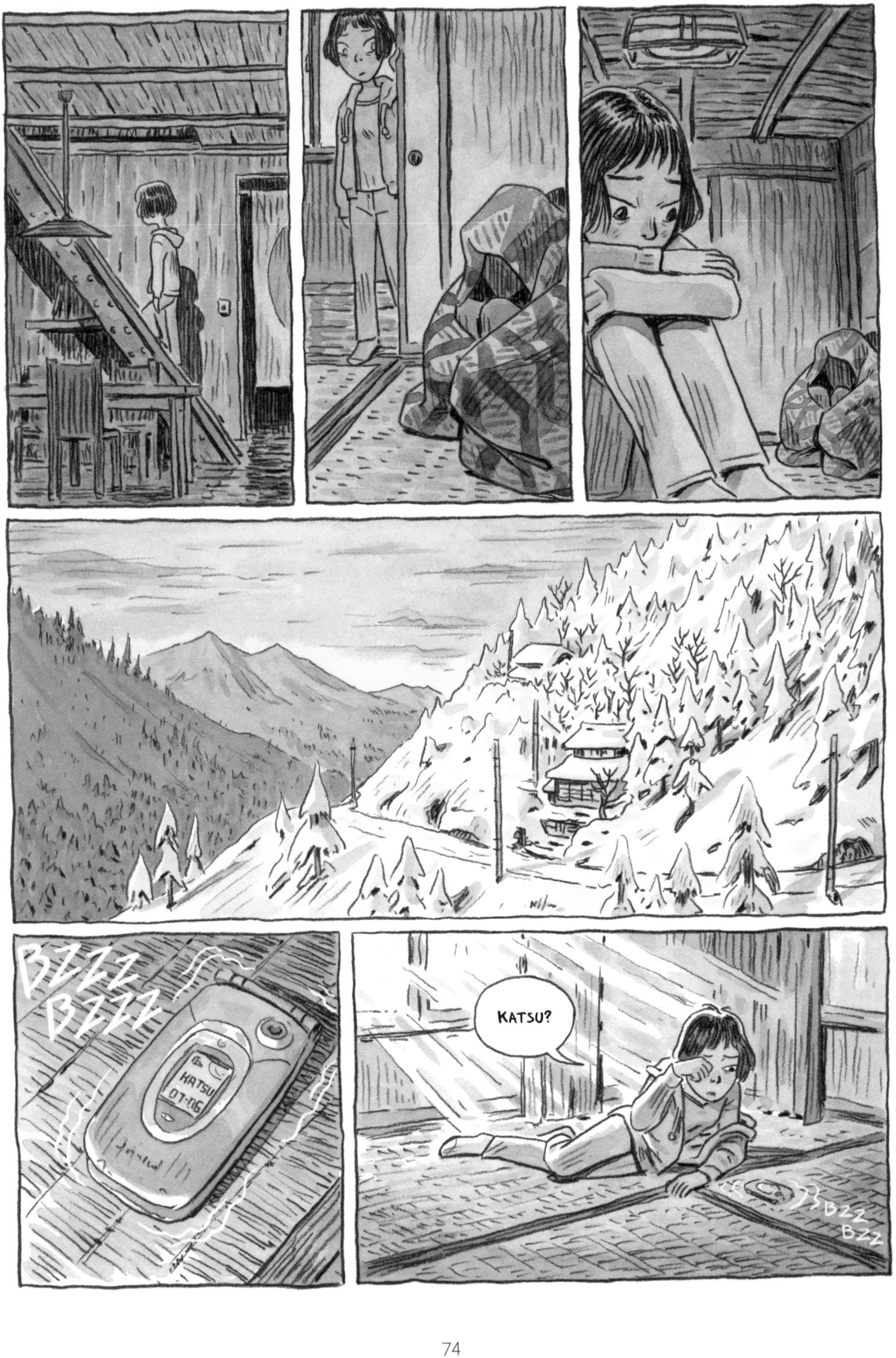
BZZZ
BZZZ
KATSU
KATSU?
BZZ
BZZ

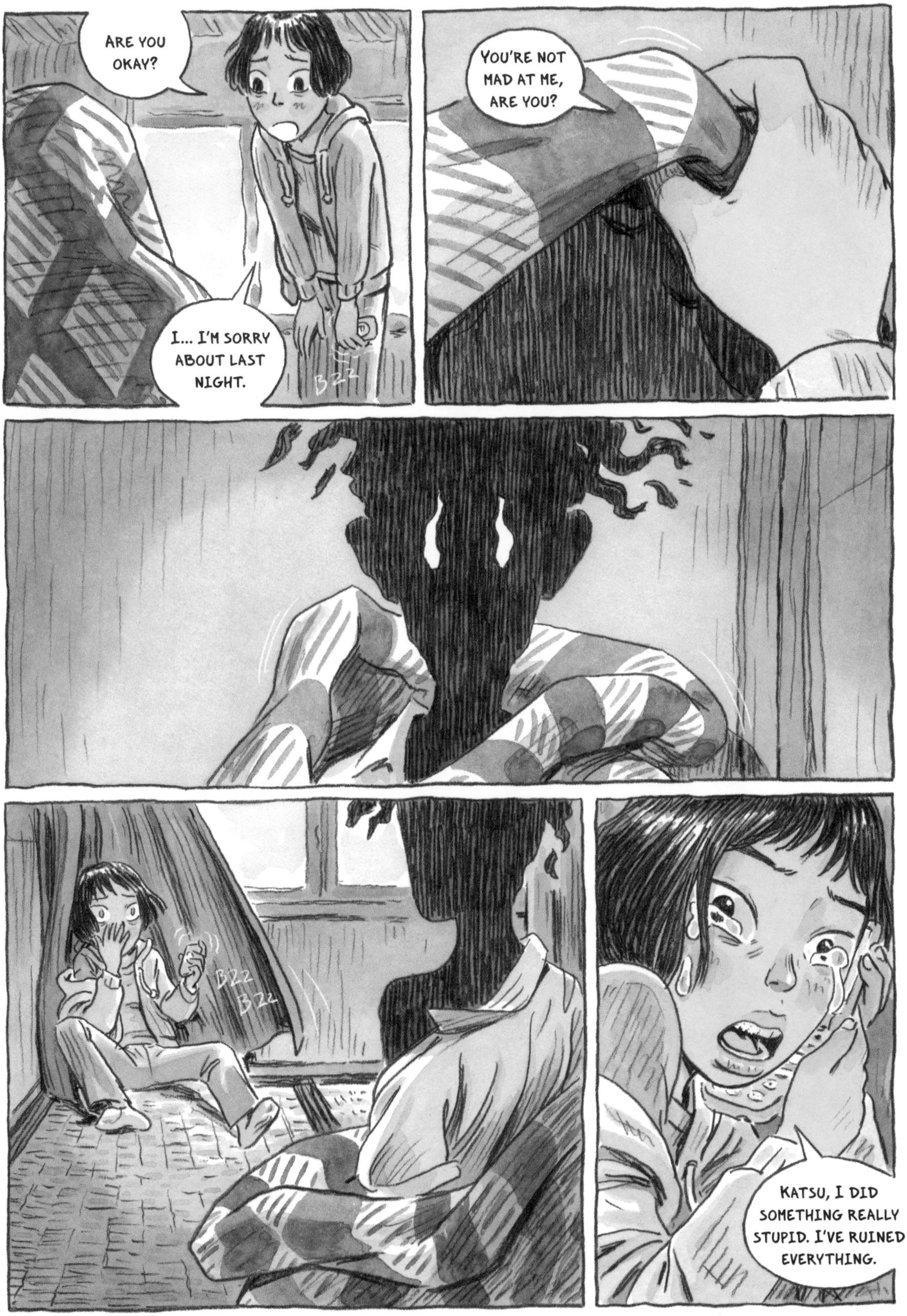
ARE YOU OKAY?
I... I'M SORRY ABOUT LAST NIGHT.
BZZ
YOU'RE NOT MAD AT ME, ARE YOU?
BZZ BZZ
KATSU, I DID SOMETHING REALLY STUPID. I'VE RUINED EVERYTHING.

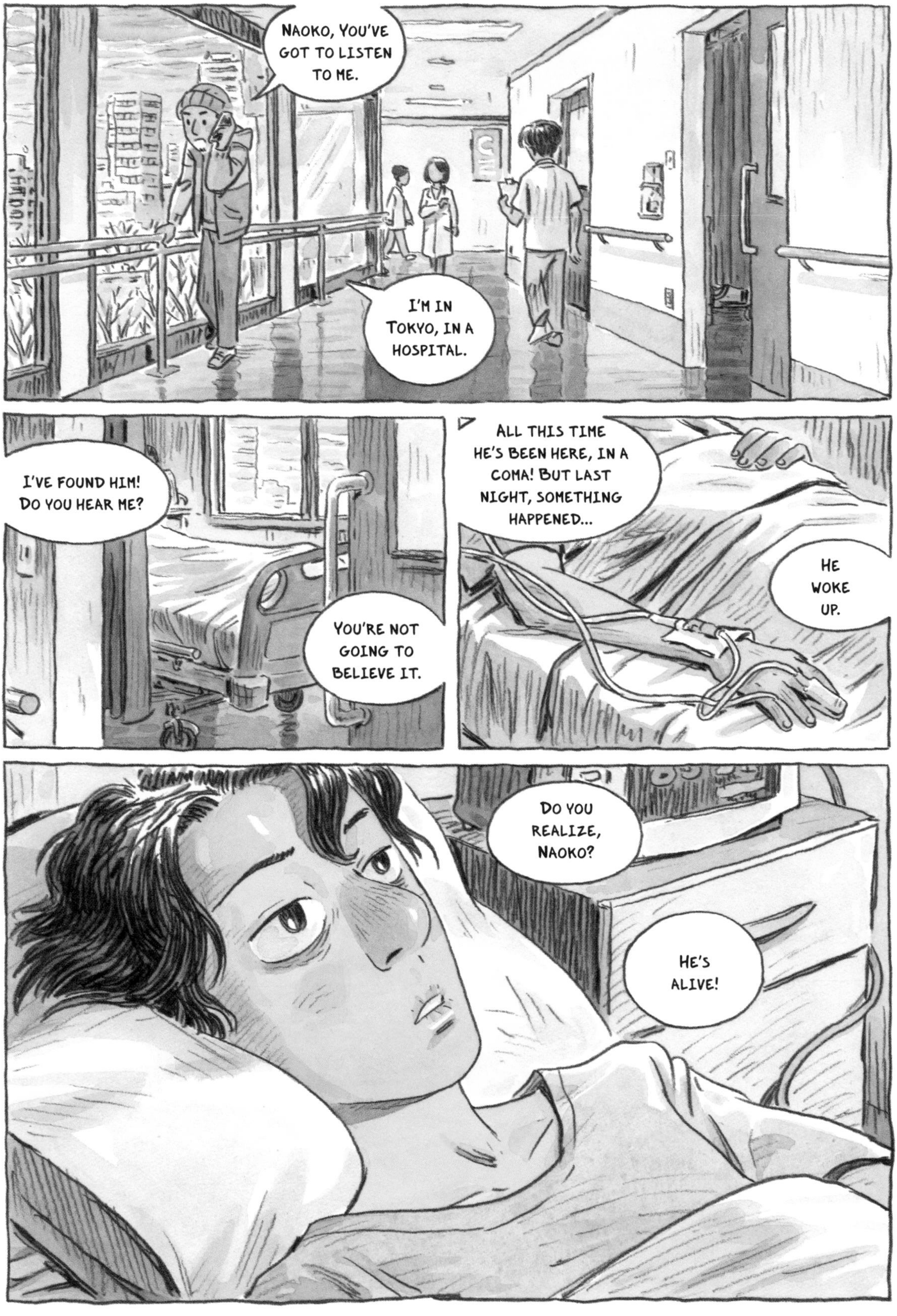
NAOKO, YOU'VE GOT TO LISTEN TO ME.
I'M IN TOKYO, IN A HOSPITAL.
I'VE FOUND HIM! DO YOU HEAR ME?
YOU'RE NOT GOING TO BELIEVE IT.
ALL THIS TIME HE'S BEEN HERE, IN A COMA! BUT LAST NIGHT, SOMETHING HAPPENED...
HE WOKE UP.
DO YOU REALIZE, NAOKO?
HE'S ALIVE!

End of part one

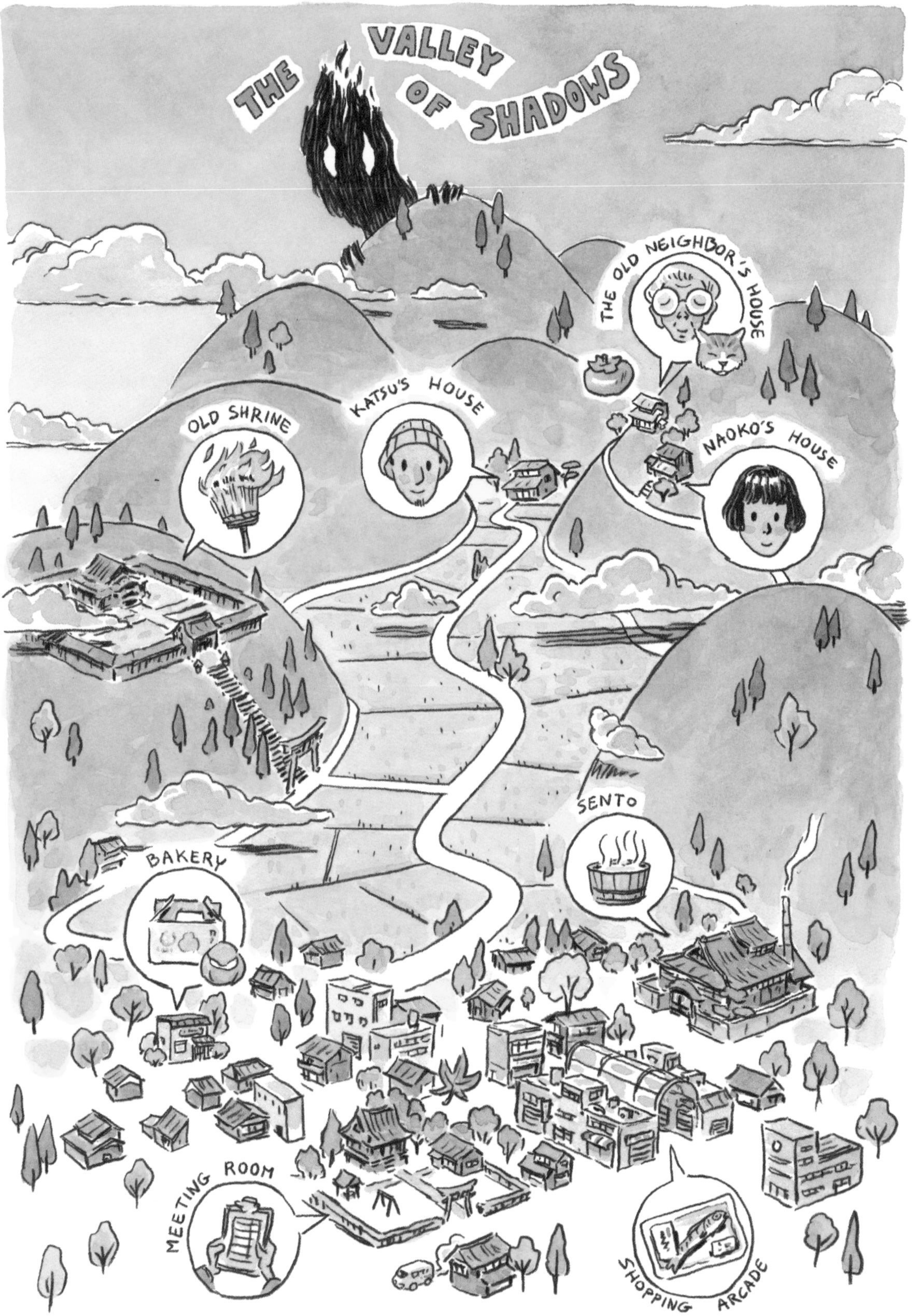
THE VALLEY OF SHADOWS
THE OLD NEIGHBOR'S HOUSE
KATSU'S HOUSE
OLD SHRINE
NAOKO'S HOUSE
SENTO
BAKERY
MEETING ROOM
SHOPPING ARCADE

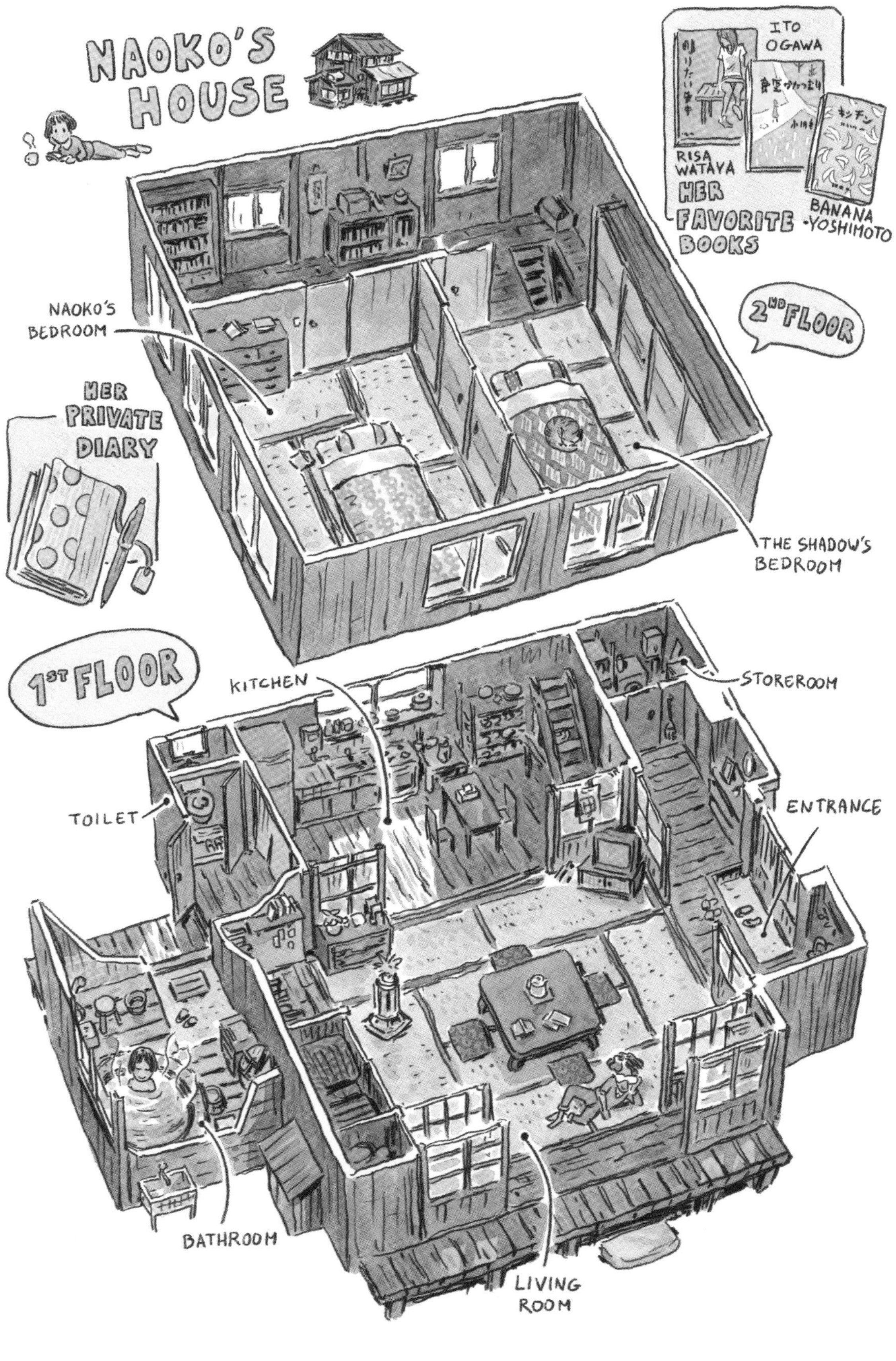
NAOKO'S HOUSE
ITO OGAWA
RISA WATAYA
HER FAVORITE BOOKS
BANANA -YOSHIMOTO
NAOKO'S BEDROOM
2ND FLOOR
HER PRIVATE DIARY
THE SHADOW'S BEDROOM
1ST FLOOR
KITCHEN
STOREROOM
TOILET
ENTRANCE
BATHROOM
LIVING ROOM

Part two

The returned

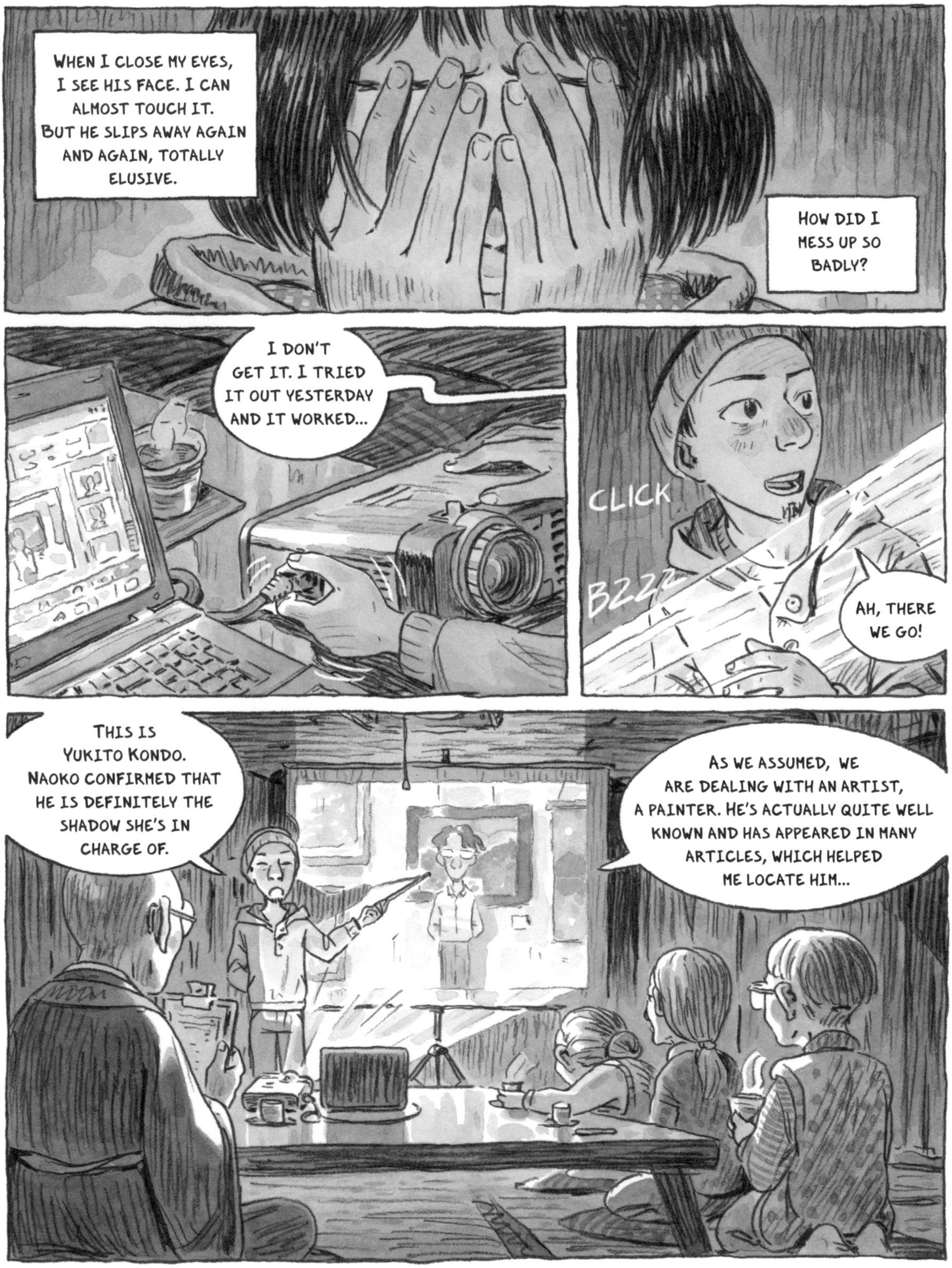

WHEN I CLOSE MY EYES, I SEE HIS FACE. I CAN ALMOST TOUCH IT. BUT HE SLIPS AWAY AGAIN AND AGAIN, TOTALLY ELUSIVE.
HOW DID I MESS UP SO BADLY?
I DON'T GET IT. I TRIED IT OUT YESTERDAY AND IT WORKED...
CLICK
BZZZ
AH, THERE WE GO!
THIS IS YUKITO KONDO. NAOKO CONFIRMED THAT HE IS DEFINITELY THE SHADOW SHE'S IN CHARGE OF.
AS WE ASSUMED, WE ARE DEALING WITH AN ARTIST, A PAINTER. HE'S ACTUALLY QUITE WELL KNOWN AND HAS APPEARED IN MANY ARTICLES, WHICH HELPED ME LOCATE HIM...

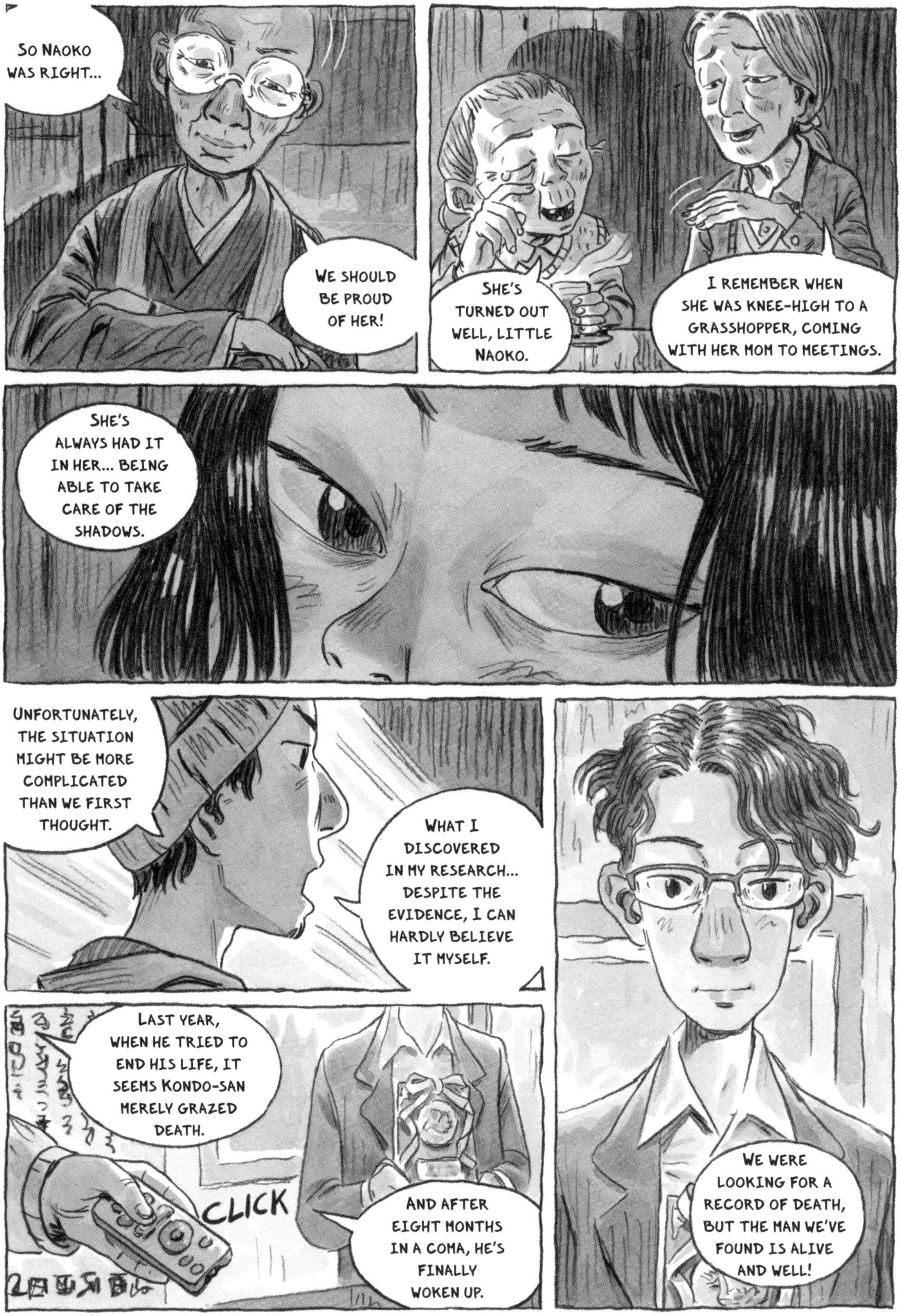
So Naoko was right...
We should be proud of her!
She's turned out well, little Naoko.
I remember when she was knee-high to a grasshopper, coming with her mom to meetings.
She's always had it in her... being able to take care of the shadows.
Unfortunately, the situation might be more complicated than we first thought.
What I discovered in my research... despite the evidence, I can hardly believe it myself.
We were looking for a record of death, but the man we've found is alive and well!
Last year, when he tried to end his life, it seems Kondo-san merely grazed death.
CLICK
And after eight months in a coma, he's finally woken up.

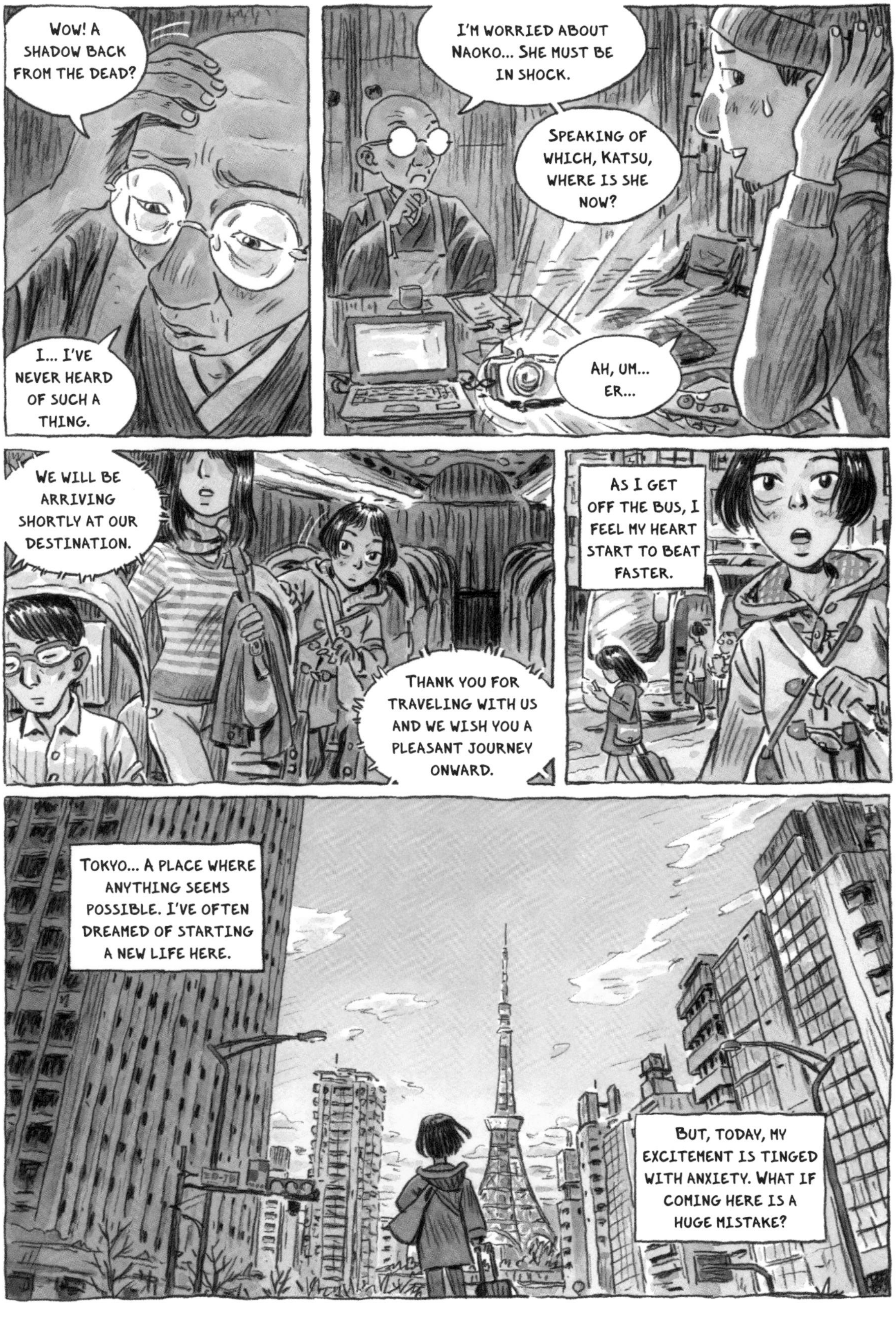
WOW! A SHADOW BACK FROM THE DEAD?
I... I'VE NEVER HEARD OF SUCH A THING.
I'M WORRIED ABOUT NAOKO... SHE MUST BE IN SHOCK.
SPEAKING OF WHICH, KATSU, WHERE IS SHE NOW?
AH, UM... ER...
WE WILL BE ARRIVING SHORTLY AT OUR DESTINATION.
THANK YOU FOR TRAVELING WITH US AND WE WISH YOU A PLEASANT JOURNEY ONWARD.
AS I GET OFF THE BUS, I FEEL MY HEART START TO BEAT FASTER.
TOKYO... A PLACE WHERE ANYTHING SEEMS POSSIBLE. I'VE OFTEN DREAMED OF STARTING A NEW LIFE HERE.
BUT, TODAY, MY EXCITEMENT IS TINGED WITH ANXIETY. WHAT IF COMING HERE IS A HUGE MISTAKE?

春

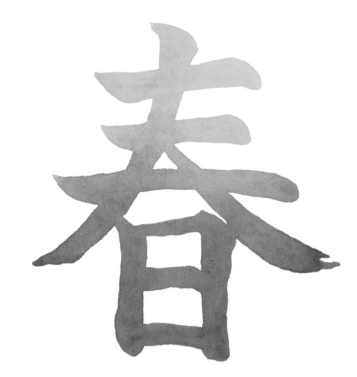

Spring

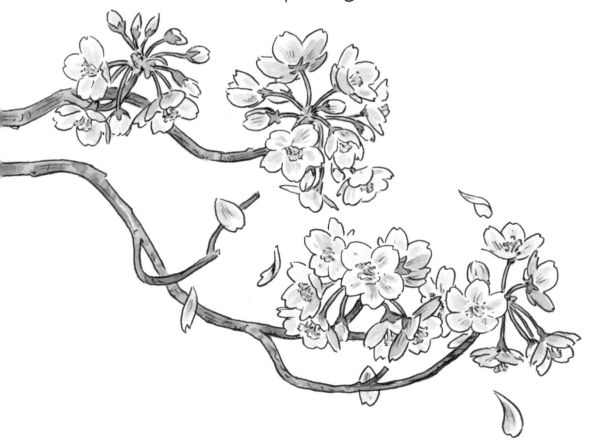

On the lookout

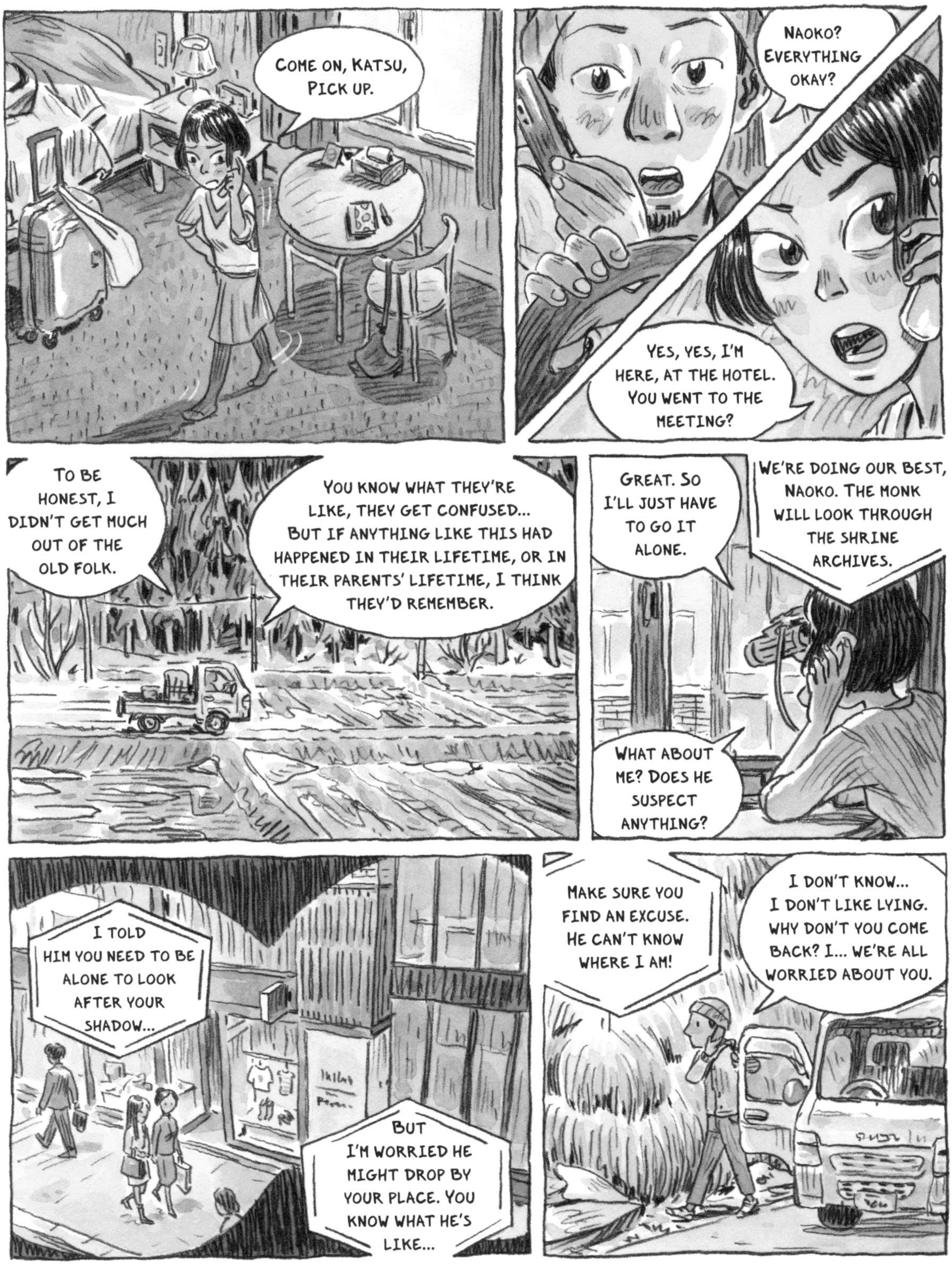
COME ON, KATSU, PICK UP.
NAOKO? EVERYTHING OKAY?
YES, YES, I'M HERE, AT THE HOTEL. YOU WENT TO THE MEETING?
TO BE HONEST, I DIDN'T GET MUCH OUT OF THE OLD FOLK.
YOU KNOW WHAT THEY'RE LIKE, THEY GET CONFUSED... BUT IF ANYTHING LIKE THIS HAD HAPPENED IN THEIR LIFETIME, OR IN THEIR PARENTS' LIFETIME, I THINK THEY'D REMEMBER.
GREAT. SO I'LL JUST HAVE TO GO IT ALONE.
WE'RE DOING OUR BEST, NAOKO. THE MONK WILL LOOK THROUGH THE SHRINE ARCHIVES.
WHAT ABOUT ME? DOES HE SUSPECT ANYTHING?
I TOLD HIM YOU NEED TO BE ALONE TO LOOK AFTER YOUR SHADOW...
BUT I'M WORRIED HE MIGHT DROP BY YOUR PLACE. YOU KNOW WHAT HE'S LIKE...
MAKE SURE YOU FIND AN EXCUSE. HE CAN'T KNOW WHERE I AM!
I DON'T KNOW... I DON'T LIKE LYING. WHY DON'T YOU COME BACK? I... WE'RE ALL WORRIED ABOUT YOU.

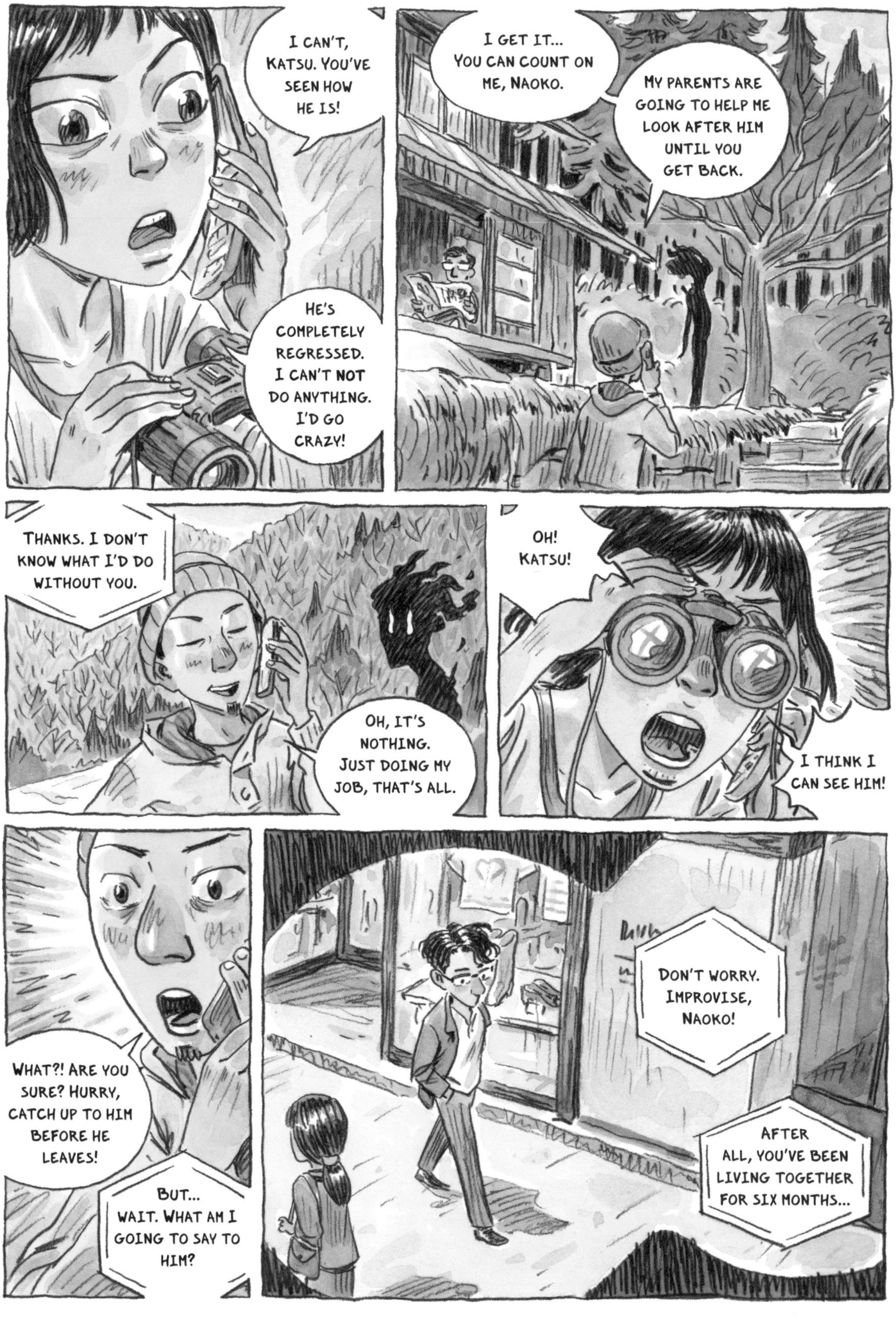
I CAN'T, KATSU. YOU'VE SEEN HOW HE IS!
HE'S COMPLETELY REGRESSED. I CAN'T NOT DO ANYTHING. I'D GO CRAZY!
I GET IT... YOU CAN COUNT ON ME, NAOKO.
MY PARENTS ARE GOING TO HELP ME LOOK AFTER HIM UNTIL YOU GET BACK.
THANKS. I DON'T KNOW WHAT I'D DO WITHOUT YOU.
OH, IT'S NOTHING. JUST DOING MY JOB, THAT'S ALL.
OH! KATSU!
I THINK I CAN SEE HIM!
WHAT?! ARE YOU SURE? HURRY, CATCH UP TO HIM BEFORE HE LEAVES!
BUT... WAIT. WHAT AM I GOING TO SAY TO HIM?
DON'T WORRY. IMPROVISE, NAOKO!
AFTER ALL, YOU'VE BEEN LIVING TOGETHER FOR SIX MONTHS...

Second chance

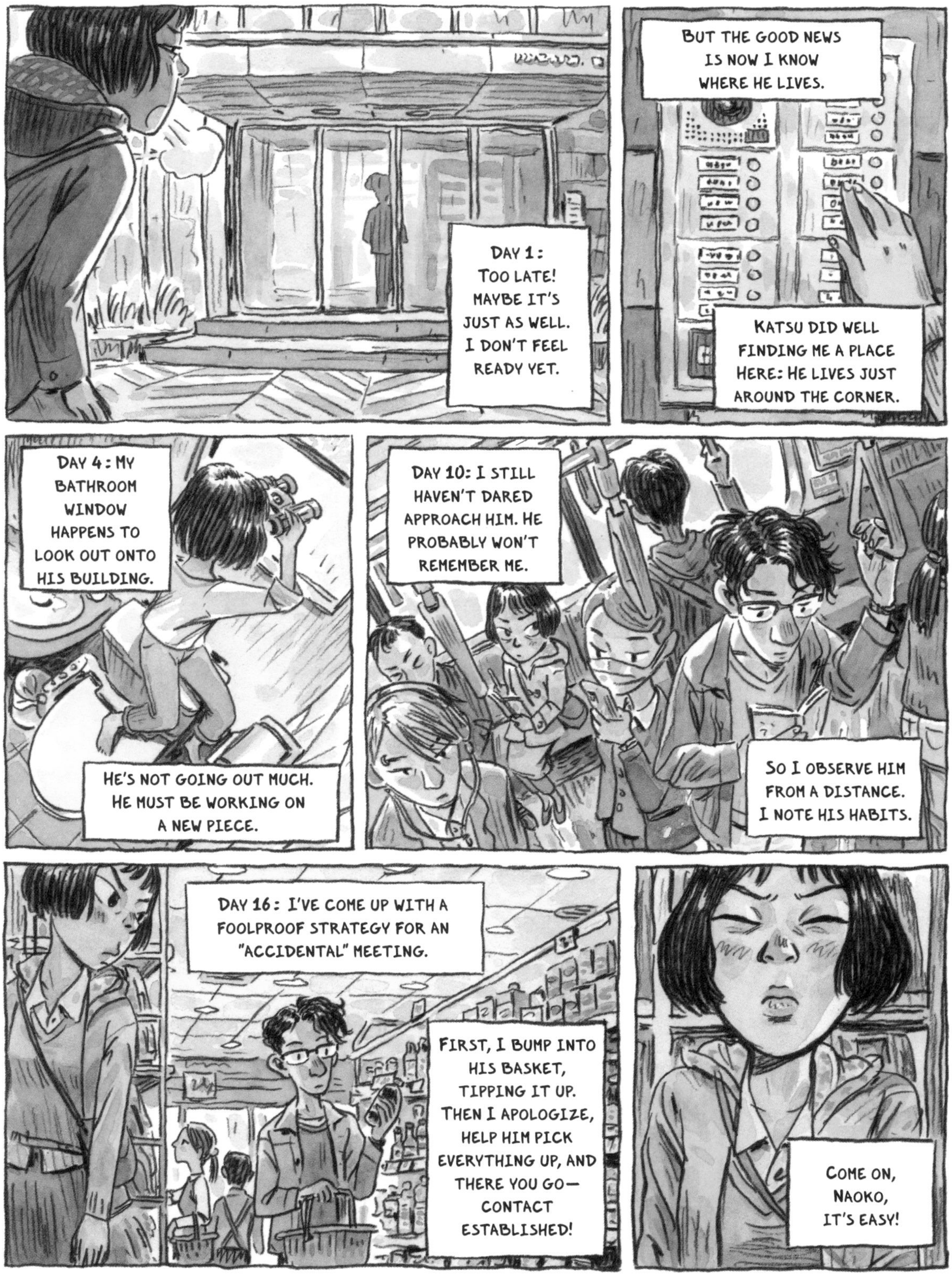
DAY 1: TOO LATE! MAYBE IT'S JUST AS WELL. I DON'T FEEL READY YET.
BUT THE GOOD NEWS IS NOW I KNOW WHERE HE LIVES.
KATSU DID WELL FINDING ME A PLACE HERE: HE LIVES JUST AROUND THE CORNER.
DAY 4: MY BATHROOM WINDOW HAPPENS TO LOOK OUT ONTO HIS BUILDING.
HE'S NOT GOING OUT MUCH. HE MUST BE WORKING ON A NEW PIECE.
DAY 10: I STILL HAVEN'T DARED APPROACH HIM. HE PROBABLY WON'T REMEMBER ME.
SO I OBSERVE HIM FROM A DISTANCE. I NOTE HIS HABITS.
DAY 16: I'VE COME UP WITH A FOOLPROOF STRATEGY FOR AN "ACCIDENTAL" MEETING.
FIRST, I BUMP INTO HIS BASKET, TIPPING IT UP. THEN I APOLOGIZE, HELP HIM PICK EVERYTHING UP, AND THERE YOU GO— CONTACT ESTABLISHED!
COME ON, NAOKO, IT'S EASY!

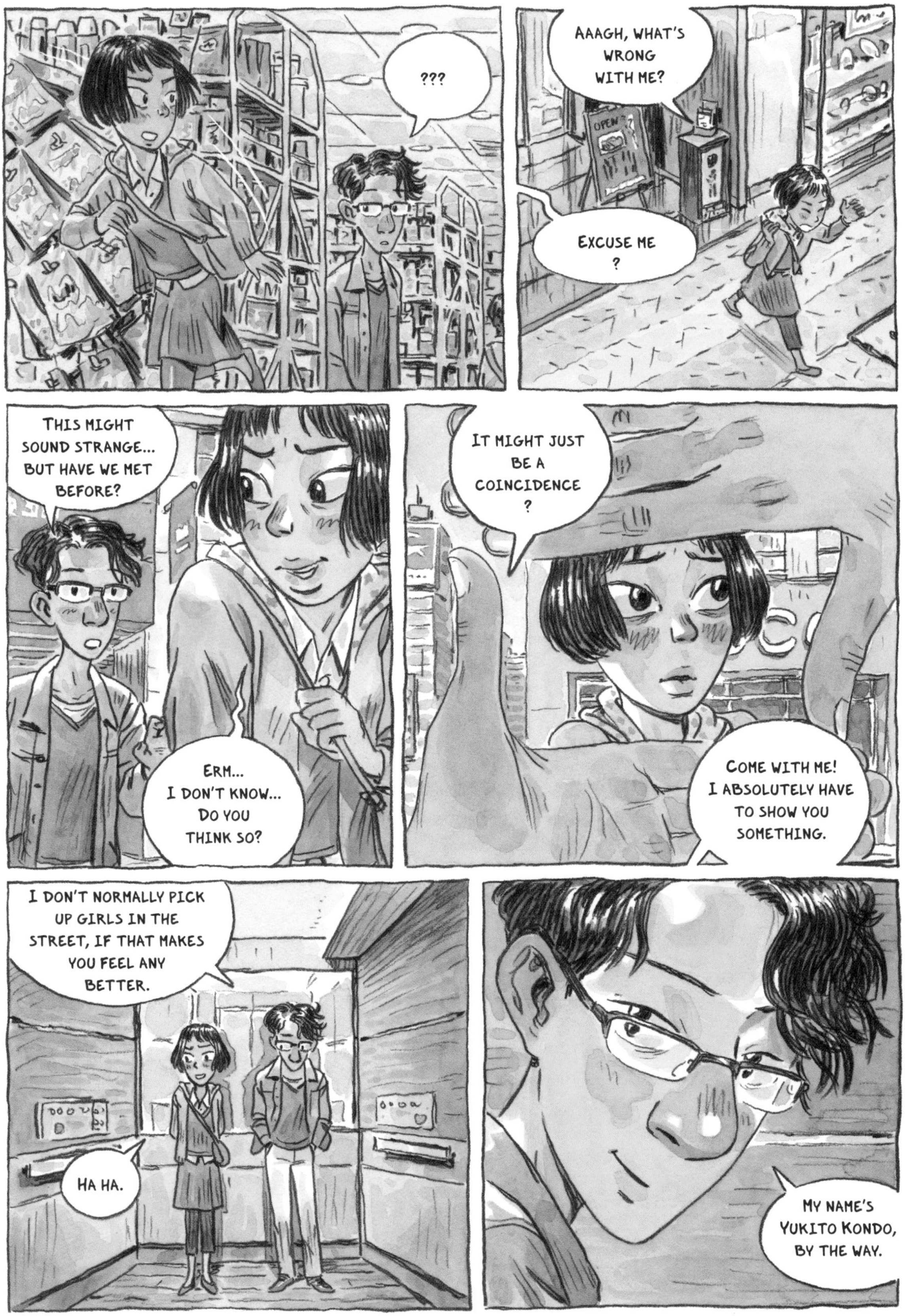
???
AAAGH, WHAT'S WRONG WITH ME?
EXCUSE ME ?
THIS MIGHT SOUND STRANGE... BUT HAVE WE MET BEFORE?
ERM... I DON'T KNOW... DO YOU THINK SO?
IT MIGHT JUST BE A COINCIDENCE ?
COME WITH ME! I ABSOLUTELY HAVE TO SHOW YOU SOMETHING.
I DON'T NORMALLY PICK UP GIRLS IN THE STREET, IF THAT MAKES YOU FEEL ANY BETTER.
HA HA.
MY NAME'S YUKITO KONDO, BY THE WAY.

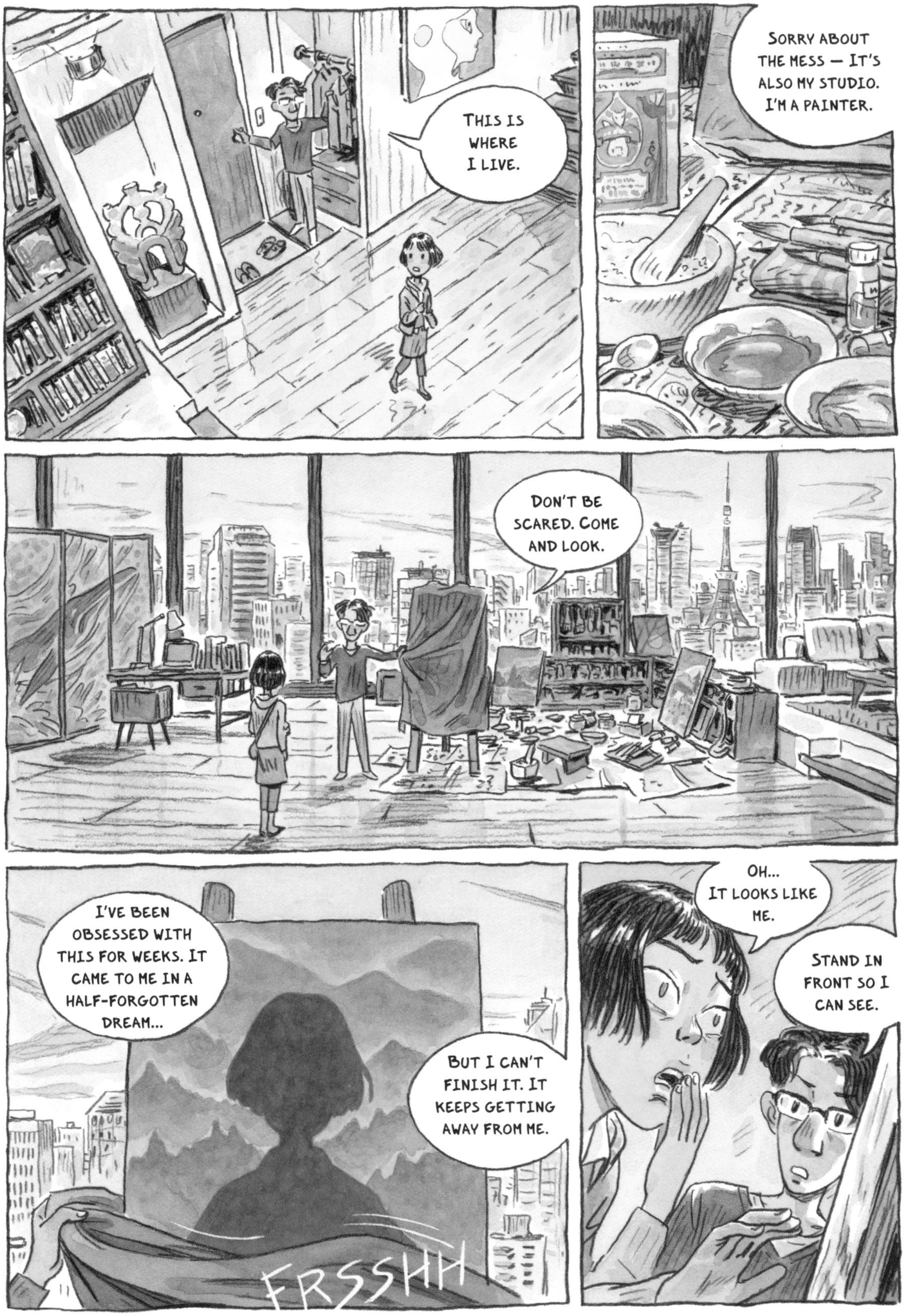
THIS IS WHERE I LIVE.
SORRY ABOUT THE MESS — IT'S ALSO MY STUDIO. I'M A PAINTER.
DON'T BE SCARED. COME AND LOOK.
I'VE BEEN OBSESSED WITH THIS FOR WEEKS. IT CAME TO ME IN A HALF-FORGOTTEN DREAM...
BUT I CAN'T FINISH IT. IT KEEPS GETTING AWAY FROM ME.
FRSSHH
OH... IT LOOKS LIKE ME.
STAND IN FRONT SO I CAN SEE.

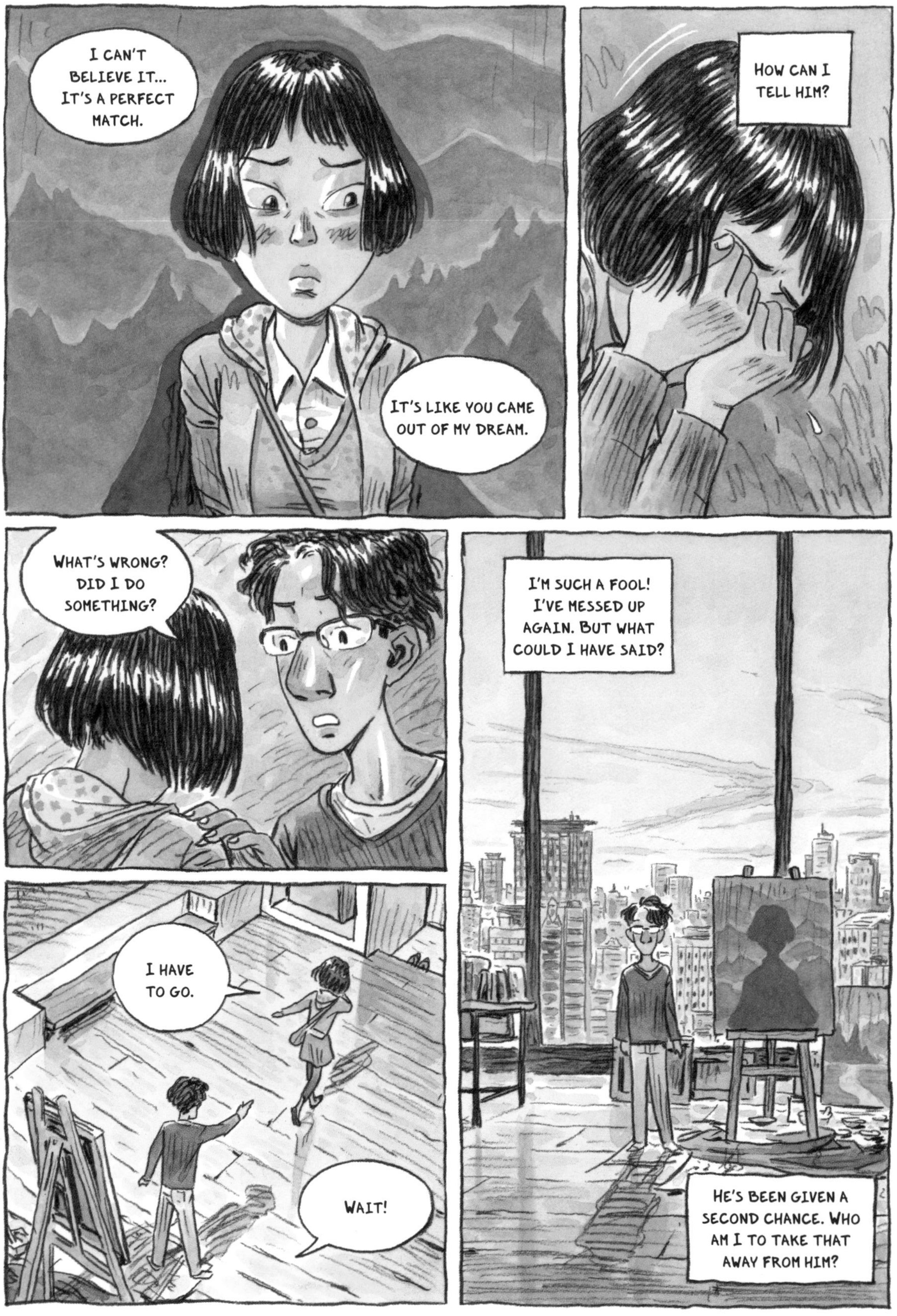
I CAN'T BELIEVE IT... IT'S A PERFECT MATCH.
IT'S LIKE YOU CAME OUT OF MY DREAM.
HOW CAN I TELL HIM?
WHAT'S WRONG? DID I DO SOMETHING?
I'M SUCH A FOOL! I'VE MESSED UP AGAIN. BUT WHAT COULD I HAVE SAID?
I HAVE TO GO.
WAIT!
HE'S BEEN GIVEN A SECOND CHANCE. WHO AM I TO TAKE THAT AWAY FROM HIM?

Refuge

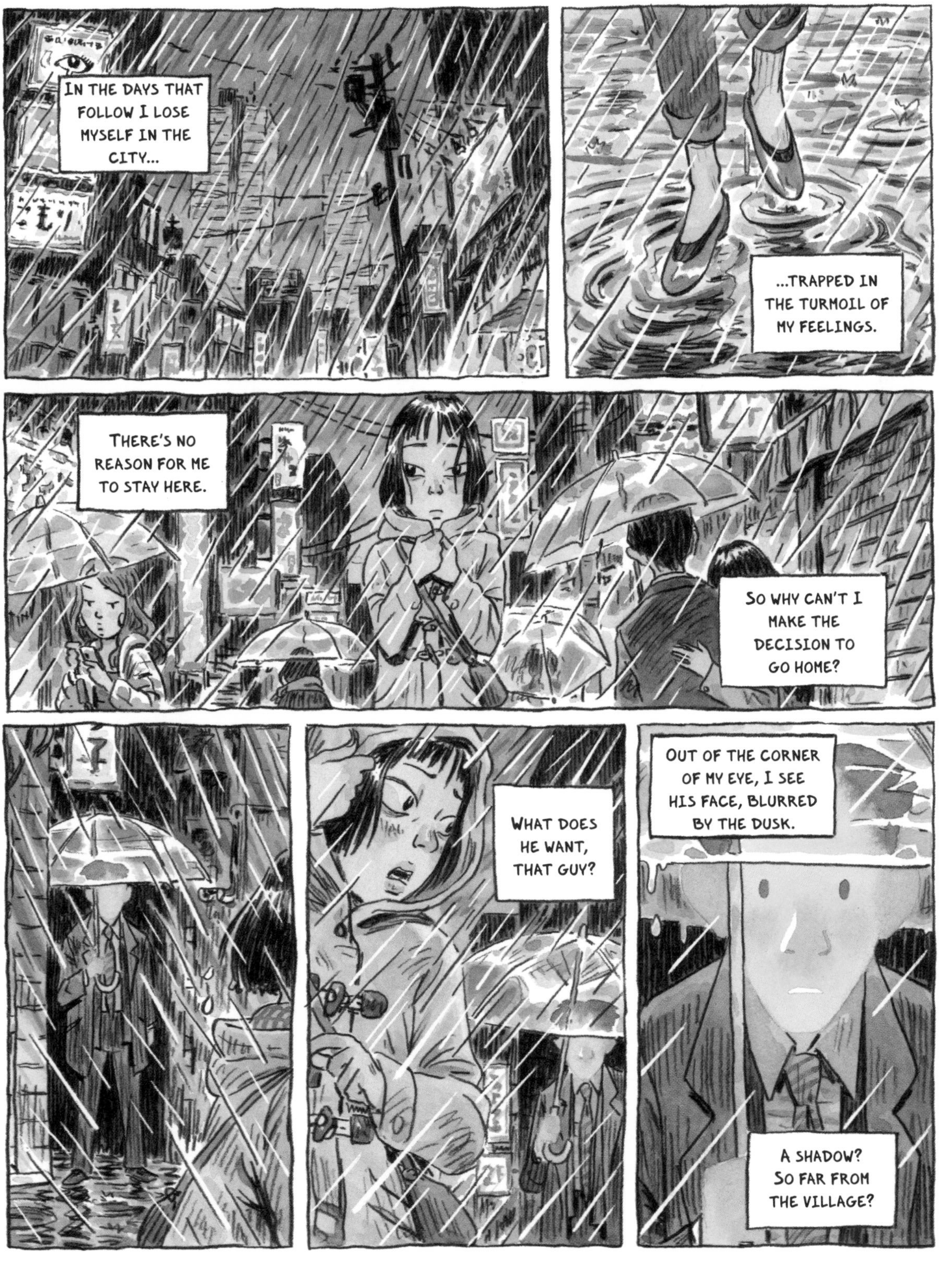
IN THE DAYS THAT FOLLOW I LOSE MYSELF IN THE CITY...
...TRAPPED IN THE TURMOIL OF MY FEELINGS.
THERE'S NO REASON FOR ME TO STAY HERE.
SO WHY CAN'T I MAKE THE DECISION TO GO HOME?
WHAT DOES HE WANT, THAT GUY?
OUT OF THE CORNER OF MY EYE, I SEE HIS FACE, BLURRED BY THE DUSK.
A SHADOW? SO FAR FROM THE VILLAGE?

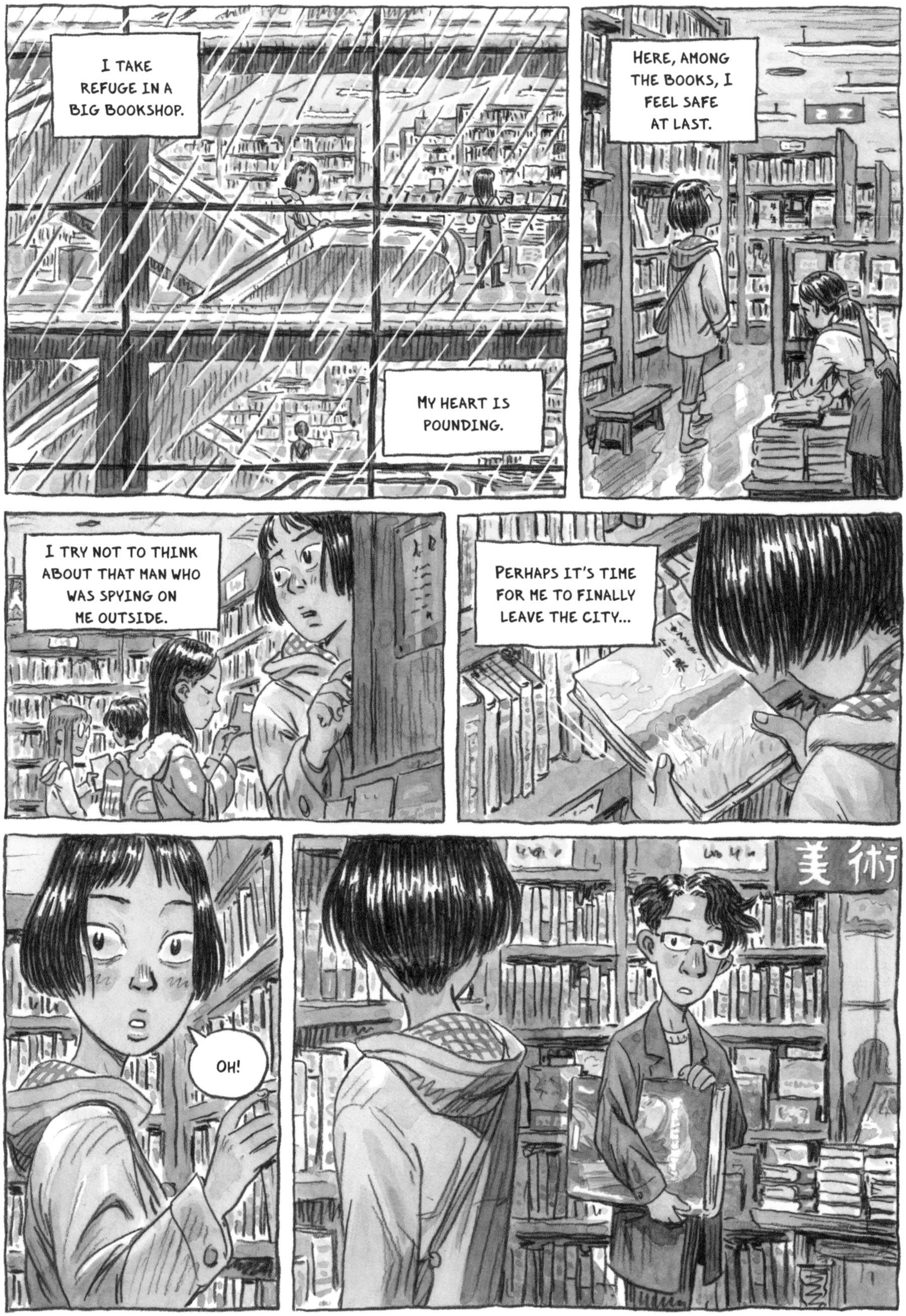
I take refuge in a big bookshop.
My heart is pounding.
Here, among the books, I feel safe at last.
I try not to think about that man who was spying on me outside.
Perhaps it's time for me to finally leave the city...
Oh!
美術

Horizons

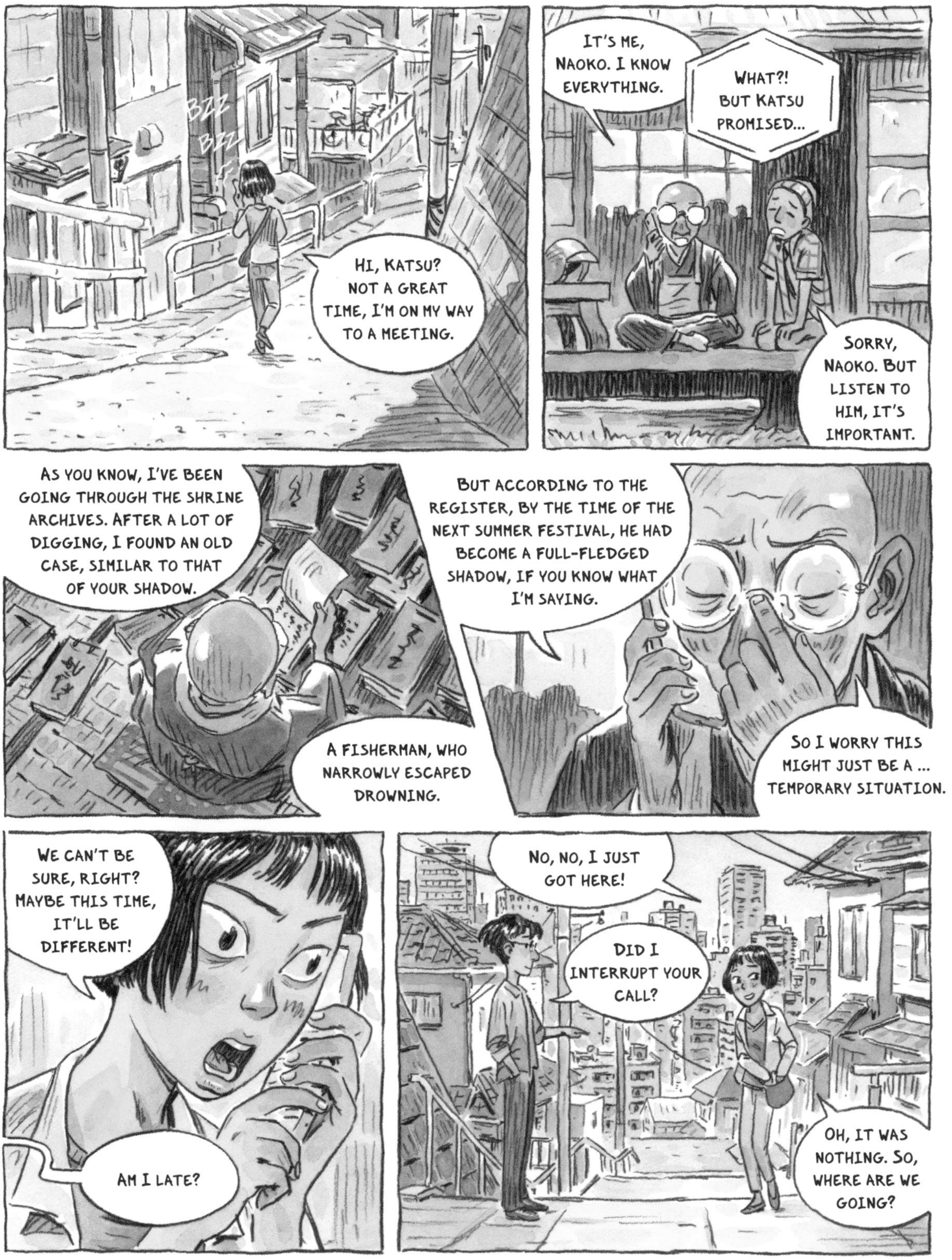
BZZ
BZZ
HI, KATSU? NOT A GREAT TIME, I'M ON MY WAY TO A MEETING.
IT'S ME, NAOKO. I KNOW EVERYTHING.
WHAT?! BUT KATSU PROMISED...
SORRY, NAOKO. BUT LISTEN TO HIM, IT'S IMPORTANT.
AS YOU KNOW, I'VE BEEN GOING THROUGH THE SHRINE ARCHIVES. AFTER A LOT OF DIGGING, I FOUND AN OLD CASE, SIMILAR TO THAT OF YOUR SHADOW.
A FISHERMAN, WHO NARROWLY ESCAPED DROWNING.
BUT ACCORDING TO THE REGISTER, BY THE TIME OF THE NEXT SUMMER FESTIVAL, HE HAD BECOME A FULL-FLEDGED SHADOW, IF YOU KNOW WHAT I'M SAYING.
SO I WORRY THIS MIGHT JUST BE A ... TEMPORARY SITUATION.
WE CAN'T BE SURE, RIGHT? MAYBE THIS TIME, IT'LL BE DIFFERENT!
AM I LATE?
NO, NO, I JUST GOT HERE!
DID I INTERRUPT YOUR CALL?
OH, IT WAS NOTHING. SO, WHERE ARE WE GOING?

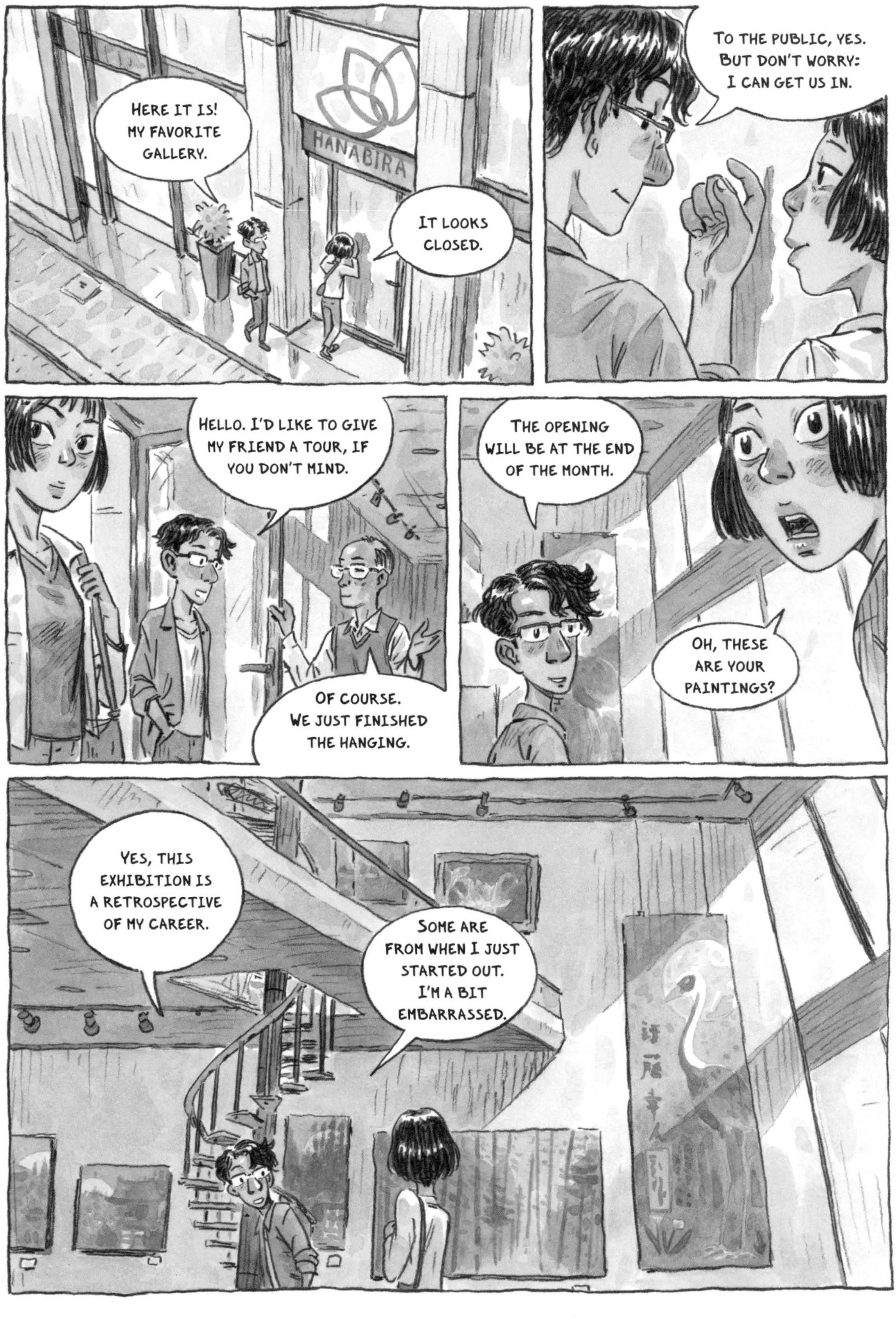
HERE IT IS! MY FAVORITE GALLERY.
HANABIRA
IT LOOKS CLOSED.
TO THE PUBLIC, YES. BUT DON'T WORRY: I CAN GET US IN.
HELLO. I'D LIKE TO GIVE MY FRIEND A TOUR, IF YOU DON'T MIND.
OF COURSE. WE JUST FINISHED THE HANGING.
THE OPENING WILL BE AT THE END OF THE MONTH.
OH, THESE ARE YOUR PAINTINGS?
YES, THIS EXHIBITION IS A RETROSPECTIVE OF MY CAREER.
SOME ARE FROM WHEN I JUST STARTED OUT. I'M A BIT EMBARRASSED.

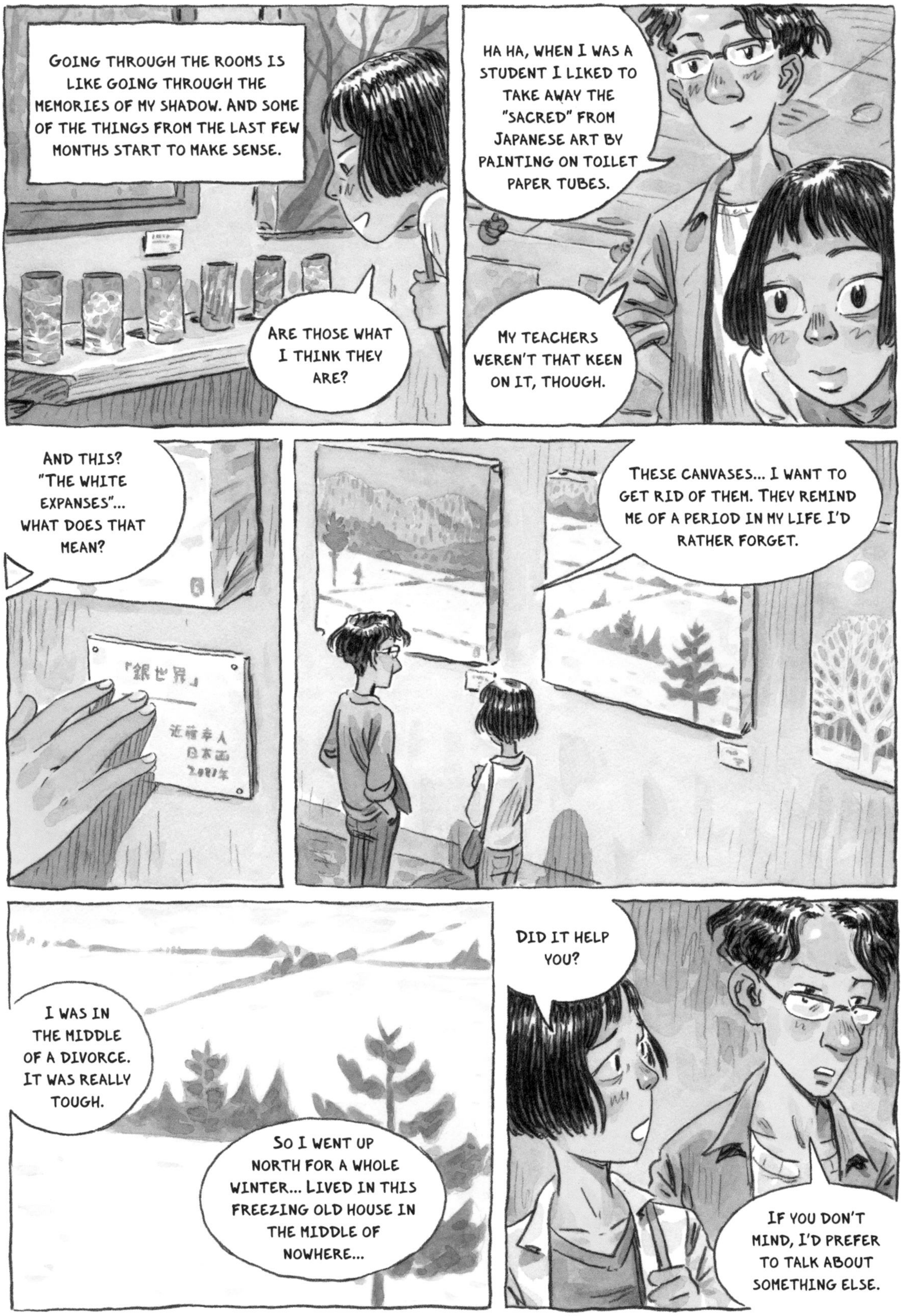
GOING THROUGH THE ROOMS IS LIKE GOING THROUGH THE MEMORIES OF MY SHADOW. AND SOME OF THE THINGS FROM THE LAST FEW MONTHS START TO MAKE SENSE.
ARE THOSE WHAT I THINK THEY ARE?
HA HA, WHEN I WAS A STUDENT I LIKED TO TAKE AWAY THE "SACRED" FROM JAPANESE ART BY PAINTING ON TOILET PAPER TUBES.
MY TEACHERS WEREN'T THAT KEEN ON IT, THOUGH.
AND THIS? "THE WHITE EXPANSES"... WHAT DOES THAT MEAN?
『銀世界』
THESE CANVASES... I WANT TO GET RID OF THEM. THEY REMIND ME OF A PERIOD IN MY LIFE I'D RATHER FORGET.
I WAS IN THE MIDDLE OF A DIVORCE. IT WAS REALLY TOUGH.
SO I WENT UP NORTH FOR A WHOLE WINTER... LIVED IN THIS FREEZING OLD HOUSE IN THE MIDDLE OF NOWHERE...
DID IT HELP YOU?
IF YOU DON'T MIND, I'D PREFER TO TALK ABOUT SOMETHING ELSE.

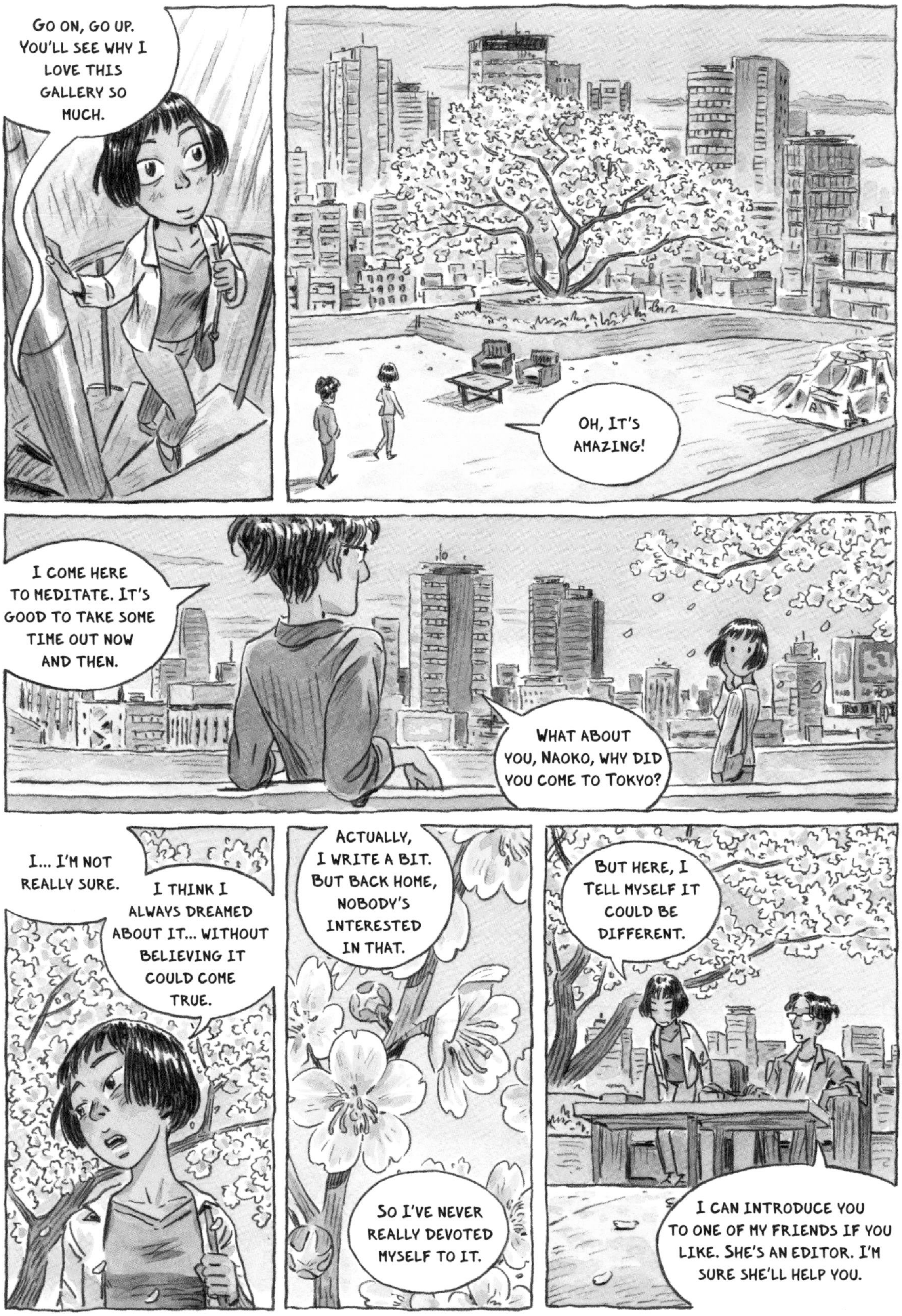
Go on, go up. You'll see why I love this gallery so much.
Oh, it's amazing!
I come here to meditate. It's good to take some time out now and then.
What about you, Naoko, why did you come to Tokyo?
I... I'm not really sure.
I think I always dreamed about it... without believing it could come true.
Actually, I write a bit. But back home, nobody's interested in that.
So I've never really devoted myself to it.
But here, I tell myself it could be different.
I can introduce you to one of my friends if you like. She's an editor. I'm sure she'll help you.

I'VE MADE YOU SOME TEA.

OH, THANK YOU.

BUT TELL ME MORE. WHAT ARE YOU WRITING? A NOVEL?

ER, NOT REALLY... WELL, KIND OF... IT'S ABOUT... A YOUNG WOMAN WHO LIVES WITH A GHOST...

SHE DIDN'T CHOOSE TO. AND GRADUALLY SHE GETS SO LOST IN IT, SHE DOESN'T EVEN KNOW IF HER LIFE'S HER OWN ANYMORE...

OR IF SHE'S JUST FOLLOWING A PREDESTINED PATH.

HMM, SOUNDS INTRIGUING. TO BE HONEST THAT'S KIND OF HOW I FEEL.

OUR LIVES CAN GET AWAY FROM US AND WE DON'T EVEN NOTICE IT.

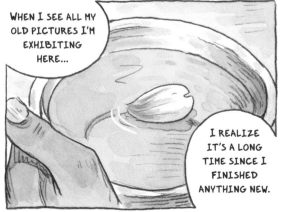

WHEN I SEE ALL MY OLD PICTURES I'M EXHIBITING HERE...

I REALIZE IT'S A LONG TIME SINCE I FINISHED ANYTHING NEW.

IT'S POSSIBLE THAT THIS EXHIBITION ...

MIGHT BE MY LAST.

Work-in-progress

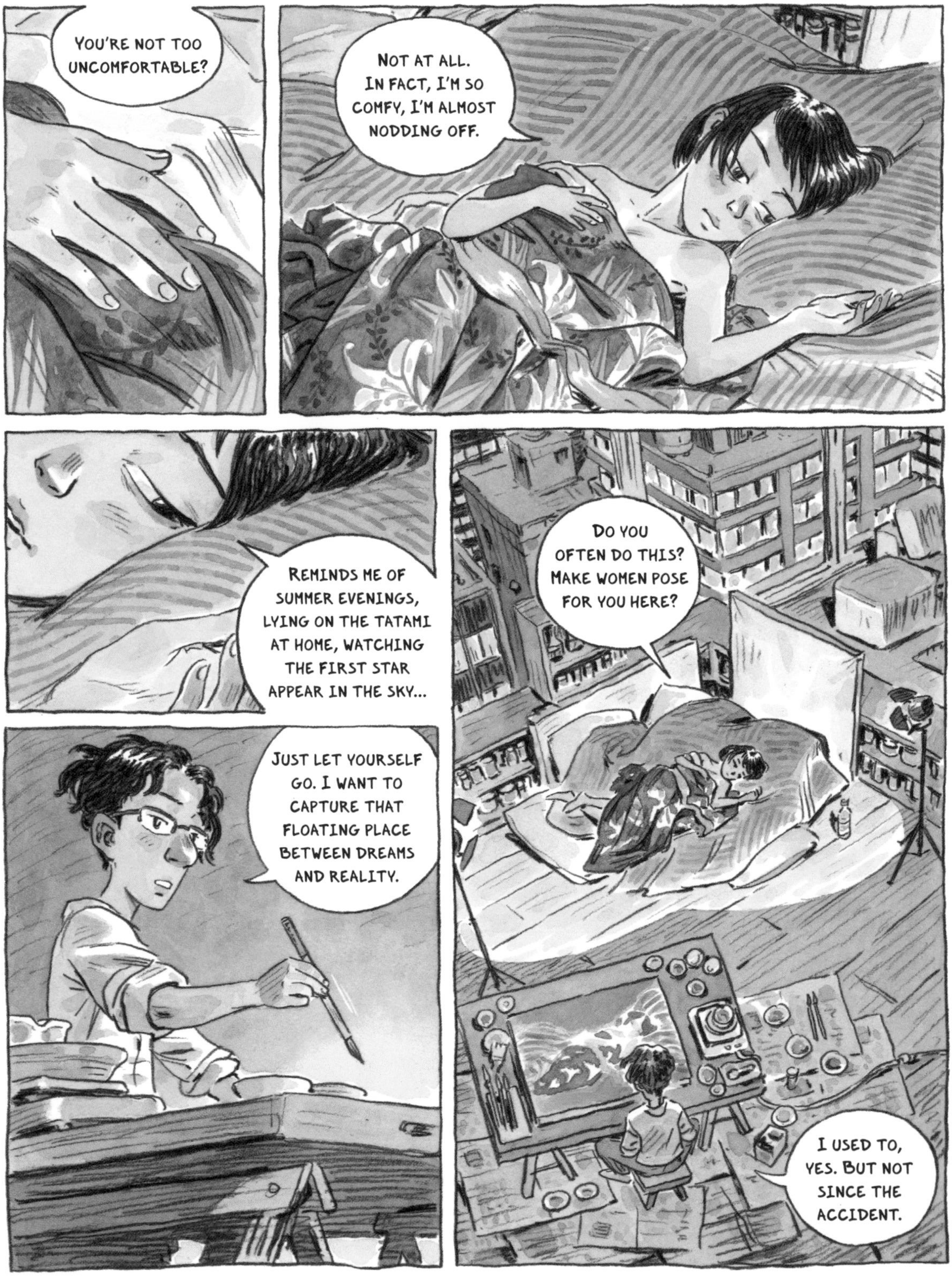
YOU'RE NOT TOO UNCOMFORTABLE?
NOT AT ALL. IN FACT, I'M SO COMFY, I'M ALMOST NODDING OFF.
REMINDS ME OF SUMMER EVENINGS, LYING ON THE TATAMI AT HOME, WATCHING THE FIRST STAR APPEAR IN THE SKY...
DO YOU OFTEN DO THIS? MAKE WOMEN POSE FOR YOU HERE?
JUST LET YOURSELF GO. I WANT TO CAPTURE THAT FLOATING PLACE BETWEEN DREAMS AND REALITY.
I USED TO, YES. BUT NOT SINCE THE ACCIDENT.

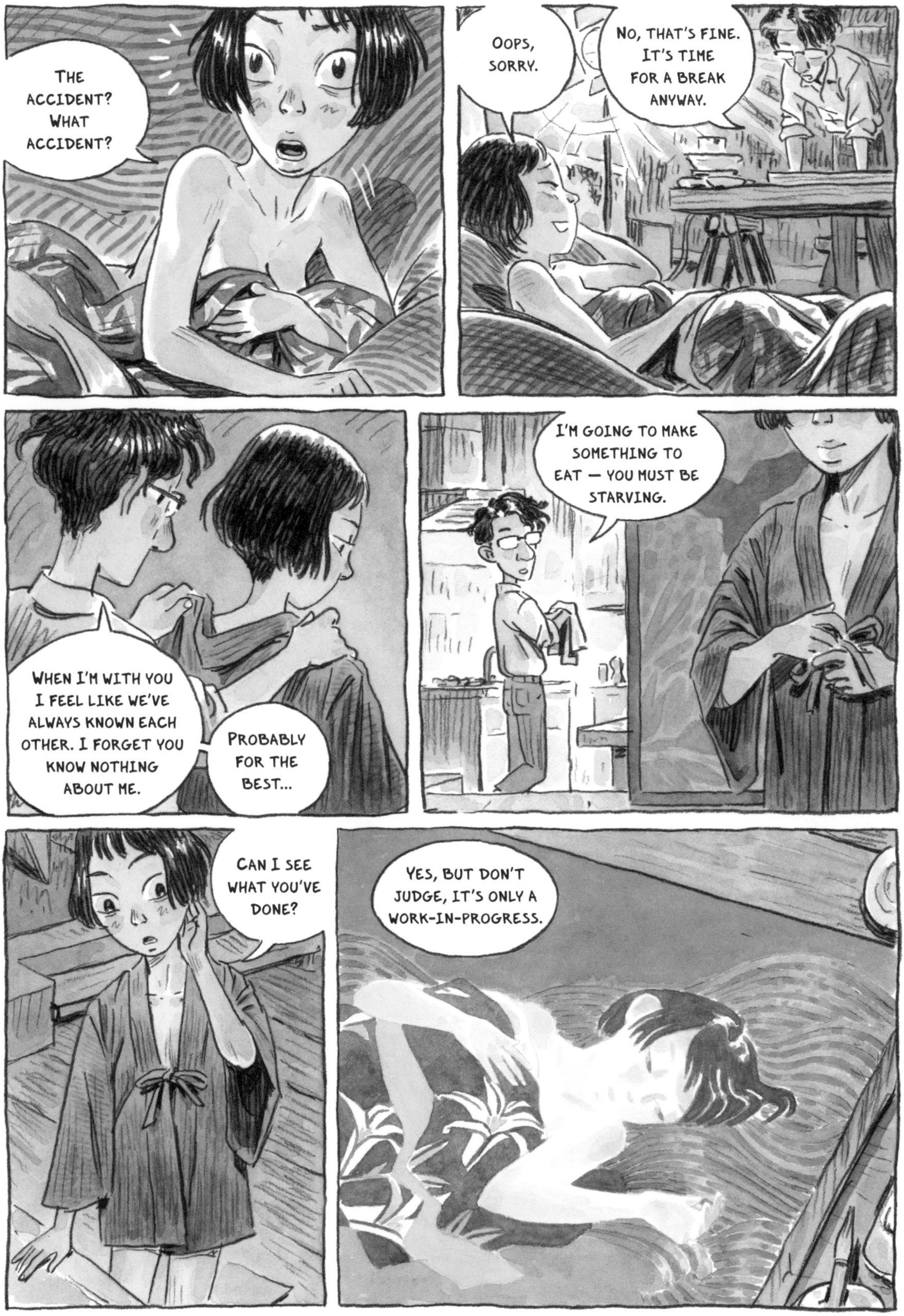
The accident? What accident?
Oops, sorry.
No, that's fine. It's time for a break anyway.
When I'm with you I feel like we've always known each other. I forget you know nothing about me.
Probably for the best...
I'm going to make something to eat — you must be starving.
Can I see what you've done?
Yes, but don't judge, it's only a work-in-progress.

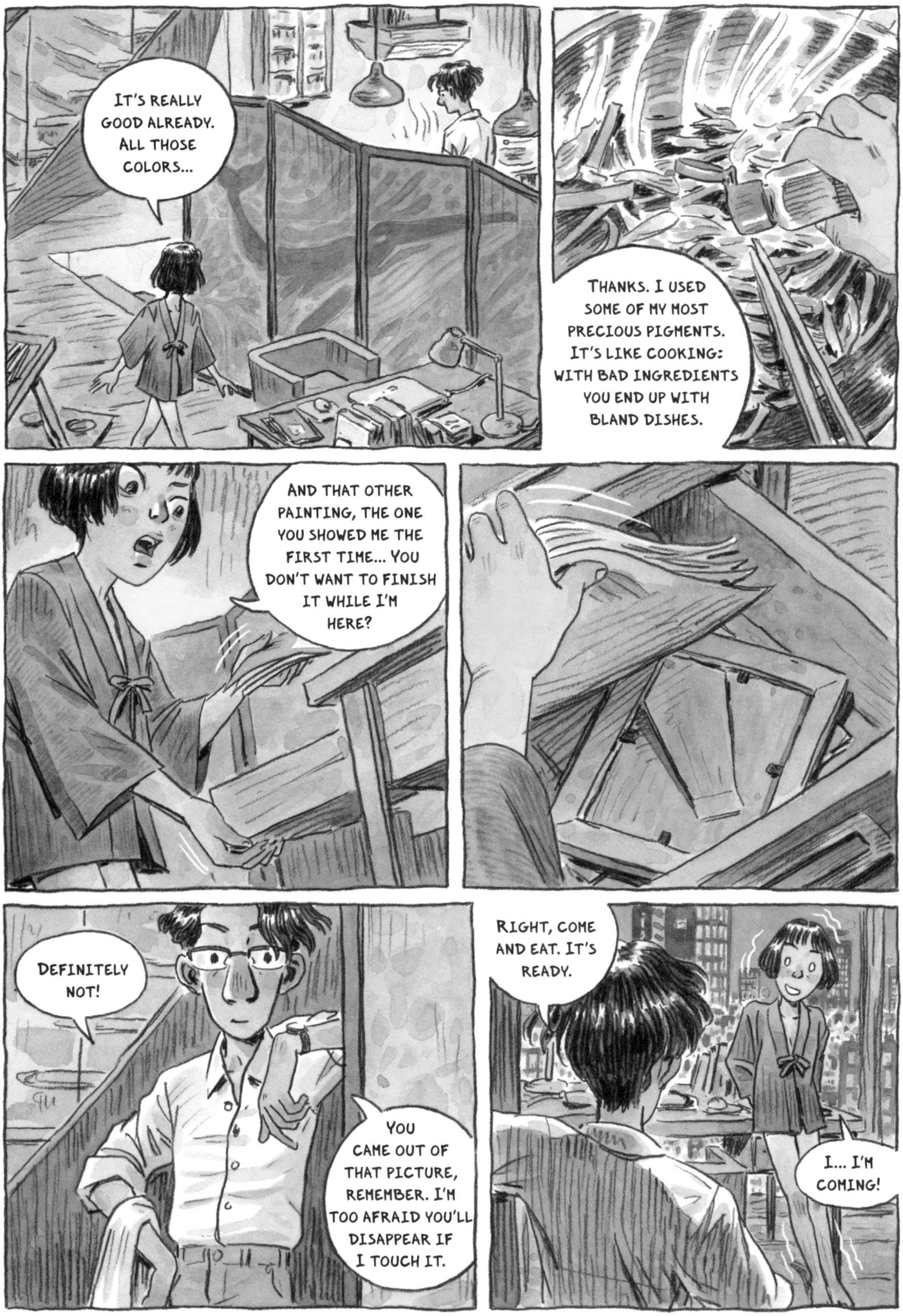
IT'S REALLY GOOD ALREADY. ALL THOSE COLORS...
THANKS. I USED SOME OF MY MOST PRECIOUS PIGMENTS. IT'S LIKE COOKING: WITH BAD INGREDIENTS YOU END UP WITH BLAND DISHES.
AND THAT OTHER PAINTING, THE ONE YOU SHOWED ME THE FIRST TIME... YOU DON'T WANT TO FINISH IT WHILE I'M HERE?
DEFINITELY NOT!
YOU CAME OUT OF THAT PICTURE, REMEMBER. I'M TOO AFRAID YOU'LL DISAPPEAR IF I TOUCH IT.
RIGHT, COME AND EAT. IT'S READY.
I... I'M COMING!

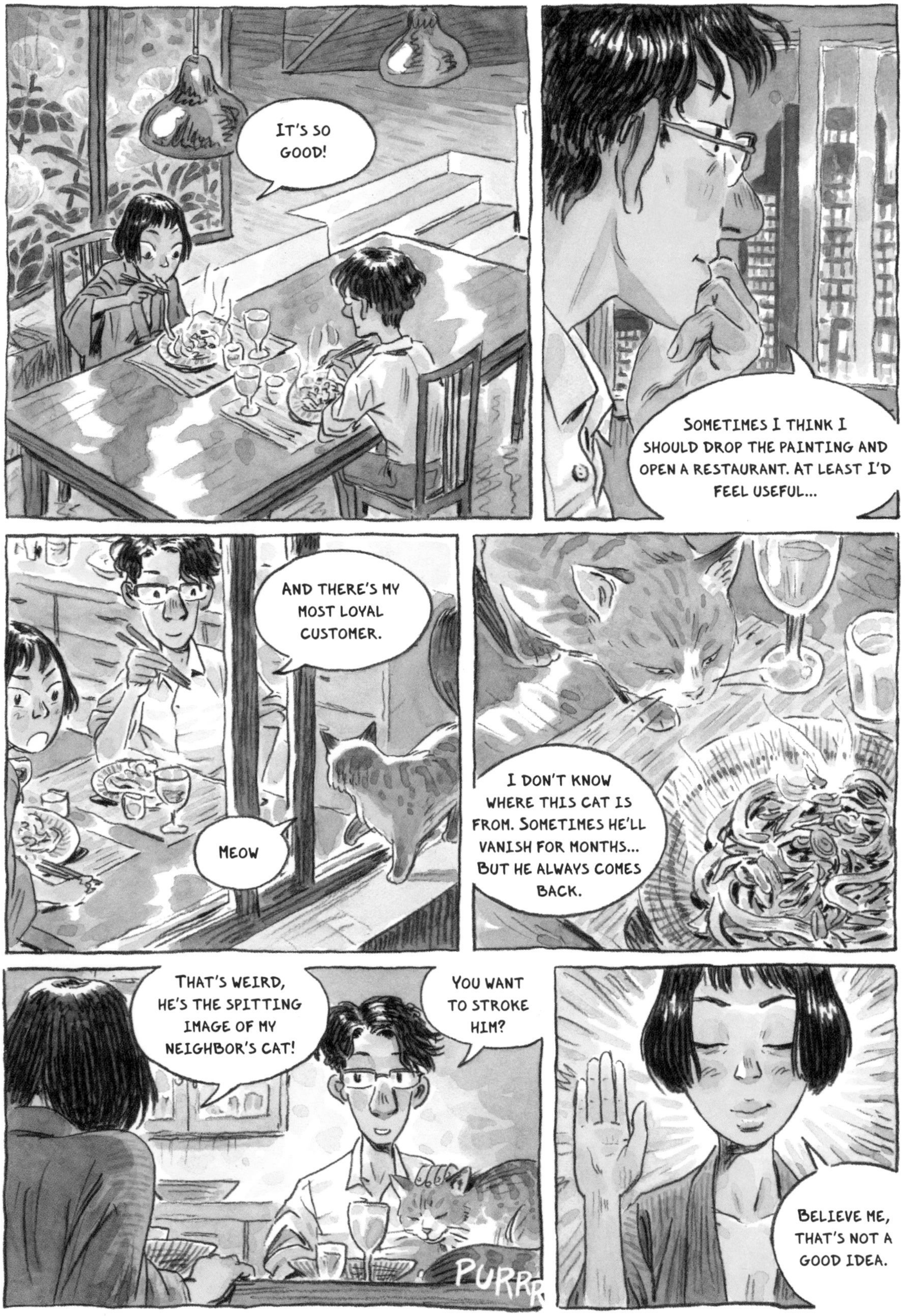
It's so good!
Sometimes I think I should drop the painting and open a restaurant. At least I'd feel useful...
And there's my most loyal customer.
Meow
I don't know where this cat is from. Sometimes he'll vanish for months... But he always comes back.
That's weird, he's the spitting image of my neighbor's cat!
You want to stroke him?
PURRR
Believe me, that's not a good idea.

Starstruck

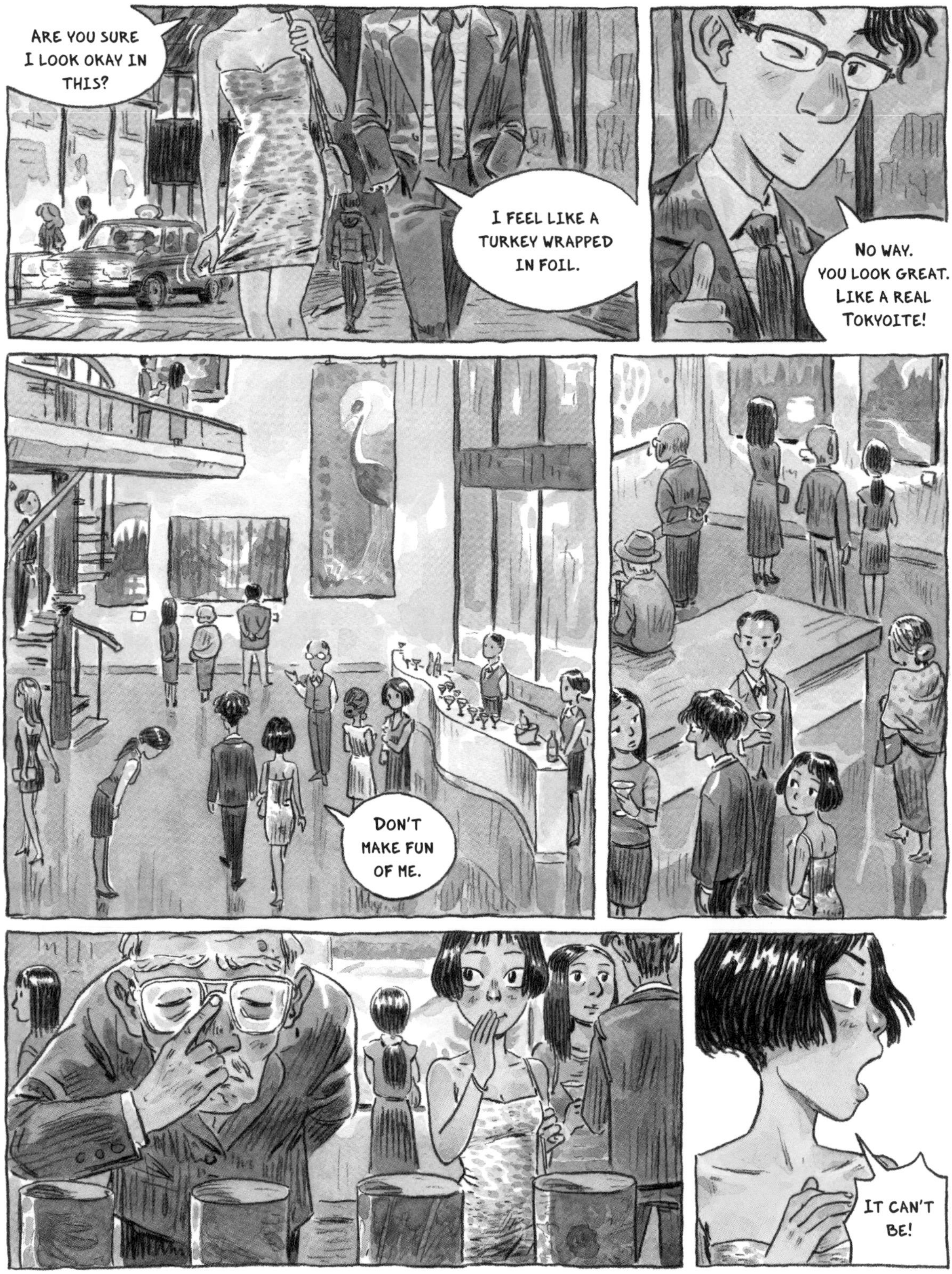

ARE YOU SURE I LOOK OKAY IN THIS?
I FEEL LIKE A TURKEY WRAPPED IN FOIL.
NO WAY. YOU LOOK GREAT. LIKE A REAL TOKYOITE!
DON'T MAKE FUN OF ME.
IT CAN'T BE!

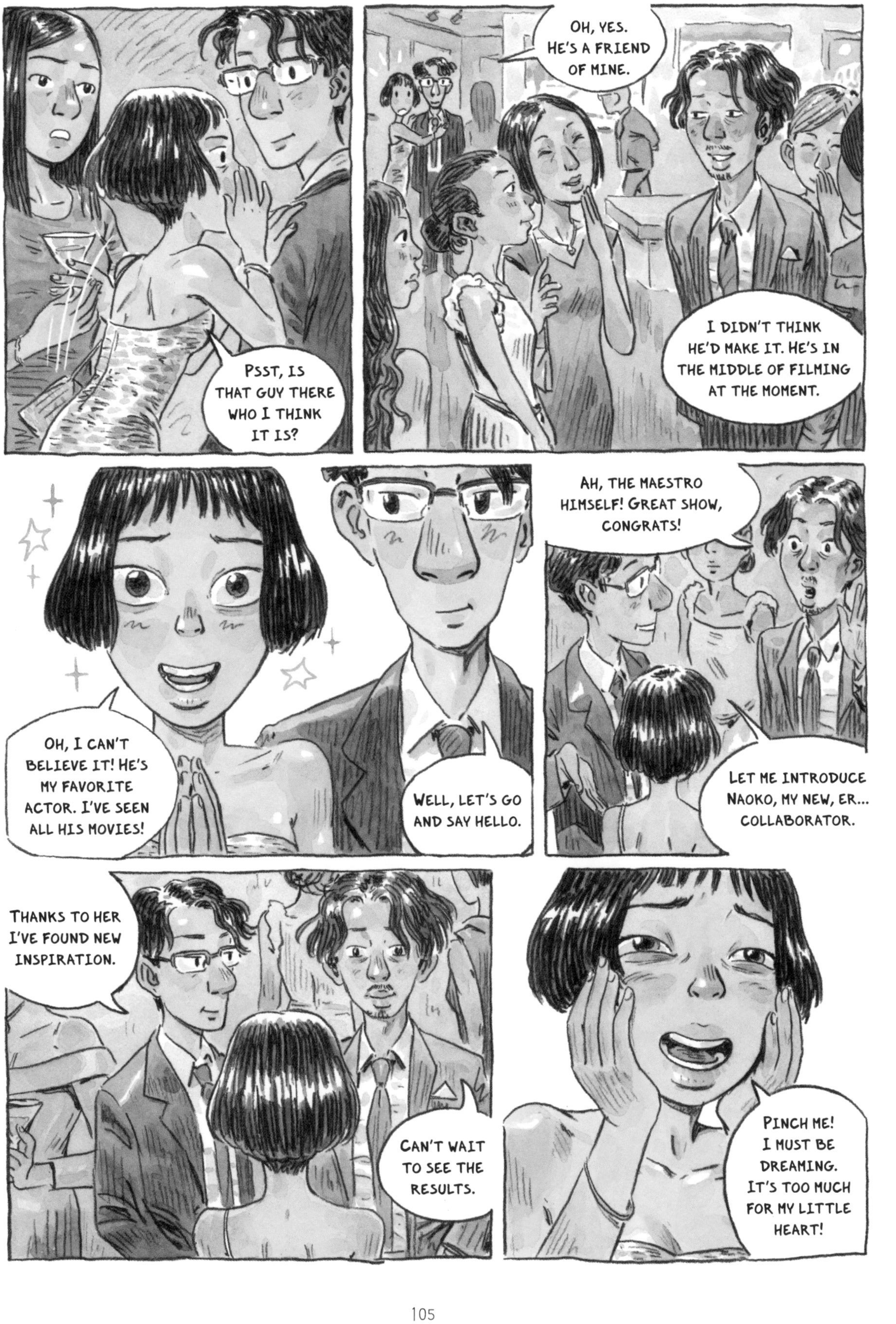
PSST, IS THAT GUY THERE WHO I THINK IT IS?
OH, YES. HE'S A FRIEND OF MINE.
I DIDN'T THINK HE'D MAKE IT. HE'S IN THE MIDDLE OF FILMING AT THE MOMENT.
OH, I CAN'T BELIEVE IT! HE'S MY FAVORITE ACTOR. I'VE SEEN ALL HIS MOVIES!
WELL, LET'S GO AND SAY HELLO.
AH, THE MAESTRO HIMSELF! GREAT SHOW, CONGRATS!
LET ME INTRODUCE NAOKO, MY NEW, ER... COLLABORATOR.
THANKS TO HER I'VE FOUND NEW INSPIRATION.
CAN'T WAIT TO SEE THE RESULTS.
PINCH ME! I MUST BE DREAMING. IT'S TOO MUCH FOR MY LITTLE HEART!

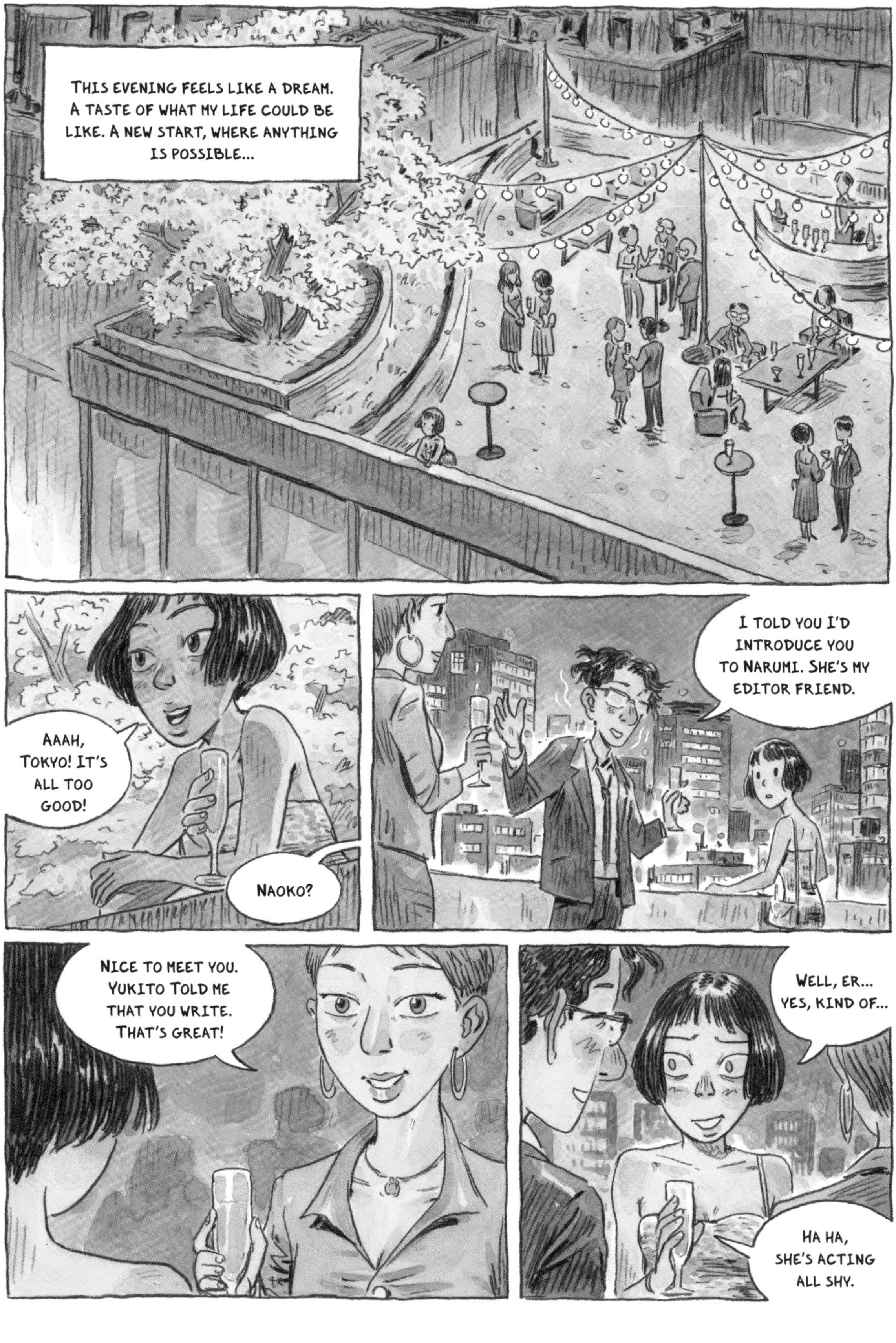
THIS EVENING FEELS LIKE A DREAM. A TASTE OF WHAT MY LIFE COULD BE LIKE. A NEW START, WHERE ANYTHING IS POSSIBLE...
AAAH, TOKYO! IT'S ALL TOO GOOD!
NAOKO?
I TOLD YOU I'D INTRODUCE YOU TO NARUMI. SHE'S MY EDITOR FRIEND.
NICE TO MEET YOU. YUKITO TOLD ME THAT YOU WRITE. THAT'S GREAT!
WELL, ER... YES, KIND OF...
HA HA, SHE'S ACTING ALL SHY.

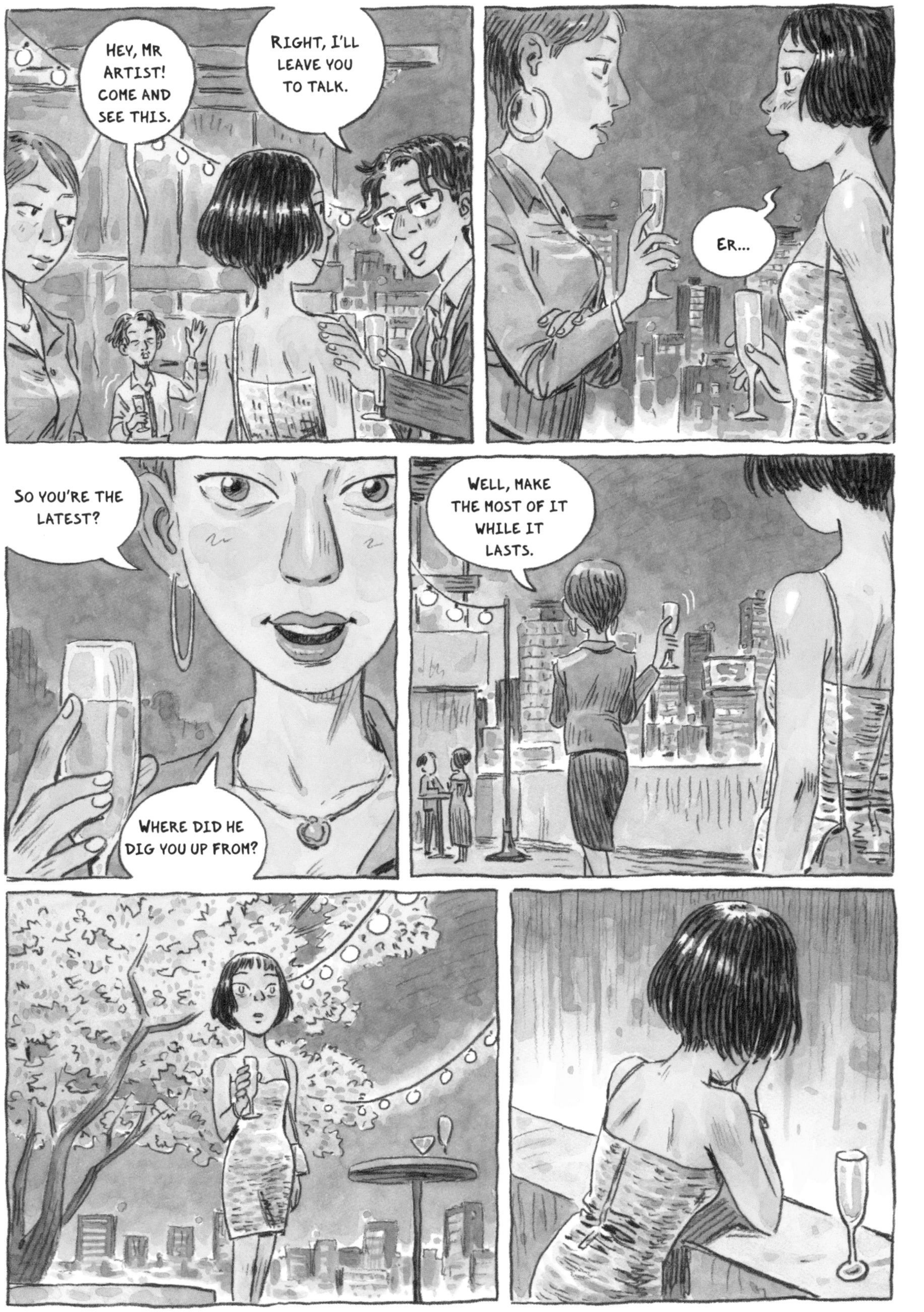
HEY, MR ARTIST! COME AND SEE THIS.
RIGHT, I'LL LEAVE YOU TO TALK.
ER...
SO YOU'RE THE LATEST?
WHERE DID HE DIG YOU UP FROM?
WELL, MAKE THE MOST OF IT WHILE IT LASTS.

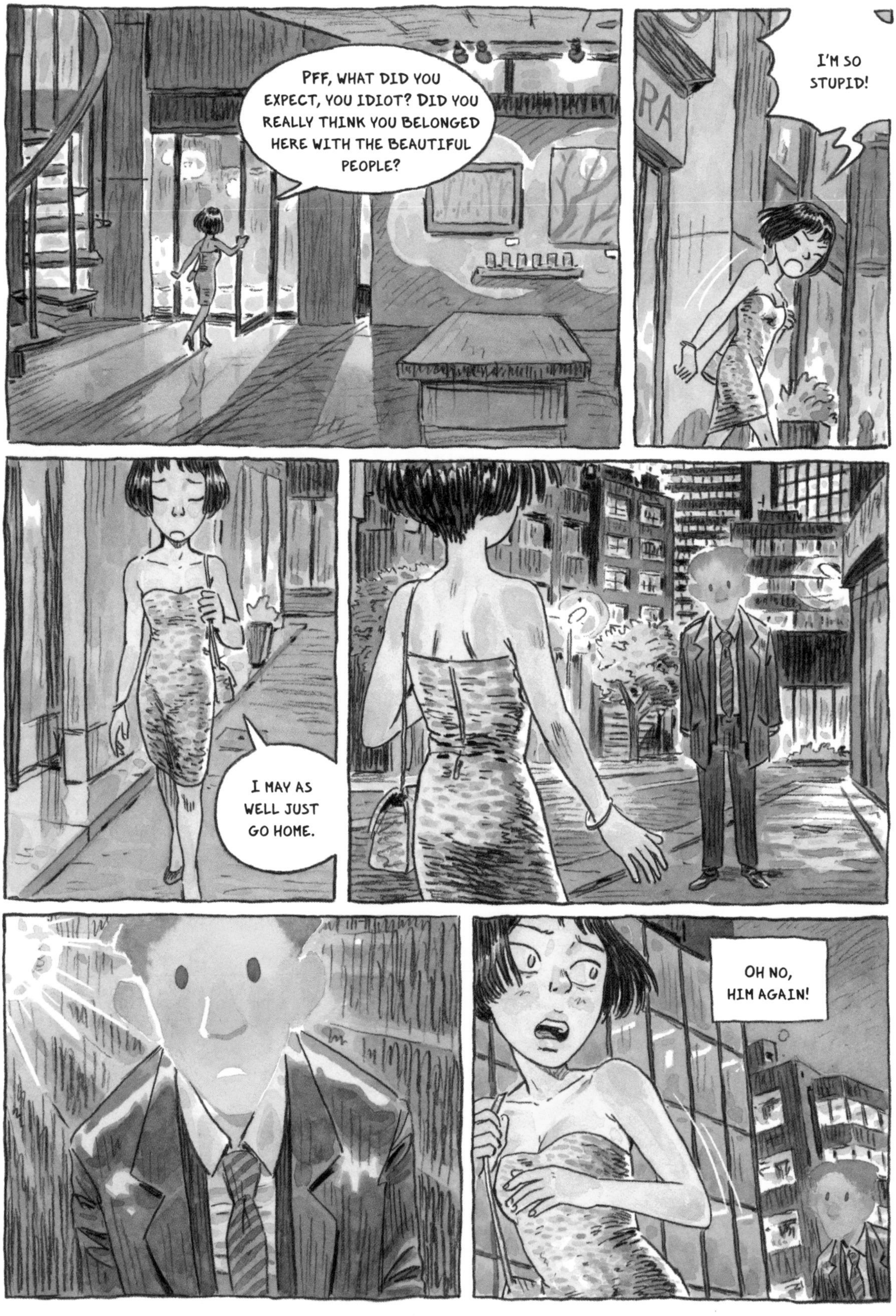
PFF, WHAT DID YOU EXPECT, YOU IDIOT? DID YOU REALLY THINK YOU BELONGED HERE WITH THE BEAUTIFUL PEOPLE?
I'M SO STUPID!
I MAY AS WELL JUST GO HOME.
OH NO, HIM AGAIN!

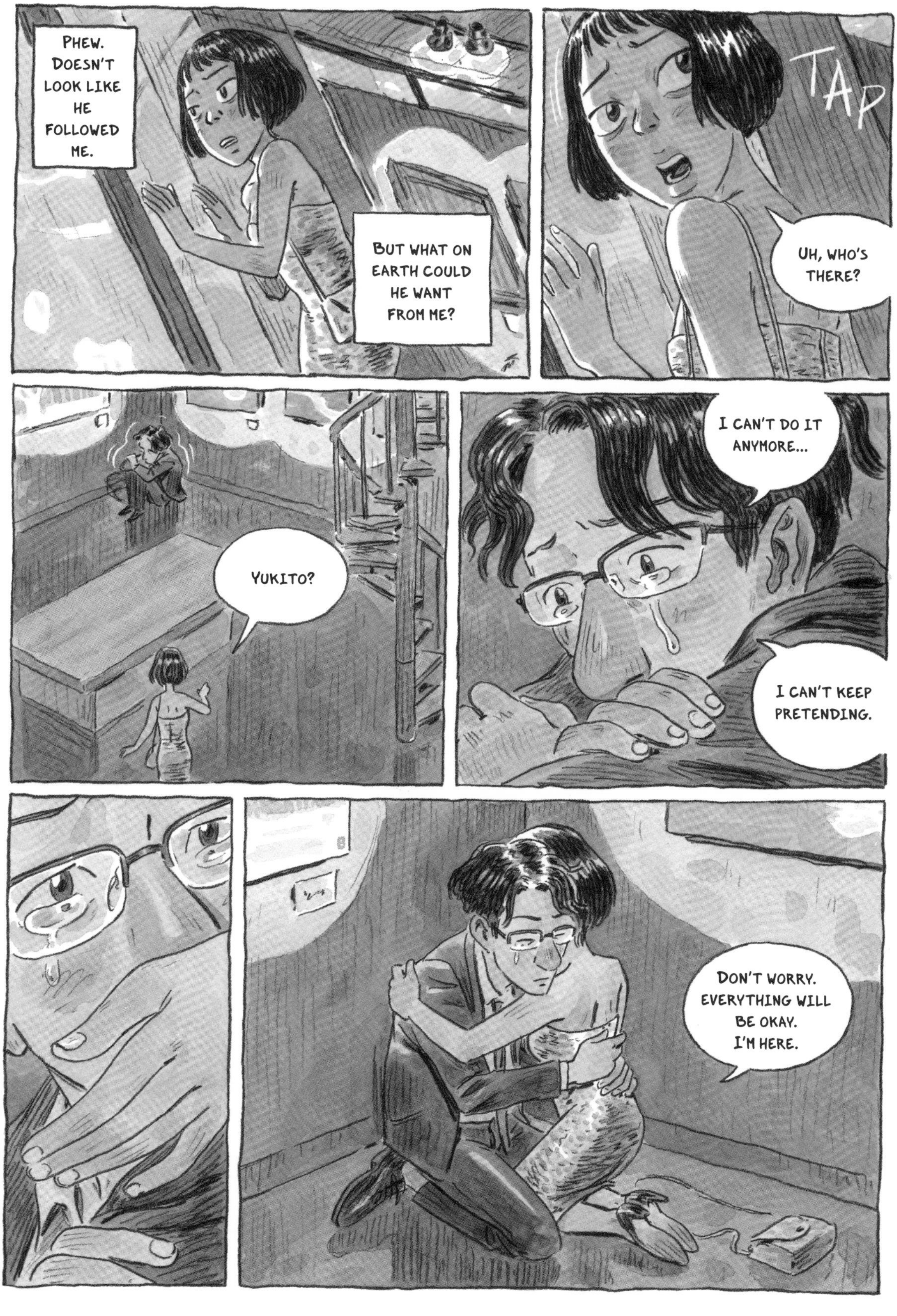
Phew. Doesn't look like he followed me.
But what on earth could he want from me?
TAP
Uh, who's there?
Yukito?
I can't do it anymore...
I can't keep pretending.
Don't worry. Everything will be okay. I'm here.

In the looking-glass

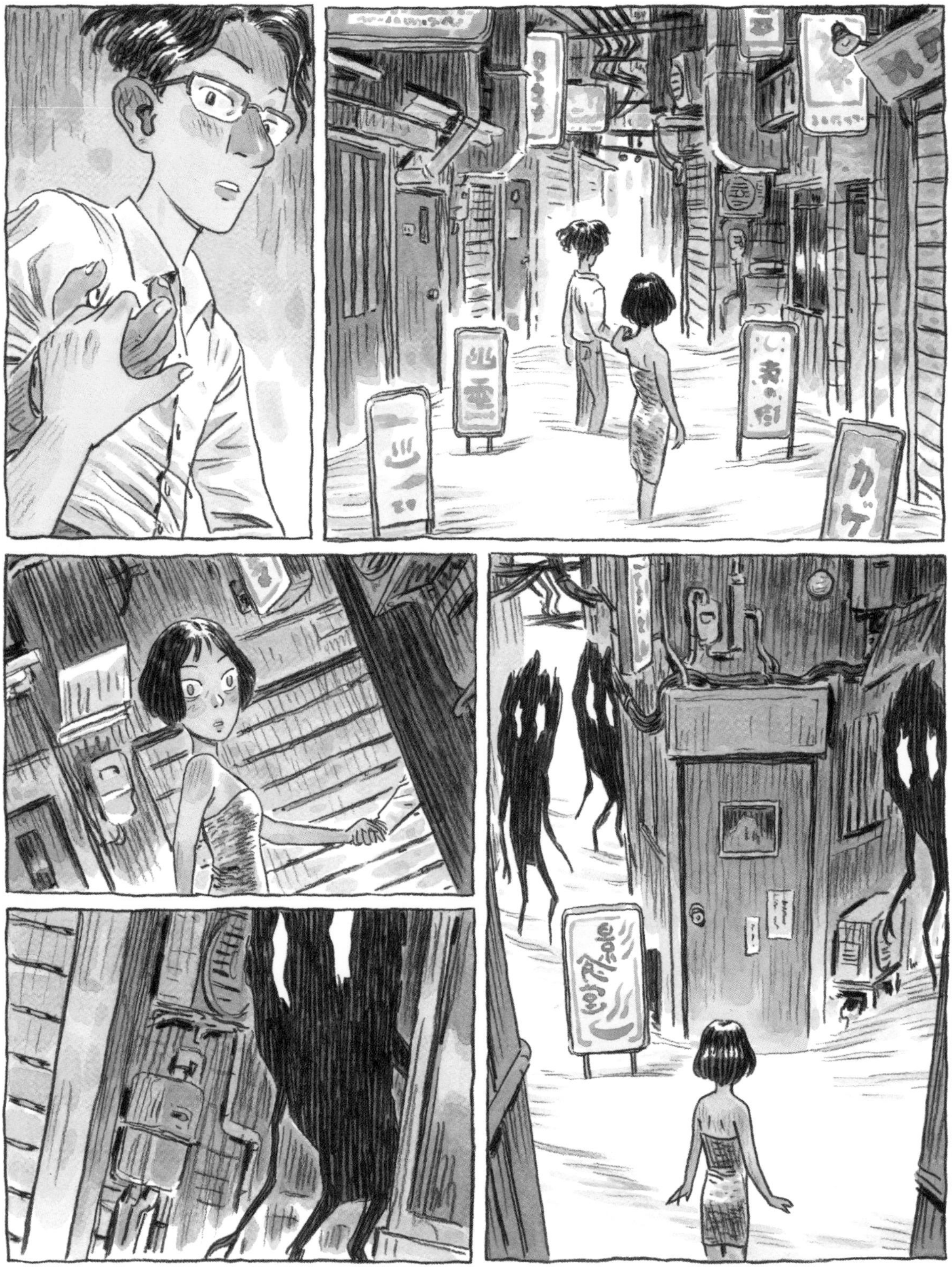
カゲ

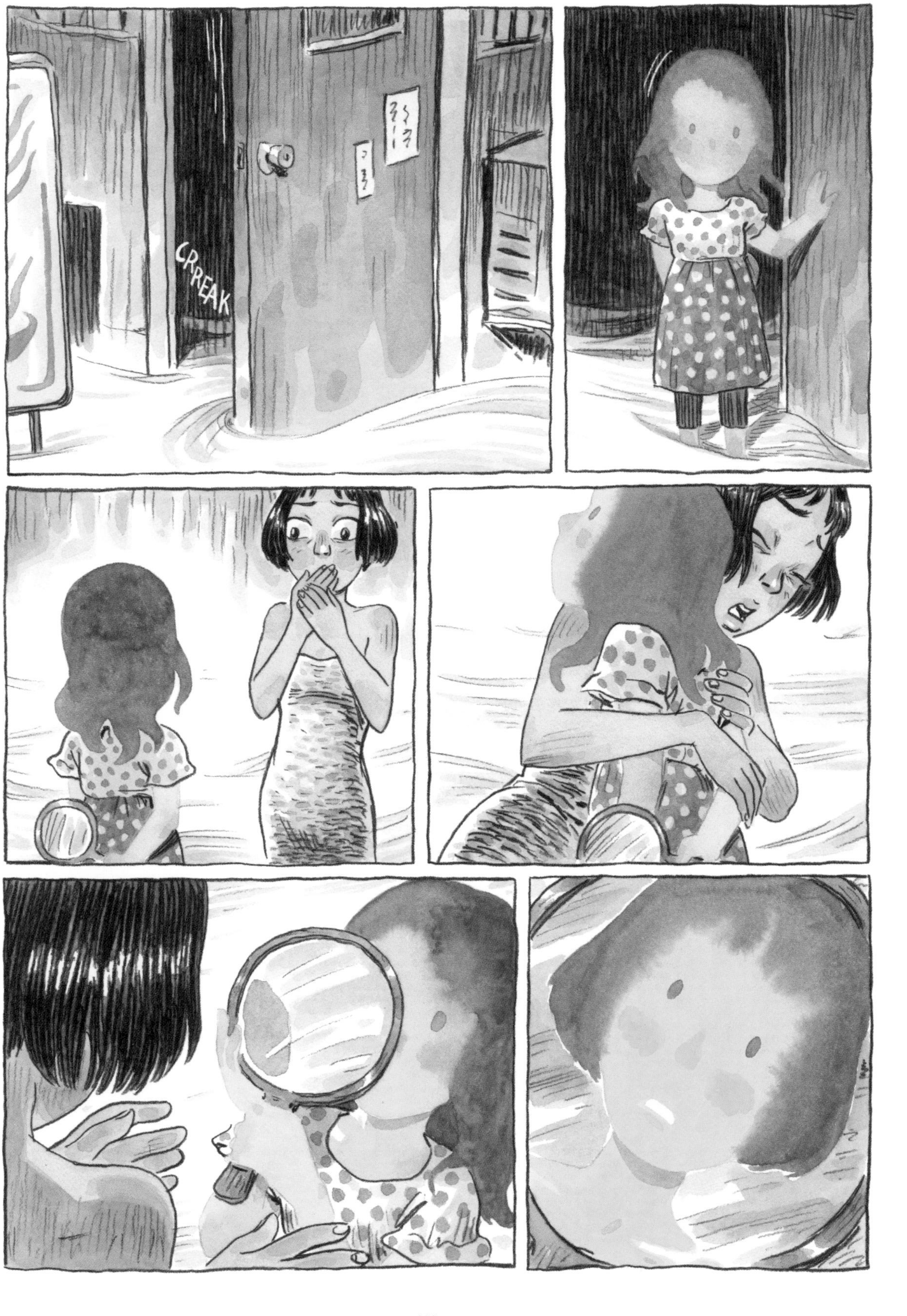
CRREAK

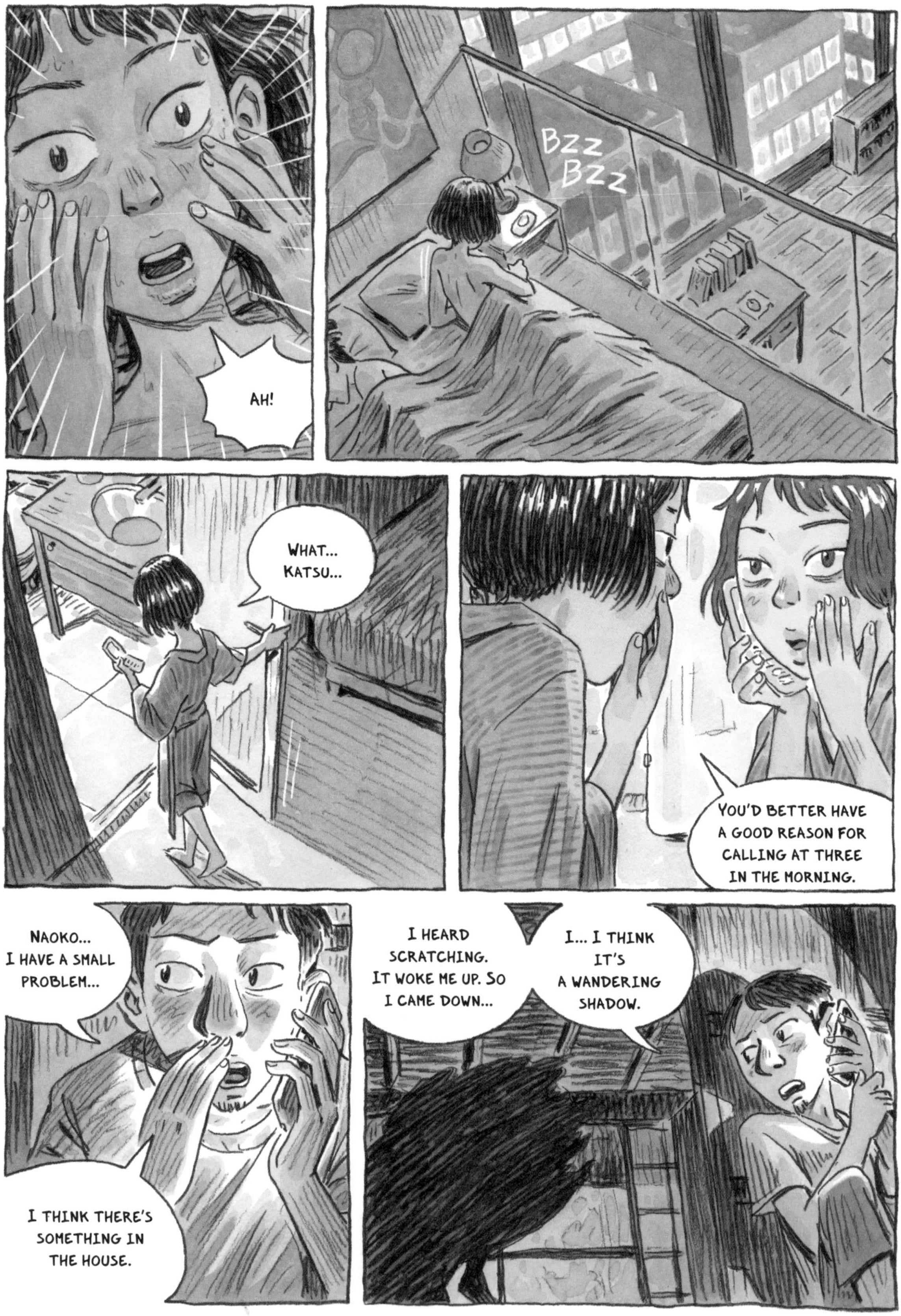
AH!
BZZ BZZ
WHAT... KATSU...
YOU'D BETTER HAVE A GOOD REASON FOR CALLING AT THREE IN THE MORNING.
NAOKO... I HAVE A SMALL PROBLEM...
I THINK THERE'S SOMETHING IN THE HOUSE.
I HEARD SCRATCHING. IT WOKE ME UP. SO I CAME DOWN...
I... I THINK IT'S A WANDERING SHADOW.

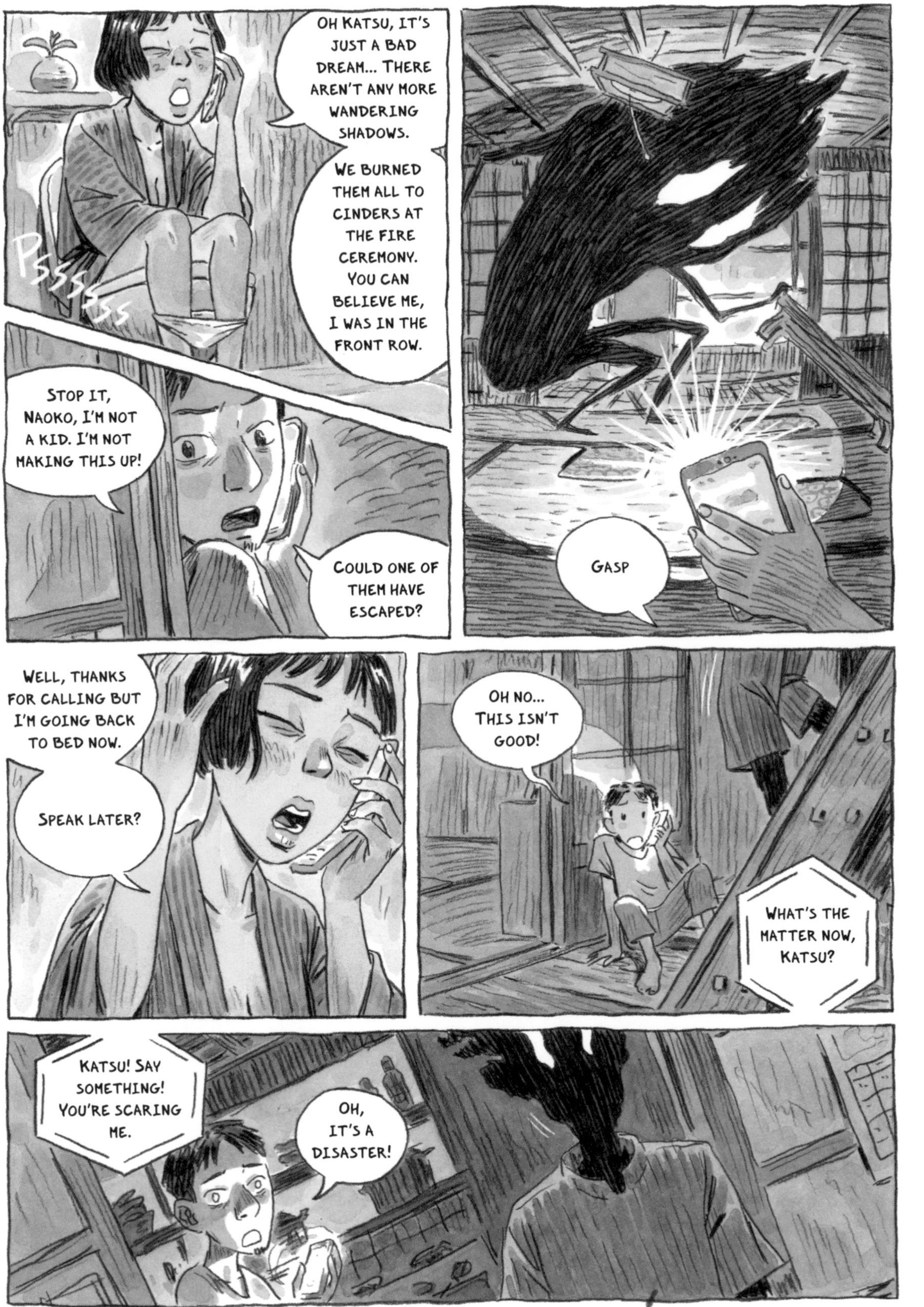
Oh Katsu, it's just a bad dream... There aren't any more wandering shadows.
We burned them all to cinders at the fire ceremony. You can believe me, I was in the front row.
Psssssss
Stop it, Naoko, I'm not a kid. I'm not making this up!
Could one of them have escaped?
Gasp
Well, thanks for calling but I'm going back to bed now.
Speak later?
Oh no... this isn't good!
What's the matter now, Katsu?
Katsu! Say something! You're scaring me.
Oh, it's a disaster!

AAAHHHH
YUKITO?!

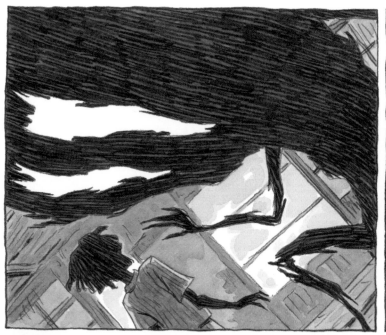

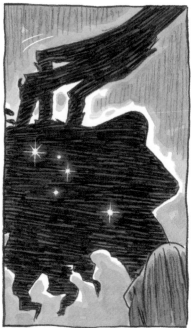

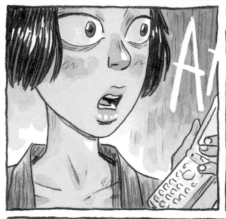

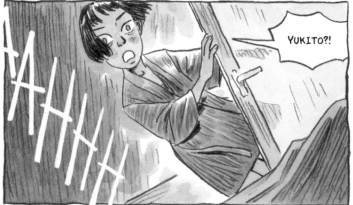

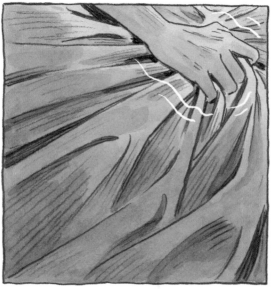

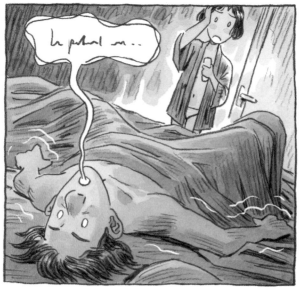

The broken frame

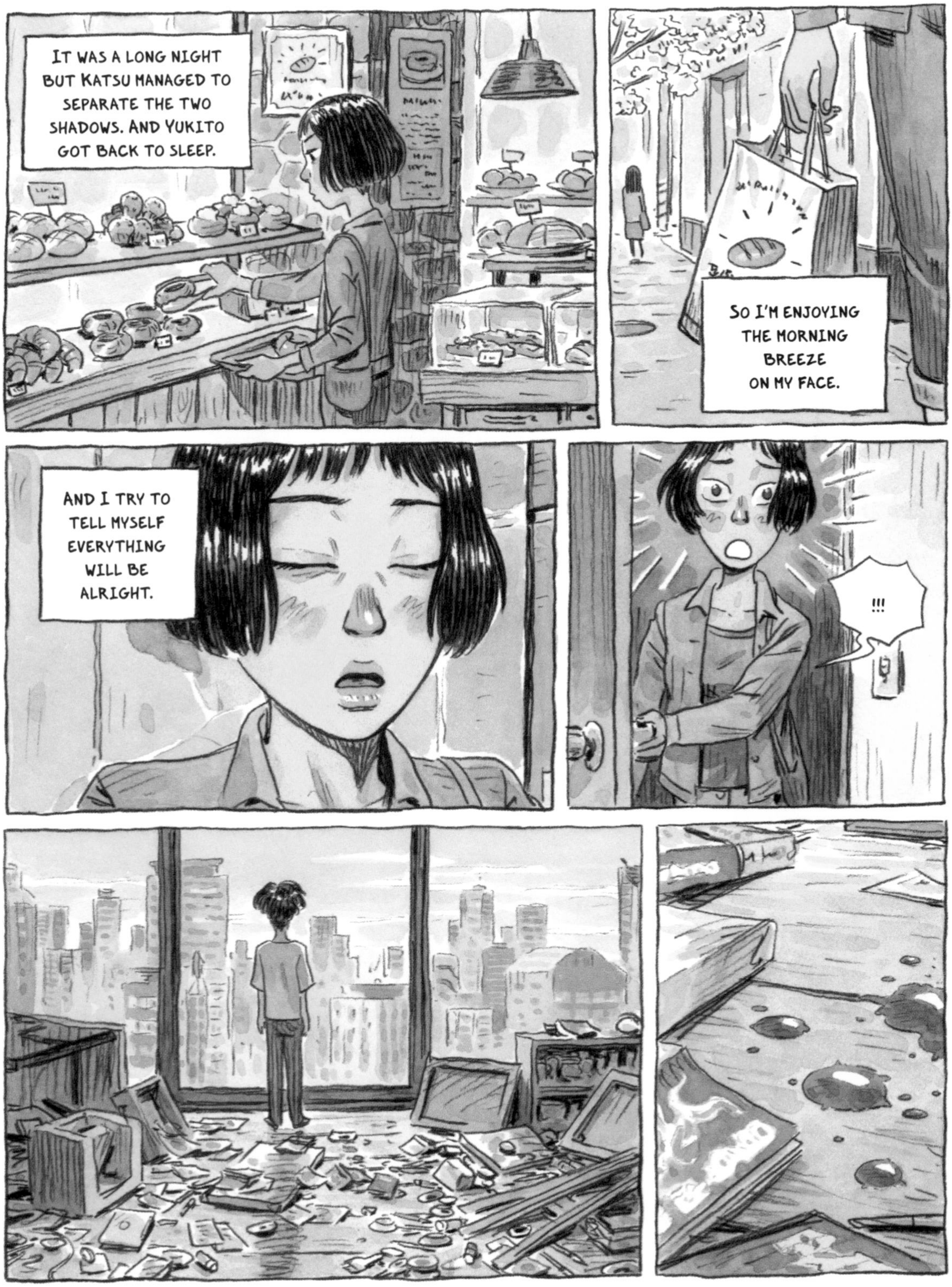

IT WAS A LONG NIGHT BUT KATSU MANAGED TO SEPARATE THE TWO SHADOWS. AND YUKITO GOT BACK TO SLEEP.
SO I'M ENJOYING THE MORNING BREEZE ON MY FACE.
AND I TRY TO TELL MYSELF EVERYTHING WILL BE ALRIGHT.
!!!

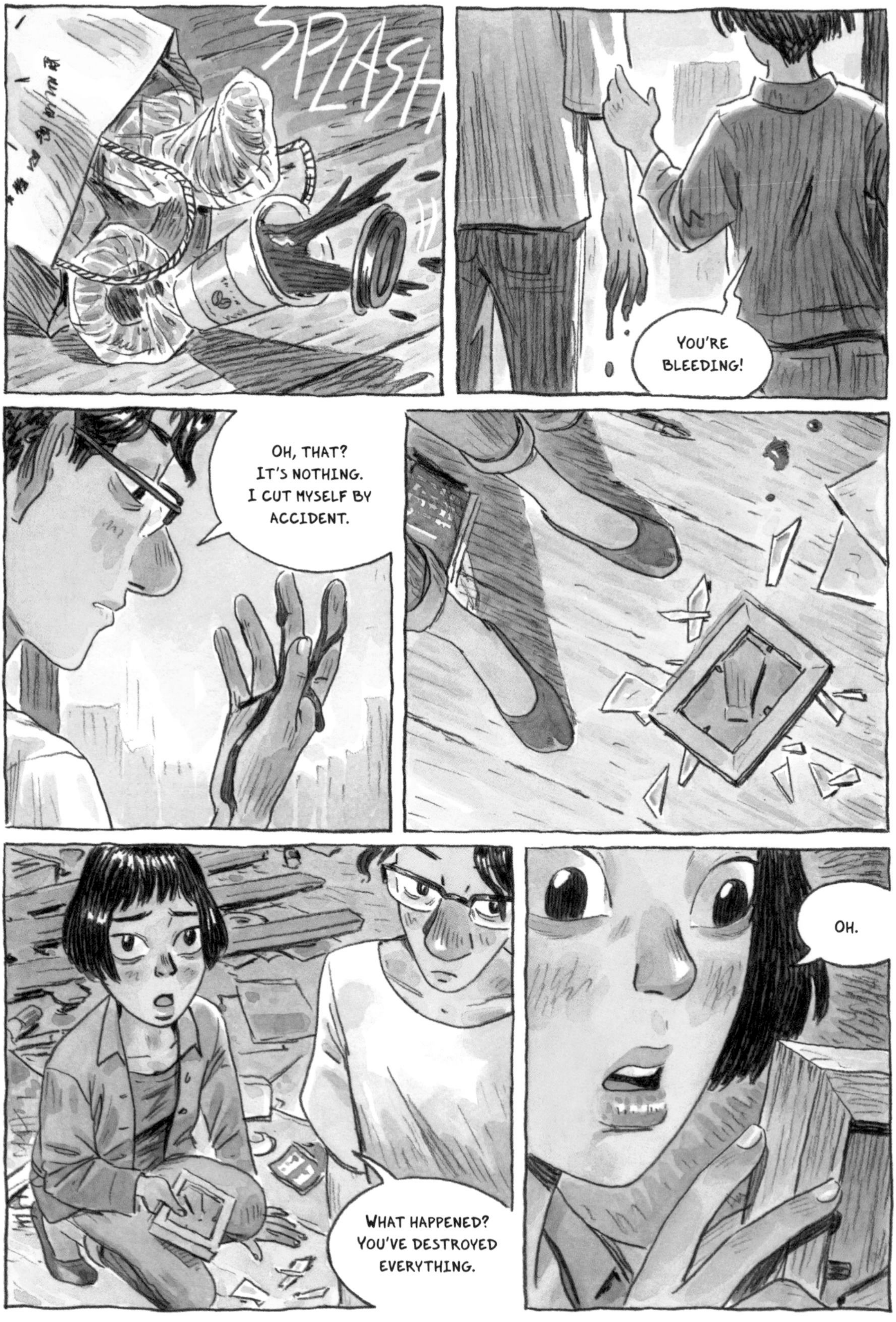
SPLASH
YOU'RE BLEEDING!
OH, THAT? IT'S NOTHING. I CUT MYSELF BY ACCIDENT.
WHAT HAPPENED? YOU'VE DESTROYED EVERYTHING.
OH.

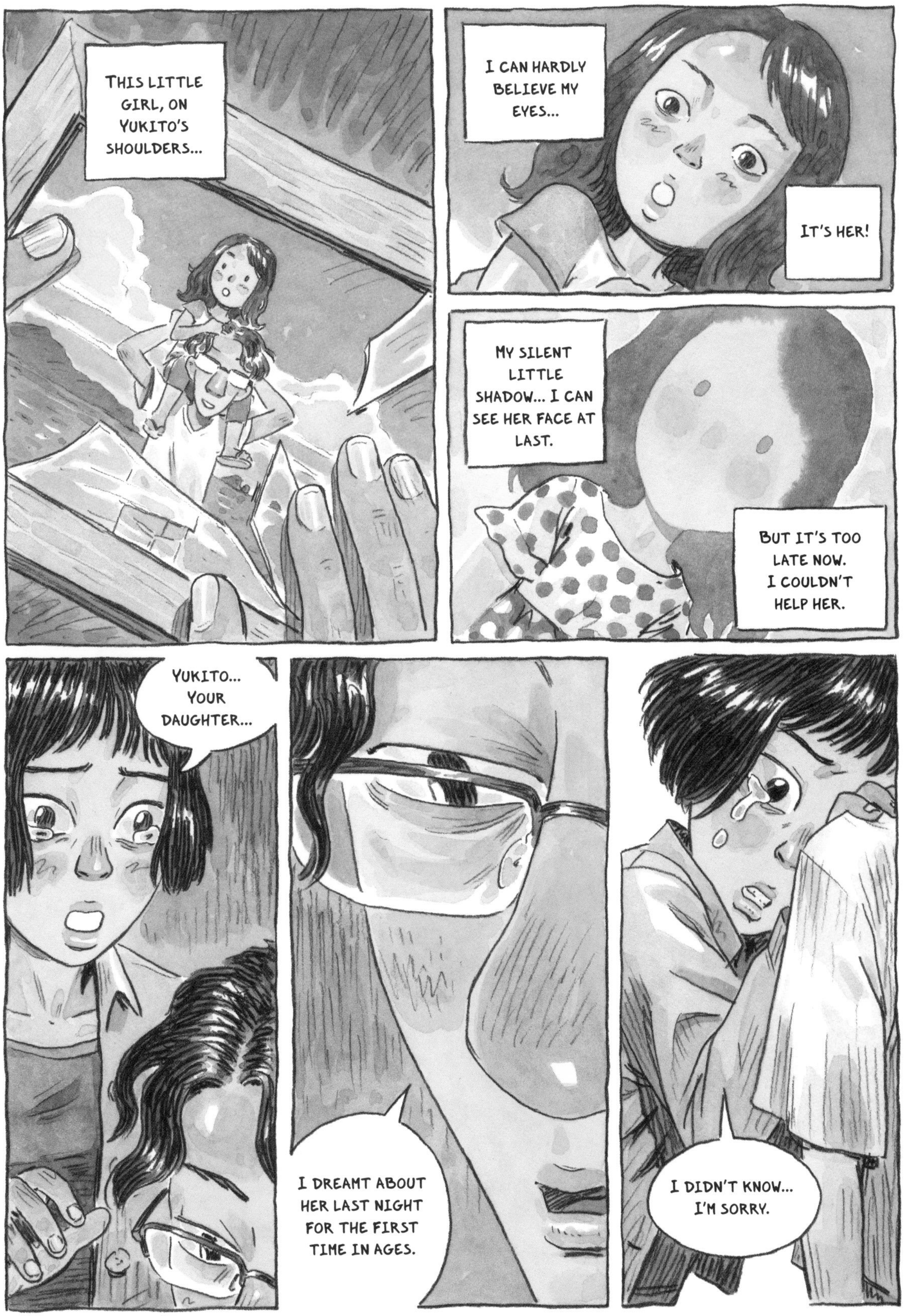
THIS LITTLE GIRL, ON YUKITO'S SHOULDERS...
I CAN HARDLY BELIEVE MY EYES...
IT'S HER!
MY SILENT LITTLE SHADOW... I CAN SEE HER FACE AT LAST.
BUT IT'S TOO LATE NOW. I COULDN'T HELP HER.
YUKITO... YOUR DAUGHTER...
I DREAMT ABOUT HER LAST NIGHT FOR THE FIRST TIME IN AGES.
I DIDN'T KNOW... I'M SORRY.

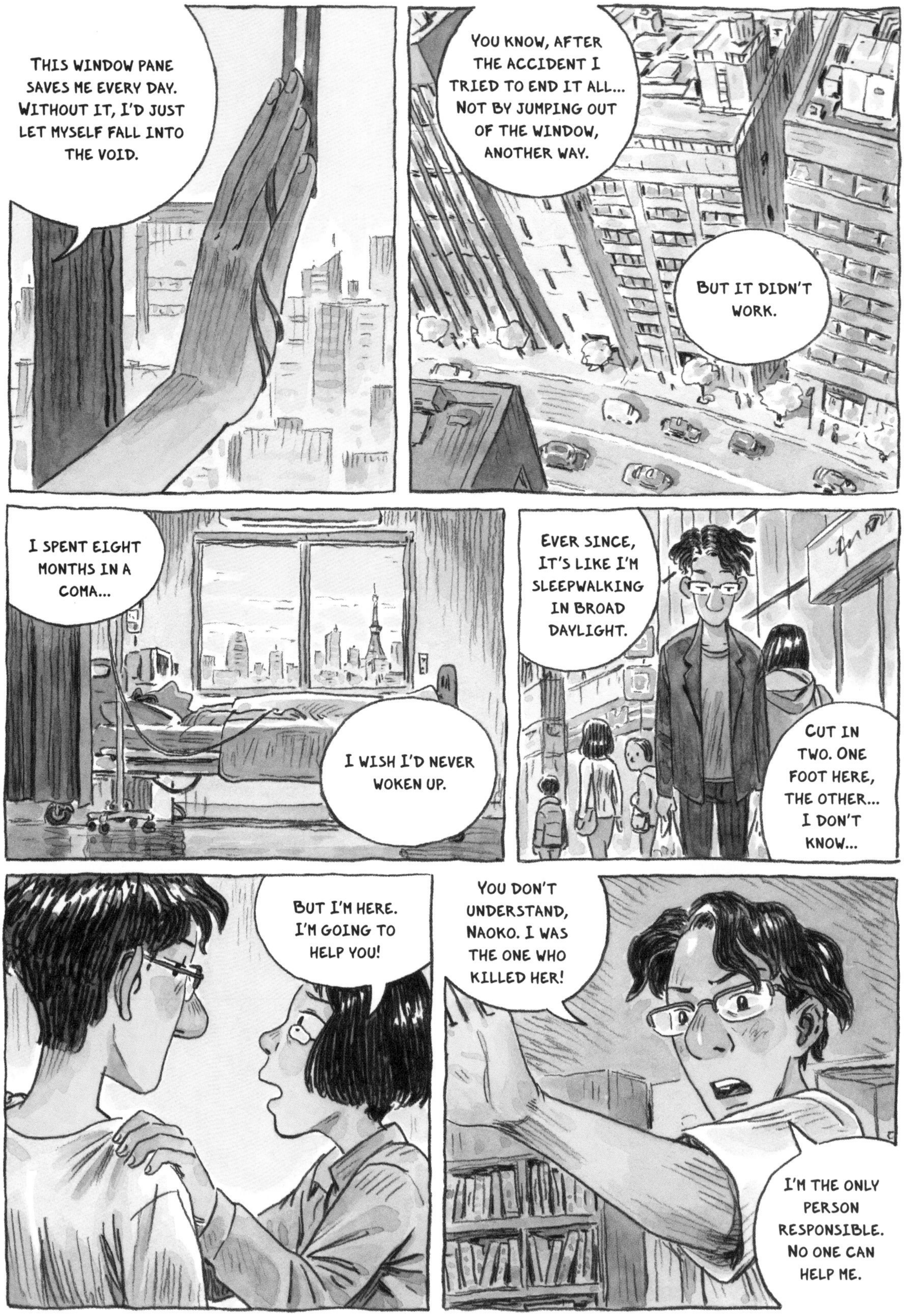
THIS WINDOW PANE SAVES ME EVERY DAY. WITHOUT IT, I'D JUST LET MYSELF FALL INTO THE VOID.
YOU KNOW, AFTER THE ACCIDENT I TRIED TO END IT ALL... NOT BY JUMPING OUT OF THE WINDOW, ANOTHER WAY.
BUT IT DIDN'T WORK.
I SPENT EIGHT MONTHS IN A COMA...
I WISH I'D NEVER WOKEN UP.
EVER SINCE, IT'S LIKE I'M SLEEPWALKING IN BROAD DAYLIGHT.
CUT IN TWO. ONE FOOT HERE, THE OTHER... I DON'T KNOW...
BUT I'M HERE. I'M GOING TO HELP YOU!
YOU DON'T UNDERSTAND, NAOKO. I WAS THE ONE WHO KILLED HER!
I'M THE ONLY PERSON RESPONSIBLE. NO ONE CAN HELP ME.

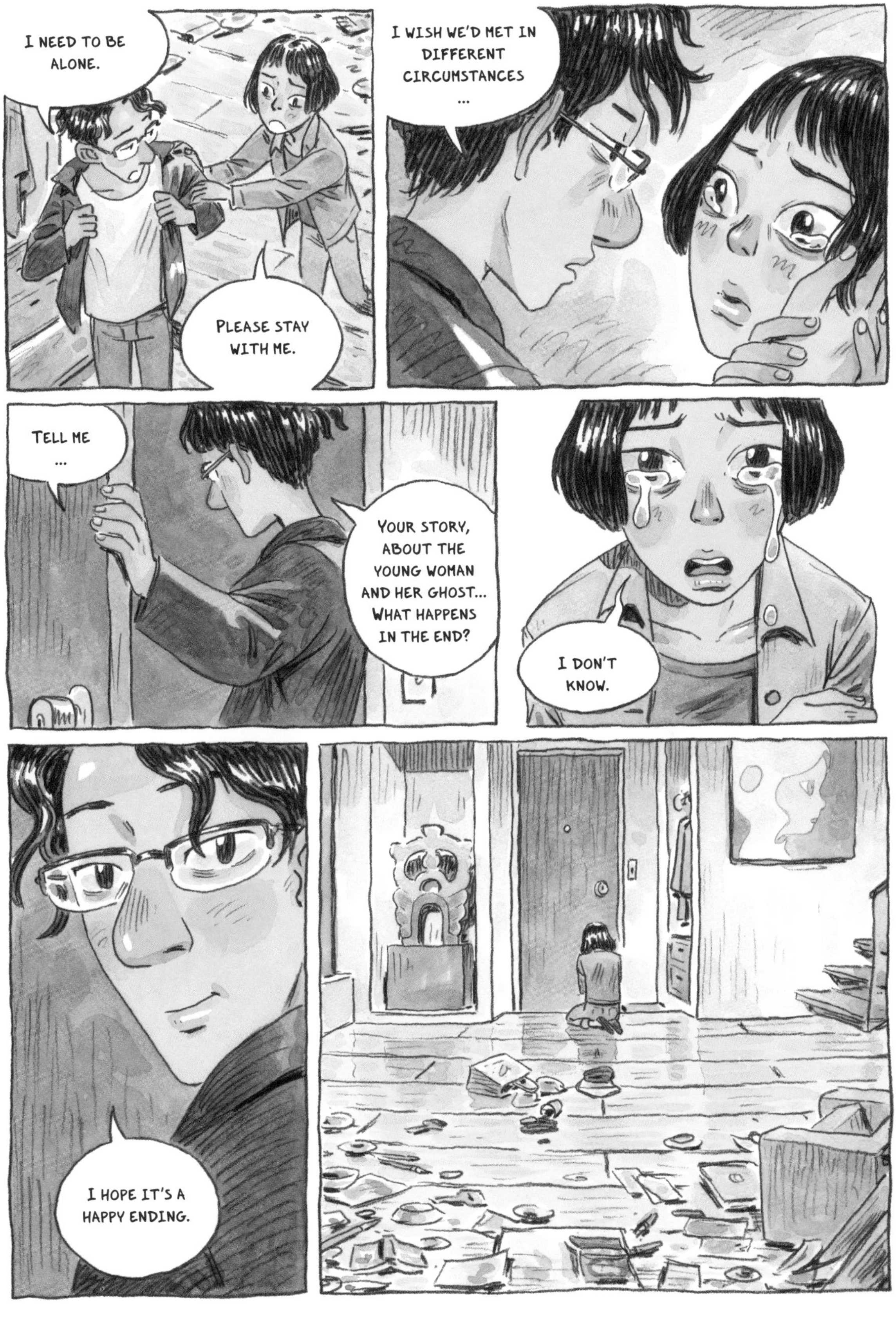
I NEED TO BE ALONE.
PLEASE STAY WITH ME.
I WISH WE'D MET IN DIFFERENT CIRCUMSTANCES ...
TELL ME ...
YOUR STORY, ABOUT THE YOUNG WOMAN AND HER GHOST... WHAT HAPPENS IN THE END?
I DON'T KNOW.
I HOPE IT'S A HAPPY ENDING.

夏

Summer

Those who stray

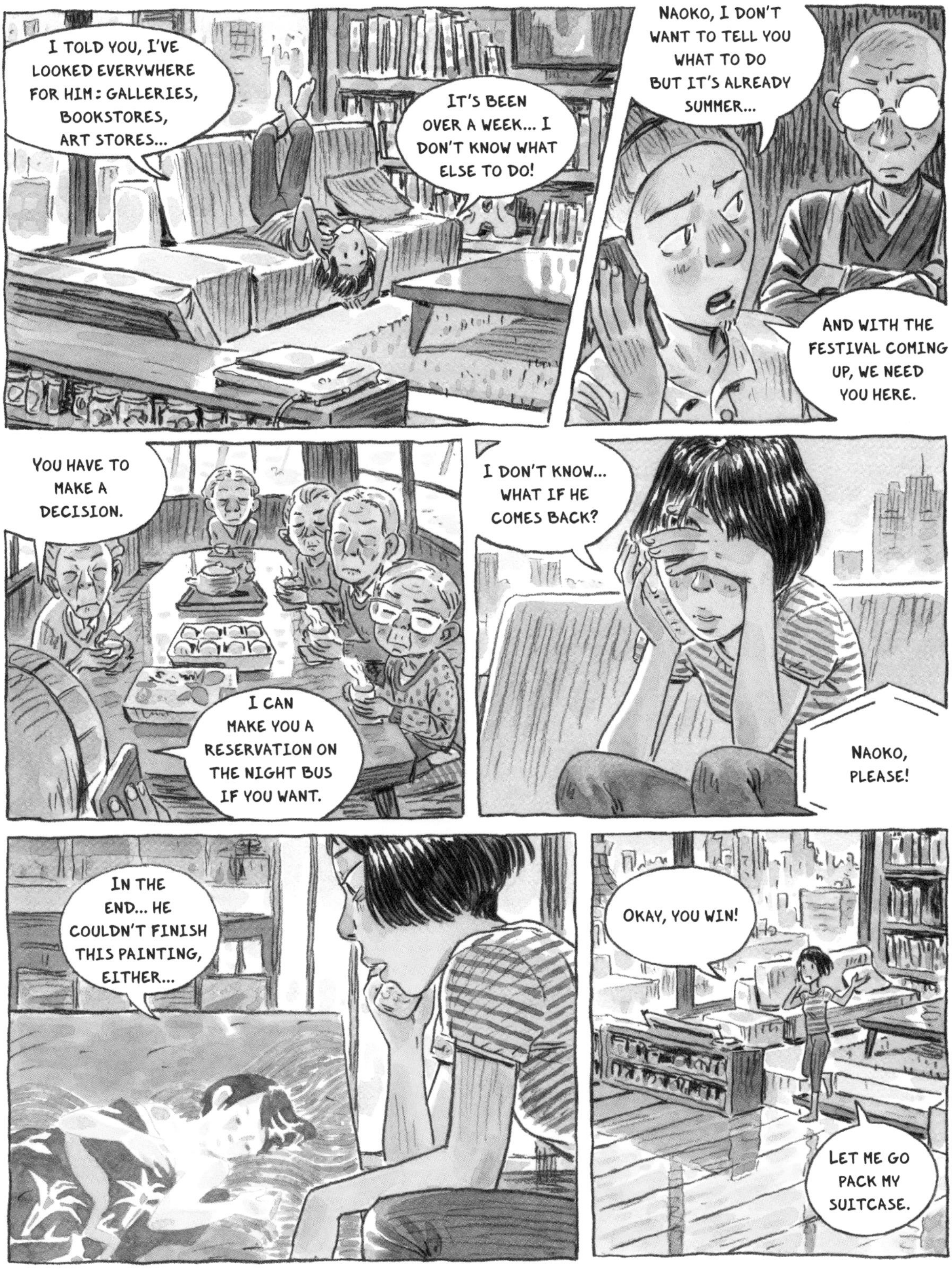
I TOLD YOU, I'VE LOOKED EVERYWHERE FOR HIM: GALLERIES, BOOKSTORES, ART STORES...
IT'S BEEN OVER A WEEK... I DON'T KNOW WHAT ELSE TO DO!
NAOKO, I DON'T WANT TO TELL YOU WHAT TO DO BUT IT'S ALREADY SUMMER...
AND WITH THE FESTIVAL COMING UP, WE NEED YOU HERE.
YOU HAVE TO MAKE A DECISION.
I CAN MAKE YOU A RESERVATION ON THE NIGHT BUS IF YOU WANT.
I DON'T KNOW... WHAT IF HE COMES BACK?
NAOKO, PLEASE!
IN THE END... HE COULDN'T FINISH THIS PAINTING, EITHER...
OKAY, YOU WIN!
LET ME GO PACK MY SUITCASE.

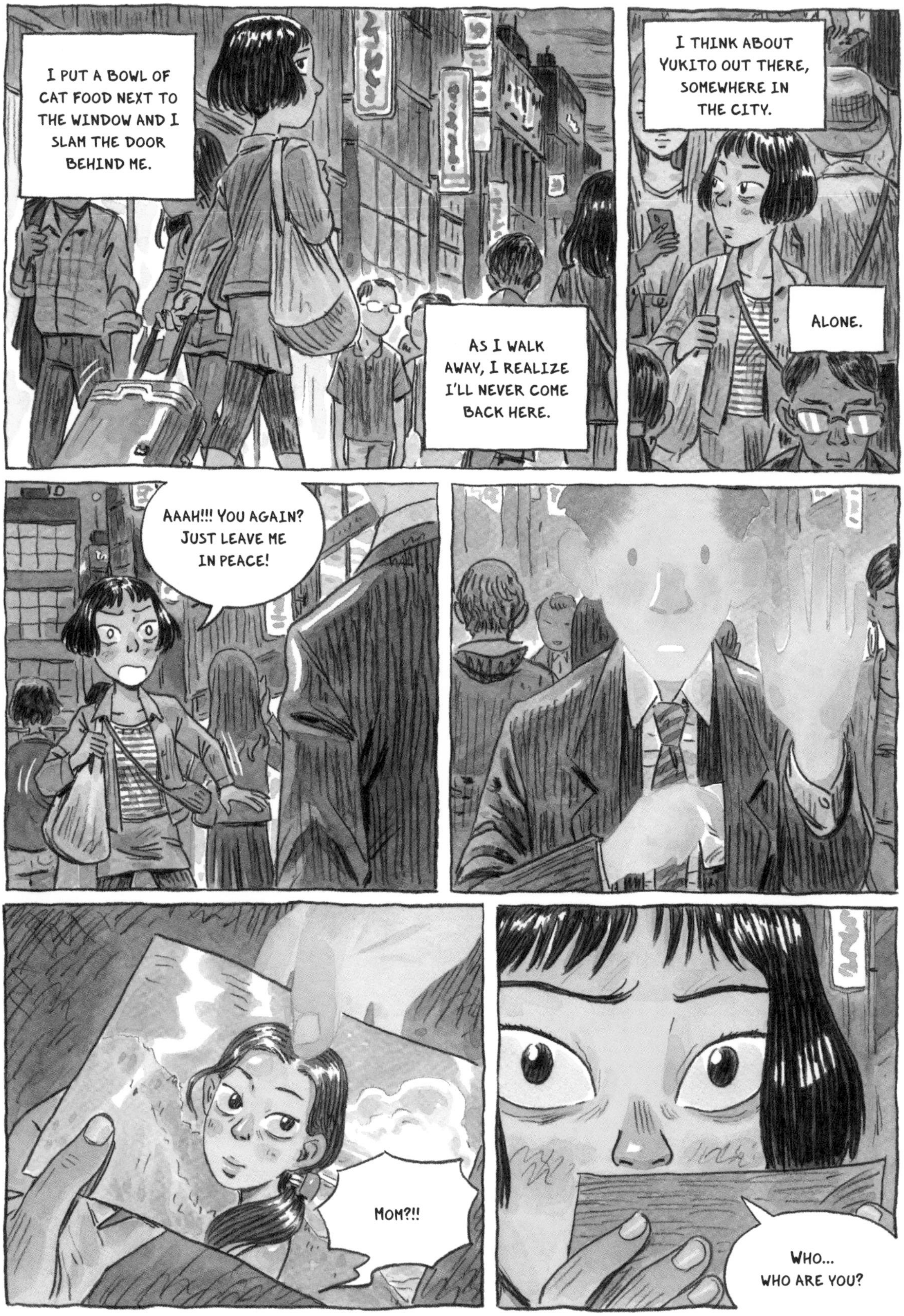
I put a bowl of cat food next to the window and I slam the door behind me.
As I walk away, I realize I'll never come back here.
I think about Yukito out there, somewhere in the city.
Alone.
Aaah!!! You again? Just leave me in peace!
Mom?!!
Who...
who are you?

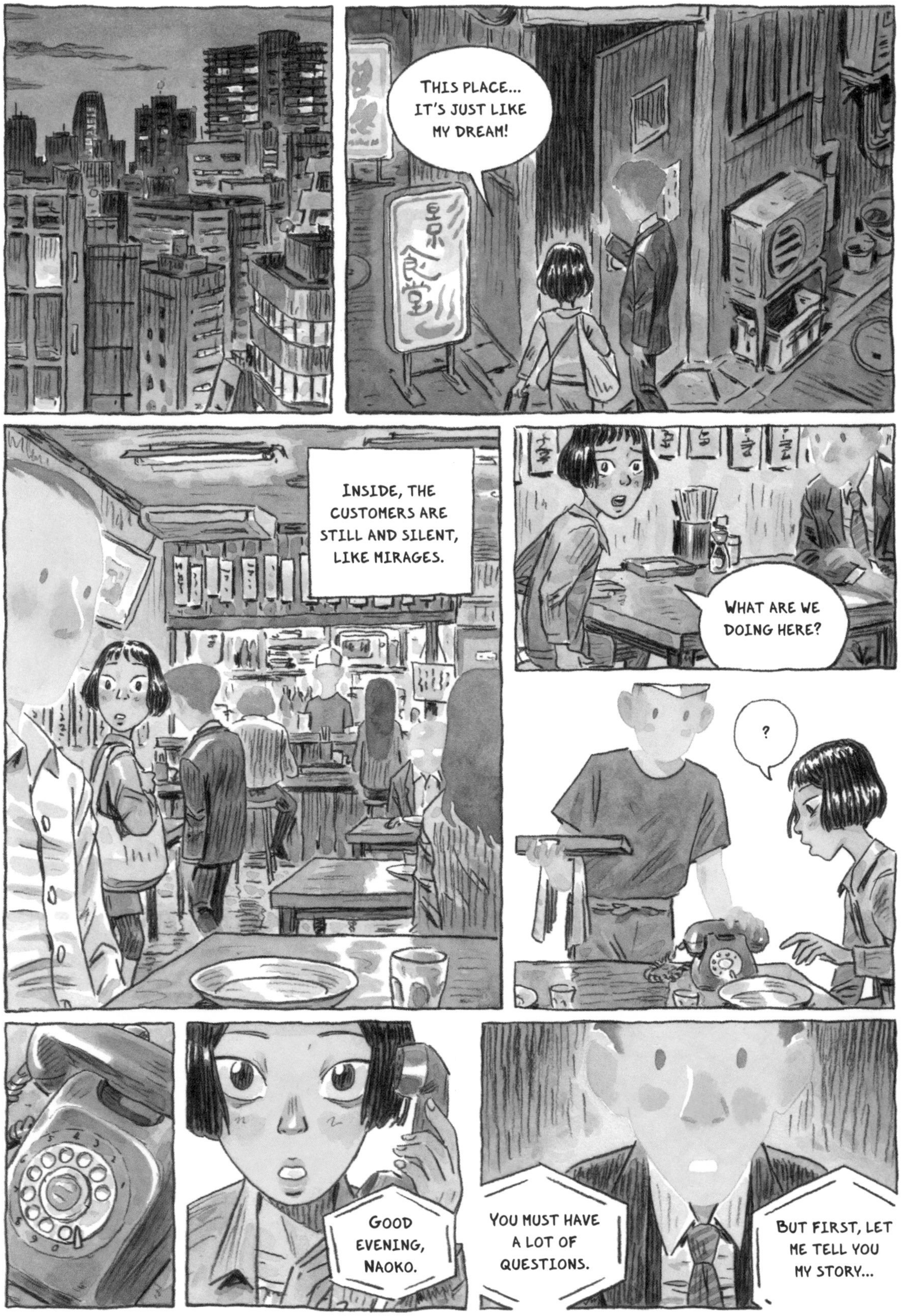
THIS PLACE... IT'S JUST LIKE MY DREAM!
INSIDE, THE CUSTOMERS ARE STILL AND SILENT, LIKE MIRAGES.
WHAT ARE WE DOING HERE?
?
GOOD EVENING, NAOKO.
YOU MUST HAVE A LOT OF QUESTIONS.
BUT FIRST, LET ME TELL YOU MY STORY...

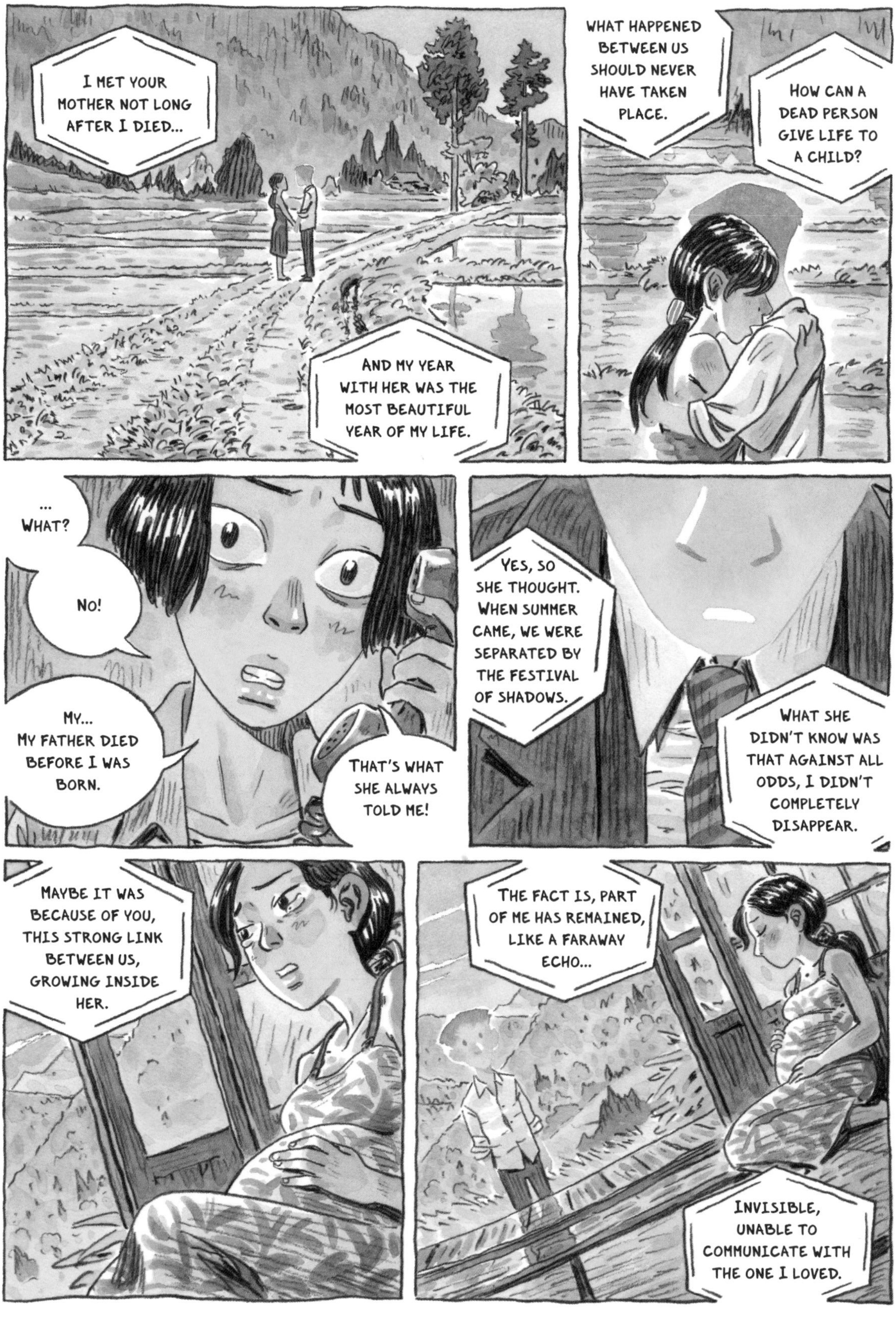
I MET YOUR MOTHER NOT LONG AFTER I DIED...
AND MY YEAR WITH HER WAS THE MOST BEAUTIFUL YEAR OF MY LIFE.
WHAT HAPPENED BETWEEN US SHOULD NEVER HAVE TAKEN PLACE.
HOW CAN A DEAD PERSON GIVE LIFE TO A CHILD?
... WHAT?
NO!
MY... MY FATHER DIED BEFORE I WAS BORN.
THAT'S WHAT SHE ALWAYS TOLD ME!
YES, SO SHE THOUGHT. WHEN SUMMER CAME, WE WERE SEPARATED BY THE FESTIVAL OF SHADOWS.
WHAT SHE DIDN'T KNOW WAS THAT AGAINST ALL ODDS, I DIDN'T COMPLETELY DISAPPEAR.
MAYBE IT WAS BECAUSE OF YOU, THIS STRONG LINK BETWEEN US, GROWING INSIDE HER.
THE FACT IS, PART OF ME HAS REMAINED, LIKE A FARAWAY ECHO...
INVISIBLE, UNABLE TO COMMUNICATE WITH THE ONE I LOVED.

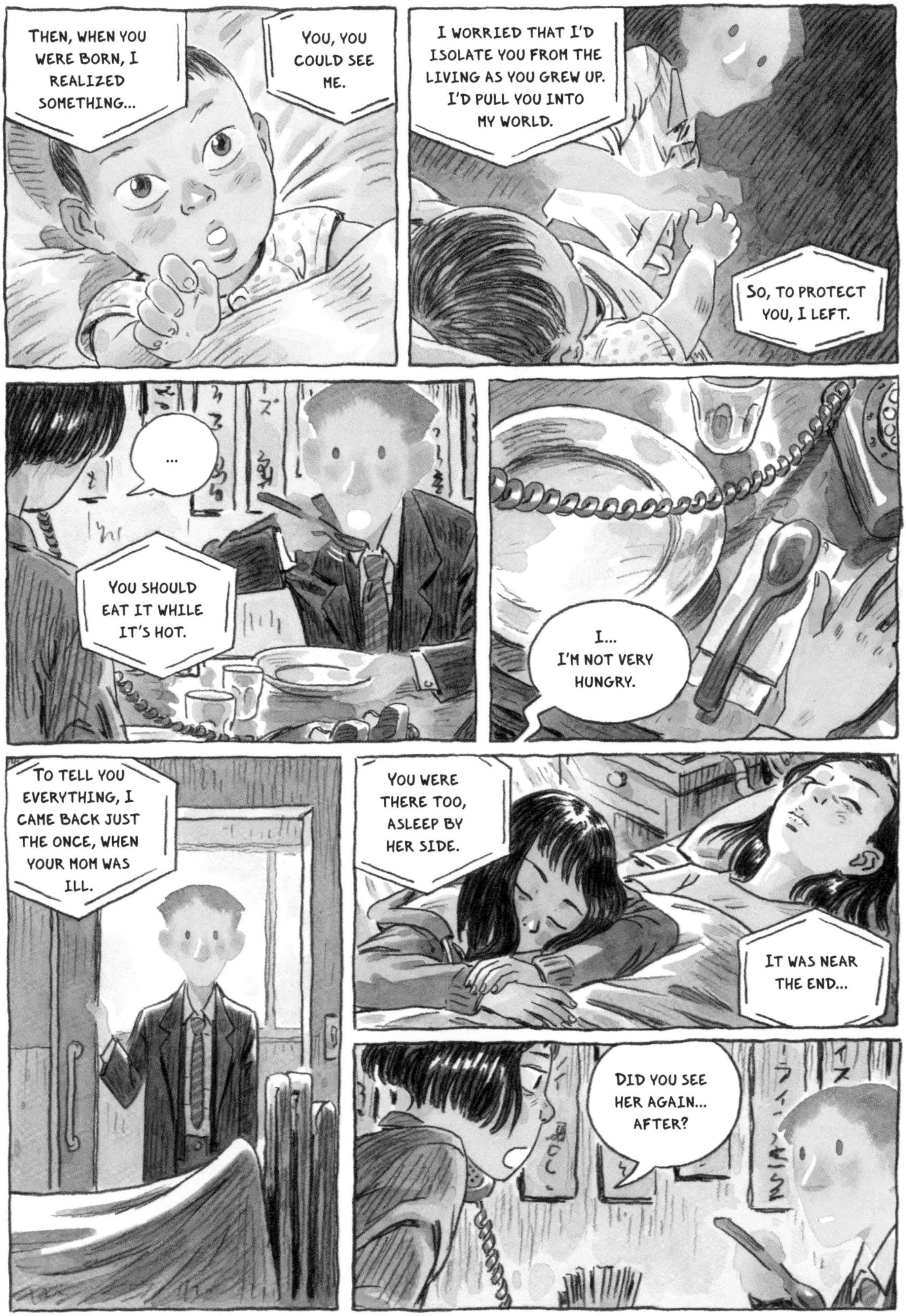

THEN, WHEN YOU WERE BORN, I REALIZED SOMETHING...
YOU, YOU COULD SEE ME.
I WORRIED THAT I'D ISOLATE YOU FROM THE LIVING AS YOU GREW UP. I'D PULL YOU INTO MY WORLD.
SO, TO PROTECT YOU, I LEFT.
...
YOU SHOULD EAT IT WHILE IT'S HOT.
I... I'M NOT VERY HUNGRY.
TO TELL YOU EVERYTHING, I CAME BACK JUST THE ONCE, WHEN YOUR MOM WAS ILL.
YOU WERE THERE TOO, ASLEEP BY HER SIDE.
IT WAS NEAR THE END...
DID YOU SEE HER AGAIN... AFTER?

NO. SHE LEFT FOR GOOD, WITH NO REGRETS.

IF ONLY YOU KNEW HOW PROUD SHE WAS OF YOU!

AAAH, THIS IS AWFUL! I'M SICK OF THIS DAMN FESTIVAL. IT TAKES EVERYTHING AND LEAVES ME WITH NOTHING!

I FEEL SO ALONE.

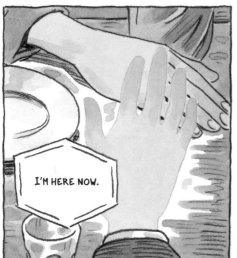

I'M HERE NOW.

NO!

I... I CAN'T.

NAOKO, WAIT!

YOU'RE WRONG...

YOU'RE NOT ALONE.

End of the road

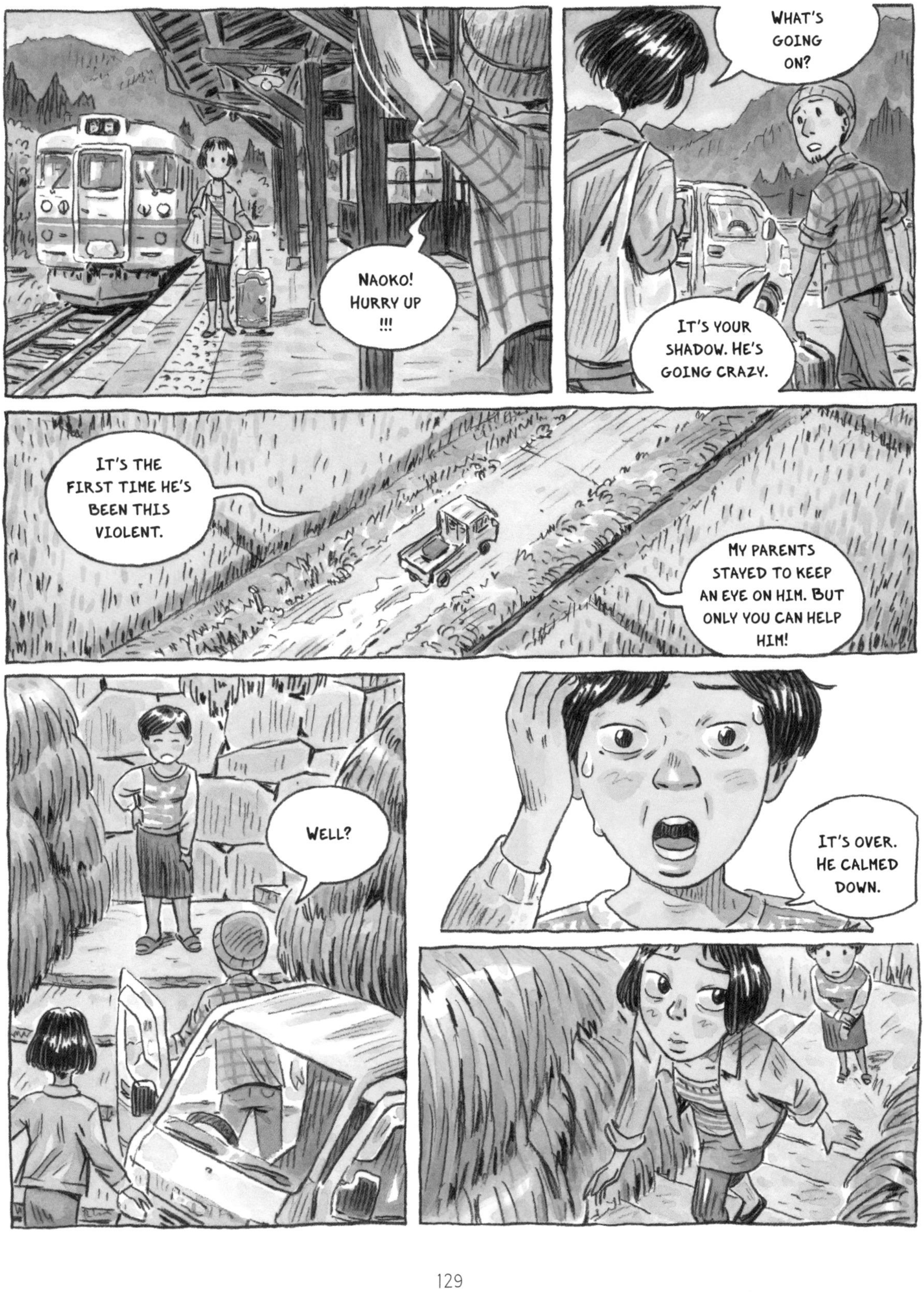
NAOKO! HURRY UP !!!
WHAT'S GOING ON?
IT'S YOUR SHADOW. HE'S GOING CRAZY.
IT'S THE FIRST TIME HE'S BEEN THIS VIOLENT.
MY PARENTS STAYED TO KEEP AN EYE ON HIM. BUT ONLY YOU CAN HELP HIM!
WELL?
IT'S OVER. HE CALMED DOWN.

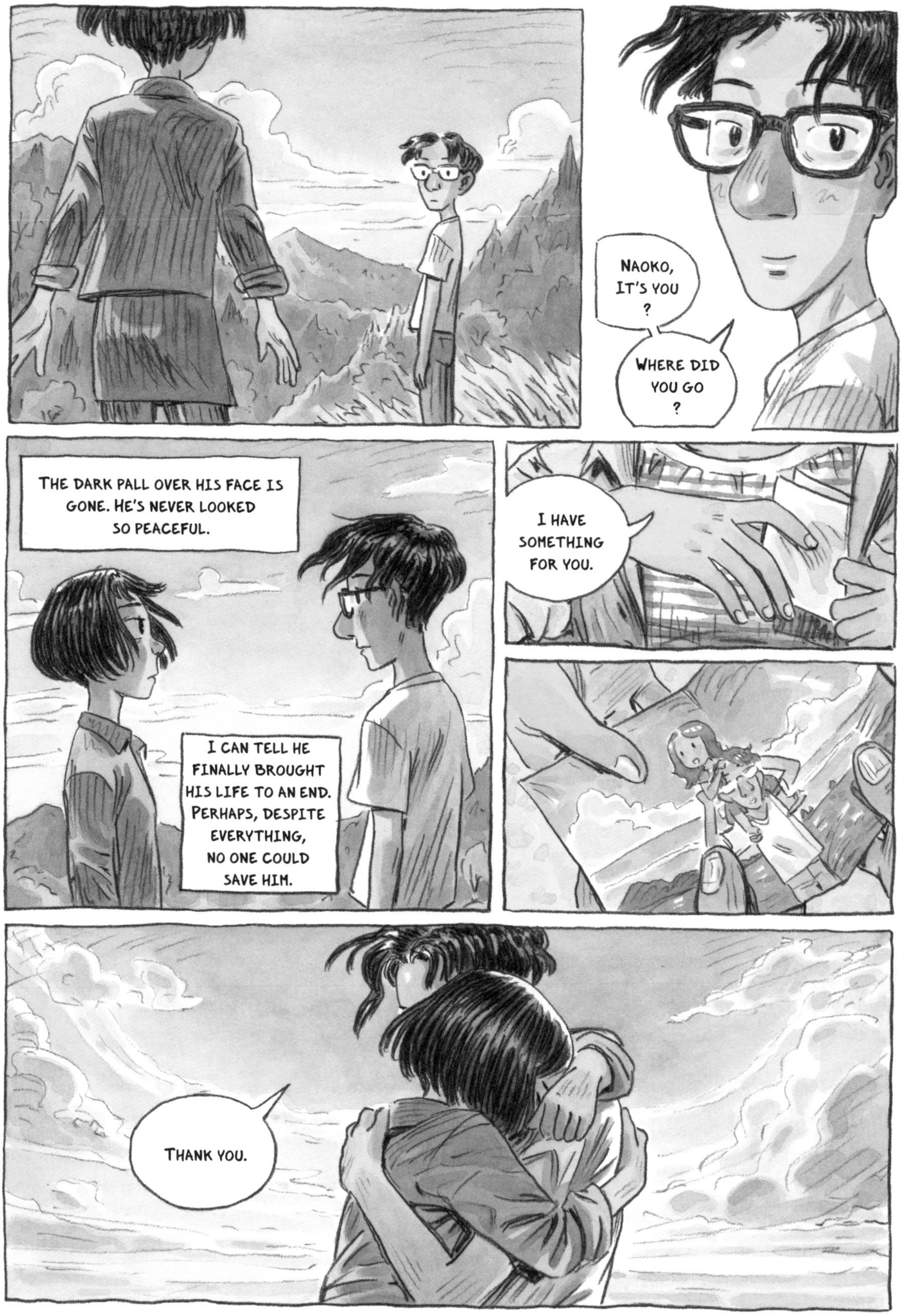
NAOKO, IT'S YOU ?
WHERE DID YOU GO ?
THE DARK PALL OVER HIS FACE IS GONE. HE'S NEVER LOOKED SO PEACEFUL.
I CAN TELL HE FINALLY BROUGHT HIS LIFE TO AN END. PERHAPS, DESPITE EVERYTHING, NO ONE COULD SAVE HIM.
I HAVE SOMETHING FOR YOU.
THANK YOU.

The season of farewells

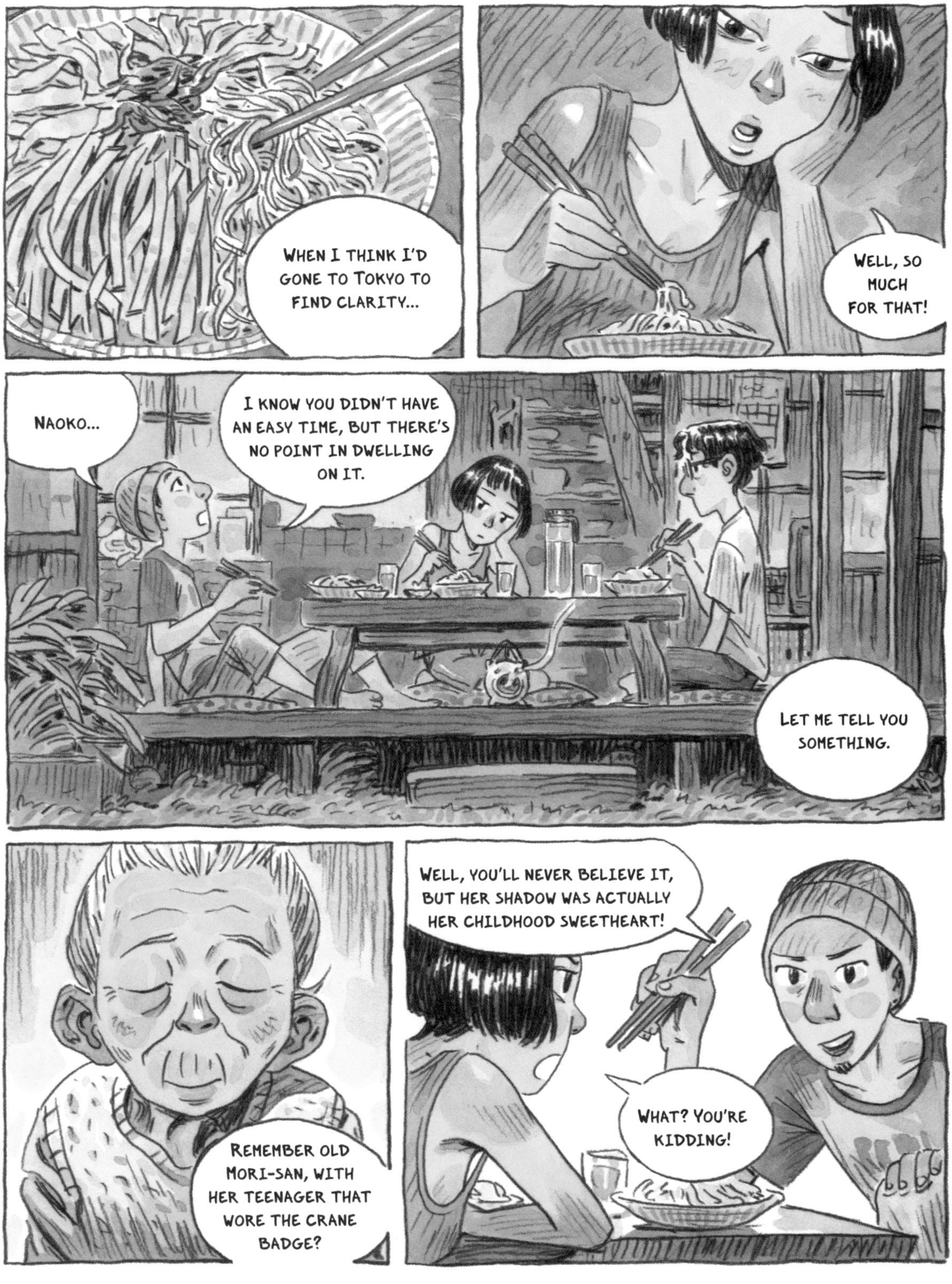

WHEN I THINK I'D GONE TO TOKYO TO FIND CLARITY...
WELL, SO MUCH FOR THAT!
NAOKO...
I KNOW YOU DIDN'T HAVE AN EASY TIME, BUT THERE'S NO POINT IN DWELLING ON IT.
LET ME TELL YOU SOMETHING.
REMEMBER OLD MORI-SAN, WITH HER TEENAGER THAT WORE THE CRANE BADGE?
WELL, YOU'LL NEVER BELIEVE IT, BUT HER SHADOW WAS ACTUALLY HER CHILDHOOD SWEETHEART!
WHAT? YOU'RE KIDDING!

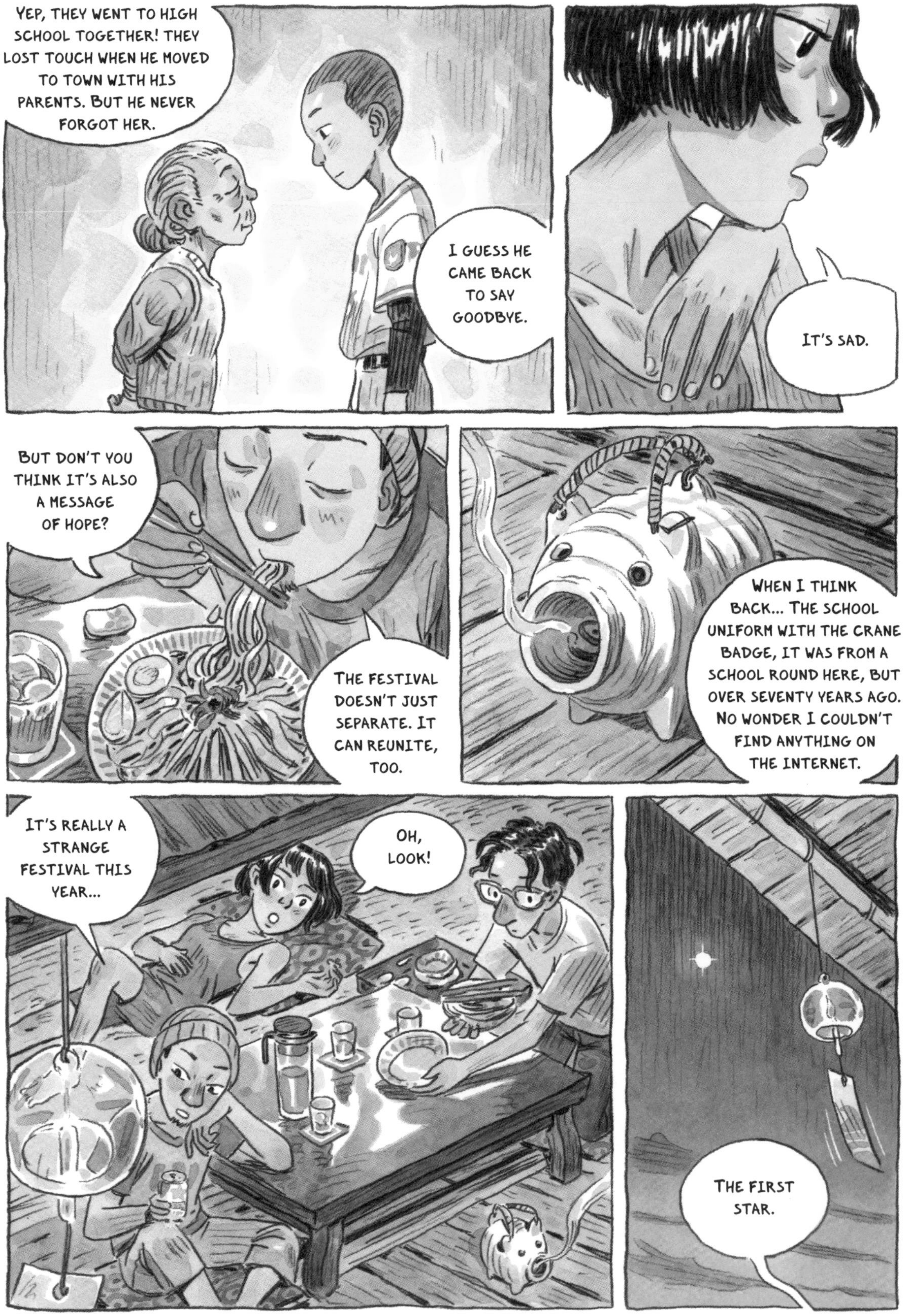
YEP, THEY WENT TO HIGH SCHOOL TOGETHER! THEY LOST TOUCH WHEN HE MOVED TO TOWN WITH HIS PARENTS. BUT HE NEVER FORGOT HER.
I GUESS HE CAME BACK TO SAY GOODBYE.
IT'S SAD.
BUT DON'T YOU THINK IT'S ALSO A MESSAGE OF HOPE?
THE FESTIVAL DOESN'T JUST SEPARATE. IT CAN REUNITE, TOO.
WHEN I THINK BACK... THE SCHOOL UNIFORM WITH THE CRANE BADGE, IT WAS FROM A SCHOOL ROUND HERE, BUT OVER SEVENTY YEARS AGO. NO WONDER I COULDN'T FIND ANYTHING ON THE INTERNET.
IT'S REALLY A STRANGE FESTIVAL THIS YEAR...
OH, LOOK!
THE FIRST STAR.

Floating

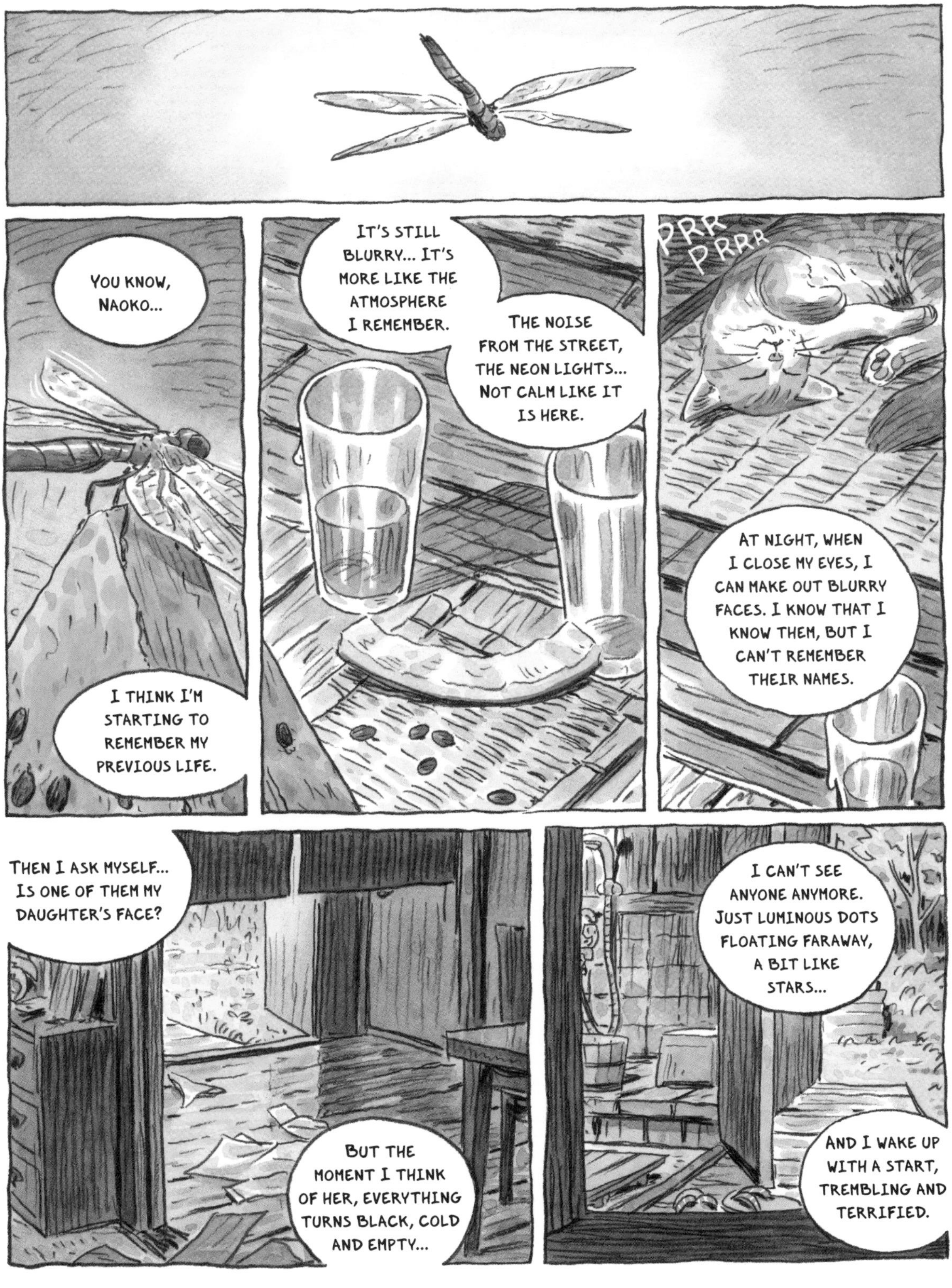
YOU KNOW, NAOKO...
I THINK I'M STARTING TO REMEMBER MY PREVIOUS LIFE.
IT'S STILL BLURRY... IT'S MORE LIKE THE ATMOSPHERE I REMEMBER.
THE NOISE FROM THE STREET, THE NEON LIGHTS... NOT CALM LIKE IT IS HERE.
PRR PRRR
AT NIGHT, WHEN I CLOSE MY EYES, I CAN MAKE OUT BLURRY FACES. I KNOW THAT I KNOW THEM, BUT I CAN'T REMEMBER THEIR NAMES.
THEN I ASK MYSELF... IS ONE OF THEM MY DAUGHTER'S FACE?
BUT THE MOMENT I THINK OF HER, EVERYTHING TURNS BLACK, COLD AND EMPTY...
I CAN'T SEE ANYONE ANYMORE. JUST LUMINOUS DOTS FLOATING FARAWAY, A BIT LIKE STARS...
AND I WAKE UP WITH A START, TREMBLING AND TERRIFIED.

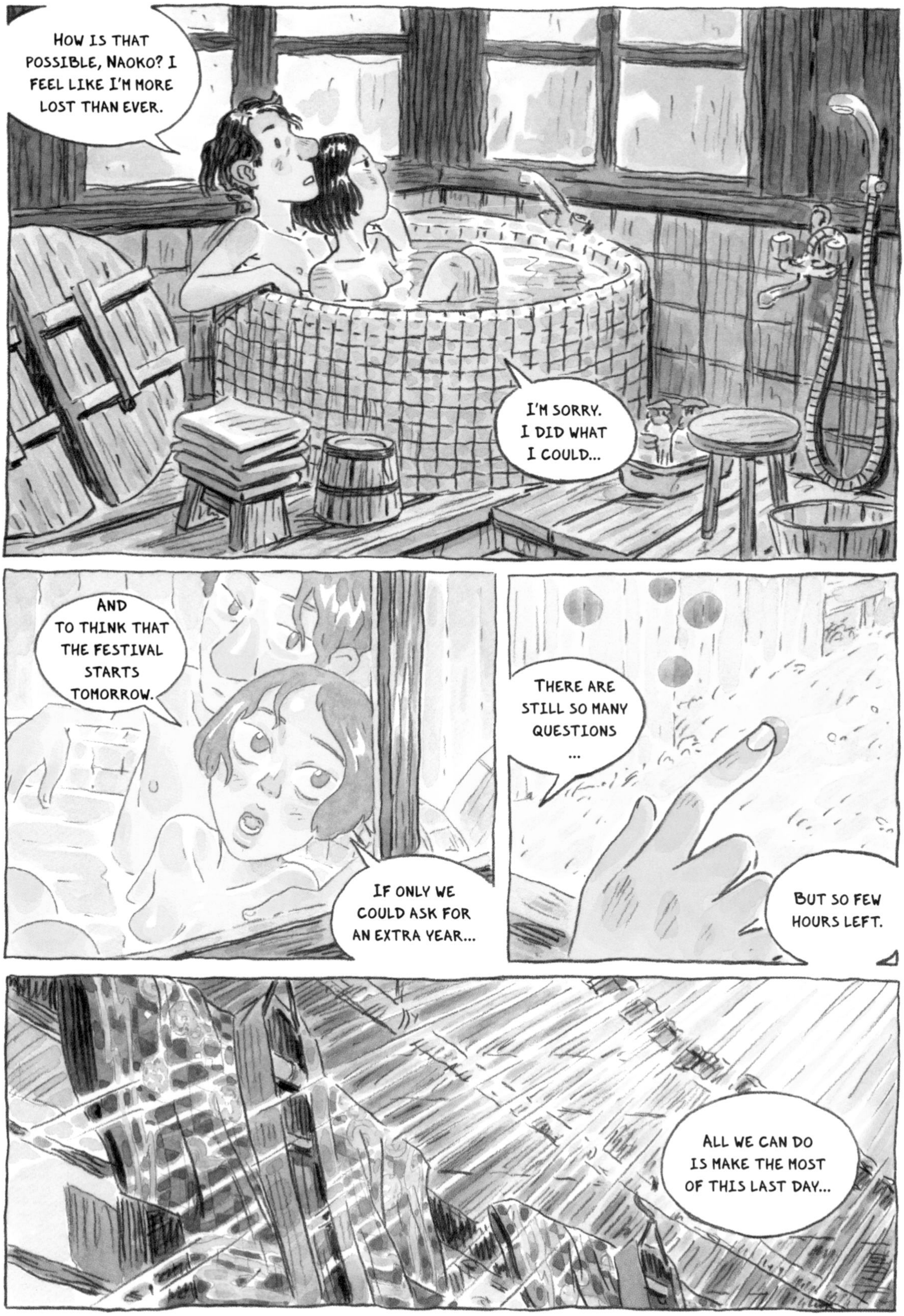
HOW IS THAT POSSIBLE, NAOKO? I FEEL LIKE I'M MORE LOST THAN EVER.
I'M SORRY. I DID WHAT I COULD...
AND TO THINK THAT THE FESTIVAL STARTS TOMORROW.
IF ONLY WE COULD ASK FOR AN EXTRA YEAR...
THERE ARE STILL SO MANY QUESTIONS ...
BUT SO FEW HOURS LEFT.
ALL WE CAN DO IS MAKE THE MOST OF THIS LAST DAY...

Festival of shadows

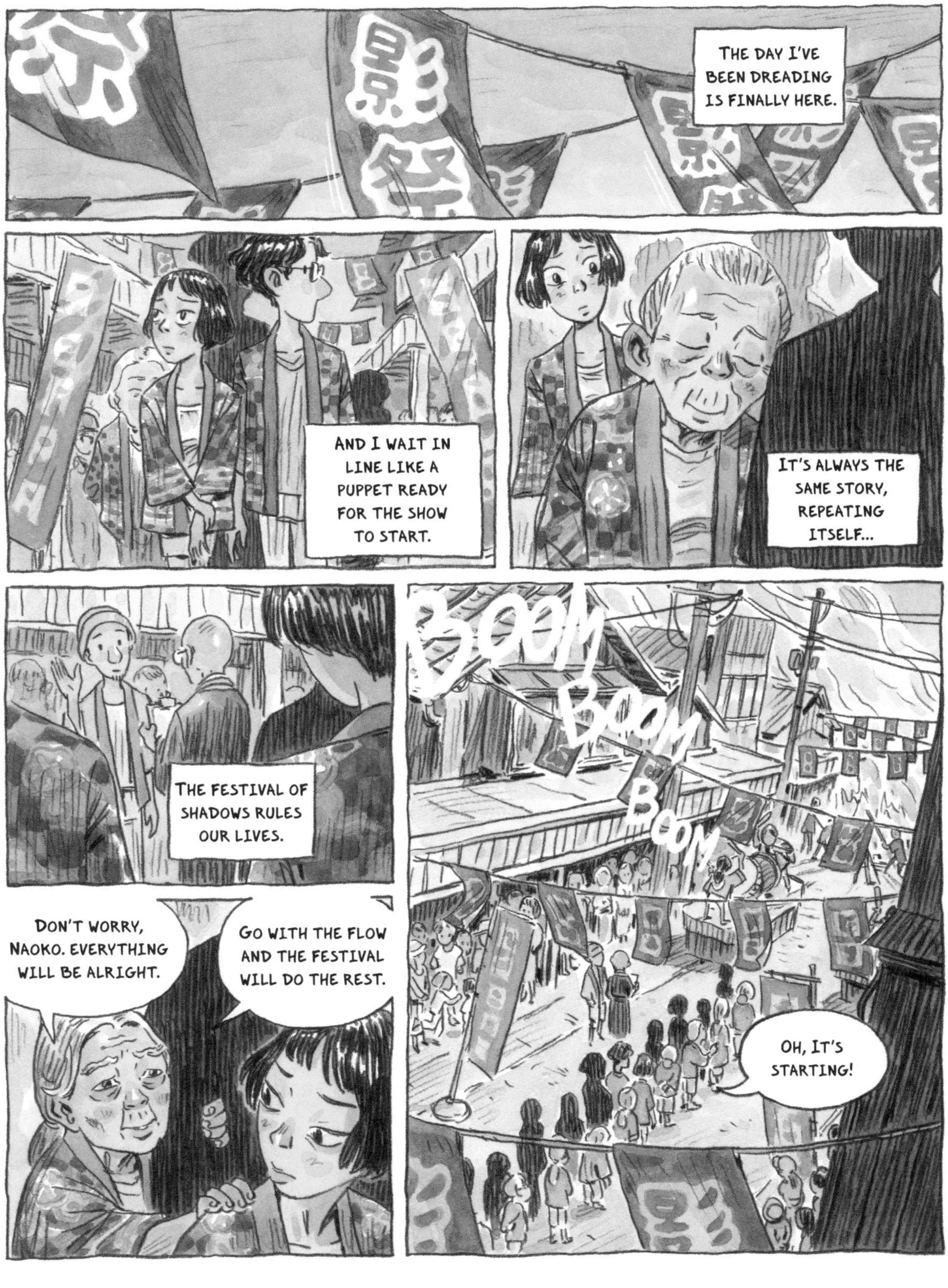
THE DAY I'VE BEEN DREADING IS FINALLY HERE.
AND I WAIT IN LINE LIKE A PUPPET READY FOR THE SHOW TO START.
IT'S ALWAYS THE SAME STORY, REPEATING ITSELF...
THE FESTIVAL OF SHADOWS RULES OUR LIVES.
DON'T WORRY, NAOKO. EVERYTHING WILL BE ALRIGHT.
GO WITH THE FLOW AND THE FESTIVAL WILL DO THE REST.
BOOM
BOOM
BOOM
OH, IT'S STARTING!

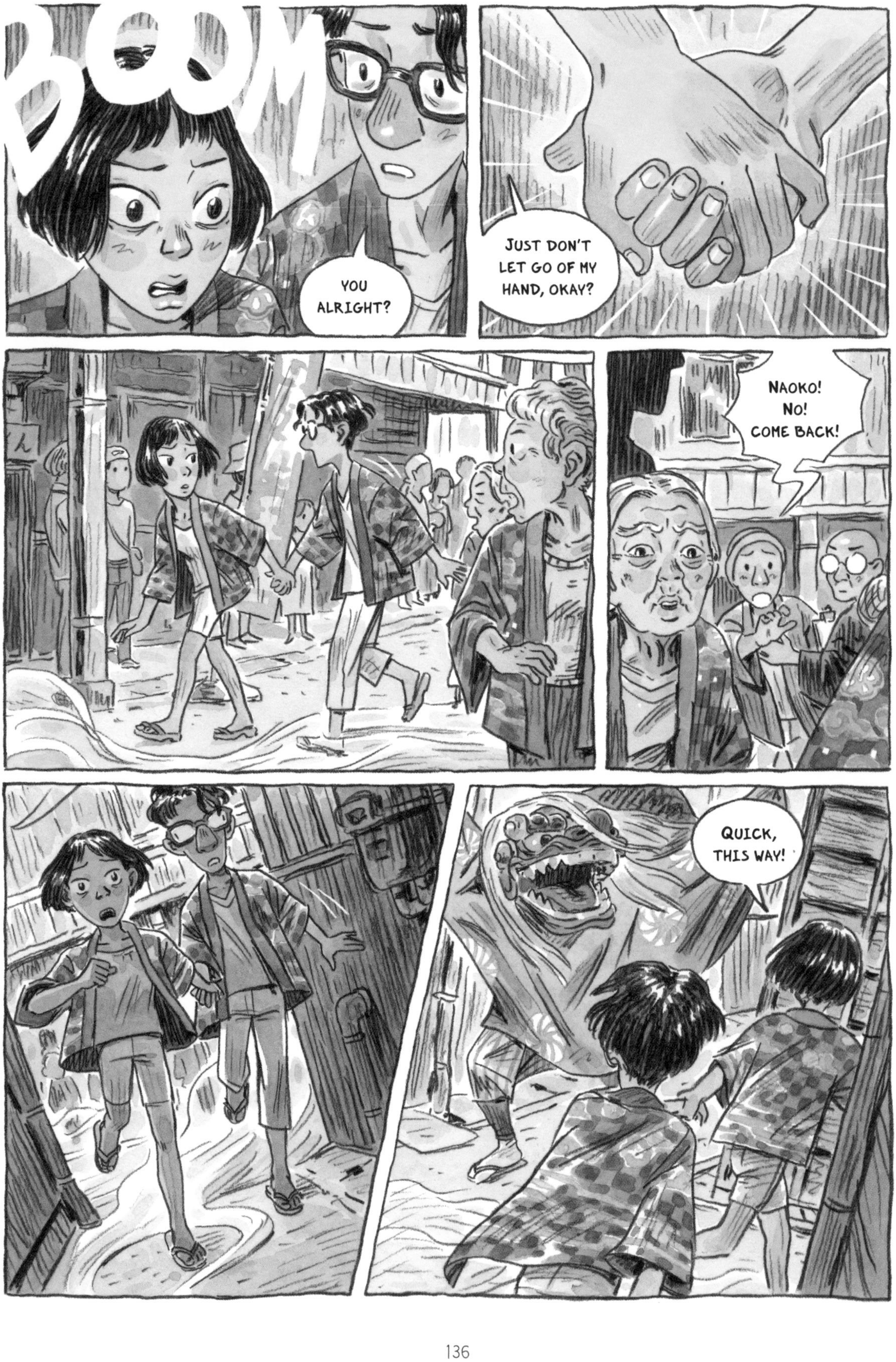
BOOM
YOU ALRIGHT?
JUST DON'T LET GO OF MY HAND, OKAY?
NAOKO! NO! COME BACK!
QUICK, THIS WAY!

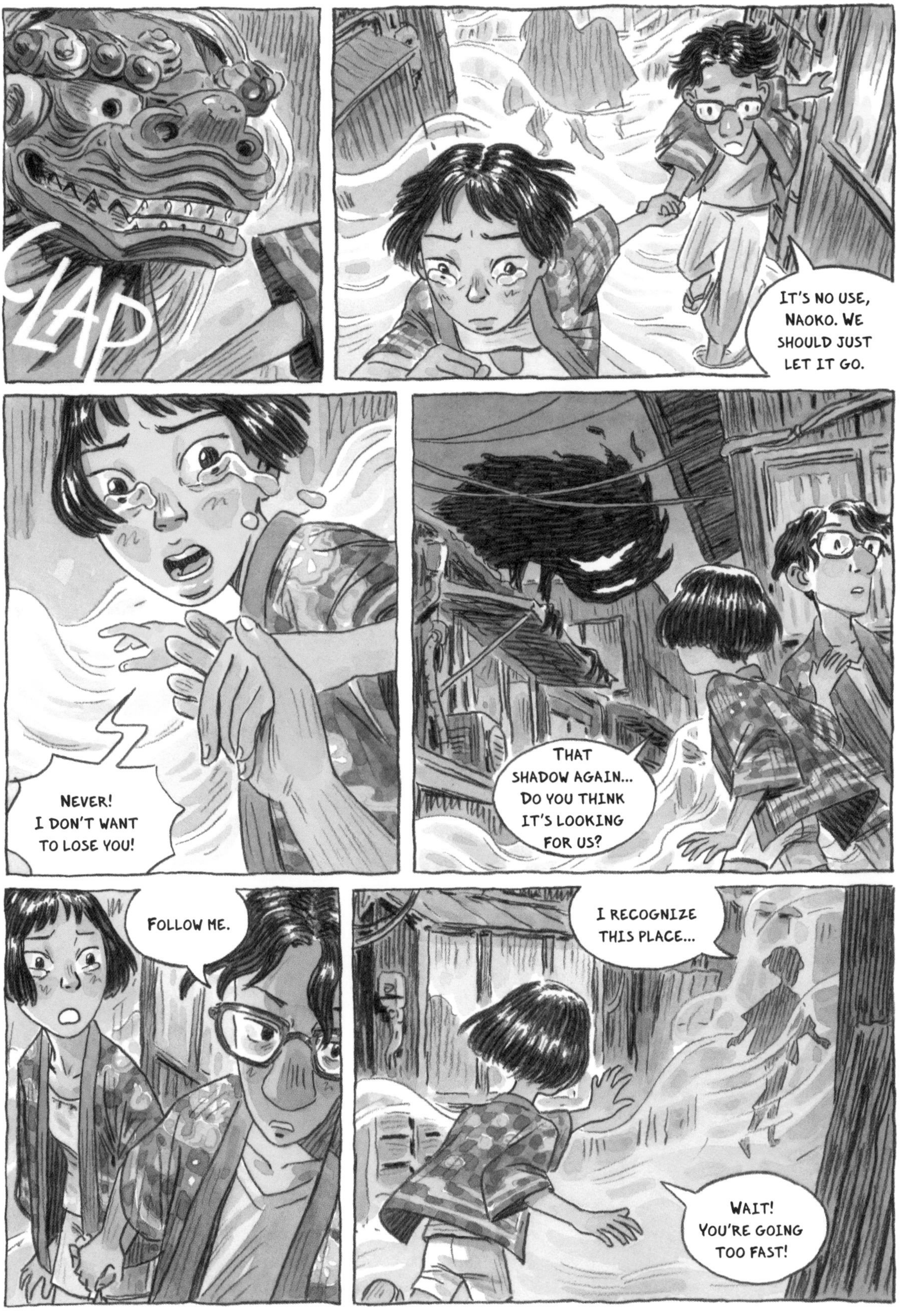
CLAP
IT'S NO USE, NAOKO. WE SHOULD JUST LET IT GO.
NEVER! I DON'T WANT TO LOSE YOU!
THAT SHADOW AGAIN... DO YOU THINK IT'S LOOKING FOR US?
FOLLOW ME.
I RECOGNIZE THIS PLACE...
WAIT! YOU'RE GOING TOO FAST!

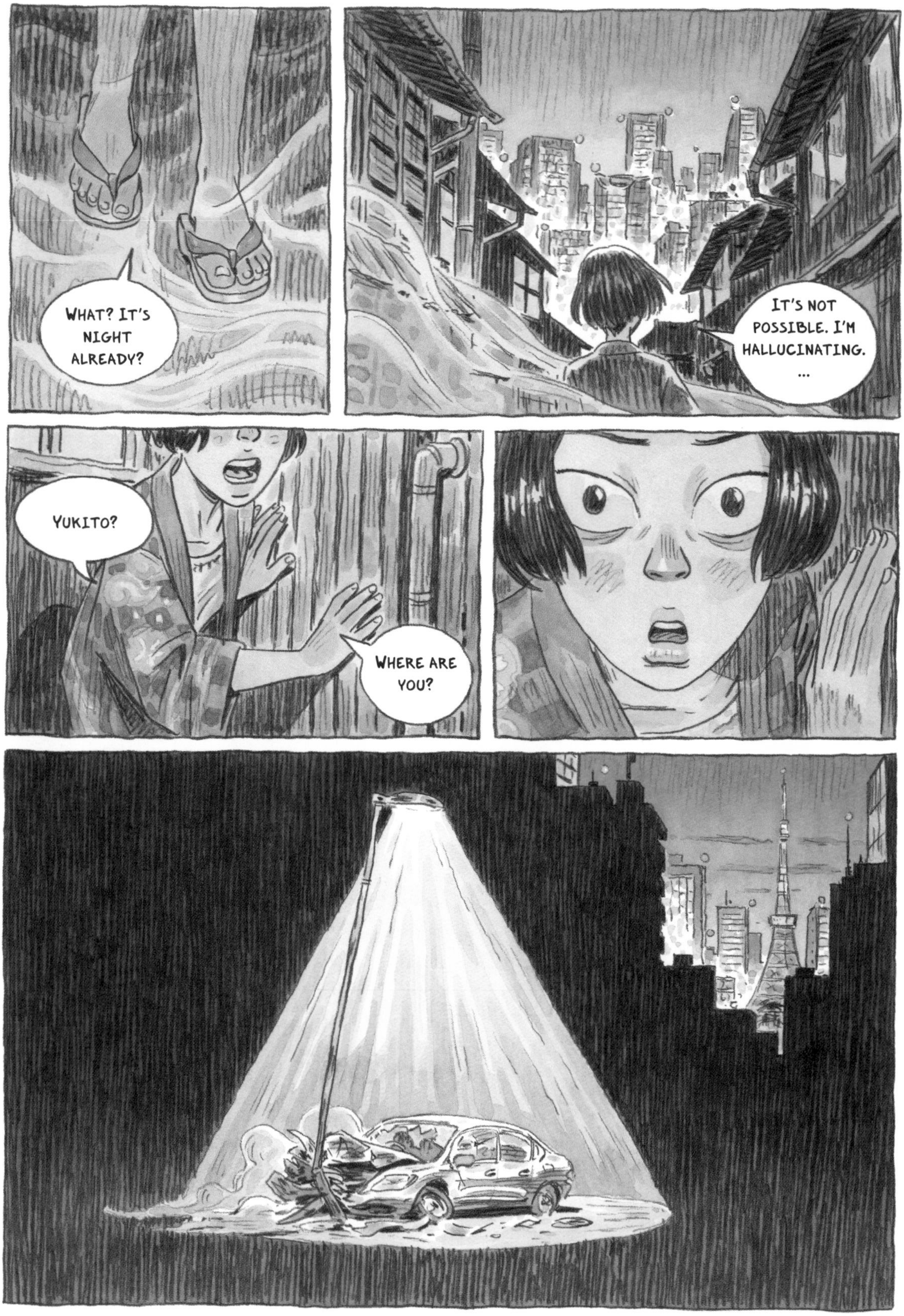
WHAT? IT'S NIGHT ALREADY?
IT'S NOT POSSIBLE. I'M HALLUCINATING. ...
YUKITO?
WHERE ARE YOU?

The crash

A SECRET WOUND HIDES IN THE HEART OF EVERY SHADOW.

ALL YEAR I'VE TRIED TO CURE THE ONE THAT'S BEEN GNAWING AT YUKITO.

MAYU?

KOFF
KOFF

BUT NOW THAT HIS MEMORIES ARE STIRRING, I'M HESITATING. COULD THIS REPRESSED SUFFERING RISK DESTROYING HIM?

I WANT TO WARN HIM...

FORCE HIM TO LOOK AWAY.

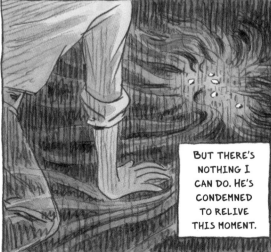

BUT THERE'S NOTHING I CAN DO. HE'S CONDEMNED TO RELIVE THIS MOMENT.

THERE ON THE TARMAC... FIVE LITTLE TEETH...

LIKE STARS IN AN EMPTY SKY.

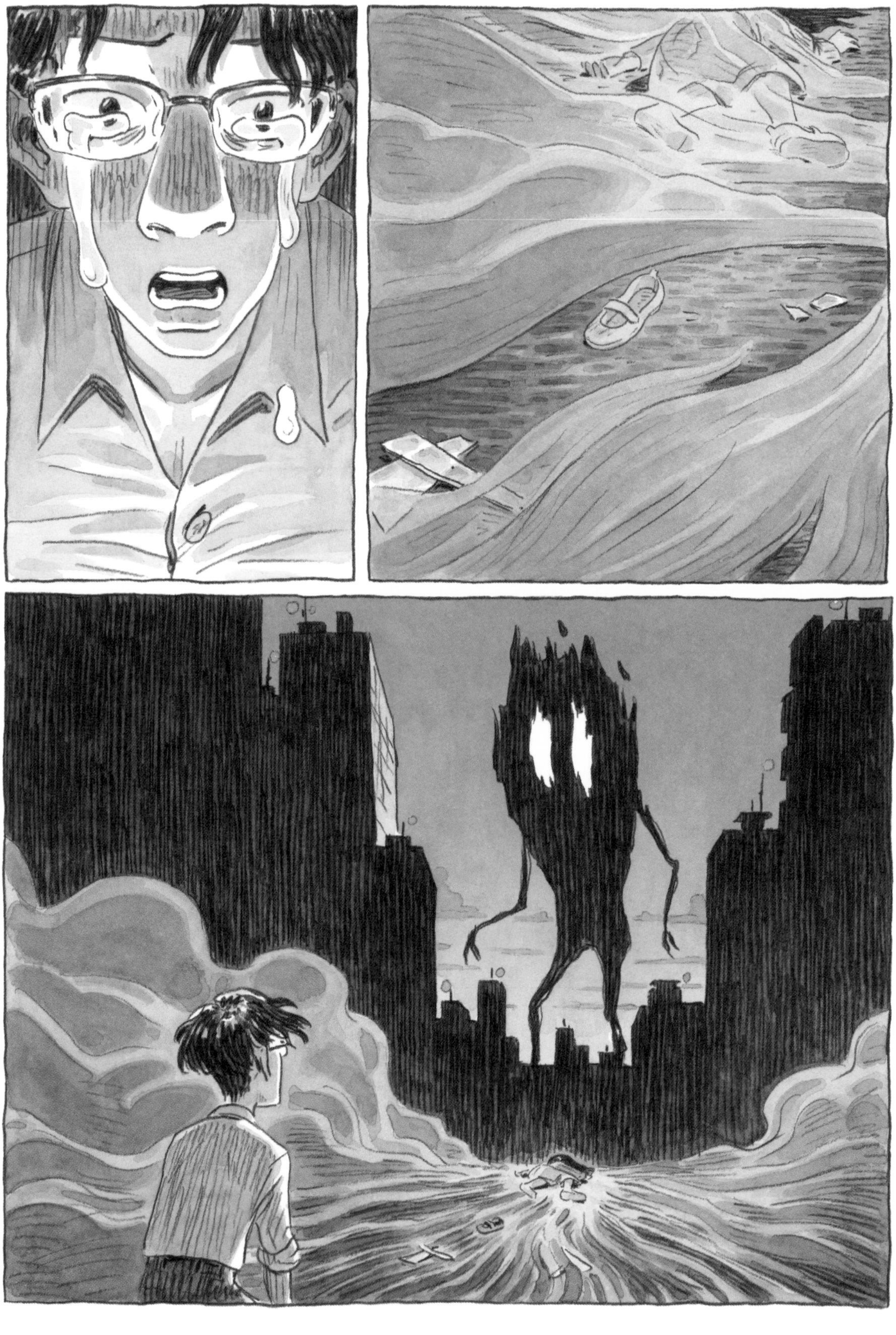

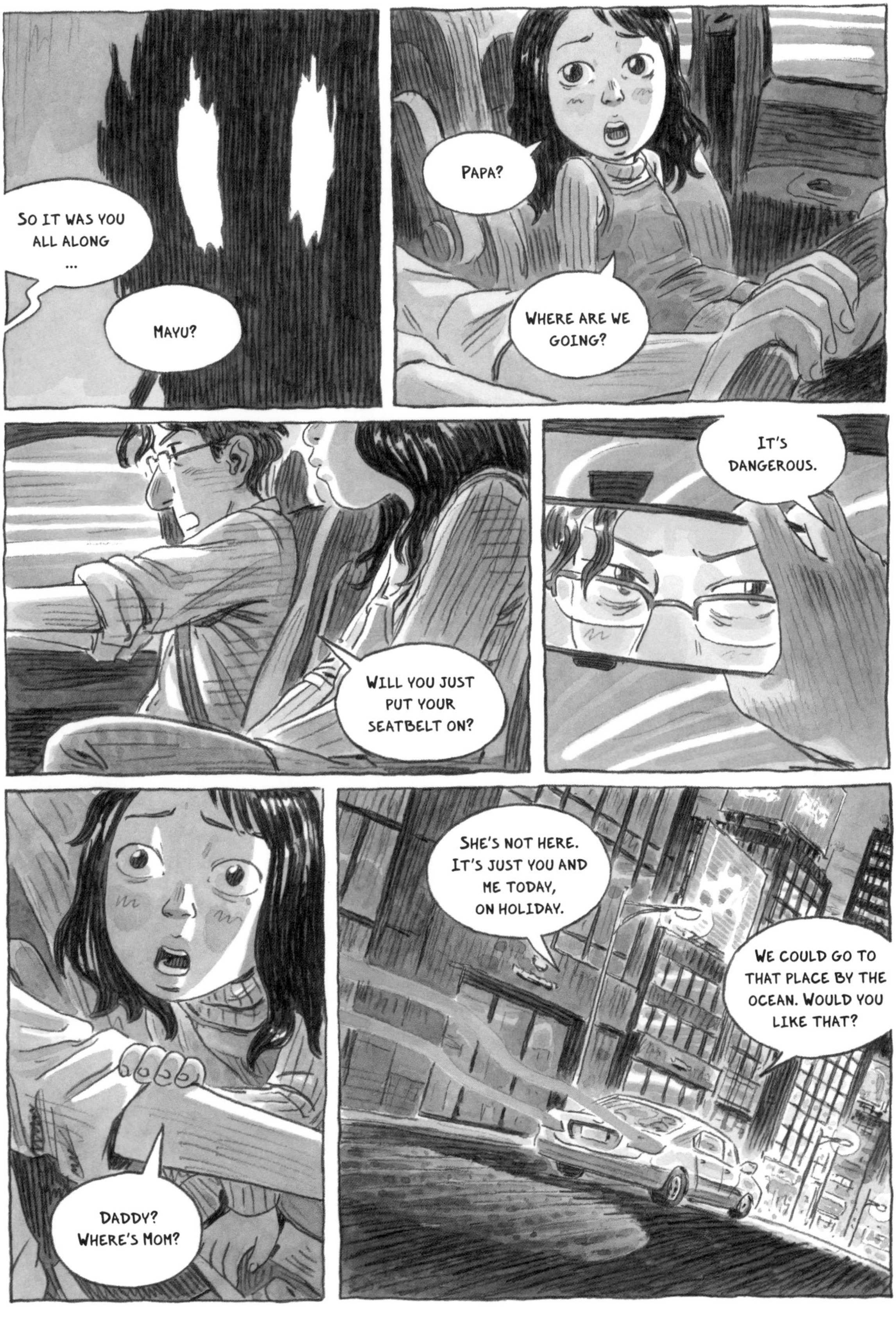
So it was you all along ...
Mayu?
Papa?
Where are we going?
Will you just put your seatbelt on?
It's dangerous.
Daddy? Where's Mom?
She's not here. It's just you and me today, on holiday.
We could go to that place by the ocean. Would you like that?

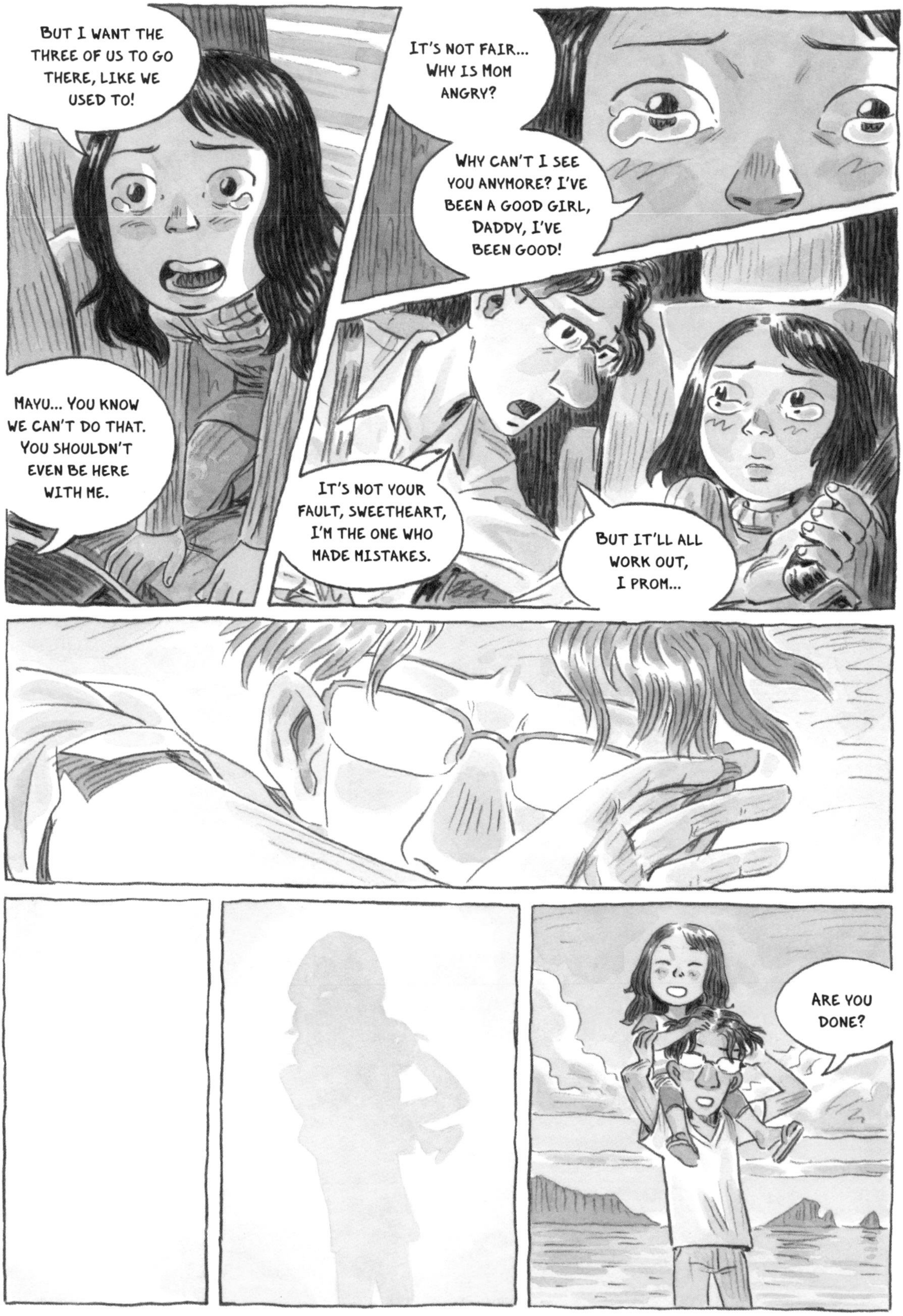
But I want the three of us to go there, like we used to!
It's not fair... Why is Mom angry?
Why can't I see you anymore? I've been a good girl, Daddy, I've been good!
Mayu... You know we can't do that. You shouldn't even be here with me.
It's not your fault, sweetheart, I'm the one who made mistakes.
But it'll all work out, I prom...
Are you done?

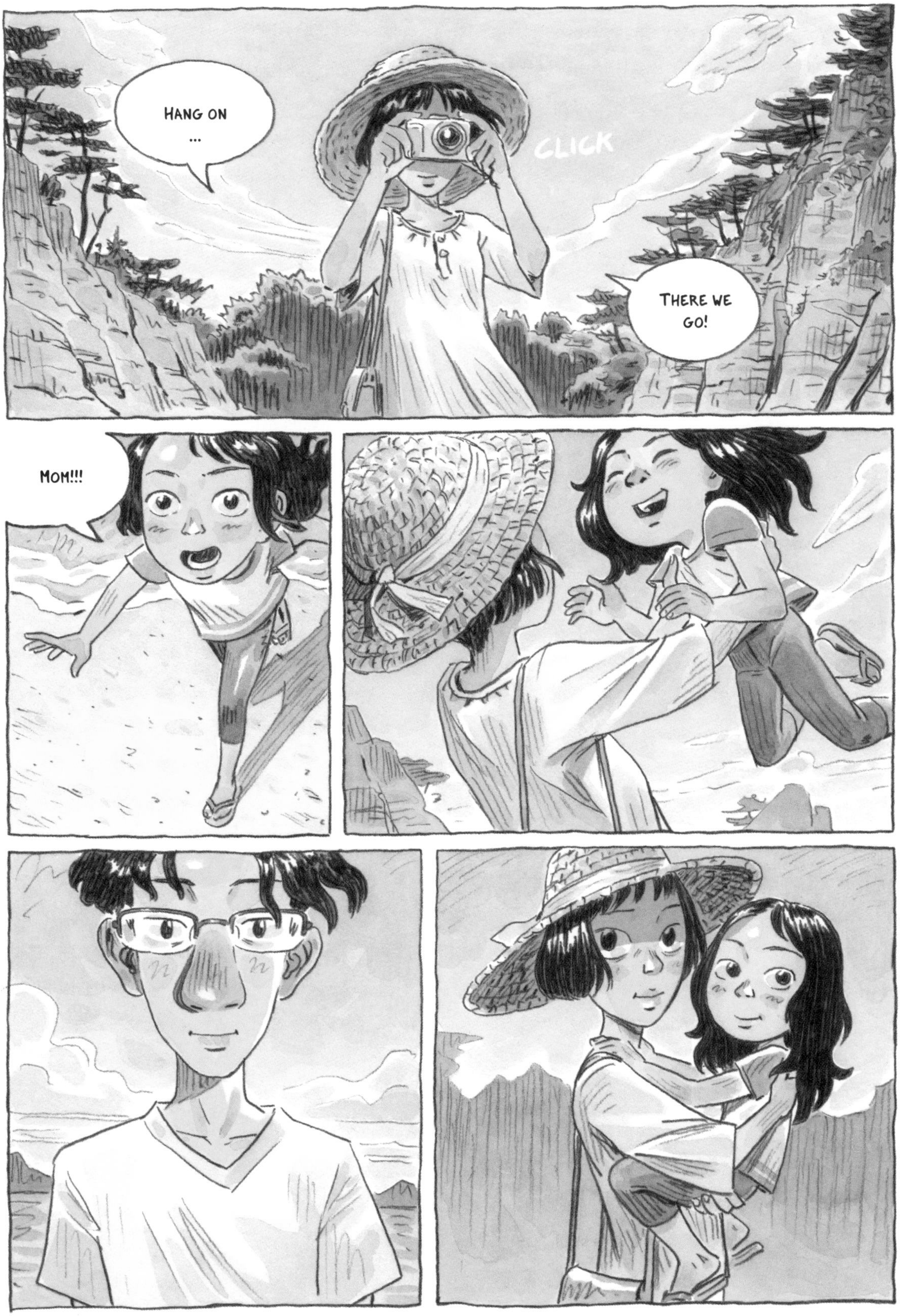
HANG ON
...
CLICK
THERE WE
GO!
MOM!!!

Happy days

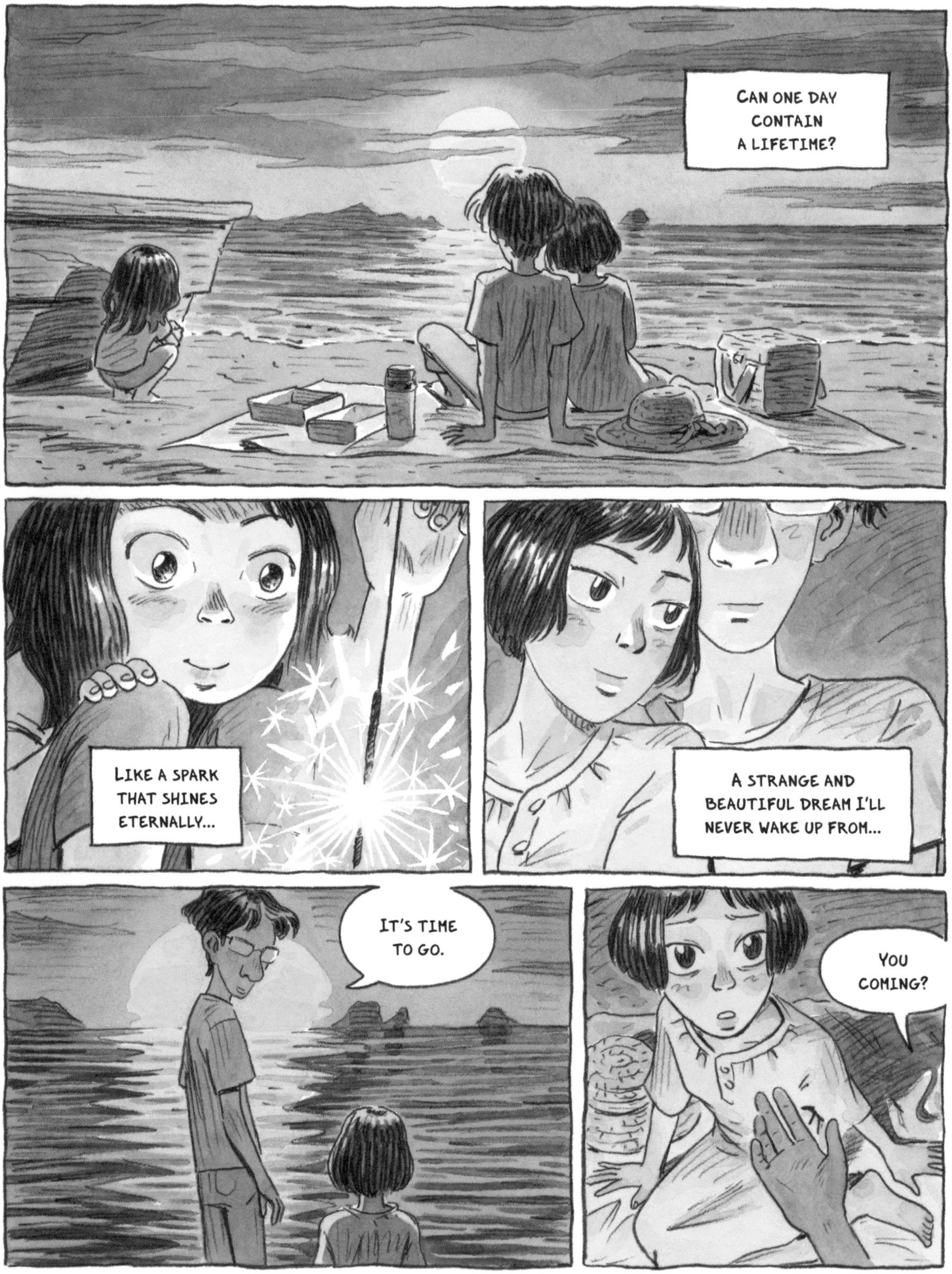
CAN ONE DAY CONTAIN A LIFETIME?
LIKE A SPARK THAT SHINES ETERNALLY...
A STRANGE AND BEAUTIFUL DREAM I'LL NEVER WAKE UP FROM...
IT'S TIME TO GO.
YOU COMING?

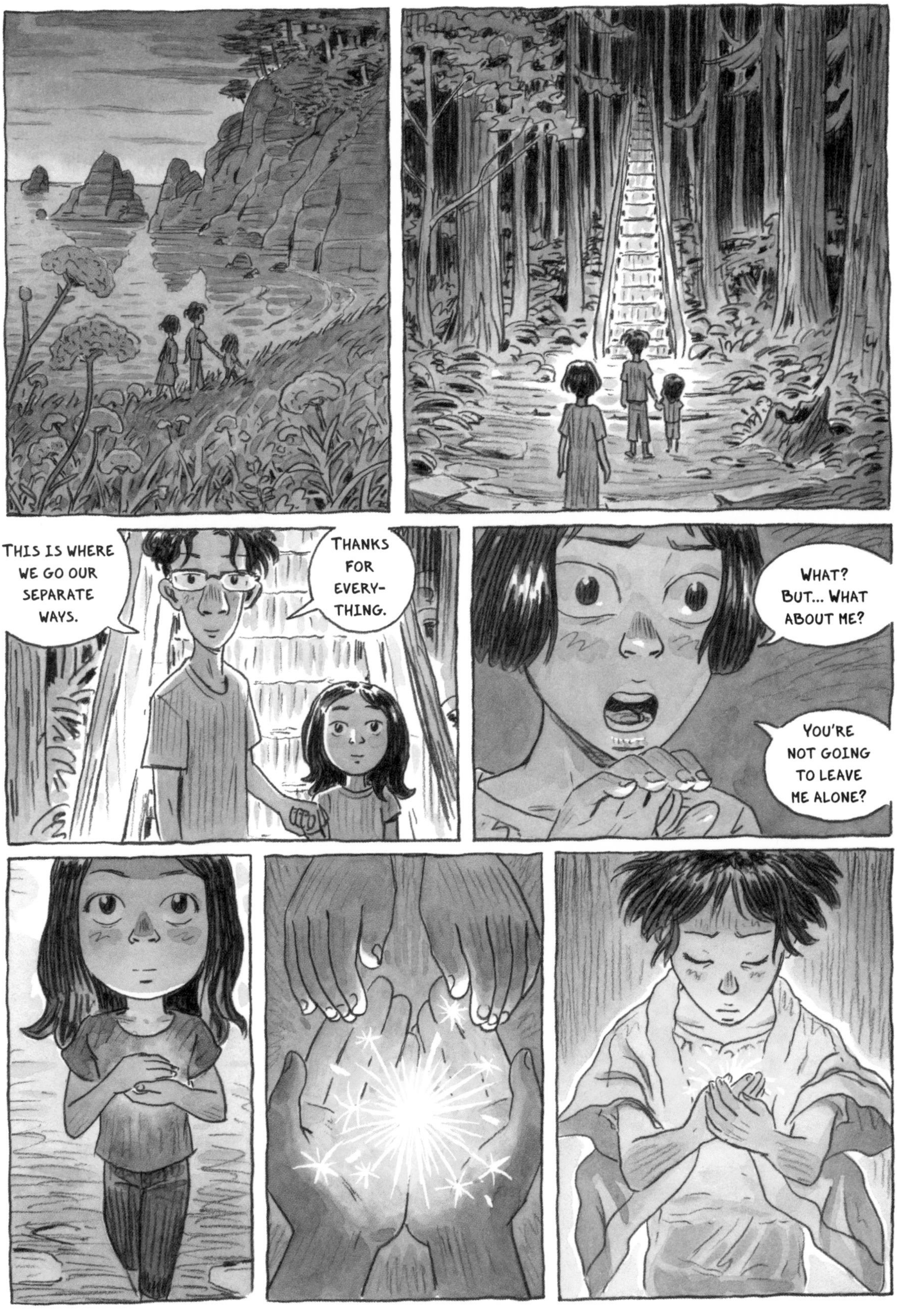
THIS IS WHERE WE GO OUR SEPARATE WAYS.
THANKS FOR EVERY-THING.
WHAT? BUT... WHAT ABOUT ME?
YOU'RE NOT GOING TO LEAVE ME ALONE?

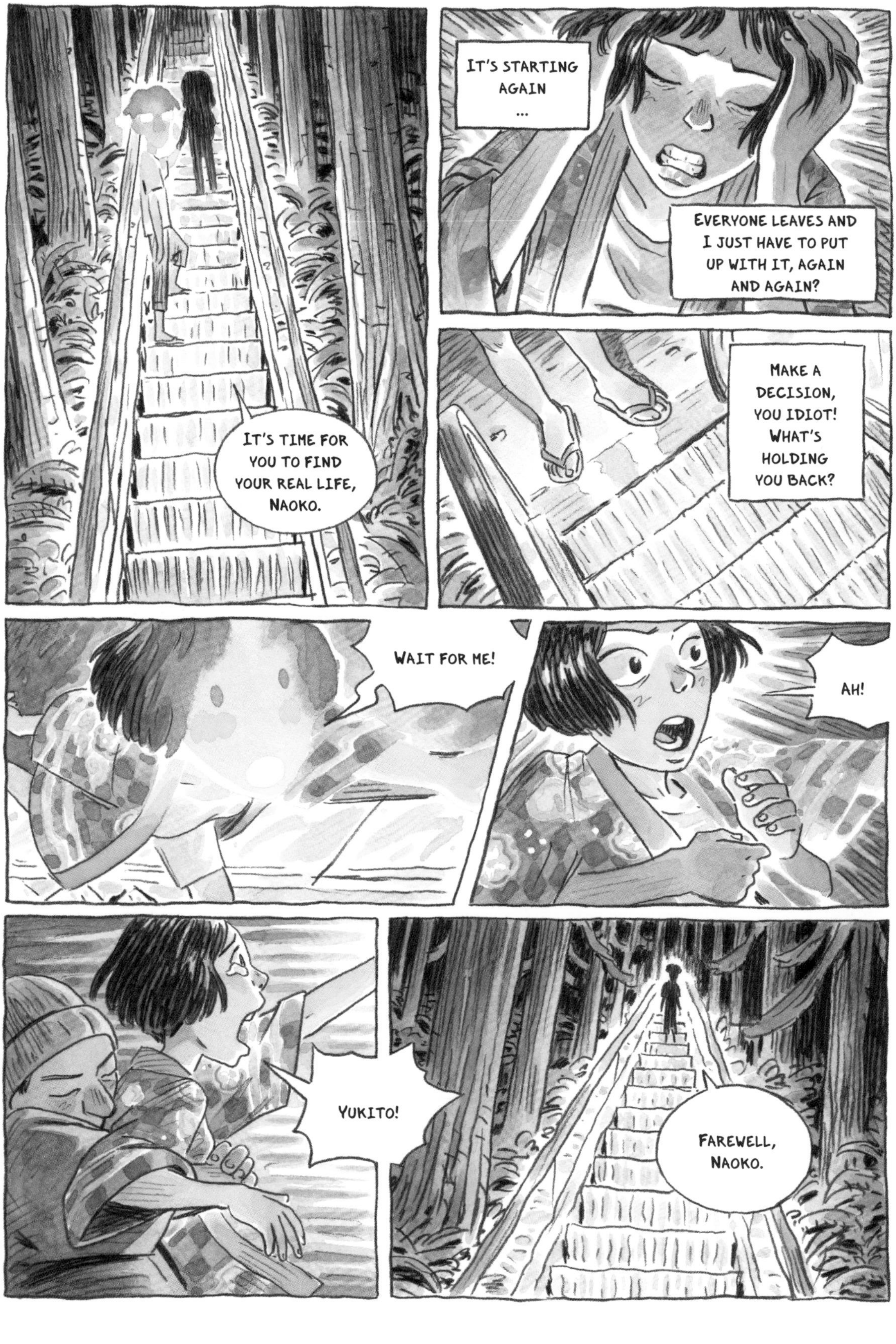
It's time for you to find your real life, Naoko.
It's starting again ...
Everyone leaves and I just have to put up with it, again and again?
Make a decision, you idiot! What's holding you back?
Wait for me!
Ah!
Yukito!
Farewell, Naoko.

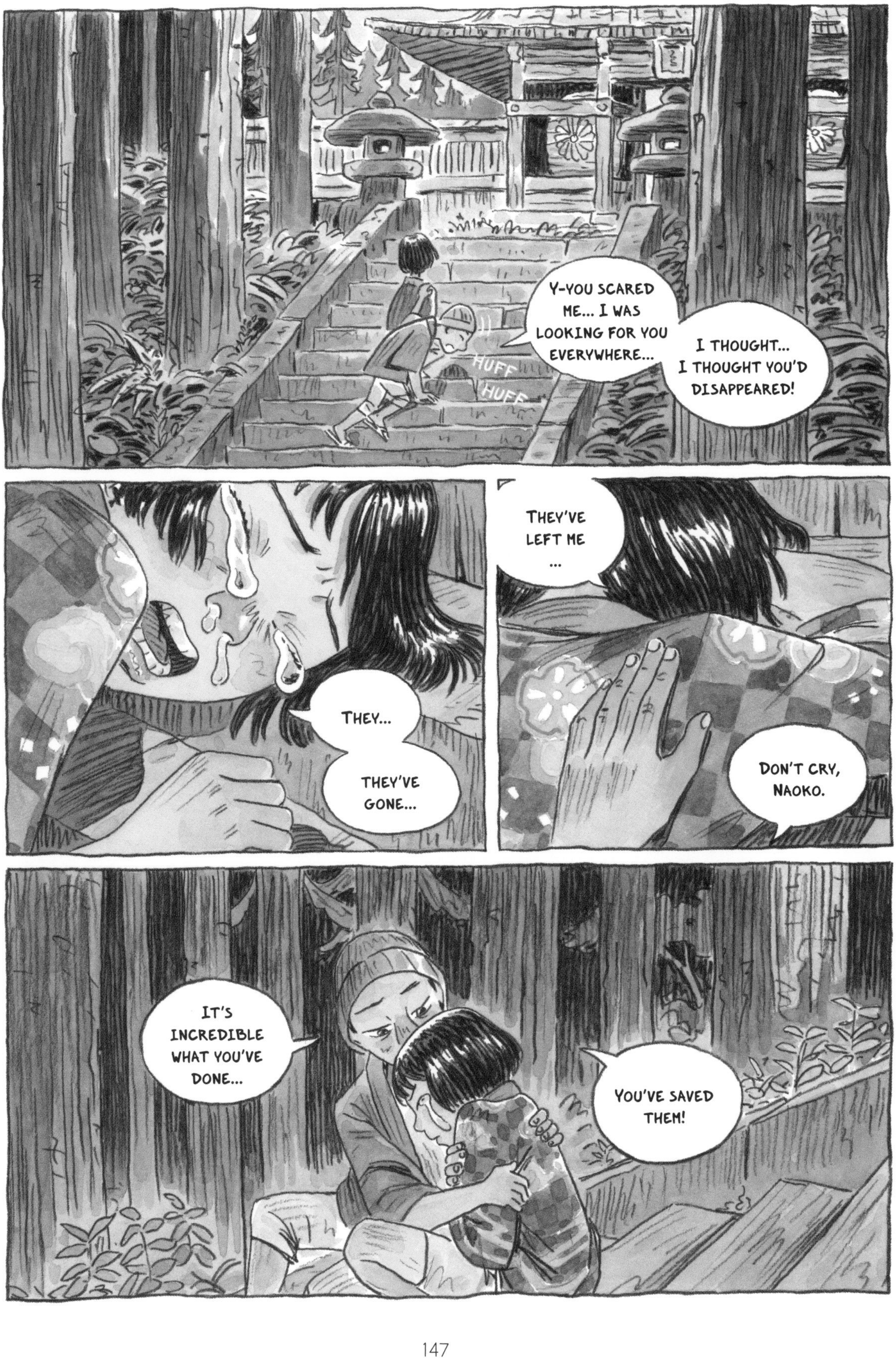
HUFF
HUFF
Y-YOU SCARED ME... I WAS LOOKING FOR YOU EVERYWHERE...
I THOUGHT... I THOUGHT YOU'D DISAPPEARED!
THEY...
THEY'VE GONE...
THEY'VE LEFT ME ...
DON'T CRY, NAOKO.
IT'S INCREDIBLE WHAT YOU'VE DONE...
YOU'VE SAVED THEM!

Airborne

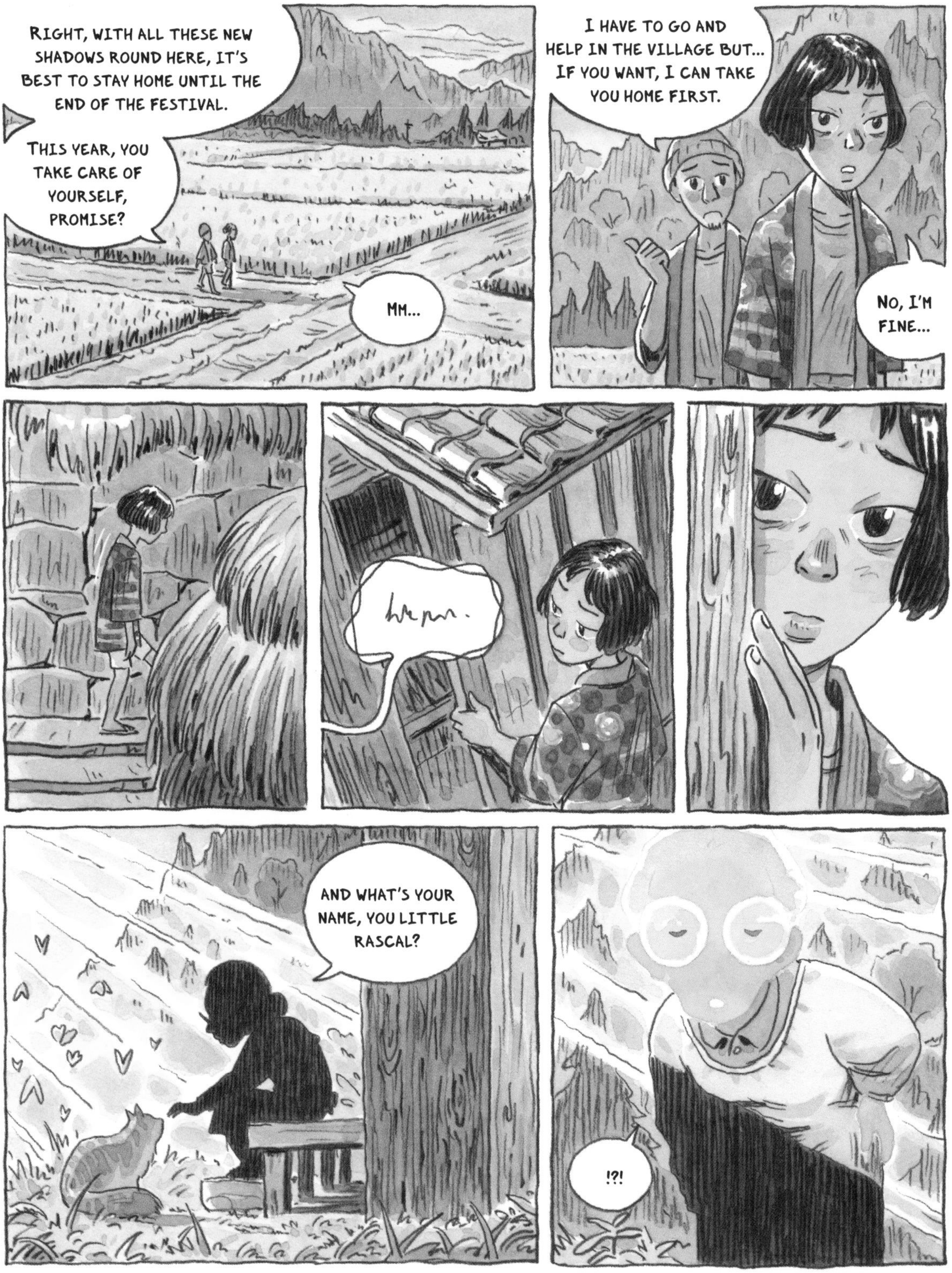

RIGHT, WITH ALL THESE NEW SHADOWS ROUND HERE, IT'S BEST TO STAY HOME UNTIL THE END OF THE FESTIVAL.
THIS YEAR, YOU TAKE CARE OF YOURSELF, PROMISE?
MM...
I HAVE TO GO AND HELP IN THE VILLAGE BUT... IF YOU WANT, I CAN TAKE YOU HOME FIRST.
NO, I'M FINE...
AND WHAT'S YOUR NAME, YOU LITTLE RASCAL?
!?!

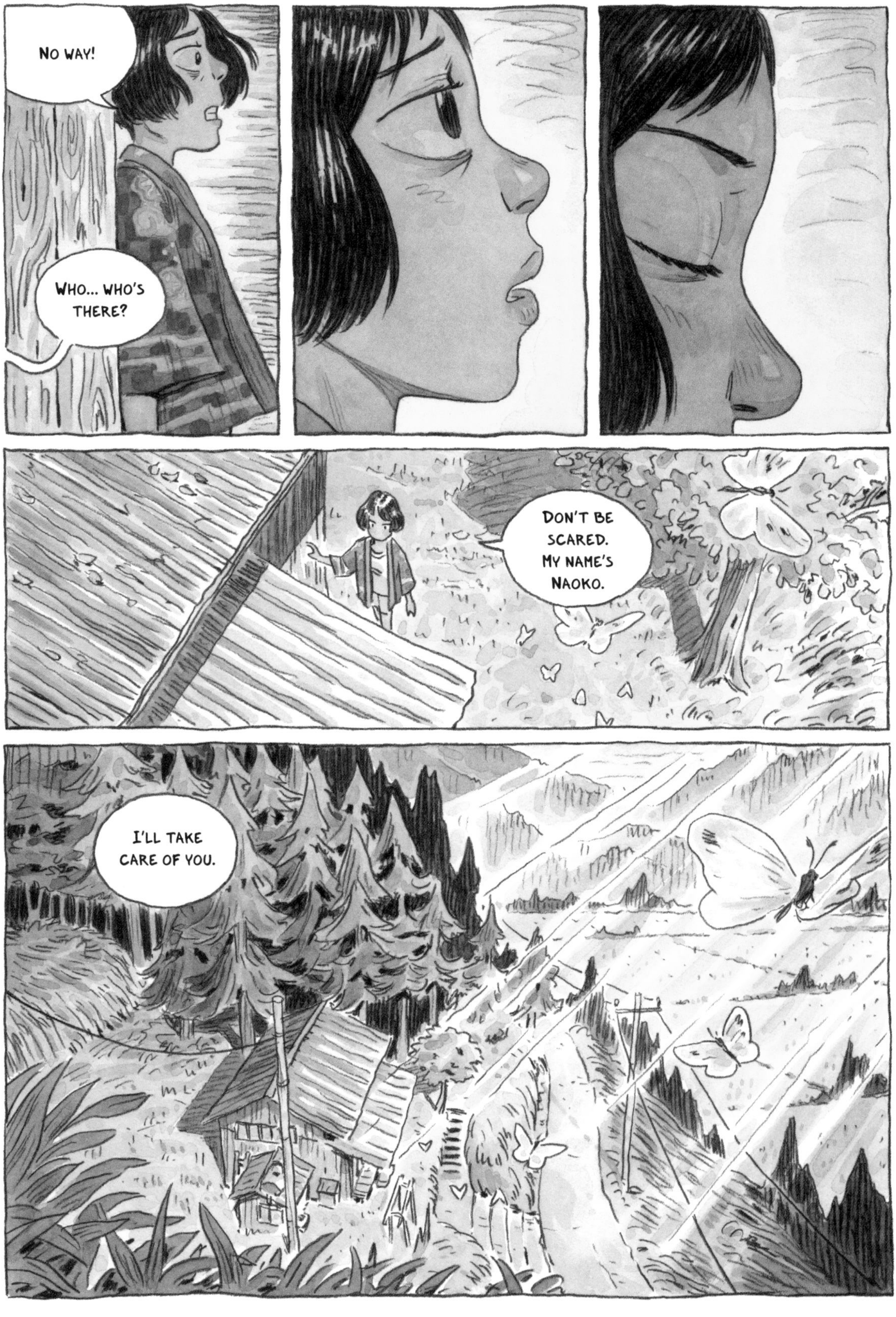
NO WAY!
WHO... WHO'S THERE?
DON'T BE SCARED. MY NAME'S NAOKO.
I'LL TAKE CARE OF YOU.

Epilogue

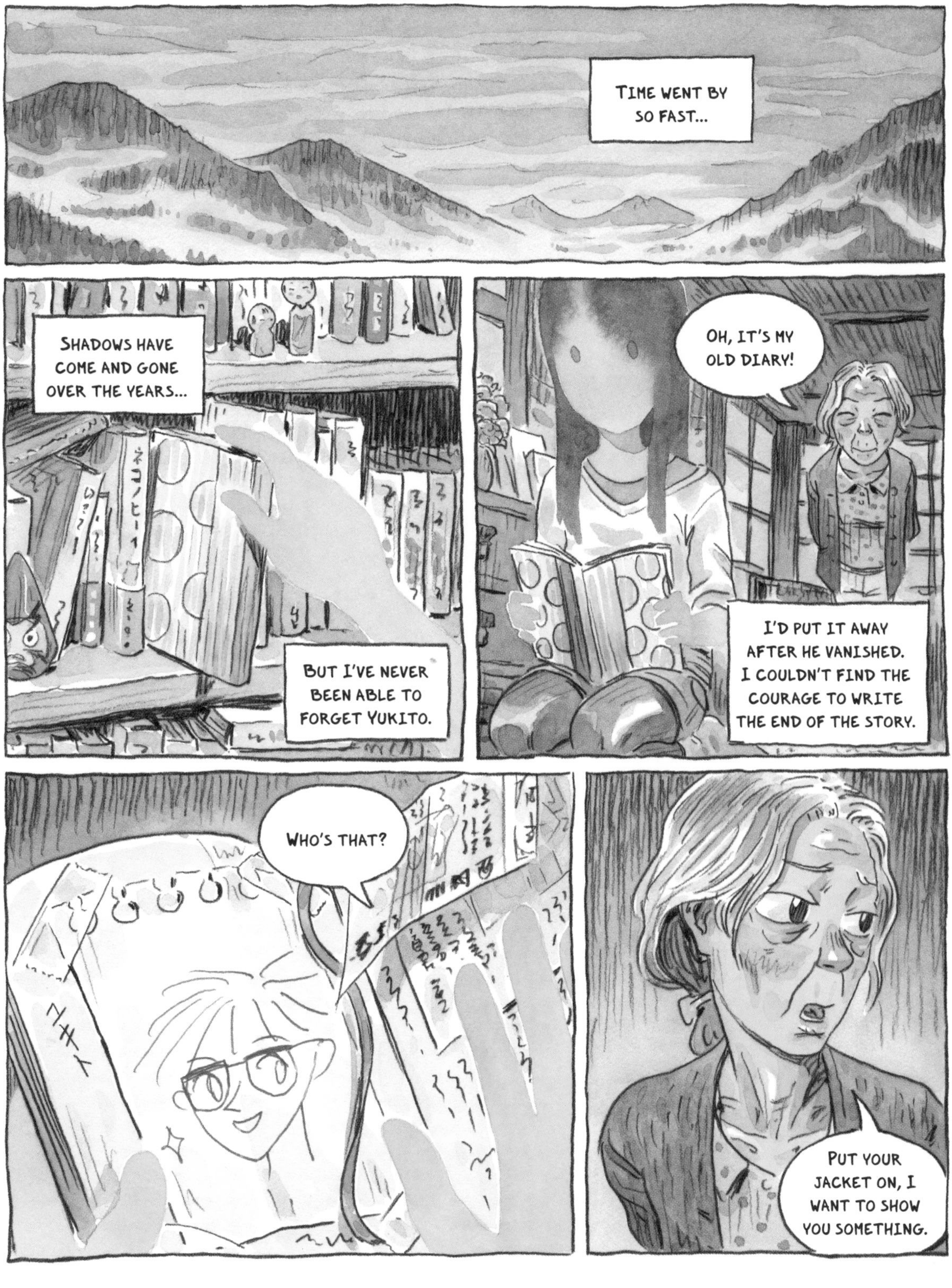

TIME WENT BY SO FAST...
SHADOWS HAVE COME AND GONE OVER THE YEARS...
BUT I'VE NEVER BEEN ABLE TO FORGET YUKITO.
OH, IT'S MY OLD DIARY!
I'D PUT IT AWAY AFTER HE VANISHED. I COULDN'T FIND THE COURAGE TO WRITE THE END OF THE STORY.
WHO'S THAT?
PUT YOUR JACKET ON, I WANT TO SHOW YOU SOMETHING.

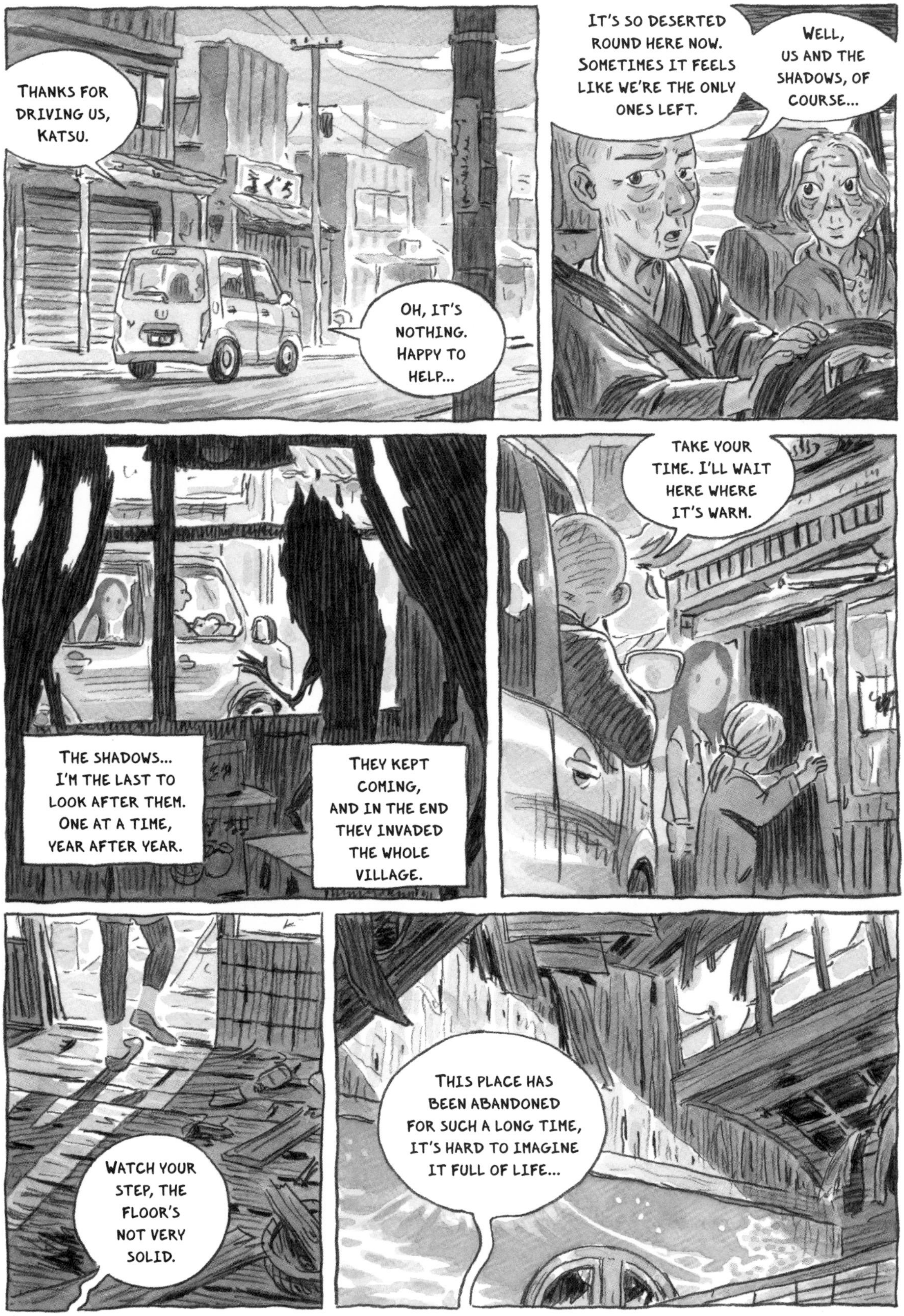
THANKS FOR DRIVING US, KATSU.
OH, IT'S NOTHING. HAPPY TO HELP...
IT'S SO DESERTED ROUND HERE NOW. SOMETIMES IT FEELS LIKE WE'RE THE ONLY ONES LEFT.
WELL, US AND THE SHADOWS, OF COURSE...
THE SHADOWS... I'M THE LAST TO LOOK AFTER THEM. ONE AT A TIME, YEAR AFTER YEAR.
THEY KEPT COMING, AND IN THE END THEY INVADED THE WHOLE VILLAGE.
TAKE YOUR TIME. I'LL WAIT HERE WHERE IT'S WARM.
WATCH YOUR STEP, THE FLOOR'S NOT VERY SOLID.
THIS PLACE HAS BEEN ABANDONED FOR SUCH A LONG TIME, IT'S HARD TO IMAGINE IT FULL OF LIFE...

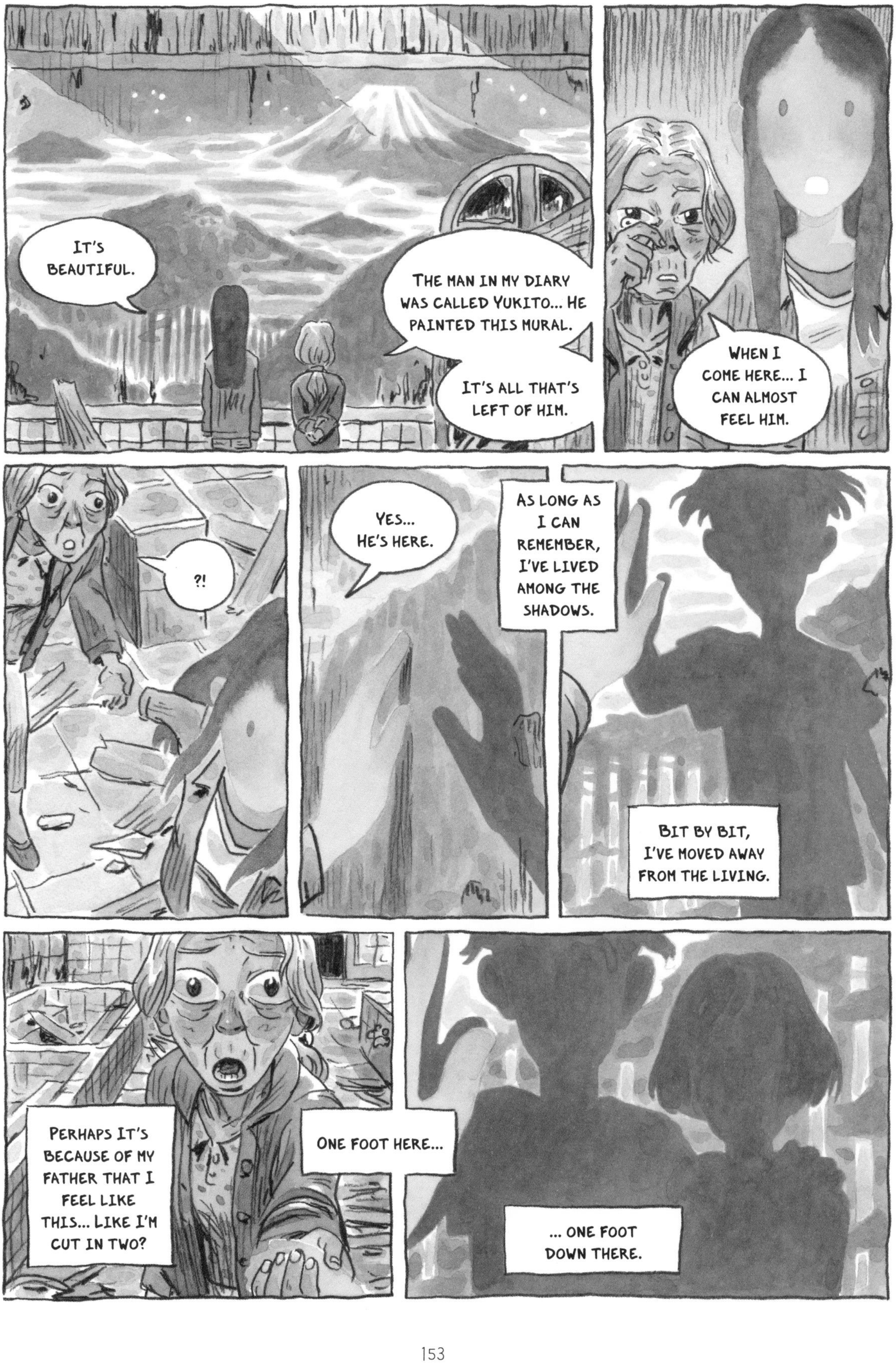

It's beautiful.
The man in my diary was called Yukito... He painted this mural.
It's all that's left of him.
When I come here... I can almost feel him.
?!
Yes... He's here.
As long as I can remember, I've lived among the shadows.
Bit by bit, I've moved away from the living.
Perhaps it's because of my father that I feel like this... Like I'm cut in two?
One foot here...
... one foot down there.

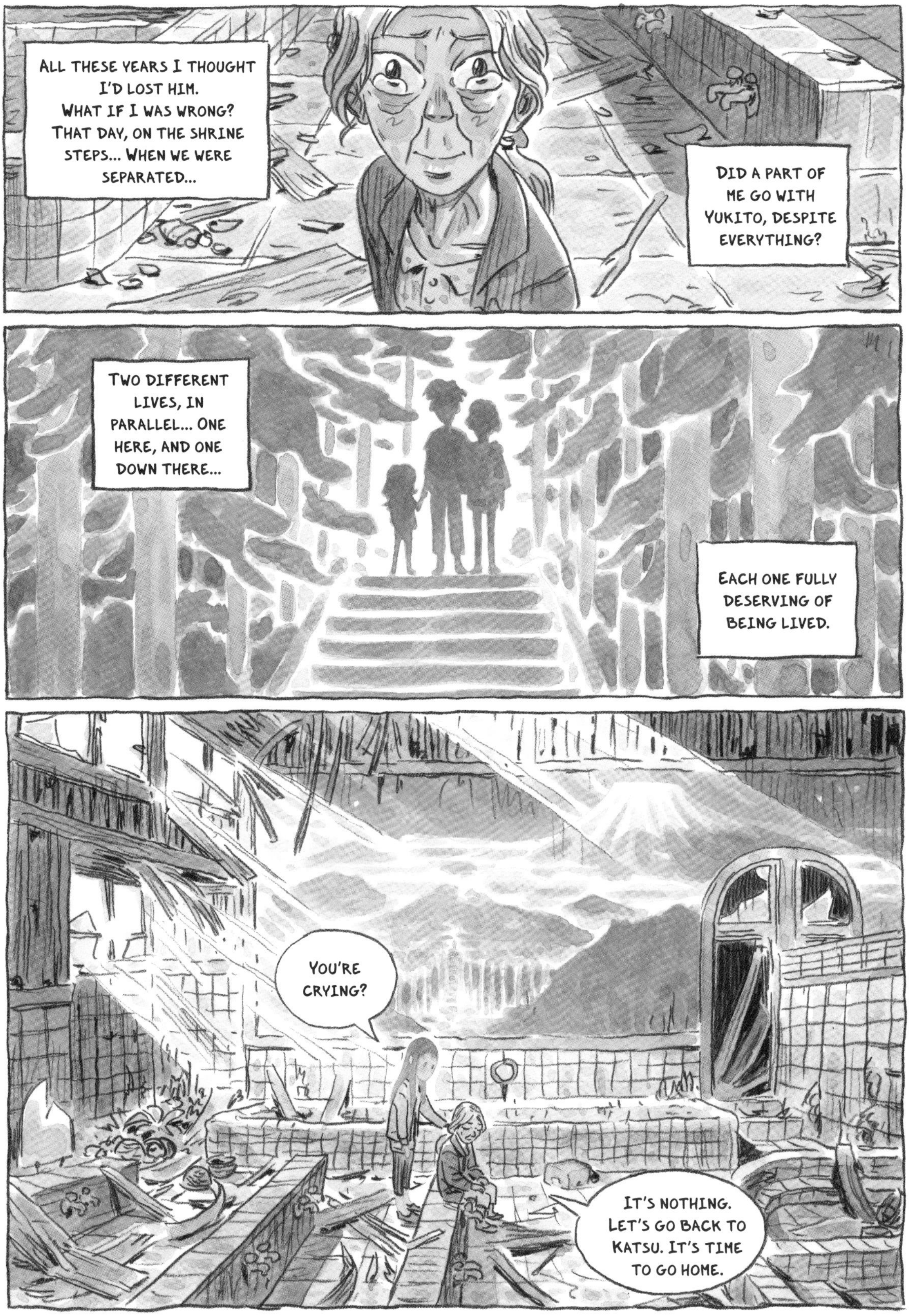
ALL THESE YEARS I THOUGHT I'D LOST HIM. WHAT IF I WAS WRONG? THAT DAY, ON THE SHRINE STEPS... WHEN WE WERE SEPARATED...
DID A PART OF ME GO WITH YUKITO, DESPITE EVERYTHING?
TWO DIFFERENT LIVES, IN PARALLEL... ONE HERE, AND ONE DOWN THERE...
EACH ONE FULLY DESERVING OF BEING LIVED.
YOU'RE CRYING?
IT'S NOTHING. LET'S GO BACK TO KATSU. IT'S TIME TO GO HOME.

The end

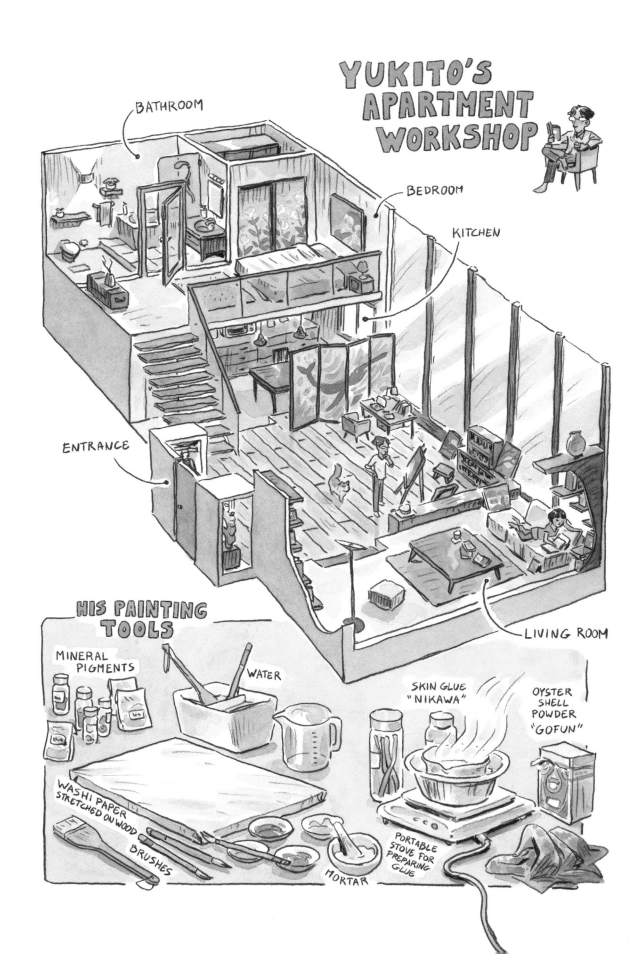

YUKITO'S APARTMENT WORKSHOP

BATHROOM

BEDROOM

KITCHEN

ENTRANCE

LIVING ROOM

HIS PAINTING TOOLS

MINERAL PIGMENTS

WATER

SKIN GLUE "NIKAWA"

OYSTER SHELL POWDER "GOFUN"

WASHI PAPER STRETCHED ON WOOD

BRUSHES

MORTAR

PORTABLE STOVE FOR PREPARING GLUE

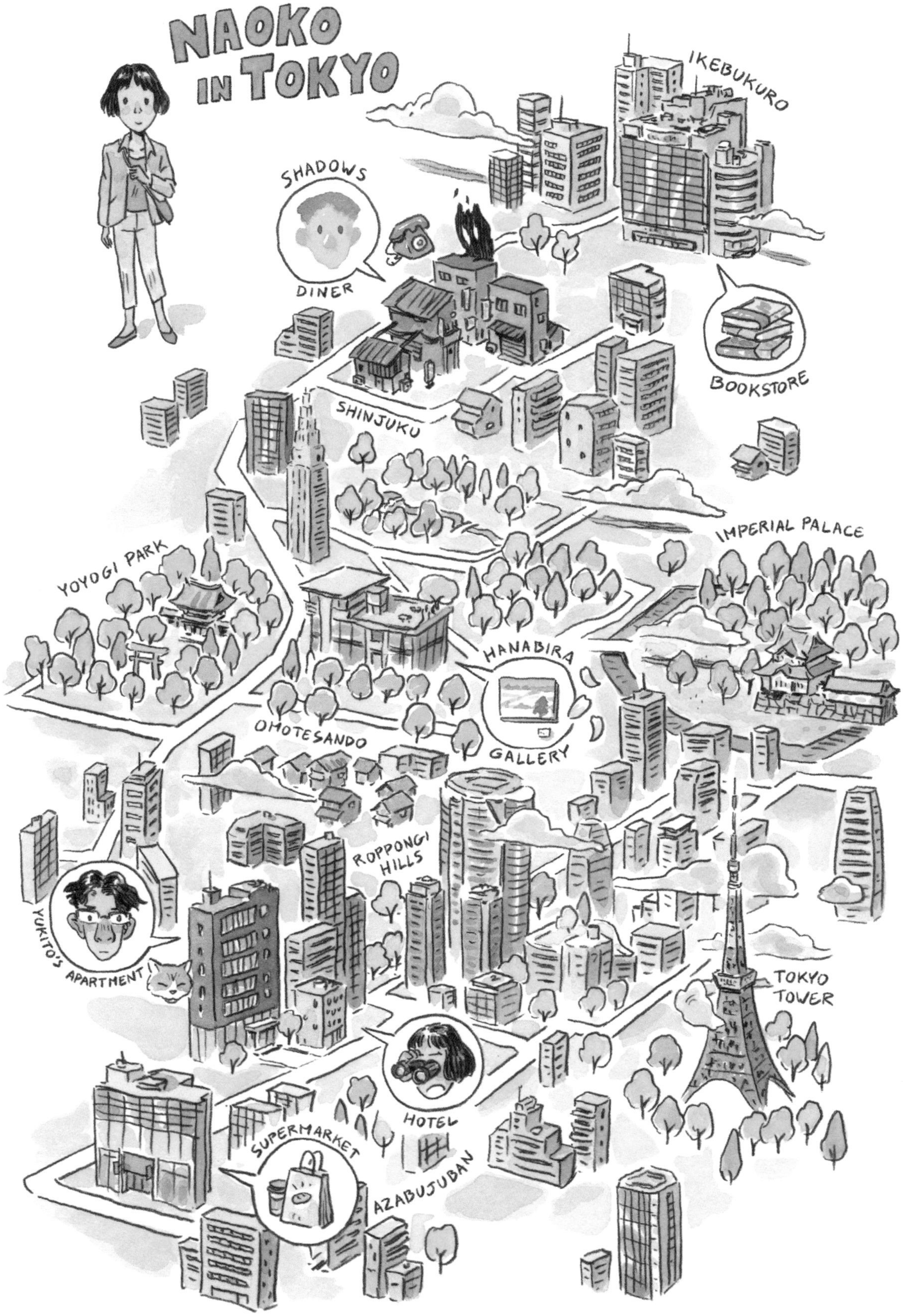
NAOKO IN TOKYO
IKEBUKURO
SHADOWS
DINER
BOOKSTORE
SHINJUKU
IMPERIAL PALACE
YOYOGI PARK
HANABIRA
GALLERY
OMOTESANDO
ROPPONGI HILLS
YUKITO'S APARTMENT
TOKYO TOWER
HOTEL
SUPERMARKET
AZABUJUBAN

Acknowledgments

The making of this book took a lot of research and we would like to thank a number of Japan-based collaborators who were kind enough to help us:

Mizuka Yagi for providing us with invaluable cultural information and for drawing the portrait on page 47.

Sakino, Mizuka's daughter, for the seasonal calligraphy at the start of every chapter.

Stéphanie Crohin (instagram.com/__stephaniemelanie__), Japanese bathhouse ambassador, and Wakame Tamago (inaca.me), who provided us with many photographs.

Yukio Kondo (yukio-kondo.com), who introduced us to the art of Japanese Nihonga paintings.

Sharp-eyed readers will have noticed in Yukito's apartment a few nods to some of our favorite artists: paintings by Yoshitaka Amano (instagram.com/yoshitaka__amano), sculptures by Miwa Neishi (instagram.com/miwaclay), and a book of collages by Masayasu Uchida (instagram.com/uchidamasayasu).

Yukito's paintings are inspired by the work of the painter Kazu Saito (saitoukazu.com).

A big thank you to Delphine and Alexandre for their investment in this project and to Josh Tierney for his help with the English translation.

© Nat Gorry

Continue experiencing the world of this book with the clip *La Poussière de l'Air*, the new song by Cécile Corbel, composer and interpreter of the music for the animated film *Arrietty* from Studio Ghibli. Her musical universe melds with that of the world illustrated in *Festival of Shadows*, evoking through an emotional score the traces of those who have left us.
Watch it at the official link: isse.cc/poussiere

Keep up to date with the latest from Atelier Sentō:

 ateliersento.com  ateliersento AtSento

"Books to Span the East and West"

Tuttle Publishing was founded in 1832 in the small New England town of Rutland, Vermont [USA]. Our core values remain as strong today as they were then—to publish best-in-class books which bring people together one page at a time. In 1948, we established a publishing office in Japan—and Tuttle is now a leader in publishing English-language books about the arts, languages and cultures of Asia. The world has become a much smaller place today and Asia's economic and cultural influence has grown. Yet the need for meaningful dialogue and information about this diverse region has never been greater. Over the past seven decades, Tuttle has published thousands of books on subjects ranging from martial arts and paper crafts to language learning and literature—and our talented authors, illustrators, designers and photographers have won many prestigious awards. We welcome you to explore the wealth of information available on Asia at **www.tuttlepublishing.com.**

Published as *La Fete des Ombres Vol. 1* and *Vol. 2* by Éditions Issekinicho, Shiltigheim, France, 2021

www.tuttlepublishing.com

ISBN: 978-4-8053-1724-2

25 24 23 22   6 5 4 3 2 1   2208TP
Printed in Singapore

Distributed by

**North America, Latin America
& Europe**
Tuttle Publishing
364 Innovation Drive
North Clarendon,
VT 05759-9436 U.S.A.
Tel: 1 (802) 773-8930
Fax: 1 (802) 773-6993
info@tuttlepublishing.com
www.tuttlepublishing.com

Japan
Tuttle Publishing
Yaekari Building, 3rd Floor
5-4-12 Osaki
Shinagawa-ku
Tokyo 141-0032
Tel: (81) 3 5437-0171
Fax: (81) 3 5437-0755
sales@tuttle.co.jp
www.tuttle.co.jp

Asia Pacific
Berkeley Books Pte. Ltd.
3 Kallang Sector #04-01
Singapore 349278
Tel: (65) 6741-2178
Fax: (65) 6741-2179
inquiries@periplus.com.sg
www.periplus.com

TUTTLE PUBLISHING® is a registered trademark of Tuttle Publishing, a division of Periplus Editions (HK) Ltd.